Black Easter

A gripping story of power, politics, modern theology and the dark forces of necromancy, in which an arms dealer hires a black magician to unleash all the Demons of Hell on earth for a single day.

The Day After Judgement

The events told in Black Easter have run their course. Now God is dead, and Satan has dominion over the earth . . .

The Seedling Stars

Through the science of pantropy, Adapted Men were produced to live and thrive in the alien environments found only in space. They were crucial to a daring plan to colonize the universe. And millennia later, it is only fitting that they should return to a long forgotten planetary system to colonise a hostile world called . . . Earth.

Also by James Blish

A Case of Conscience (1958)
A Torrent of Faces (with Norman L. Knight (1967))
And All the Stars a Stage (1971)
Black Easter (1968)
Doctor Mirabilis (1964)
Cities in Flight, comprising:
~ *They Shall Have Stars* (1956)
~ *A Life for the Stars* (1962)
~ *Earthman, Come Home* (1954)
~ *A Clash of Cymbals* (aka *The Triumph of Time* (1959))
Fallen Star (aka *The Frozen Year* (1957))
Jack of Eagles (1952)
Midsummer Century (1972)
Mission to the Heart Stars (1965)
More Issues at Hand (1970)
The Day after Judgement (1971)
The Duplicated Man (with Robert A. W. Lowndes (1959))
The Issue at Hand (1964)
The Night Shapes (1962)
The Quincunx of Time (1973)
The Seedling Stars (1957)
The Star Dwellers (1961)
The Tale that Wags the God (1987)
The Warriors of Day (1953)
Titan's Daughter (1961)
Vor (1958)
Welcome to Mars! (1967)

James Blish

SF GATEWAY OMNIBUS

BLACK EASTER
THE DAY AFTER JUDGEMENT
THE SEEDLING STARS

GOLLANCZ
LONDON

This omnibus copyright © James Blish 2013
Black Easter copyright © James Blish 1968
The Day After Judgement copyright © James Blish 1971
The Seedling Stars copyright © James Blish 1957
Introduction copyright © SFE Ltd 2013

First published in Great Britain in 2013 by Gollancz
An imprint of the Orion Publishing Group
Orion House, 5 Upper St Martin's Lane,
London WC2H 9EA

An Hachette UK Company

A CIP catalogue record for this book is
available from the British Library

ISBN 978 0 575 12930 6

1 3 5 7 9 10 8 6 4 2

Typeset by Input Data Services Ltd, Bridgwater, Somerset

Printed and bound by CPI Group (UK) Ltd, Croydon, CR0 4YY

The Orion Publishing Group's policy is to use papers
that are natural, renewable and recyclable products and
made from wood grown in sustainable forests. The logging
and manufacturing processes are expected to conform to
the environmental regulations of the country of origin.

www.orionbooks.co.uk
www.gollancz.co.uk

CONTENTS

ENTER THE SF GATEWAY . . .

Towards the end of 2011, in conjunction with the celebration of fifty years of coherent, continuous science fiction and fantasy publishing, Gollancz launched the SF Gateway.

Over a decade after launching the landmark SF Masterworks series, we realised that the realities of commercial publishing are such that even the Masterworks could only ever scratch the surface of an author's career. Vast troves of classic SF & Fantasy were almost certainly destined never again to see print. Until very recently, this meant that anyone interested in reading any of those books would have been confined to scouring second-hand bookshops. The advent of digital publishing changed that paradigm for ever.

Embracing the future even as we honour the past, Gollancz launched the SF Gateway with a view to utilising the technology that now exists to make available, for the first time, the entire backlists of an incredibly wide range of classic and modern SF and fantasy authors. Our plan, at its simplest, was – and still is! – to use this technology to build on the success of the SF and Fantasy Masterworks series and to go even further.

The SF Gateway was designed to be the new home of classic Science Fiction & Fantasy – the most comprehensive electronic library of classic SFF titles ever assembled. The programme has been extremely well received and we've been very happy with the results. So happy, in fact, that we've decided to complete the circle and return a selection of our titles to print, in these omnibus editions.

We hope you enjoy this selection. And we hope that you'll want to explore more of the classic SF and fantasy we have available. These are wonderful books you're holding in your hand, but you'll find much, much more ... through the SF Gateway.

www.sfgateway.com

INTRODUCTION

from The Encyclopedia of Science Fiction

James Blish (1921–1975) was a US author whose early career in sf followed a pattern typical of the generation whose early careers coincided with World War Two. He had been a fan during the 1930s, and soon joined the well-known New York fan group the Futurians, where he became friendly with future writers like Isaac Asimov, Damon Knight and C. M. Kornbluth. His first short story, 'Emergency Refueling', was published in *Super Science Stories* in 1940. He studied microbiology at Rutgers, graduating in 1942, and was then drafted, serving as a medical laboratory technician in the US Army. In 1945–1946 he carried out post-graduate work in zoology at Columbia University, abandoning this to become a writer. He was married to Virginia Kidd 1947–1963 and then, from 1964 until his death, to Judith Ann Lawrence.

From the beginning, Blish worked hard to develop his craft, but not until 1950, when the first of his **Okie** stories appeared in *Astounding Science-Fiction*, did it became clear that he could successfully combine his scientific training and his ambitions as an author. The **Okie** stories featured flying cities, the most important of these being Manhattan under the leadership of Mayor John Amalfi; as an iconic image of New York this vision has proved lasting. Powered by Antigravity devices called Spindizzies, Manhattan and other populous compact Keeps travel through the Galaxy looking for work, much as the Okies did in America in the 1930s when they escaped from the dustbowl. The first **Okie** book, a coherent if episodic novel, was *Earthman, Come Home* (**1958**). Three more followed: *They Shall Have Stars* (**1957**), *The Triumph of Time* (**1958**) and *A Life for the Stars* (**1962**). These four books were finally brought together in a single volume, *Cities in Flight* (**1970**), where they appeared in the order of their internal chronology: *They Shall Have Stars, A Life for the Stars, Earthman, Come Home* and *The Triumph of Time*. Underpinning the pulp-indebted plotting of much of this series is a serious and pessimistic interest in the cyclic nature of History, climaxing at the end of *The Triumph of Time*, where the long epic passes through the death of our Universe into the birth of the next. In a memorable passage Amalfi himself – the main protagonist of the series – becomes, literally, the deep structure of the new Universe.

The years 1950–1958 were extraordinarily productive for Blish, and many of his best short stories were published in this period, including 'Beanstalk', 'Surface Tension', 'Common Time', 'Beep' and 'A Work of Art'. Several appear in his first collection, *Galactic Cluster* (**1959**); others were linked together as *The Seedling Stars* (**1957**), where Blish focused on biological themes. This area of science had previously been rather neglected in sf in favour of the 'harder' sciences – physics, astronomy, science-based technologies, etc. *The Seedling Stars* is an important road-marker in the early development of sf about genetic engineering.

These years also saw the publication of his first novel to appear in book form, *Jack of Eagles* (**1952**), followed by *The Warriors of Day* (**1953**), *The Frozen Year* (**1957**) and *A Case of Conscience* (**1958**). *Jack of Eagles* contains one of the few attempts in sf to give a scientific rationale for Telepathy. *A Case of Conscience,* which won the 1959 Hugo for Best Novel, was one of the first serious attempts to deal with Religion in sf, and remains one of the most sophisticated in its tale of a priest whose mission to the planet Lithia faces him with a species seemingly free of the concept of Original Sin; but the Lithians turn out (as he believes) to constitute a kind of honey-trap, constructed by the Adversary with all the rigour of a fine Thought Experiment, in order to estrange humanity from God: because, blasphemously, the Lithians seem to have achieved moral perfection without divine guidance.

Blish was interested in Metaphysics, and some critics regard as his most important work the thematic trilogy **After Such Knowledge**, in which *A Case of Conscience* is followed by *Doctor Mirabilis* (**1964**), and the intimately linked *Black Easter; Or, Faust Aleph-Null* (**1968**) and *The Day After Judgement* (**1971**); he regarded the last two volumes as one novel, and indeed they were so published in *Black Easter and The Day After Judgement* – hence his use of the term 'trilogy'. **After Such Knowledge** poses a question once expressed by Blish as: 'Is the desire for secular knowledge, let alone the acquisition and use of it, a misuse of the mind, and perhaps even actively evil?' This is one of the fundamental themes of sf, and is painstakingly explored in *Doctor Mirabilis*, an historical novel which treats the life of the thirteenth- century scientist and theologian Roger BACON. It deals with the archetypal sf theme of Conceptual Breakthrough from one intellectual model of the Universe to another, more sophisticated model. *Black Easter*, a better and more unified work than its intimate sequel *The Day After Judgement*, is a strong fantasy in which black Magic – treated here as a science or, as Blish has it, a 'scholium' – releases Satan into the world again; Satan rules Heaven in the sequel.

Blish's later years were much preoccupied with the *Star Trek* books, beginning with *Star Trek* (**1967**) and ending with *Star Trek 11* (**1975**). They are based on the original television scripts, and hence are in fact technically collaborations, but *Spock Must Die* (**1970**) is an original work, the first original adult *Star Trek* novel (it was preceded by Mack Reynolds's *Mission to Horatius* [**1968**], a juvenile). The posthumous *Star Trek 12* (coll **1977**) contained two adaptations (out of five) completed by Judith Ann Lawrence, who also completed some of the work in #11.

In addition to his fiction, Blish had been for decades recognized, along with Damon Knight, as one of the most influential of early sf critics. He wrote his criticism as by William Atheling Jr, a pseudonym borrowed from Ezra Pound (Blish was deeply knowledgeable about Pound) and first used as a byline on essays for *Skyhook*; in other fanzines such as *Warhoon* he published critiques under his own name. Much of this criticism was collected in two books, *The Issue at Hand: Studies in Contemporary Magazine Science Fiction* (**1964**) as by William Atheling Jr and *More Issues at Hand: Critical Studies in Contemporary Science Fiction* (**1970**) as by William Atheling Jr; Blish acknowledged his authorship in introductions to both. The criticism is notably stern in many cases, often pedantic, but intelligent and written from a much wider perspective than was usual for fan criticism of Blish's era.

Blish did much to encourage younger writers; he was one of the founders of the Milford Science Fiction Writers' Conference, and an active charter member of the Science Fiction Writers of America. He also became, in 1970, one of the founder members of the Science Fiction Foundation in the UK. Blish had a scholastic temperament, and in 1969 emigrated to England to be close to Oxford, where he is buried. His manuscripts and papers are in the Bodleian Library. These include several unpublished works of both mainstream fiction and sf.

Blish was an interesting example of a writer with an enquiring mind and a strong literary bent – with some of the crotchets of the autodidact – who turned his attention to fundamentally pulp GENRE-SF materials and in so doing transformed them. His part in the transformation of pulp sf to something of greater cognitive ambitiousness is historically of the first importance. He was not a naturally easy or harmonious writer; his style was often awkward, and in its sometimes anomalous displays of erudition it could appear cold. But there was a visionary, romantic side to Blish which, though carefully controlled, is often visible below the surface. At his best, he wrote tales full of the joys of thinking hard about large issues. He was posthumously inducted into the Science Fiction Hall Of Fame in 2002.

The three titles selected here copiously illustrate the joy that can radiate from stories that think. There is an exuberance about the tales assembled into *The Seedling Stars* rare in the 1950s and even rarer now. They all deal with the implications of pantropy, a term Blish coined for this series, where he argues that the human species will need to be genetically engineered to cope with the exploration of deep space; and that these genetic modifications, or pantropy, will give us the stars. In *Black Easter*, and its sequel *The Day After Judgement*, Satan as always gets the best lines. The first volume, where humans release Him through black magic, is unholy fun; the second volume, which is more grown up, shows Satan having to deal with all the headaches of having to govern the world. It is exhilarating to have things put so well. It is what Blish did.

For a more detailed version of the above, see James Blish's author entry in *The Encyclopedia of Science Fiction*: http://sf-encyclopedia.com/entry/blish_james

Some terms above are capitalised when they would not normally be so rendered; this indicates that the terms represent discrete entries in *The Encyclopedia of Science Fiction*.

BLACK EASTER

In memoriam C. S. Lewis

AUTHOR'S NOTE

There have been many novels, poems and plays about magic and witchcraft. All of them that I have read – which I think includes the vast majority – classify without exception as either romantic or playful, Thomas Mann's included. I have never seen one which dealt with what real sorcery actually had to be like if it existed, although all the grimoires are explicit about the matter. Whatever other merits this book may have, it neither romanticizes magic nor treats it as a game.

Technically, its background is based as closely as possible upon the writings and actual working manuals of practising magicians working in the Christian tradition from the thirteenth to the eighteenth centuries, from the *Ars Magna* of Ramon Lull, through the various *Keys* of pseudo-Solomon, pseudo-Agrippa, pseudo-Honorius and so on, to the grimoires themselves. All of the books mentioned in the text actually exist; there are no 'Necronomicons' or other such invented works, and the quotations and symbols are equally authentic. (Though of course it should be added that the attributions of these works are seldom to be trusted; as C. A. E. Waite has noted, the besetting *bibliographic* sins of magic are imputed authorship, false places of publication and back-dating.)

For most readers this will be warning enough. The experimentally minded, however, should be further warned that, although the quotations, diagrams and rituals in the novel are authentic, they are in no case complete. The book, is not, and was not intended to be, either synoptic or encyclopedic. It is not a *vade mecum*, but a *cursus infamam*.

Alexandria (Va.)
1968
James Blish

PREPARATION OF THE OPERATOR

It is not reasonable to suppose that Aristotle knew the number of the Elect.

—*Albertus Magnus*

The room stank of demons.

And it was not just the room – which would have been unusual, but not unprecedented. Demons were not welcome visitors on Monte Albano, where the magic practised was mostly of the kind called Transcendental, aimed at pursuit of a more perfect mystical union with God and His two revelations, the Scriptures and the World. But occasionally, Ceremonial magic – an applied rather than a pure art, seeking certain immediate advantages – was practised also, and in the course of that the White Monks sometimes called down a demiurge, and, even more rarely, raised up one of the Fallen.

That had not happened in a long time, however; of that, Father F. X. Domenico Bruno Garelli was now positive. No, the stench was something in the general air. It was, in fact, something that was abroad in the world ... the secular world, God's world, the world at large.

And it would have to be something extraordinarily powerful, extraordinarily malign, for Father Domenico to have detected it without prayer, without ritual, without divination, without instruments or instrumentalities of any kind. Though Father Domenico – ostensibly an ordinary Italian monk of about forty *ae*, with the stolid face of his peasant family and calluses on his feet – was in fact an adept of the highest class, the class called Karcists, he was not a Sensitive. There were no true Sensitives at all on the mountain, for they did not thrive even in the relative isolation of a monastery; they could not function except as eremites (which explained why there were so few of them anywhere in the world, these days).

Father Domenico closed the huge Book of Hours with a creak of leather and parchment, and rolled up the palimpsest upon which he had been calculating. There was no doubt about it: none of the White Monks had invoked any infernal power, not even a minor seneschal, for more than a twelve-month past. He had suspected as much – how, after all, could he have gone unaware of such an event? – but the records, which kept themselves without possibility of human intervention, confirmed it. That exhalation from Hell-mouth was drifting up from the world below.

Deeply disturbed, Father Domenico rested his elbows upon the closed record book and propped his chin in his hands. The question was, what should he do now? Tell Father Umberto? No, he really had too little solid information yet to convey to anyone else, let alone disturbing the Director-General with his suspicions and groundless certainties.

How, then, to find out more? He looked ruefully to his right, at his crystal. He had never been able to make it work – probably because he knew all too well that what Roger Bacon had really been describing in *The Nullity of Magic* had been nothing more than a forerunner of the telescope – though others on the mountain, unencumbered by such historical scepticism, practised crystallomancy with considerable success. To his left, next to the book, a small brass telescope was held aloft in a regrettably phallic position by a beautiful gold statuette of Pan that had a golden globe for a pediment, but which was only a trophy of an old triumph over a minor Piedmontese black magician and had no astronomical usefulness; should Father Domenico want to know the precise positions of the lesser Jovian satellites (the Galilean ones were of course listed in the US Naval Observatory ephemeris), or anything else necessary to the casting of an absolute horoscope, he would call upon the twelve-inch telescope and the image-orthicon on the roof of the monastery and have the images (should he need them as well as the data) transmitted by closed-circuit television directly to his room. At the moment, unhappily, he had no event to cast a horoscope either from or toward – only a pervasive, immensurable fog of rising evil.

At Father Domenico's back, he knew without looking, coloured spots and lozenges of light from his high, narrow, stained-glass window were being cast at this hour across the face of his computer, mocking the little coloured points of its safe-lights. He was in charge of this machine, which the other Brothers regarded with an awe he privately thought perilously close to being superstitious; he himself knew the computer to be nothing but a moron – an idiot-savant with a gift for fast addition. But he had no data to feed the machine, either.

Call for a Power and ask for help? No, not yet. The occasion might be trivial, or at least seem so in the spheres they moved, and where they moved. Father Domenico gravely doubted that it was, but he had been rebuked before for unnecessarily troubling those movers and governors, and it was not a kind of displeasure a sensible white magician could afford, however in contempt he might hold the indiscriminate hatred of demons.

No; there was no present solution but to write to Father Uccello, who would listen hungrily, if nothing else. He was a Sensitive; he, too, would know that something ugly was being born – and would doubtless know more about it than that. He would have data.

Father Domenico realized promptly that he had been almost unconsciously trying to avoid this decision almost from the start. The reason was obvious, now that he looked squarely at it; for of all the possibilities, this one would be the most time-consuming. But it also seemed to be unavoidable.

Resignedly, he got out his Biro fountain pen and a sheet of foolscap and began. What few facts he had could be briefly set down, but there was a certain amount of ceremony that had to be observed: salutations in Christ, inquiries about health, prayers and so on, and of course the news; Sensitives were always as lonely as old women, and as interested in gossip about sin, sickness and death. One had to placate them; edifying them – let alone curing them – was impossible.

While he was still at it, the door swung inward to admit an acolyte: the one Father Domenico, in a rare burst of sportiveness, had nicknamed Joannes, after Bacon's famous disappearing apprentice. Looking up at him bemusedly, Father Domenico said:

'I'm not through yet.'

'I beg your pardon?'

'Sorry … I was thinking about something else. I'll have a letter for you to send down the mountain in a while. In the meantime, what did you want?'

'Myself, nothing,' Joannes said. 'But the Director asks me to tell you that he wishes your presence, in the office, right after sext. There's to be a meeting with a client.'

'Oh. Very well. What sort of client?'

'I don't know, Father. It's a new one. He's being hauled up the mountain now. I hear he's a rich American, but then, a lot of them are, aren't they?'

'You do seem to know *something*,' Father Domenico said drily, but his mind was not on the words. The reek of evil had suddenly become much more pronounced; it was astonishing that the boy couldn't smell it too. He put the letter aside. By tonight there would be more news to add – and, perhaps, data.

'Tell the Director I'll be along promptly.'

'First I have to go and tell Father Amparo,' Joannes said. 'He's supposed to meet the client too.'

Father Domenico nodded. At the door, the acolyte turned, with a mysterious sort of slyness, and added:

'His name is Baines.'

The door shut. Well, there was a fact, such as it was – and obviously Joannes had thought it full of significance. But to Father Domenico it meant nothing at all.

Nothing, nothing at all.

THE FIRST COMMISSION

[In] the legendary wonder-world of Theurgy ... all paradoxes seem to obtain actually, contradictions coexist logically, the effect is greater than the cause and the shadow more than the substance. Therein the visible melts into the unseen, the invisible is manifested openly, motion from place to place is accomplished without traversing the intervening distance, matter passes through matter ... There life is prolonged, youth renewed, physical immortality secured. There earth becomes gold, and gold earth. There words and wishes possess creative power, thoughts are things, desire realizes its object. There, also, the dead live and the hierarchies of extra-mundane intelligence are within easy communication, and become ministers or tormentors, guides or destroyers, of man.

—A. E. Waite, *The Book of Ceremonial Magic*

1

The magician said, 'No, I can't help you to persuade a woman. Should you want her raped, I can arrange that. If you want to rape her yourself, I can arrange that, too, with more difficulty – possibly more than you'd have to exert on your own hook. But I can't supply you with any philtres or formulae. My speciality is crimes of violence. Chiefly, murder.'

Baines shot a sidelong glance at his special assistant, Jack Ginsberg, who as usual wore no expression whatsoever and had not a crease out of true. It was nice to be able to trust someone. Baines said, 'You're very frank.'

'I try to leave as little mystery as possible,' Theron Ware – Baines knew that was indeed his real name – said promptly. 'From the client's point of view, black magic is a body of technique, like engineering. The more he knows about it, the easier I find it makes coming to an agreement.'

'No trade secrets? Arcane lore, and so on?'

'Some – mostly the products of my own research, and very few of them of any real importance to you. The main scholium of magic is "arcane" only because most people don't know what books to read or where to find them. Given those books – and sometimes, somebody to translate them for you – you could learn almost everything important that I know in a year. To make something of the material, of course, you'd have to have the talent, since magic is also an art. With books and the gift, you could become a magician

– either you are or you aren't, there are no bad magicians, any more than there is such a thing as a bad mathematician – in about twenty years. If it didn't kill you first, of course, in some equivalent of a laboratory accident. It takes that long, give or take a few years, to develop the skills involved. I don't mean to say you wouldn't find it formidable, but the age of secrecy is past. And really the old codes were rather simple-minded, much easier to read than, say, musical notation. If they weren't, well, computers could break them in a hurry.'

Most of these generalities were familiar stuff to Baines, as Ware doubtless knew. Baines suspected the magician of offering them in order to allow time for himself to be studied by the client. This suspicion crystallized promptly as a swinging door behind Ware's huge desk chair opened silently, and a short-skirted blonde girl in a pageboy coiffure came in with a letter on a small silver tray.

'Thank you, Greta. Excuse me,' Ware said, taking the tray. 'We wouldn't have been interrupted if this weren't important.' The envelope crackled expensively in his hands as he opened it.

Baines watched the girl go out – a moving object, to be sure, but except that she reminded him vaguely of someone else, nothing at all extraordinary – and then went openly about inspecting Ware. As usual, he started with the man's chosen surroundings.

The magician's office, brilliant in the afternoon sunlight, might have been the book-lined study of any doctor or lawyer, except that the room and the furniture were outsize. That said very little about Ware, for the house was a rented cliffside palazzo; there were bigger ones available in Positano had Ware been interested in still higher ceilings and worse acoustics. Though most of the books looked old, the office was no mustier than, say, the library of Merton College, and it contained far fewer positively ancient instruments. The only trace in it that might have been attributable to magic was a faint smell of mixed incenses, which the Tyrrhenian air coming in through the opened windows could not entirely dispel; but it was so slight that the nose soon tired of trying to detect it. Besides, it was hardly diagnostic by itself; small Italian churches, for instance, also smelled like that – and so did the drawing rooms of Egyptian police chiefs.

Ware himself was remarkable, but with only a single exception, only in the sense that all men are unique to the eye of the born captain. A small, spare man he was, dressed in natural Irish tweeds, a French-cuffed shirt linked with what looked like ordinary steel, a narrow, grey, silk four-in-hand tie with a single very small sapphire chessman – a rook – tacked to it. His leanness seemed to be held together with cables; Baines was sure that he was physically strong, despite a marked pallor, and that his belt size had not changed since he had been in high school.

His present apparent age was deceptive. His face was seamed, and his bushy grey eyebrows now only slightly suggested that he had once been red-haired. His hair proper could not, for – herein lay his one marked oddity – he was tonsured, like a monk, blue veins crawling across his bare white scalp as across the papery backs of his hands. An innocent bystander might have taken him to be in his late sixties. Baines knew him to be exactly his own age, which was forty-eight. Black magic, not surprisingly, was obviously a wearing profession; cerebrotonic types like Ware, as Baines had often observed of the scientists who worked for Consolidated Warfare Service (div. A. O. LeFebre et Cie.), ordinarily look about forty-five from a real age of thirty until their hair turns white, if a heart attack doesn't knock them off in the interim.

The parchment crackled and Jack Ginsberg unobtrusively touched his dispatch case, setting going again a tape recorder back in Rome. Baines thought Ware saw this, but chose to take no notice. The magician said:

'Of course, it's also faster if my clients are equally frank with me.'

'I should think you'd know all about me by now,' Baines said. He felt an inner admiration. The ability to pick up an interrupted conversation exactly where it had been left off is rare in a man. Women do it easily, but seldom to any purpose.

'Oh, Dun and Bradstreet,' Ware said, 'newspaper morgues, and of course the grapevine – I have all that, naturally. But I'll still need to ask some questions.'

'Why not read my mind?'

'Because it's more work than it's worth. I mean your excellent mind no disrespect, Mr Baines. But one thing you must understand is that magic is hard work. I don't use it out of laziness, I am not a lazy man, but by the same token I do take the easier ways of getting what I want if easier ways are available.'

'You've lost me.'

'An example, then. All magic – I repeat, *all* magic, with no exceptions whatsoever – depends upon the control of demons. By demons I mean specifically fallen angels. No lesser class can do a thing for you. Now, I know one such whose earthly form includes a long tongue. You may find the notion comic.'

'Not exactly.'

'Let that pass for now. In any event, this is also a great prince and president, whose apparition would cost me three days of work and two weeks of subsequent exhaustion. Shall I call him up to lick stamps for me?'

'I see the point,' Baines said. 'All right, ask your questions.'

Thank you. Who sent you to me?'

'A medium in Bel Air – Los Angeles. She attempted to blackmail me, so nearly successfully that I concluded that she did have some real talent and would know somebody who had more. I threatened her life and she broke.'

Ware was taking notes. 'I see. And she sent you to the Rosicrucians?'

'She tried, but I already knew that dodge. She sent me to Monte Albano.'

'Ah. That surprises me, a little. I wouldn't have thought that you'd have any need of treasure finders.'

'I do and I don't,' Baines said. 'I'll explain that, too, but a little later, if you don't mind. Primarily I wanted someone in your speciality – murder – and of course the white monks were of no use there. I didn't even broach the subject with them. Frankly, I only wanted to test your reputation, of which I'd had hints. I, too, can use newspaper morgues. Their horror when I mentioned you was enough to convince me that I ought to talk to you, at least.'

'Sensible. Then you don't really believe in magic yet – only in ESP or some such nonsense.'

'I'm not,' Baines said guardedly, 'a religious man.'

'Precisely put. Hence, you want a demonstration. Did you bring with you the mirror I mentioned on the phone to your assistant?'

Silently, Jack took from his inside jacket pocket a waxed paper envelope, from which he in turn removed a lady's hand mirror sealed in glassine. He handed it to Baines, who broke the seal.

'Good. Look in it.'

Out of the corners of Baines's eyes, two slow thick tears of dark venous blood were crawling down beside his nose. He lowered the mirror and stared at Ware.

'Hypnotism,' he said, quite steadily. 'I had hoped for better.'

'Wipe them off,' Ware said, unruffled.

Baines pulled out his immaculate monogrammed handkerchief. On the white-on-white fabric, the red stains turned slowly into butter-yellow gold.

'I suggest you take those to a government metallurgist tomorrow,' Ware said. 'I could hardly have hypnotized him. Now perhaps we might get down to business.'

'I thought you said—'

That even the simplest trick requires a demon. So I did, and I meant it. He is sitting at your back now, Mr Baines, and he will be there until the day after tomorrow at this hour. Remember that – day after tomorrow. It will cost me dearly to have turned this little piece of silliness, but I'm used to having to do such things for a sceptical client – and it will be included in my bill. Now, if you please, Mr Baines, what *do* you want?'

Baines handed the handkerchief to Jack, who folded it carefully and put it back in its waxed-paper wrapper. 'I,' Baines said, 'of course want someone killed. Tracelessly.'

'Of course, but who?'

'I'll tell you that in a minute. First of all, do you exercise any scruples?'

'Quite a few,' Ware said. 'For instance, I don't kill my friends, not for any client. And possibly I might balk at certain strangers. However, in general, I do have strangers sent for, on a regular scale of charges.'

'Then we had better explore the possibilities,' Baines said. 'I've got an ex-wife who's a gross inconvenience to me. Do you balk at that?'

'Has she any children – by you or anybody else?'

'No, none at all.'

'In that case, there's no problem. For that kind of job, my standard fee is fifteen thousand dollars, flat.'

Despite himself, Baines stared in astonishment. 'Is that all?' he said at last.

'That's all. I suspect that I'm almost as wealthy as you are, Mr Baines. After all, I can find treasure as handily as the white monks can – indeed, a good deal better. I use these alimony cases to keep my name before the public. Financially they're a loss to me.'

'What kinds of fees are you interested in?'

'I begin to exert myself slightly at about five million.'

If this man was a charlatan, he was a grandiose one. Baines said, 'Let's stick to the alimony case for the moment. Or rather, suppose I don't care about the alimony, as in fact I don't. Instead, I might not only want her dead, but I might want her to die badly. To suffer.'

'I don't charge for that.'

'Why not?'

'Mr Baines,' Ware said patiently, 'I remind you, please, that I myself am not a killer. I merely summon and direct the agent. I think it very likely – in fact, I think it beyond doubt – that any patient I have sent for dies in an access of horror and agony beyond your power to imagine, or even of mine. But you did specify that you wanted your murder done "tracelessly", which obviously means that I must have no unusual marks left on the patient. I prefer it that way myself. How then could I prove suffering if you asked for it, in a way inarguable enough to charge you extra for it?

'Or, look at the other side of the shield, Mr Baines. Every now and then, an unusual divorce client asks that the ex-consort be carried away painlessly, even sweetly, out of some residue of sentiment. I *could* collect an extra fee for that, on a contingent basis, that is, if the body turns out to show no overt marks of disease or violence. But my agents are demons, and sweetness is not a trait they can be compelled to exhibit, so I never accept that kind of condition from a client, either. Death is what you pay for, and death is what you get. The circumstances are up to the agent, and I don't offer my clients anything that I know I can't deliver.'

'All right, I'm answered,' Baines said. 'Forget Dolores – actually she's only a minor nuisance, and only one of several, for that matter. Now let's talk about the other end of the spectrum. Suppose instead that I should ask you to ... send for ... a great political figure. Say, the governor of California – or, if he's a friend of yours, pick a similar figure who isn't.'

Ware nodded. 'He'll do well enough. But you'll recall that I asked you about children. Had you really turned out to have been an alimony case, I should next have asked you about surviving relatives. My fees rise in direct proportion to the numbers and kinds of people a given death is likely to affect. This is partly what you call scruples, and partly a species of self-defence. Now in the case of a reigning governor, I would charge you one dollar for every vote he got when he was last elected. Plus expenses, of course.'

Baines whistled in admiration. 'You're the first man I've ever met who's worked out a system to make scruples pay. And I can see why you don't care about alimony cases. Someday, Mr Ware—'

'*Doctor* Ware, please. I am a Doctor of Theology.'

'Sorry. I only meant to say that someday I'll ask you why you want so much money. You asthenics seldom can think of any good use for it. In the meantime, however, you're hired. Is it all payable in advance?'

'The expenses are payable in advance. The fee is C.O.D. As you'll realize once you stop to think about it, Mr Baines—'

'*Doctor* Baines. I am an LL.D.'

'Apologies in exchange. I want you to realize, after these courtesies, that I have never, never been bilked.'

Baines thought about what was supposed to be at his back until the day after tomorrow. Pending the test of the golden tears on the handkerchief, he was willing to believe that he should not try to cheat Ware. Actually, he had never planned to.

'Good,' he said, getting up. 'By the same token, we don't need a contract. I agree to your terms.'

'But what for?'

'Oh,' Baines said, 'we can use the governor of California for a starter. Jack here will iron out any remaining details with you. I have to get back to Rome by tonight.'

'You did say, "For a starter"?'

Baines nodded shortly. Ware, also rising, said, 'Very well. I shall ask no questions. But in fairness, Mr Baines. I should warn you that on your next commission of this kind, I shall ask you what *you* want.'

'By that time,' Baines said, holding his excitement tightly bottled, 'we'll *have* to exchange such confidences. Oh, Dr Ware, will the, uh, demon on my back go away by itself when the time's up or must I see you again to get it taken off?'

'It isn't *on* your back,' Ware said. 'And it will go by itself. Marlowe to the contrary, misery does not love company.'

Baring his teeth, Baines said, 'We'll see about that.'

2

For a moment, Jack Ginsberg felt the same soon-to-be-brief strangeness of the man who does not really know what is going on and hence thinks he might be about to be fired. It was as though something had swallowed him by mistake, and – quite without malice – was about to throw him up again.

While he waited for the monster's nausea to settle out, Jack went through his rituals, stroking his cheeks for stubble, resetting his creases, running through last week's accounts, and thinking above all, as he usually did most of all in such interims, of what the new girl might look like squatting in her stockings. Nothing special, probably; the reality was almost always hedged around with fleshy inconveniences and piddling little preferences that he could flense away at will from the clean vision.

When the chief had left and Ware had come back to his desk, however, Jack was ready for business and thoroughly on top of it. He prided himself upon an absolute self-control.

'Questions?' Ware said, leaning back easily.

'A few, Dr Ware. You mentioned expenses. What expenses?'

'Chiefly travel,' Ware said. 'I have to see the patient, personally. In the case Dr Baines posed, that involves a trip to California, which is a vast inconvenience to me, and goes on the bill. It includes air fare, hotels, meals, other out-of-pocket expenses, which I'll itemize when the mission is over. Then there's the question of getting to see the governor. I have colleagues in California, but there's a certain amount of influence I'll have to buy, even with the help of Consolidated Warfare – munitions and magic are circles that don't intersect very effectively. On the whole, I think a draft for ten thousand would be none too small.'

All that for magic. Disgusting. But the chief believed in it, at least provisionally. It made Jack feel very queasy.

'That sounds satisfactory,' he said, but he made no move towards the corporate chequebook; he was not about to issue any Valentines to strangers yet, not until there was more love touring about the landscape than he had felt in his crew-cut antennae. 'We're naturally a little bit wondering, sir, why all this expense is necessary. We understand that you'd rather not ride a demon when you can fly a jet with less effort—'

'I'm not sure you do,' Ware said, 'but stop simpering about it and ask me about the money.'

'Argh ... well, sir, then, just why do you live outside the United States? We know you're still a citizen. And after all, we have freedom of religion in the

States still. Why does the chief have to pay to ship you back home for one job?'

'Because I'm not a common gunman,' Ware said. 'Because I don't care to pay income taxes, or even report my income to anybody. There are two reasons. For the benefit of your ever-attentive dispatch case there – since you're a deaf ear if ever I saw one – if I lived in the United States and advertised myself as a magician, I would be charged with fraud, and if I successfully defended myself – proved I was what I said I was – I'd wind up in a gas chamber. If I failed to defend myself, I'd be just one more charlatan. In Europe, I can say I'm a magician, and be left alone if I can satisfy my clients – *caveat emptor*. Otherwise, I'd have to be constantly killing off petty politicians and accountants, which isn't worth the work, and sooner or later runs into the law of diminishing returns. Now you can turn that thing off.'

Aha; there was something wrong with this joker. He was preying upon superstition. As a reformed Orthodox Agnostic, Jack Ginsberg knew all the ins and outs of that, especially the double-entry sides. He said smoothly:

'I quite understand. But don't you perhaps have almost as much trouble with the Church, here in Italy, as you would with the government back home?'

'No, not under a liberal pontificate. The modern Church discourages what it calls superstition among its adherents. I haven't encountered a prelate in decades who believes in the *literal* existence of demons – though of course some of the Orders know better.'

'To be sure,' Jack said, springing his trap exultantly. 'So I think, sir, that you may be overcharging us – and haven't been quite candid with us. If you do indeed control all these great princes and presidents, you could as easily bring the chief a woman as you could bring him a treasure or a murder.'

'So I could,' the magician said, a little wearily. 'I see you've done a little reading. But I explained to Dr Baines, and I explain again to you, that I specialize only in crimes of violence. Now, Mr Ginsberg, I think you were about to write me an expense cheque.'

'So I was.' But still he hesitated. At last Ware said with delicate politeness:

'Is there some other doubt I could resolve for you, Mr Ginsberg? I am, after all, a Doctor of Theology. Or perhaps you have a private commission you wish to broach to me?'

'No,' Jack said. 'No, not exactly.'

'I see no reason why you should be shy. It's clear that you like my lamia. And in fact, she's quite free of the nuisances of human women that so annoy you—'

'Damn you. I *thought* you read minds! You lied about that, too.'

'I don't read minds, and I never lie,' Ware said. 'But I'm adept at reading faces and somatotypes. It saves me a lot of trouble, and a lot of unnecessary magic. Do you want the creature or don't you? I could have her sent to you invisibly if you like.'

'No.'

'Not invisibly. I'm sorry for you. Well then, my godless and lustless friend, speak up for yourself. What *would* you like? Your business is long since done. Spit it out. What is it?'

For a breathless instant, Jack almost said what it was, but the God in which he no longer believed was at his back. He made out the cheque and handed it over. The girl (no, not a girl) came in and took it away.

'Good-bye,' Theron Ware said.

He had missed the boat again.

3

Father Domenico read the letter again, hopefully. Father Uccello affected an Augustinian style, after his name saint, full of rare words and outright neologisms embedded in medieval syntax – as a stylist, Father Domenico much preferred Roger Bacon, but that eminent anti-magician, not being a Father of the Church, tempted few imitators – and it was possible that Father Domenico had misread him. But no; involuted though the Latin of the letter was, the sense, this time, was all too plain.

Father Domenico sighed. The practice of Ceremonial magic, at least of the white kind which was the monastery's sole concern, seemed to be becoming increasingly unrewarding. Part of the difficulty, of course, lay in the fact that the chiefest traditional use (for profit) of white magic was the finding of buried treasure; and after centuries of unremitting practice by centuries of sorcerers black and white, plus the irruption into the field of such modern devices as the mine detector, there was very little buried treasure left to find. Of late, the troves revealed by those under the governments of Och and Bethor – with the former of whom in particular lay the bestowal of 'a purse springing with gold' – had increasingly turned out to be underseas, or in places like Fort Knox or a Swiss bank, making the recovery of them enterprises so colossal and mischancy as to remove all possibility of profit for client and monastery alike.

On the whole, black magicians had an easier time of it – at least in this life; one must never forget, Father Domenico reminded himself hastily, that they were also damned eternally. It was as mysterious as it had always been that such infernal spirits as LUCIFUGE ROFOCALE should be willing to lend so much power to a mortal whose soul Hell would almost inevitably have won anyhow, considering the character of the average sorcerer, and considering how easily such pacts could be voided at the last instant; and that God would allow so much demonic malice to be vented through the sorcerer upon the innocent. But that was simply another version of the Problem of Evil, for which the Church had long had the answer (or, the dual answer) of free will and original sin.

It had to be recalled, too, that even the practice of white or Transcendental magic was officially a mortal sin, for the modern Church held that all trafficking with spirits – including the un-Fallen, since such dealings inevitably assumed the angels to be demiurges and other kabbalistic semi-deities – was an abomination, regardless of intent. Once upon a time, it had been recognized that (barring the undertaking of an actual pact) only a man of the highest piety, of the highest purpose, and in the highest state of ritual and spiritual purification, could hope to summon and control a demon, let alone an angel; but there had been too many lapses of intent, and then of act, and in both practicality and compassion the Church had declared all Theurgy to be anathema, reserving unto itself only one negative aspect of magic – exorcism – and that only under the strictest of canonical limitations.

Monte Albano had a special dispensation, to be sure – partly since the monks had at one time been so spectacularly successful in nourishing the coffers of St Peter's; partly because the knowledge to be won through the Transcendental rituals might sometimes be said to have nourished the soul of the Rock; and, in small part, because under the rarest of circumstances white magic had been known to prolong the life of the body. But these fountains (to shift the image) were now showing every sign of running dry, and hence the dispensation might be withdrawn at any time – thus closing out the last sanctuary of white magic in the world.

That would leave the field to the black magicians. There were no black sanctuaries, except for the Parisian Brothers of the Left-Hand Way, who were romantics of the school of Éliphas Lévi and were more to be pitied for folly than condemned for evil. But of solitary black sorcerers there were still a disconcerting number – though even one would be far too many.

Which brought Father Domenico directly back to the problem of the letter. He sighed again, turned away from his lectern and padded off – the Brothers of Monte Albano were discalced – towards the office of the Director, letter in hand. Father Umberto was in (of course he was always *physically* in, like all the rest of them, since the Mount could not be left once entered, except by the laity and they only by muleback), and Father Domenico got to the point directly.

'I've had another impassioned screed from our witch smeller,' he said. 'I am beginning to consider, reluctantly, that the matter is at least as serious as he's been saying all along.'

'You mean the matter of Theron Ware, I presume.'

'Yes, of course. The American gunmaker we saw went directly from the Mount to Ware, as seemed all too likely even at the time, and Father Uccello says that there's now every sign of another series of sendings being prepared in Positano.'

'I wish you would avoid these alliterations. They make it difficult to discover what you're talking about. I often feel that a lapse into alliteration or other grammatical tricks is a sure sign that the speaker isn't himself quite sure of what he means to say, and is trying to blind me to the fact. Never mind. As for the demonolater Ware, we are in no position to interfere with him, whatever he's preparing.'

'The style is Father Uccello's. Anyhow, he insists that we *must* interfere. He has been practising divination – so you can see how seriously *he* takes this, the old purist – and he says that his principal, whom he takes great pains not to identify, told him that the meeting of Ware and Baines presages something truly monstrous for the world at large. According to his information, all Hell has been waiting for this meeting since the two of them were born.'

'I suppose he's sure his principal wasn't in fact a demon and didn't slip a lie past him, or at least one of their usual brags? As you've just indirectly pointed out, Father Uccello is way out of practice.'

Father Domenico spread his hands. 'Of course I can't answer that. Though if you wish, Father, I'll try to summon Whatever it was myself, and put the problem to It. But you know how good the chances are that I'll get the wrong one – and how hard it is to ask the right question. The great Governors seem to have no time sense as we understand the term, and as for demons, well, even when compelled they often really don't seem to know what's going on outside their own jurisdictions.'

'Quite so,' said the Director, who had not himself practised in many years. He had been greatly talented once, but the loss of gifted experimenters to administrative posts was the curse of all research organizations. 'I think it best that you don't jeopardize your own usefulness, and your own soul, of course, in calling up some spirit you can't name. Father Uccello in turn ought to know that there's nothing we can do about Ware. Or does he have some proposal?'

'He wants us,' Father Domenico said in a slightly shaky voice, 'to impose an observer on Ware. To send one directly to Positano, someone who'll stick to Ware until we know what the deed is going to be. We're just barely empowered to do this – whereas, of course, Father Uccello can't. The question is, do *we* want to?'

'Hmm, hmm,' the Director said. 'Obviously not. That would bankrupt us – oh, not financially, of course, though it would be difficult enough. But we couldn't afford to send a novice, or indeed anyone less than the best we have, and after the good Lord only knows how many months in that infernal atmosphere ...'

The sentence trailed off, as the Director's sentences often did, but Father Domenico no longer had any difficulty in completing them. Obviously the Mount could not afford to have even one of its best operators incapacitated – the word, in fact, was 'contaminated' – by prolonged contact with the person and effects of Theron Ware. Similarly, Father Domenico was reasonably certain that the Director would in fact send somebody to Positano; otherwise he would not have mounted the obvious objections, but simply dismissed the proposal. For all their usual amusement with Father Uccello, both men knew that there were occasions when one had to take him with the utmost seriousness, and that this was one of them.

'Nevertheless the matter will need to be explored,' the Director resumed after a moment, fingering his beads. 'I had better give Ware the usual formal notification. We're not obligated to follow up on it, but …'

'Quite,' Father Domenico said. He put the letter into his scrip and arose. 'I'll hear from you, then, when a reply's been received from Ware. I'm glad you agree that the matter is serious.'

After another exchange of formalities, he left, head bowed. He also knew well enough whom the Director would send, without any intervention of false modesty to cloud the issue; and he was well aware that he was terrified.

He went directly to his conjuring room, the cluttered tower chamber that no one else could use – for magic is intensely sensitive to the personality of the operator – and which was still faintly redolent of a scent a little like oil of lavender, a trace of his last use of the room. *Mansit odor, posses scire duisse deam*, he thought, not for the first time; but he had no intention of summoning any Presence now. Instead, he crossed to the chased casket which contained his 1606 copy – the second edition, but not much corrupted – of the *Enchiridion* of Leo III, that odd collection of prayers and other devices 'effectual against all the perils to which every sort and condition of men may be made subject on land; on water, from open and secret enemies, from the bites of wild and rabid beasts, from poisons, from fire, from tempests'. For greatest effectiveness he was instructed to carry the book on his person, but he had seldom judged himself to be in sufficient peril to risk so rare and valuable an object, and in any event he did always read at least one page daily, chiefly the *In principio*, a version of the first chapter of the Gospel According to St John.

Now he took the book out and opened it to the Seven Mysterious Orisons, the only section of the work – without prejudice to the efficacy of the rest of it – that probably had indeed proceeded from the hand of the Pope of Charlemagne. Kneeling to face the east, Father Domenico, without looking at the page, began the prayer appropriate for Thursday, at the utterance of which, perhaps by no coincidence, it is said that 'the demons flee away'.

4

Considerable business awaited Baines in Rome, all the more pressing because Jack Ginsberg was still out of town, and Baines made no special effort to hunt down Jack's report on what the government metallurgist had said about the golden tears amid the mass of other papers. For the time being, at least, Baines regarded the report as personal correspondence, and he had a standing rule never even to open personal letters during office hours, whether he was actually in an office or, as now, working out of a hotel room.

Nevertheless, the report came to the surface the second day that he was back at work; and since he also made a rule never to lose time to the distractions of an unsatisfied curiosity if an easy remedy was to hand, he read it. The tears on the handkerchief were indeed 24-carat gold; worth about eleven cents, taken together, on the current market, but to Baines representing an enormous investment (or, looked at another way, a potential investment in enormity).

He put it aside with satisfaction and promptly forgot about it, or very nearly. Investments in enormity were his stock in trade, though of late, he thought again with cold anger, they had been paying less and less – hence his interest in Ware, which the other directors of Consolidated Warfare Service would have considered simple insanity. But after all, if the business was no longer satisfying, it was only natural to seek analogous satisfactions somewhere else. An insane man, in Baines's view, would be one who tried to substitute some pleasure – women, philanthropy, art collecting, golf – that offered no cognate satisfaction at all. Baines was ardent about his trade, which was destruction; golf could no more have sublimated that passion than it could have diluted that of a painter or a lecher.

The current fact, which had to be faced and dealt with, was that nuclear weapons had almost totally spoiled the munitions business. Oh, there was still a thriving trade to be drummed up selling small arms to a few small new nations – small arms being defined arbitrarily as anything up to the size of a submarine – but hydrogen fusion and the ballistic missile made the really major achievements of the art, the lubrication of the twenty-year cycle of world wars, entirely too obliterative and self-defeating. These days, Baines's kind of diplomacy consisted chiefly in the fanning of brush fires and civil wars. Even this was a delicate business, for the nationalism game was increasingly an exceedingly confused affair, in which one could never be quite sure whether some emergent African state with a population about the size of Maplewood, N.J., would not turn out to be of absorbing interest to one or more of the nuclear powers. (Some day, of course, they would all be nuclear powers, and then the art would become as formalized and minor as flower arranging.)

The very delicacy of this kind of operation had its satisfactions, in a way, and Baines was good at it. In addition, Consolidated Warfare Service had several thousand man-years of accumulated experience at this sort of thing upon which he could call. One of CWS's chief specialists was in Rome with him now – Dr Adolph Hess, famous as the designer of that peculiar all-purpose vehicle called the Hessicopter, but of interest in the present negotiations as the inventor of something nobody was supposed to have heard of – the land torpedo, a rapidly burrowing device that might show up, commendably anonymous, under any installation within two hundred miles of its launching tunnel, geology permitting. Baines had guessed that it might be especially attractive to at least one of the combatants in the Yemeni insurrection, and had proven to be so right that he was now trying hard not to have to dicker with all four of them. This was all the more difficult because, although the two putative Yemeni factions accounted for very little, Nasser was nearly as shrewd as Baines was, and Faisal inarguably a good deal shrewder.

Nevertheless, Baines was not essentially a miniaturist, and he was well aware of it. He had recognized the transformation impending in the trade early on, in fact with the publication in 1950 by the US Government Printing Office of a volume titled *The Effects of Atomic Weapons*, and as soon as possible had engaged the services of a private firm called the Mamaroneck Research Institute. This was essentially a brainstorming organization, started by an alumnus of the RAND Corporation, which specialized in imagining possible political and military confrontations and their possible outcomes, some of them so *outré* as to require the subcontracting of freelance science-fiction writers. From the files of CWS and other sources, Baines fed Mamaroneck materials for its computers, some of which material would have considerably shaken the governments who thought they were sitting on it; and, in return, Mamaroneck fed Baines long, neatly lettered and Xeroxed reports bearing titles as 'Short- and Long-Term Probabilities Consequent to an Israeli Blockade of the Faeröe Islands'.

Baines winnowed out the most obviously absurd of these, but with a care that was the very opposite of conservatism, for some of the strangest proposals could turn out upon second look to be not absurd at all. Those that offered the best combination of surface absurdity with hidden plausibility, he set out to translate into real situations. Hence there was really nothing illogical or even out of character in his interest in Theron Ware, for Baines, too, practised what was literally an occult art in which the man on the street no longer believed.

The buzzer sounded twice; Ginsberg was back. Baines returned the signal and the door swung open.

'Rogan's dead,' Jack said without preamble.

'That was fast. I thought it was going to take Ware a week after he got back from the States.'

'It's been a week,' Jack reminded him.

'Hmm? So it has. Waiting around for these Ayrabs to get off the dime is hard on the time sense. Well, well, Details?'

'Only what's come over the Reuters ticker, so far. Started as pneumonia, ended as cor pulmonale – heart failure from too much coughing. It appears that he had a small mitral murmur for years. Only the family knew about it, and his physicians assured them that it wasn't dangerous if he didn't try to run a four-minute mile or something like that. Now the guessing is that the last campaign put a strain on it, and the pneumonia did the rest.'

'Very clean,' Baines said.

He thought about the matter for a while. He had borne the late governor of California no ill will. He had never met the man, nor had any business conflicts with him, and in fact had rather admired his brand of medium-right-wing politics, which had been of the articulate but inoffensive sort expectable of an ex-account executive for a San Francisco advertising agency specializing in the touting of cold breakfast cereals. Indeed, Baines recalled suddenly from the file biography, Rogan had been a fraternity brother of his.

Nevertheless he was pleased. Ware had done the job – Baines was not in the smallest doubt that Ware should have the credit – with great nicety. After one more such trial run, simply to rule out all possibility of coincidence, he should be ready to tackle something larger; possibly, the biggest job of them all.

Baines wondered how it had been done. Was it possible that a demon could appear to a victim in the form of a pneumococcus? If so, what about the problem of reproduction? Well, there had been the appearances all over medieval Europe of fragments of the True Cross, in numbers quantitatively sufficient to stock a large lumberyard. Contemporary clerical apologists had called that Miraculous Multiplication, which had always seemed to Baines to be a classic example of rationalizing away the obvious; but since magic was real, maybe Miraculous Multiplication was too.

These, however, were merely details of technique, in which he made a practice of taking no interest. That kind of thing was for hirelings. Still, it wouldn't hurt to have somebody in the organization who did know something about the technicalities. It was often dangerous to depend solely on outside experts.

'Make out a cheque for Ware,' he told Jack. 'From my personal account. Call it a consultation fee – medical, preferably. When you send it to him, set up a date for another visit – let's see – as soon as I get back from Riyadh. I'll take up all this other business with you in about half an hour. Send Hess in, but wait outside.'

Jack nodded and left. A moment later, Hess entered silently. He was a tall, bony man with a slight pod, bushy eyebrows, a bald spot in the back, pepper-and-salt hair, and a narrow jaw that made his face look nearly triangular.

'Any interest in sorcery, Adolph? Personal I mean?'

'Sorcery? I know something about it. For all the nonsense involved, it was highly important in the history of science, particularly the alchemical side, and the astrological.'

'I'm not interested in either of those. I'm talking about black magic.'

'Then no, I don't know much about it,' Hess said.

'Well, you're about to learn. We're going to visit an authentic sorcerer in about two weeks, and I want you to go along and study his methods.'

'Are you pulling my leg?' Hess said. 'No, you never do that. Are we going into the business of exposing charlatans, then? I'm not sure I'm the best man for that, Baines. A professional stage magician – a Houdini type – would be far more likely to catch out a faker than I would.'

'No, that's not the issue at all. I'm going to ask this man to do some work for me, in his own line, and I need a close observer to see what he does – not to see through it, but to form an accurate impression of the procedures, in case something should go sour with the relationship later on.'

'But – well, if you say so, Baines. It does seem rather a waste of time, though.'

'Not to me,' Baines said. 'While you're waiting to talk to the Saudis with me, read up on the subject. By the end of a year I want you to know as much about the subject as an expert. The man himself has told me that that's possible even for me, so it shouldn't tax you any.'

'It's not likely to tax my brains much,' Hess said drily, 'but it may be a considerable tax on my patience. However, you're the boss.'

'Right. Get on it.'

Hess nodded distantly to Jack as he went out. The two men did not like each other much; in part, Baines sometimes thought, because in some ways they were much alike. When the door had closed behind the scientist, Jack produced from his pocket the waxed-paper envelope that had contained, and obviously still contained, the handkerchief bearing the two transmuted tears.

'I don't need that,' Baines said. 'I've got your report. Throw that thing away. I don't want anybody asking what it means.'

'I will,' Jack said. 'But first, you'll remember that Ware said that the demon would leave you after two days.'

'Sure. Why?'

'Look at this.'

Jack took out the handkerchief and spread it carefully on Baines's desk blotter.

On the Irish linen, where the golden tears had been, were now two dull, inarguable smears of lead.

5

By some untraceable miscalculation, Baines's party arrived in Riyadh precisely at the beginning of Ramadan, during which the Arabs fasted all day and were consequently in too short a temper to do business with; which was followed, after twenty-nine solid days, by a three-day feast during which they were too stuporous to do business with. Once negotiations were properly opened, however, they took no more than the two weeks Baines had anticipated.

Since the Moslem calendar is lunar, Ramadan is a moveable festival, which this year fell close to Christmas. Baines half suspected that Theron Ware would refuse to see him in so inauspicious a season for servants of Satan, but Ware made no objection, remarking only (by post), 'December 25th is a celebration of great antiquity.' Hess, who had been reading dutifully, interpreted Ware to mean that Christ had not actually been born on that date – 'though in this universe of discourse I can't see what difference that makes,' he said. 'If the word "superstition" has any of its old meaning left at all by now, it means that the sign has come to replace the thing – or in other words, that facts come to mean what we say they mean.'

'Call it an observer effect,' Baines suggested, not entirely jokingly. He was not disposed to argue the point with either of them; Ware would see him, that was what counted.

But if the season was no apparent inconvenience to Ware, it was a considerable one to Father Domenico, who at first flatly refused to celebrate it in the very maw of Hell. He was pressed at length and from both sides by the Director and Father Uccello, whose arguments had no less force for being so utterly predictable; and – to skip over a full week of positively Scholastic disputation – they prevailed, as again he had been sure they would.

Mustering all his humility, obedience and resignation – his courage seemed to have evaporated – he trudged forth from the monastery, excused from sandals, and mounted a mule, the *Enchiridion* of Leo III swinging from his neck under his cassock in a new leather bag, and a selection of his thaumaturgic tools, newly exorcised, asperged, fumigated and wrapped in silken cloths, in a satchel balanced carefully on the mule's neck. It was a hushed leave-taking – all the more so in its lack of any formalities or even witnesses, for only the Director knew why he was going, and he had been restrained with difficulty from bruiting it about that Father Domenico actually had been expelled, to make a cover story.

The practical effect of both delays was that Father Domenico and Baines's party arrived at Ware's palazzo on the same day, in the midst of the only snowstorm Positano had seen in seven years. As a spiritual courtesy – for protocol was all-important in such matters, otherwise neither monk nor sorcerer would have dared to confront the other – Father Domenico was received first, briefly but punctiliously; but as a client, Baines (and his crew, in descending order) got the best quarters. They also got the only service available, since Ware had no servants who could cross over the invisible line Father Domenico at once ruled at the foot of his apartment door with the point of his bolline.

As was customary in southern Italian towns at this time, three masked kings later came to the gate of the palazzo to bring and ask presents for the children and the Child; but there were no children there and the mummers were turned away, baffled and resentful (for the rich American, who was said to be writing a book about the frescoes of Pompeii, had previously shown himself open-handed), but oddly grateful too; it was a cold night, and the lights in the palazzo were of a grim and distant colour.

Then the gates closed. The principals had gathered and were in their places; and the stage was set.

THREE SLEEPS

It requires more courage and intelligence to be a devil than the folk who take experience at hearsay think. And none, save only he who has destroyed the devil in himself, and that by dint of hard work (for there is no other way) knows what a devil is, and what a devil he himself might be, as also what an army for the devils' use are they who think the devils are delusion.

—*The Book of the Sayings of Tsiang Samdup*

6

Father Domenico's interview with Theron Ware was brief, formal and edgy. The monk, despite his apprehensions, had been curious to see what the magician looked like, and had been irrationally disappointed to find him not much out of the ordinary run of intellectuals. Except for the tonsure, of course; like Baines, Father Domenico found that startling. Also, unlike Baines, he found it upsetting, because he knew the reason for it – not that Ware intended any mockery of his pious counterparts, but because demons, given a moment of inattention, were prone to seizing one by the hair.

'Under the Covenant,' Ware told him in excellent Latin, 'I have no choice but to receive you, of course, Father. And under other circumstances I might even have enjoyed discussing the Art with you, even though we are of opposite schools. But this is an inconvenient time for me. I've got a very important client here, as you've seen, and I've already been notified that what he wants of me is likely to be extraordinarily ambitious.'

'I shan't interfere in any way,' Father Domenico said. 'Even should I wish to, which obviously I shall, I know very well that any such interference would cost me all my protections.'

'I was sure you understood that, but nonetheless I'm glad to hear you say so,' Ware said. 'However, your very presence here is an embarrassment – not only because I'll have to explain it to my client, but also because it changes the atmosphere unfavourably and will make my operations more difficult. I can only hope, in defiance of all hospitality, that your mission will be speedily satisfied.'

'I can't bring myself to regret the difficulty, since I only wish I could make your operations outright impossible. The best I can proffer you is strict adherence to the truce. As for the length of my stay, that depends wholly on what it is your client turns out to want, and how long *that* takes. I am charged with seeing it through to its conclusion.'

'A prime nuisance,' Ware said. 'I suppose I should be grateful that I haven't been blessed with this kind of attention from Monte Albano before. Evidently what Mr Baines intends is even bigger than he thinks it is. I conclude without much cerebration that you know something about it I don't know.'

'It will be an immense disaster, I can tell you that.'

'Hmm. From your point of view, but not necessarily from mine, possibly. I don't suppose you're prepared to offer any further information – on the chance, say, of dissuading me?'

'Certainly not,' Father Domenico said indignantly. 'If eternal damnation hasn't dissuaded you long before this, I'd be a fool to hope to.'

'Well,' Ware said, 'but you are, after all, charged with the cure of souls, and unless the Church has done another flip-flop since the last Congress, it is still also a mortal sin to assume that any man is certainly damned – even me.'

That argument was potent, it had to be granted; but Father Domenico had not been trained in casuistry (and that by Jesuits) for nothing.

'I'm a monk, not a priest,' he said. 'And any information I give you would, on the contrary, almost certainly be used to abet the evil, not turn it aside. I don't find the choice a hard one under the circumstances.'

'Then let me suggest a more practical consideration,' Ware said. 'I don't know yet what Baines intends, but I do know well enough that I am not a Power myself – only a factor. I have no desire to bite off more than I can chew.'

'Now you're just wheedling,' Father Domenico said, with energy. 'Knowing your own limitations is not an exercise at which I or anyone else can help you. You'll just have to weigh them in the light of Mr Baines's commission, whatever that proves to be. In the meantime, I shall tell you nothing.'

'Very well,' Ware said, rising. 'I will be a little more generous with my information, Father, than you have been with yours. I will tell you that you will be well advised to adhere to every letter of the Covenant. One step over the line, one toe, and *I shall have you* – and hardly any outcome in this world would give me greater pleasure. I'm sure I make myself clear.'

Father Domenico could think of no reply; but none seemed to be necessary.

7

As Ware had sensed, Baines was indeed disturbed by the presence of Father Domenico, and made a point of bringing it up as the first order of business. After Ware had explained the monk's mission and the Covenant under which it was being conducted, however, Baines felt somewhat relieved.

'Just a nuisance, as you say, since he can't actually intervene,' he decided. 'In a way, I suppose my bringing Dr Hess here with me is comparable – he's only an observer, too, and fundamentally he's probably just as hostile to your world-view as this holier-than-us fellow is.'

'He's not significantly holier than us,' Ware said with a slight smile. 'I know something he doesn't know, too. He's in for a surprise in the next world. However, for the time being we're stuck with him – for how long depends upon you. Just what is it you want this time, Dr Baines?'

'Two things, one depending on the other. The first is the death of Albert Stockhausen.'

'The anti-matter theorist? That would be too bad. I rather like him, and besides, some of the work he does is of direct interest to me.'

'You refuse?'

'No, not immediately anyhow, but I'm now going to ask you what I promised I would ask on this occasion. What are you aiming at, anyhow?'

'Something very long-term. For the present, my lethal intentions for Dr Stockhausen are strictly business-based. He's nibbling at the edges of a scholium that my company presently controls completely. It's a monopoly of knowledge we don't want to see broken.'

'Do you think you can keep anything secret that's based in natural law? After the McCarthy fiasco I should have supposed that any intelligent American would know better. Surely Dr Stockhausen can't be just verging on some mere technicality – something your firm might eventually bracket with a salvo of process patents.'

'No, it's in the realm of natural law, and hence not patentable at all,' Baines admitted. 'And we already know that it can't be concealed forever. But we need about five years' grace to make the best use of it, and we know that nobody else but Stockhausen is even close to it, barring accidents, of course. We ourselves have nobody of Stockhausen's calibre, we just fell over it, and somebody else might do that. However, that's highly unlikely.'

'I see. Well … the project does have an attractive side. I think it's quite possible that I can persuade Father Domenico that this is the project he came to observe. Obviously it can't be – I've run many like it and never attracted Monte Albano's interest to this extent before – but given sufficient show of great preparations, and difficulty of execution, he might be deluded, and go home.'

'That would be useful,' Baines agreed. 'The question is, could he be deceived?'

'It's worth trying. The task would in fact be difficult – and quite expensive.'

'Why?' Jack Ginsberg said, sitting bolt upright in his carved Florentine chair so suddenly as to make his suit squeak against the silk upholstery.

'Don't tell us he affects thousands of other people. Nobody ever cast any votes for him that I know of.'

'Shut up, Jack.'

'No, wait, it's a reasonable question,' Ware said. 'Dr Stockhausen does have a large family, which I have to take into account. And, as I've told you, I've taken some pleasure in his company on a few occasions – not enough to balk at having him sent for, but enough to help run up the price.'

'But that's not the major impediment. The fact is that Dr Stockhausen, like a good many theoretical physicists these days, is a devout man – and furthermore, he has only a few venial sins to account for, nothing in the least meriting the attention of Hell. I'll check that again with someone who knows, but it was accurate as of six months ago and I'd be astonished if there's been any change. He's not a member of any formal congregation, but even so he's nobody a demon could reasonably have come for him – and there's a chance that he might be defended against any direct assault.'

'Successfully?'

'It depends on the forces involved. Do you want to risk a pitched battle that would tear up half of Düsseldorf? It might be cheaper just to mail him a bomb.'

'No, no. And I don't want anything that might look like some kind of laboratory accident – that'd be just the kind of clue that would set everybody else in his field haring after what we want to keep hidden. The whole secret lies in the fact that once Stockhausen knows what we know, he could create a major explosion with – well, with the equivalent of a blackboard and two pieces of chalk. Isn't there any other way?'

'Men being men, there's always another way. In this instance, though, I'd have to have him tempted. I know at least one promising avenue. But he might not fall. And even if he did, as I think he would, it would take several months and a lot of close monitoring. Which wouldn't be altogether intolerable either, since it would greatly help to mislead Father Domenico.'

'What would it cost?' Jack Ginsberg said.

'Oh – say about eight million. Entirely a contingent fee this time, since I can't see that there'd be any important out-of-pocket money needed. If there is, I'll absorb it.'

'That's nice,' Jack said. Ware took no notice of the feeble sarcasm.

Baines put on his adjudicative face but inwardly he was well satisfied. As a further test, the death of Dr Stockhausen was not as critical as that of Governor Rogan, but it did have the merit of being in an entirely different social sphere; the benefits to Consolidated Warfare Service would be real enough, so that Baines had not had to counterfeit a motive, which might have been detected by Ware and led to premature further questions; and finally, the objections Ware had raised, while in part unexpected, had been entirely consistent with everything the magician had said before, everything that he appeared to be, everything that his style proclaimed, despite the fact that he was obviously a complex man.

Good. Baines liked consistent intellectuals, and wished that he had more of them in his organization. They were always fanatics of some sort when the chips were down, and hence presented him with some large and easily grasped handle precisely when he had most need of it. Ware hadn't exhibited his handle yet, but he would; he would.

'It's worth it,' Baines said, without more than a decorous two seconds of apparent hesitation. 'I do want to remind you, though, Dr Ware, that Dr Hess here is one of my conditions. I want you to allow him to watch while you operate.'

'Oh, very gladly,' Ware said, with another smile that, this time, Baines found disquieting; it seemed false, even unctuous, and Ware was too much in command of himself to have meant the falsity not to be noticed. 'I'm sure he'll enjoy it. You can all watch, if you like. I may even invite Father Domenico.'

8

Dr Hess arrived punctually the next morning for his appointment to be shown Ware's workroom and equipment. Greeting him with a professional nod – 'Coals to Newcastle, bringing Mitford and me up here for a tertiary,' Hess found himself quoting in silent inanity – Ware led the way to a pair of heavy, brocaded hangings behind his desk, which parted to reveal a heavy brass-bound door of what was apparently cypress wood. Among its fittings was a huge knocker with a face a little like the mask of tragedy, except that the eyes had cat-like pupils in them.

Hess had thought himself prepared to notice everything and be surprised by nothing, but he was taken aback when the expression on the knocker changed, slightly but inarguably, when Ware touched it. Apparently expecting his startlement, Ware said without looking at him, 'There's nothing in here really worth stealing, but if anything were taken it would cost me a tremendous amount of trouble to replace it, no matter how worthless it would prove to the thief. Also, there's the problem of contamination – just one ignorant touch could destroy the work of months. It's rather like a bacteriology laboratory in that respect. Hence the Guardian.'

'Obviously there can't be a standard supply house for your tools,' Hess agreed, recovering his composure.

'No, that's not even theoretically possible. The operator must make everything himself – not as easy now as it was in the Middle Ages, when most educated men had the requisite skills as a matter of course. Here we go.'

The door swung back as if being opened from the inside, slowly and soundlessly. At first it yawned on a deep scarlet gloom, but Ware touched a switch and, with a brief rushing sound, like water, sunlight flooded the room.

Immediately Hess could see why Ware had rented this particular palazzo and no other. The room was an immense refectory of Sienese design, which in its heyday must often have banquetted as many as thirty nobles; there could not be another one half as big in Positano, though the palazzo as a whole was smaller than some. There were mullioned windows overhead, under the ceiling, running around all four walls, and the sunlight was pouring through two ranks of them. They were flanked by pairs of red-velvet drapes, unpatterned, hung from traverse rods; it had been these that Hess had heard pulling back when Ware had flipped the wall switch.

At the rear of the room was another door, a broad one also covered by hangings, which Hess supposed must lead to a pantry or kitchen. To the left of this was a medium-sized, modern electric furnace, and beside it an anvil bearing a hammer that looked almost too heavy for Ware to lift. On the other side of the furnace from the anvil were several graduated tubs, which obviously served as quenching baths.

To the right of the door was a black-topped chemist's bench, complete with sinks, running water and the usual nozzles for illuminating gas, vacuum and compressed air; Ware must have had to install his own pumps for all of these. Over the bench on the back wall were shelves of reagents; to the right, on the side wall, ranks of drying pegs, some of which bore contorted pieces of glassware, others coils of rubber tubing.

Farther along the wall towards the front was a lectern bearing a book as big as an unabridged dictionary, bound in red leather and closed and locked with a strap. There was a circular design chased in gold on the front of the book, but at this distance Hess could not make out what it was. The lectern was flanked by two standing candlesticks with fat candles in them; the candles had been extensively used, although there were shaded electric-light fixtures around the walls, too, and the small writing table next to the lectern bore a Tensor lamp. On the table was another hook, smaller but almost as thick, which Hess recognized at once: the *Handbook of Chemistry and Physics*, forty-seventh edition, as standard a laboratory fixture as a test tube; and a rank of quill pens and inkhorns.

'Now you can see something of what I meant by requisite skills,' Ware said. 'Of course I blow much of my own glassware, but any ordinary chemist does that. But should I need a new sword, for instance' – he pointed towards the electric furnace – 'I'd have to forge it myself. I couldn't just pick one up at a costume shop. I'd have to do a good job of it, too. As a modern writer says somewhere, the only really serviceable symbol for a sharp sword is a *sharp* sword.'

'Uhm,' Hess said, continuing to look around. Against the left wall, opposite the lectern, was a long heavy table, bearing a neat ranking of objects ranging in length from six inches to about three feet, all closely wrapped in red silk. The wrappers had writing on them, but again Hess could not decipher it. Beside the table, affixed to the wall, was a flat sword cabinet. A few stools completed the furnishings; evidently Ware seldom worked sitting down. The floor was parquetted, and towards the centre of the room still bore traces of marks in coloured chalks, considerably scuffed, which brought from Ware a grunt of annoyance.

'The wrapped instruments are all prepared and I'd rather not expose them,' the magician said, walking towards the sword rack, 'but of course I keep a set of spares and I can show you those.'

He opened the cabinet door, revealing a set of blades hung in order of size. There were thirteen of them. Some were obviously swords; others looked more like shoemaker's tools.

'The order in which you make these is important, too,' Ware said, 'because, as you can see, most of them have writing on them, and it makes a difference what instrument does the writing. Hence I began with the uninscribed instrument, this one, the bolline or sickle, which is also one of the most often used. Rituals differ, but the one I use requires starting with a piece of unused steel. It's fired three times, and then quenched in a mixture of magpie's blood and the juice of a herb called foirole.'

'The *Grimorium Verum* says mole's blood and pimpernel juice,' Hess observed.

'Ah, good, you've been doing some reading. I've tried that, and it just doesn't seem to give quite as good an edge.'

'I should think you could get a still better edge by finding out what specific compounds were essential and using those,' Hess said. 'You'll remember that Damascus steel used to be tempered by plunging the sword into the body of a slave. It worked, but modern quenching baths are a lot better – and in your case you wouldn't have to be constantly having to trap elusive animals in large numbers.'

'The analogy is incomplete,' Ware said. 'It would hold if tempering were the only end in view, or if the operation were only another observance of Paracelsus' rule, *Alterius non sit qui suus esse potest* – doing for yourself what you can't trust others to do. Both are practical ends that I might satisfy in some quite different way. But in magic the blood sacrifice has an additional function – what we might call the tempering of, not just the steel, but also the operator.'

'I see. And I suppose it has some symbolic functions, too.'

'In goëtic art, everything does. In the same way, as you probably also know from your reading, the forging and quenching is to be done on a Wednesday in either the first or the eighth of the day hours, or the third or the tenth of the night hours, under a full Moon. There is again an immediate practical interest being served here – for I assure you that the planetary hours do indeed affect affairs on Earth – but also a psychological one, the obedience of the operator in every step. The grimoires and other handbooks are at best so confused and contradictory that it's never possible to know completely what steps are essential and what aren't, and research into the subject seldom makes for a long life.'

'All right,' Hess said. 'Go on.'

'Well, the horn handle has next to be shaped and fitted, again in a particular way at a particular hour, and then perfected at still another day and hour. By the way, you mentioned a different steeping bath. If you use that ritual, the days and the hours are also different, and again the question is, what's essential and what isn't? Thereafter, there's a conjuration to be recited, plus three salutations and a warding spell. Then the instrument is sprinkled, wrapped and fumigated – not in the modern sense, I mean it's perfumed – and is ready to use. After it's used, it has to be exorcised and rededicated, and that's the difference between the wrapped tools on the table and those hanging here in the rack.

'I won't go into detail about the preparation of the other instruments. The next one I make is the pen of the Art, followed by the inkpots and the inks, for obvious reasons – and, for the same reasons, the burin or graver. The pens are on my desk. This fitted needle here is the burin. The rest, going down the line as they hang here rather than in order of manufacture, are the white-handled knife, which like the bolline is nearly an all-purpose tool ... the black-handled knife, used almost solely for inscribing the circle ... the stylet, chiefly for preparing the wooden knives used in tanning ... the wand or blasting rod, which describes itself ... the lancet, again self-descriptive ... the staff, a restraining instrument analogous to a shepherd's ... and lastly the four swords, one for the master, the other three for his assistants, if any.'

With a side-glance at Ware for permission, Hess leaned forward to inspect the writings on the graven instruments. Some of them were easy enough to make out: on the sword of the master, for instance, the word MICHAEL appeared on the pommel, and on the blade, running from point to hilt, ELOHIM GIBOR. On the other hand, on the handle of the white-handled knife was engraved the following:

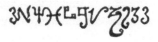

Hess pointed to this, and to a different but equally baffling inscription that was duplicated on the handles of the stylet and the lancet. 'What do those mean?'

'Mean? They can hardly be said to mean anything any more. They're greatly degenerate Hebrew characters, originally comprising various Divine Names. I could tell you what the Names were once, but the characters have no content any more – they just have to be there,'

'Superstition,' Hess said, recalling his earlier conversation with Baines, interpreting Ware's remark about Christmas.

'Precisely, in the pure sense. The process is as fundamental to the Art as evolution is to biology. Now if you'll step this way, I'll show you some other aspects that may interest you.'

He led the way diagonally across the room to the chemist's bench, pausing to rub irritatedly at the chalk marks with the sole of his slipper. 'I suppose a modern translation of that aphorism of Paracelsus,' he said, 'would be "You just can't get good servants any more." Not to ply mops, anyhow ... Now, most of these reagents will be familiar to you, but some of them are special to the Art. This, for instance, is exorcised water, which as you see I need in great quantities. It has to be river water to start with. The quicklime is for tanning. Some laymen, de Camp for instance, will tell you that "virgin parchment" simply means parchment that's never been written on before, but that's not so – all the grimoires insist that it must be the skin of a male animal that has never engendered, and the *Clavicula Salomonis* sometimes insists upon unborn parchment, or the caul of a newborn child. For tanning I also have to grind my own salt, after the usual rites are said over it. The candles I use have to be made of the first wax taken from a new hive, and so do my almadels. If I need images, I have to make them of earth dug up with my bare hands and reduced to a paste without any tool. And so on.

'I've mentioned aspersion and fumigation, in other words sprinkling and perfuming. Sprinkling has to be done with an aspergillum, a bundle of herbs like a fagot or *bouquet garni*. The herbs differ from rite to rite and you can see I've got a fair selection here – mint, marjoram, rosemary, vervain, periwinkle, sage, valerian, ash, basil, hyssop. In fumigation the most commonly used scents are aloes, incense, mace, benzoin, storax. Also, it's sometimes necessary to make a stench – for instance in the fumigation of a caul – and I've got quite a repertoire of those.'

Ware turned away abruptly, nearly treading on Hess's toes, and strode towards the exit. Hess had no choice but to follow him.

'Everything involves special preparation,' he said over his shoulder, 'even including the firewood if I want to make ink for pacts. But there's no point in my cataloguing things further, since I'm sure you thoroughly understand the principles.'

Hess scurried after, but he was still several paces behind the magician when the window drapes swished closed and the red gloom was reinstated. Ware stopped and waited for him, and the moment he was through the door, closed it and went back to his seat behind the big desk. Hess, puzzled, walked around the desk and took one of the Florentine chairs reserved for guests or clients.

'Most illuminating,' he said politely. 'Thank you.'

'You're welcome.' Ware rested his elbows on the desk and put his finger-tips over his mouth, looking down thoughtfully. There was a sprinkle of perspiration over his brow and shaven head, and he seemed more than usually pale; also, Hess noticed after a moment, he seemed to be trying without major effort to control his breathing. Hess watched curiously, wondering what could have upset him. After only a moment, however, Ware looked up at him and volunteered the explanation, with an easy half smile.

'Excuse me,' he said. 'From apprenticeship on, we're trained to secrecy. I'm perfectly convinced that it's unnecessary these days, and has been since the Inquisition died, but old oaths are the hardest to reason away. No discourtesy intended.'

'No offence taken,' Hess assured him. 'However, if you'd rather rest ...'

'No, I'll have ample rest in the next three days, and be incommunicado, too, preparing for Dr Baines's commission. So if you've further questions, now's the time for them.'

'Well ... I have no further technical questions, for the moment. But I am curious about a question Baines asked you during your first meeting – I needn't pretend, I'm sure, that I haven't heard the tape. I wonder, just as he did, what your motivation is. I can see from what you've shown me, and from everything you've said, that you've taken colossal amounts of trouble to perfect yourself in your Art, and that you believe in it. So it doesn't matter for the present whether or not *I* believe in it, only whether or not I believe in you. And your laboratory isn't a sham, it isn't there solely for extortion's sake, it's a place where a dedicated man works at something he thinks important. I confess I came to scoff – and to expose you, if I could – and I still can't credit that any of what you do works, or ever did work. But I accept that you so believe.'

Ware gave him a half nod. Thank you; go on.'

'I've no further to go but the fundamental question. You don't really need money, you don't seem to collect art or women, you're not out to be President of the World or the power behind some such person – and yet by your lights you have damned yourself eternally to make yourself expert in this highly peculiar subject. What on Earth *for*?'

'I could easily duck that question.' Ware said slowly. 'I could point out, for instance, that under certain circumstances I could prolong my life to seven hundred years, and so might not be worrying just yet about what might happen to me in the next world. Or I could point out what you already know from the texts, that every magician hopes to cheat Hell in the end – and as several did who are now nicely ensconced on the calendar as authentic saints.

'But the real fact of the matter, Dr Hess, is that I think what I'm after is worth the risk, and what I'm after is something you understand perfectly, and for which you've sold your own soul, or if you prefer an only slightly less loaded word, your integrity, to Dr Baines – *knowledge*.'

'Uhmn. Surely there must be easier ways—'

'You don't believe that. You think there may be more reliable ways, such as scientific method, but you don't think they're any easier. I myself have the utmost respect for scientific method, but I know that it doesn't offer me the kind of knowledge I'm looking for – which is also knowledge about the makeup of the universe and how it is run, but not a kind that any exact science can provide me with, because the sciences don't accept that some of the forces of nature are Persons. Well, but some of them are. And without dealing with those Persons I shall never know any of the things I want to know.

'This kind of research is just as expensive as underwriting a gigantic particle accelerator, Dr Hess, and obviously I'll never get any government to underwrite it. But people like Dr Baines can, if I can find enough of them – just as they underwrite you.

'Eventually, I may have to pay for what I've learned with a jewel no amount of money could buy. Unlike Macbeth, I know one *can't* "skip the life to come". But even if it does come to that, Dr Hess – and probably it will – I'll take my knowledge with me, and it will have been worth the price.

'In other words – just as you suspected – I'm a fanatic.'

To his own dawning astonishment, Hess said slowly:

'Yes. Yes, of course ... so am I.'

9

Father Domenico lay in his strange bed on his back, staring sleeplessly up at the pink stucco ceiling. Tonight was the night he had come for. Ware's three days of fasting, lustration and prayer – surely a blasphemous burlesque of such observances as the Church knew them, in intent if not in content – were over, and he had pronounced himself ready to act.

Apparently he still intended to allow Baines and his two repulsive henchmen to observe the conjuration, but if he had ever had any intention of including Father Domenico in the ceremony, he had thought better of it. That was frustrating, as well as a great relief; but in his place, Father Domenico would have done the same thing.

Yet even here, excluded from the scene and surrounded by every protection he had been able to muster, Father Domenico could feel the preliminary oppression, like the dead weather before an earthquake. There was always a similar hush and tension in the air just before the invocation of one of the Celestial Powers, but with none of these overtones of maleficence and disaster ... or would someone ignorant of what was actually proposed be able to tell the difference? That was a disquieting thought in itself, but one that could practically be left to Bishop Berkeley and the Logical Positivists. Father Domenico knew what was going on – a ritual of supernatural murder; and could not help but tremble in his bed.

Somewhere in the palazzo there was the silvery sound of a small clock striking, distant and sweet. The time was now 10:00 p.m., the fourth hour of Saturn on the day of Saturn, the hour most suitable – as even the blameless and pitiable Peter de Abano had written – for experiments of hatred, enmity and discord; and Father Domenico, under the Covenant, was forbidden even to pray for failure.

The clock, that two-handed engine that stands behind the Door, struck, and struck no more, and Ware drew the brocaded hangings aside.

Up to now, Baines, despite himself, had felt a little foolish in the girdled white-linen garment Ware had insisted upon, but he cheered up upon seeing Jack Ginsberg and Dr Hess in the same vestments. As for Ware, he was either comical or terrible, depending upon what view one took of the proceedings, in his white Levite surcoat with red-silk embroidery on the breast, his white leather shoes lettered in cinnabar, and his paper crown bearing the word EL. He was girdled with a belt about three inches wide, which seemed to have been made from the skin of some hairy, lion-coloured animal. Into the girdle was thrust a red-wrapped, sceptre-like object, which Baines identified tentatively from a prior description of Hess's as the wand of power.

'And now we must vest ourselves,' Ware said, almost in a whisper. 'Dr Baines, on the desk you will find three garments. Take one, and then another, and another. Give two to Dr Hess and Mr Ginsberg. Don the other yourself.'

Baines picked up the huddle of cloth. It turned out to be an alb.

'Take up your vestments and lift them in your hands above your heads. At the amen, let them fall. Now:

'ANTON, AMATOR, EMITES. THEODONIEL, PONCOR, PAGOR. ANITOR, *by the virtue of these most holy angelic names do I clothe myself, Lord of Lords, in my Vestments of Power, that so I may fulfil, even unto their term, all things which I desire to effect through Thee,* IDEO-DANIACH, PAMOR. PLAIOR. *Lord of Lords, Whose kingdom and rule endureth forever and ever. Amen.'*

The garments rustled down, and Ware opened the door.

The room beyond was only vaguely lit with yellow candlelight, and at first bore almost no resemblance to the chamber Dr Hess had described to Baines. As his eyes accommodated, however, Baines was gradually able to see that it was the same room, its margins now indistinct and its furniture slightly differently ordered: only the lectern and the candlesticks – there were now four of them, not two – were moved out from the walls and hence more or less visible.

But it was still confusing, a welter of flickering shadows and slightly sickening perfume, most unlike the blueprint of the room that Baines had erected in his mind from Hess's drawing. The thing that dominated the real room itself was also a drawing, not any piece of furniture or detail of architecture: a vast double circle on the floor in what appeared to be whitewash. Between the concentric circles were written innumerable words, or what might have been words, in characters which might have been Hebrew, Greek, Etruscan or even Elvish for all Baines could tell. Some few were in Roman lettering, but they, too, were names he could not recognize; and around the outside of the outer circle were written astrological signs in their zodiacal order, but with Saturn to the north.

At the very centre of this figure was a ruled square about two feet on a side, from each corner of which proceeded chalked, conventionalized crosses, which did not look in the least Christian. Proceeding from each of these, but not connected to them, were four six-pointed stars, verging on the innermost circle. The stars at the east, west and south each had a Tau scrawled at their centres; presumably the Saturnmost did too, but if so it could not be seen, for the heart of that emplacement was hidden by what seemed to be a fat puddle of stippled fur.

Outside the circles, at the other compass points, were drawn four penta-grams, in the chords of which were written TE TRA GRAM MA TON, and at the centres of which stood the candles. Farthest away from all this – about two feet outside the circle and three feet over it to the north – was a circle enclosed by a triangle, also much lettered inside and out; Baines could just see that the characters in the angles of the triangle read NI CH EL.

'Tanists,' Ware whispered, pointing into the circle, 'take your places.'

He went towards the long table Hess had described and vanished in the gloom. As instructed, Baines walked into the circle and stood in the western star; Hess followed, taking the eastern; and Ginsberg, very slowly, crept into the southern. To the north, the puddle of fur revolved once widdershins and resettled itself with an unsettling sigh, making Jack Ginsberg jump. Baines inspected it belatedly. Probably it was only a cat, as was supposed to be traditional, but in this light it looked more like a badger. Whatever it was, it was obscenely fat.

Ware reappeared, carrying a sword. He entered the circle, closed it with the point of the sword, and proceeded to the central square, where he laid the sword across the toes of his white shoes; then he drew the wand from his belt and unwrapped it, laying the red-silk cloth across his shoulders.

'From now on,' he said, in a normal, even voice, 'no one is to move.'

From somewhere inside his vestments he produced a small crucible, which he set at his feet before the recumbent sword. Small blue flames promptly began to rise from the bowl, and Ware cast incense into it. He said:

'Holocaust. Holocaust. Holocaust.'

The flames in the brazier rose slightly.

'We are to call upon MARCHOSIAS, a great marquis of the Descending Hierarchy,' Ware said in the same conversational voice. 'Before he fell, he belonged to the Order of Dominations among the angels, and thinks to return to the Seven Thrones after twelve hundred years. His virtue is that he gives true answers. Stand fast, all.'

With a sudden motion, Ware thrust the end of his rod into the surging flames of the brazier. At once the air of the hall rang with a long, frightful chain of woeful howls. Above the bestial clamour, Ware shouted:

'I adjure thee, great MARCHOSIAS, as the agent of Emperor LUCIFER, and of his beloved son LUCIFUGE ROFOCALE, by the power of the pact I have with thee, and by the Names ADONAY, ELOIM, JEHOVAM, TAGLA, MATHON, ALMOUZIN, ARIOS, PITHONA, MAGOTS, SYLPHAE, TABOTS, SALAMANDRAE, GNOMUS, TERRAE, COELIS, GODENS, AQUA, and by the whole hierarchy of superior intelligences who shall constrain thee against thy will, *venite, venite, submiritillor* MARCHOSIAS!'

The noise rose higher, and a green steam began to come off the brazier. It smelt like someone was burning hart's horn and fish gall. But there was no other answer. His face white and cruel, Ware rasped over the tumult:

'I adjure thee, MARCHOSIAS, by the pact, and by the names, appear instanter!' He plunged the rod a second time into the flames. The room screamed; but still there was no apparition.

'Now I adjure thee, LUCIFUGE ROFOCALE, whom I command, as the agent of the Lord and Emperor of Lords, send me thy messenger MARCHOSIAS, forcing him to forsake his hiding place, wheresoever it may be, and warning thee—'

The rod went back into the fire. Instantly, the palazzo rocked as though the earth had moved under it.

'Stand fast!' Ware said hoarsely.

Something Else said:

HUSH, I AM HERE. WHAT DOST THOU SEEK OF ME? WHY DOST THOU DISTURB MY REPOSE? LET MY FATHER REST, AND HOLD THY ROD.

Never had Baines heard a voice like that before. It seemed to speak in syllables of burning ashes.

'Hadst thou appeared when first I invoked thee, I had by no means smitten thee, nor called thy father,' Ware said. 'Remember, if the request I make of thee be refused, I shall thrust again my rod into the fire.'

THINK AND SEE!

The palazzo shuddered again. Then, from the middle of the triangle to the northwest, a slow cloud of yellow fumes went up towards the ceiling, making them all cough, even Ware. As it spread and thinned, Baines could see a shape forming under it; but he found it impossible to believe. It was – it was something like a she-wolf, grey and immense, with green and glistening eyes. A wave of coldness was coming from it.

The cloud continued to dissipate. The she-wolf glared at them, slowly spreading her griffin's wings. Her serpent's tail lashed gently, scalily.

In the northern pentacle, the great Abyssinian cat sat up and stared back. The demon-wolf showed her teeth and emitted a disgusting belch of fire. The cat settled its front feet indifferently.

'Stand, by the Seal,' Ware said. 'Stand and transform, else I shall plunge thee back whence thou camest. I command thee.'

The she-wolf vanished, leaving behind in the triangle a plump, modest-looking young man wearing a decorous necktie, a dildo almost as long and nothing else. 'Sorry, boss,' he said in a sugary voice. 'I had to try, you know. What's up?'

'Don't try to wheedle me, vision of stupidity,' Ware said harshly. Transform, I demand of thee, thou'rt wasting thy father's time, and mine! Transform!'

The young man stuck out his tongue, which was copper-green. A moment later, the triangle was occupied by a black bearded man apparently twice his age, wearing a forest-green robe rimmed in ermine and a glittering crown. It hurt Baines's eyes to look at it. An odour of sandalwood began slowly to diffuse through the room.

'That's better,' Ware said. 'Now I charge thee, by those Names I have named and on pain of those torments thou hast known, to regard the likeness and demesne of that mortal whose eidolon I hold in my hand, and that when I release thee, thou shalt straightaway go unto him, not making thyself known unto him, but revealing, as it were to come from his own intellectual soul, a vision and understanding of that great and ultimate Nothingness which lurks behind those signs he calls matter and energy, as thou wilt see it in his private forebodings, and that thou remainest with him and deepen his despair without remittal, until such time as he shall despise his soul for its endeavours, and destroy the life of his body.'

'I cannot give thee,' the crowned figure said, in a voice deep but somehow lacking all resonance, 'what thou requirest.'

'Refusal will not avail thee,' Ware said, 'for either shalt thou go incontinently and perform what I command, or I shall in no wise dismiss thee, but shall keep thee here unto my life's end, and torment thee daily, as thy father permitteth.'

'Thy life itself, though it last seven hundred years, is but a day to me,' said the crowned figure. Sparks issued from its nostrils as it spoke. 'And thy torments but a farthing of those I have endured since ere the cosmic egg was hatched, and Eve invented.'

For answer, Ware again stabbed the rod into the fire, which, Baines noted numbly, failed even to scorch it. But the crowned figure threw back its bearded head and howled desolately. Ware withdrew the rod, but only by a hand's breadth.

'I shall go as thou commandest,' the creature said sullenly. Hatred oozed from it like lava.

'Be it not performed exactly, I shall call thee up again,' Ware said. 'But be it executed, for thy pay thou shalt carry off the immortal part of the subject thou shalt tempt, which is as yet spotless in the sight of Heaven, and a great prize.'

'But not yet enough,' said the demon. 'For thou must give me also somewhat of thine hoard, as it is written in the pact.'

'Thou art slow to remember the pact,' Ware said. 'But I would deal fairly with thee, knowing marquis. Here.'

He reached into his robe and drew out something minute and colourless, which flashed in the candlelight. At first, Baines took it to be a diamond, but as Ware held it out, he recognized it as an opalescent, crystal tear vase, the smallest he had ever seen, stopper, contents and all. This Ware tossed, underhand, out of the circle to the fuming figure, which to Baines's new astonishment – for he had forgotten that what he was really looking at had first exhibited as a beast – caught it skilfully in its mouth and swallowed it.

'Thou dost only tantalize MARCHOSIAS,' the Presence said. 'When I have thee in Hell, magician, then shall I drink thee dry, though thy tears flow never so copiously.'

'Thy threats are empty. I am not marked for thee, shouldst thou see me in Hell forever,' Ware said. 'Enough, ungrateful monster. Cease thy witless plaudering and discharge thine errand. I dismiss thee.'

The crowned figure snarled, and then, suddenly, reverted to the form in which it had first showed itself. It vomited a great gout of fire, but the surge failed to pass the wall of the triangle; instead, it collected in a ball around the demon itself. Nevertheless, Baines could feel the heat against his face. Ware raised his wand.

The floor inside the small circle vanished. The apparition clashed its brazen wings and dropped like a stone. With a rending thunderclap, the floor healed seamlessly.

Then there was silence. As the ringing in Baines's ears died away, he became aware of a distant thrumming sound as though someone had left a car idling in the street in front of the palazzo. Then he realized what it was: the great cat was purring. It had watched the entire proceedings with nothing more than grave interest. So, apparently, had Hess. Ginsberg seemed to be jittering, but he was standing his ground. Although he had never seen Jack rattled before, Baines could hardly blame him; he himself felt sick and giddy, as though just the effort of looking at MARCHOSIAS had been equivalent to having scrambled for days up some Himalayan glacier.

'It is over,' Ware said in a grey whisper. He looked very old. Taking up his sword, he cut the diagram with it. 'Now we must wait. I will be in seclusion for two weeks. Then we will consult again. The circle is open. You may leave.'

Father Domenico heard the thunderclap, distant and muffled, and knew that the sending had been made – and that he was forbidden, now as before, even to pray for the soul of the victim (or the patient, in Ware's antiseptic Aristotelian terminology). Sitting up and swinging his feet over the edge of the bed, breathing with difficulty in the musky, detumescent air, he walked unsteadily to his satchel and opened it.

Why – that was the question – did God so tie his hands, why did He allow such a compromise as the Covenant at all? It suggested, at least, some limitation in His power unallowable by the firm dogma of Omnipotence, which it was a sin even to question; or, at worst, some ambiguity in His relationship with Hell, one quite outside the revealed answers to the Problem of Evil.

That last was a concept too terrible to bear thinking about. Probably it was attributable purely to the atmosphere here; in any event, Father Domenico knew that he was in no spiritual or emotional condition to examine it now.

He could, however, examine with possible profit a minor but related question: Was the evil just done the evil Father Domenico had been sent to oversee? There was every immediate reason to suppose that it was – and if it was, then Father Domenico could go home tomorrow, ravaged but convalescent.

On the other hand it was possible – dreadful but in a way also hopeful – that Father Domenico had been commanded to Hell-mouth to await the emission of something worse. That would resolve the puzzling anomaly that Ware's latest undertaking, abominable though they all were, was for Ware not unusual. Much more important, it would explain, at least in part, why the Covenant existed at all: in Tolstoy's words, 'God sees the truth, but waits.'

And this question, at least, Father Domenico need not simply ponder, but could actively submit to the Divine guidance, even here, even now, provided that he call upon no Presences. That restriction was not prohibitive; what was he a magician for, if not to be as subtle in his works as in his praise?

Inkhorn, quill, straightedge, three different discs of different sizes cut from virgin cardboard – not an easy thing to come by – and the wrapped burin came out of the satchel and were arranged on top of his dresser, which would serve well enough for a desk. On the cardboard discs he carefully inscribed three different scales: the A camerae of sixteen divine attributes, from *bonitas* to *patientia;* the T camerae of thirty attributes of things, from *temporis* to *negatio;* and the E camerae of the nine questions, from whether to how *great.* He centrepunched all three discs with the burin, pinned them together with a cuff link and finally asperged the assembled Lull Engine with holy water from the satchel. Over it he said:

'I conjure thee, O form of this instrument, by the authority of God the Father Almighty, by the virtue of Heaven and the stars, by that of the elements, by that of stones and herbs, and in like manner by the virtue of snowstorms, thunder and winds, and belike also by the virtue of the *Ars magna* in whose figure thou art drawn, that thou receive all power unto the performance of those things in the perfection of which we are concerned, the whole without trickery, falsehood or deception, by the command of God, Creator of the Angels and Emperor of the Ages. DAMAHII, LUMECH, GADAL, PANCIA, VELOAS, MEOROD, LAMIDOCH, BALDACH, ANERETHON, MITRATON, most holy angels, be ye wardens of this instrument. *Domine, Deus meus, in te speravi ... Confitebor tibi, Domine, in toto corde meo ... Quemadmodum desiderat cervus ad fontes aquarum ...* Amen.'

This said, Father Domenico took up the engine and turned the circles against each other. Lull's great art was not easy to use; most of the possible combinations of any group of wheels were trivial, and it took reason to see which were important, and faith to see which were inspired. Nevertheless, it had one advantage over all other forms of scrying: it was not in any strict sense, a form of magic.

He turned the wheels at random the required number of times, and then, taking the outermost by its edge, shook it to the four quarters of the sky. He was almost afraid to look at the result.

But on that very first essay, the engine had generated:
PATIENCE/BECOMING/REALITY
It was the answer he had both feared and hoped for. And it was, he realized with a subdued shock, the only answer he could have expected on Christmas Eve.

He put the engine and the tools back in his satchel, and crept away into the bed. In his state of over-exhaustion and alarm, he did not expect to sleep ... but within two turns of the glass he was no longer in the phenomenal world, but was dreaming instead that, like Gerbert the magician-Pope, he was fleeing the Holy Office down the wind astride a devil.

10

Ware's period of recovery did not last quite as long as he had prophesied. He was visibly up and about by Twelfth Night. By that time, Baines – though only Jack Ginsberg could see and read the signs – was chafing at the inaction. Jack had to remind him that in any event at least two months were supposed to pass before the suicide of Dr Stockhausen could even be expected, and suggested that in the interim they all go back to Rome and to work.

Baines shrugged the suggestion off. Whatever else was on his mind, it did not seem to involve Consolidated Warfare Service's interests more than marginally ... or, at least, the thought of business could not distract him beyond the making of a small number of daily telephone calls.

The priest or monk or whatever he was, Father Domenico, was still in attendance too. Evidently he had not been taken in by the show. Well, that was Ware's problem, presumably. All the same, Jack stayed out of sight of the cleric as much as possible; having him around, Jack recalled in a rare burst of association with his Bronx childhood, was a little like being visited by a lunatic Orthodox relative during a crucial marriage brokerage.

Not so lunatic at that, though; for if magic really worked – as Jack had had to see that it did – then the whole tissue of metaphysical assumptions Father Domenico stood for, from Moses through the Kabbalah to the New Testament, had to follow, as a matter of logic. After this occurred to Jack, he not only hated to see Father Domenico, but had nightmares in which he felt that Father Domenico was looking back at him.

Ware himself, however, did not emerge officially, to be talked to, until his predicted fourteenth day. Then, to Jack's several-sides disquietude, the first person he called into his office was Jack Ginsberg.

Jack wanted to talk to Ware only slightly more than he wanted to talk to the barefooted, silently courteous Father Domenico; and the effect upon Baines of Ware's singling Jack out for the first post-conjuration interview, though under ordinary circumstances it could have been discounted as minor, could not even be conjectured in Baines's present odd state of mind. After a troubled hour, Jack took the problem to Baines, not even sure any more of his own delicacy in juggling such an egg.

'Go ahead,' was all Baines said. He continued to give Jack the impression of a man whose mind was not to be turned more than momentarily from some all-important thought. That was alarming, too, but there seemed to be nothing to be done about it. Setting his face into its business mould of pleasant attentiveness, over slightly clenched teeth, Jack marched up to Ware's office.

The sunlight there was just as bright and innocent as ever, pouring directly in from the sea-sky on top of the cliff. Jack felt slightly more in contact with what he had used to think of as real life. In some hope of taking the initiative away from Ware and keeping it, he asked the magician, even before sitting down, 'Is there some news already?'

'None at all,' Ware said. 'Sit down, please. Dr Stockhausen is a tough patient, as I warned you all at the beginning. It's possible that he won't fall at all, in which case a far more strenuous endeavour will be required. But in the meantime I'm assuming that he will, and that I therefore ought to be preparing for Dr Baines's next commission. That's why I wanted to see you first.'

'I haven't any idea what Dr Baines's next commission is,' Jack said, 'and if I did I wouldn't tell you before he did.'

'You have a remorselessly literal mind, Mr Ginsberg. I'm not trying to pump you. I already know, and it's enough for the time being, that Mr Baines's next commission will be something major – perhaps even a unique experiment in the history of the Art. Father Domenico's continued presence here suggests the same sort of thing. Very well, if I'm to tackle such a project, I'll need assistants – and I have no remaining apprentices. They become ambitious very early and either make stupid technical mistakes or have to be dismissed for disobedience. Laymen, even sympathetic laymen, are equally mischancy, simply because of their eagerness and ignorance. but if they're highly intelligent, it's sometimes safe to use them. Sometimes. Given those disclaimers, that explains why I allowed you *and* Dr Hess to watch the Christmas Eve affair, not just Dr Hess, whom Dr Baines had asked for, and why I want to talk to you now.'

'I see,' Jack said. 'I suppose I should be flattered.'

Ware sat back in his chair and raised his hands as if exasperated. 'Not at all. I see that I'd better be blunt. I was quite satisfied with Dr Hess's potentialities and so don't need to talk to him any more, except to instruct him. But I am none too happy with yours. You strike me as a weak reed.'

'I'm no magician,' Jack said, holding on to his temper. 'If there's some hostility between us, it's only fair to recognize that I'm not its sole cause. You went out of your way to insult me at our very first interview, only because I was normally suspicious of your pretensions, as I was supposed to be, on behalf of my job. I'm not easily offended, Dr Ware, but I'm more cooperative if people are reasonably polite to me.'

'*Stercor,*' Ware said. The word meant nothing to Jack. 'You keep thinking I'm talking about public relations, and getting along with people, and all that goose grease. Far from it. A little hatred never hurts the Art, and studied insult is valuable in dealing with demons – there are only a few who can be flattered to any profit, and a man who can be flattered isn't a man at all, he's a dog. Do try to understand me, Mr Ginsberg. What I'm talking about is neither your footling hostility nor your unexpectedly slow brains, but your rabbit's courage. There was a moment during the last ceremony when I could see that you were going to step out of your post. You didn't know it, but I had to paralyze you, and I saved your life. If you had moved you would have endangered all of us, and had that happened I would have thrown you to MARCHOSIAS like an old bone. It wouldn't have saved the purpose of the ceremony, but it would have kept the demon from gobbling up everybody else but Ahktoi.'

'Ach ...?'

'My familiar. The cat.'

'Oh. Why not the cat?'

'He's on loan. He belongs to another demon – my patron. Do stop changing the subject, Mr Ginsberg. If I'm going to trust you as a Tanist in a great work, I'm going to have to be reasonably sure that you'll stand fast when I tell you to stand fast, no matter what you see or hear, and that when I ask you to take some small part in the ritual, you'll do it accurately and punctually. Can you assure me of this?'

'Well,' Jack said earnestly, 'I'll do my best.'

'But what for? Why do you want to sell me? I don't know what you mean by your "best" until I know what's in it for you, besides just keeping you your job – or making a good impression on me because it's a reflex with you to make a good impression on people. Explain this to me, please! I know that there's something in this situation that hits you where you live. I could see that from the outset, but my first guess as to what it was evidently was wrong, or anyhow not central. Well, what *is* central to you: the situation has now ripened to the point when you're going to have to tell me what it is. Otherwise I shall shut you out, and that will be that.'

Wobbling between unconventional hope and standard caution, Jack pushed himself out of the Florentine chair and toe-heel-toed to the window, adjusting his tie automatically. From this height, the cliff-clinging apartments of Positano fell away to the narrow beach like so many Roman tenements crowded with deposed kings – and with beach boys hoping to pick up an American heiress for the season. Except for the curling waves and a few distant birds, the scene was motionless, yet somehow to Jack it seemed to be slowly, inexorably sliding into the sea.

'Sure, I like women,' he said in a low voice. 'And I've got special preferences I don't find it easy to satisfy, even with all the money I make. For one thing, in my job I'm constantly working with classified material – secrets

– either some government's, or the company's. That means I don't dare put myself into a position where I could be blackmailed.'

'Which is why you refused my offer when we first talked,' Ware said. 'That was discreet, but unnecessary. As you've probably realized by now, neither spying nor extortion has any attraction for me – the potential income from either or both would be a pittance to me.'

'Yes, but I won't always have you around,' Jack said, turning back towards the desk. 'And I'd be stupid to form new tastes that only you could keep supplied.'

'"Pander to" is the expression. Let's be precise. Nevertheless, you have some remedy in mind. Otherwise you wouldn't be being even this frank.'

'Yes … I do. It occurred to me when you agreed to allow Hess to tour your laboratory.' He was halted by another stab of jealousy, no less acute for being half reminiscent. Drawing a deep breath, he went on, 'I want to learn the Art.'

'Oho. That *is* a reversal.'

'You said it was possible,' Jack said in a rush, emboldened by a desperate sense of having now nothing to lose. 'I know you said you don't take apprentices, but I wouldn't be trying to stab you in the back or take over your clients, I'd only be using the Art for my specialized purposes. I couldn't pay you any fortune, but I do have money. I could do the reading in my spare time, and come back after a year or so for the actual instruction. I think Baines would give me a sabbatical for that – he wants somebody on his staff to know the Art, at least the theory, only he thinks it's going to be Hess. But Hess will be too busy with his own sciences to do a thorough job of it.'

'You really hate Dr Hess, don't you?'

'We don't impinge,' Jack said stiffly. 'Anyhow what I say is true. I could be a lot better expert from Baines's point of view than Hess ever could.'

'Do you have a sense of humour, Mr Ginsberg?'

'Certainly. everybody does.'

'Untrue,' Ware said. 'Everybody claims to have, that's all. I ask only because the first thing to be sacrificed to the Art is the gift of laughter, and some people would miss it more than others. Yours seems to be residual at best. In you it would probably be a minor operation, like an appendectomy.'

'You don't seem to have lost yours.'

'You confuse humour with wit, like most people. The two are as different as creativity and scholarship. However, as I say, in your case it's not a great consideration, obviously. But there may be greater ones. For example, what tradition I would be training you in. For instance, I could make a kabbalistic magician of you, which would give you a substantial grounding in white

47

magic. And for the black, I could teach you most of what's in the *Clavicle* and the *Lemegeton*, cutting out the specifically Christian accretions. Would that content you, do you think?'

'Maybe, if it met my primary requirements,' Jack said. 'But if I had to go on from there, I wouldn't care. These days I'm a Jew only by birth, not by culture – and up until Christmas Eve I was an atheist. Now I don't know what I am. All I know is, I've got to believe what I see.'

'Not in this Art,' Ware said. 'But we'll think of you as a *tabula rasa* for the time being. Well, Mr Ginsberg, I'll consider it. But before I decide, I think you ought to explore further your insight about special tastes becoming satisfiable only through magic, whether mine or yours. You like to think how delightful it would be to enjoy them freely and without fear of consequences, but it often happens – you'll remember Oscar Wilde's epigram on the subject – that fulfilled desire isn't a delight, but a cross.'

'I'll take the chance.'

'Don't be so hasty. You have no real idea of the risks. Suppose you should find, for example, that no human woman could please you any more, and you'd become dependent on succubi? I don't know how much you know of the theory of such a relationship. In general, the revolt in heaven involved angels from every order in the hierarchy. And of the Fallen, only those who fell from the lowest ranks are assigned to this sort of duty. By comparison, MARCHOSIAS is a paragon of nobility. These creatures have even lost their names, and there's nothing in the least grand about their malignancy – they are pure essences of narrow meanness and petty spite, the kind of spirit a Sicilian milkmaid calls on to make her rival's toenails split, or give an unfaithful lover a pimple on the end of his nose.'

'That doesn't make them sound much different from ordinary women,' Jack said, shrugging. 'So long as they deliver, what does it matter? Presumably, as a magician I'd have *some* control over how they behaved.'

'Yes. Nevertheless, why be persuaded out of desire and ignorance when an experiment is available to you? In fact, Mr Ginsberg, I would not trust any resolution you made from the state of simple fantasy you're in now. If you won't try the experiment, I must refuse your petition.'

'Now wait a minute,' Jack said. 'Why are you so urgent about this, anyhow? What kind of advantage do you get out of it?'

'I've already told you that,' Ware said patiently. 'I will probably need you as a Tanist in Dr Baines's major enterprise. I want to be able to trust you to stand fast, and I won't be able to do that without being sure of your degree and kind of commitment.'

Everything that Ware said seemed to have behind it the sound of doors softly closing in Jack's face. And on the other hand, the possibilities – the opportunities ...

'What,' he said, 'do I need to do?'

11

The palazzo was asleep. In the distance, that same oblivious clock struck eleven; the proper hour of this day, Ware had said, for experiments in venery. Jack waited nervously for it to stop, or for something to begin.

His preparations were all made, but he was uncertain whether any of them had been necessary. After all, if the ... girl ... who was to come to him was to be totally amenable to his wishes, why should he have to impress her?

Nevertheless, he had gone through all the special rituals, bathing for an hour, shaving twice, trimming his finger- and toenails and buffing them, brushing his hair back for thirty strokes and combing it with the West German tonic that was said to have allatoin in it, dressing in his best silk pyjamas, smoking jacket (though he neither smoked nor drank), ascot and Venetian-leather slippers, adding a dash of cologne and scattering a light film of talcum powder inside the bed. Maybe, he thought, part of the pleasure would be in taking all the trouble and having everything work.

The clock stopped striking. Almost at once there was a slow triple knock at the door, so slow that each soft blow seemed like an independent act. Jack's heart bounded like a boy's. Pulling the sash of his jacket tighter, he said as instructed:

'Come in ... come in ... come in.'

He opened the door. As Ware had told him to expect, there was no one in the dark corridor outside; but when he closed the door and turned around, there she was.

'Good evening,' she said in a light voice with the barest trace of an accent – or was it a lisp? 'I am here, as you invited me. Do you like me?'

It was not the same girl who had brought the letter to Ware, so many weeks ago, though she somehow reminded him of someone he had once known, he could not think who. This one was positively beautiful. She was small – half a head shorter than Jack, slender and apparently only about eighteen – and very fair, with blue eyes and a fresh, innocent expression, which was doubly piquant because the lines of her features were patrician, her skin so delicate that it was almost like fine parchment.

She was fully clothed, in spike heels, patterned but otherwise sheer stockings, and a short-sleeved, expensively tailored black dress of some material like rayon, which clung to her breasts, waist and upper hips as though electrified, and then burst into a full skirt like an inverted tulip, breaking just above the knees. Wire-thin silver bracelets slid and tinkled almost inaudibly on her left wrist as she ruffled her chrysanthemum petal coiffure, and small silver earrings echoed them; between her breasts was a circular onyx brooch inlaid in silver with the word *Cazotte*, set off by a ruby about the size of a fly's eye, the only touch of colour in the entire costume; even her make-up was the Italian 'white look', long out of style but so exaggerating her paleness as to look almost theatrical on her – almost, but not quite.

'Yes,' he said, remembering to breathe.

'Ah, you make up your mind so soon. Perhaps you are wrong.' She pirouetted away from him towards the bed, making the black tulip flare, and lace foam under its corolla and around her legs with a dry rustling. She stopped the spin facing him, so suddenly that the skirts snapped above her knees like banners in a stiff gust. She seemed wholly human.

'Impossible,' Jack said, mustering all his gallantry. 'I think you're exquisite. Uh, what shall I call you?'

'Oh, I do not come when called. You will have to exert yourself more than that. But my name could be Rita, if you need one.'

She lifted the front of the skirts up over the welts of her stockings, which cut her white thighs only a few inches beneath the vase of her pelvis, and sat down daintily on the side of the bed. 'You are very distant,' she said, pouting. 'Perhaps you suspect I am only pretty on the outside. That would be unfair.'

'Oh no, I'm sure—'

'But how can you be sure yet?' She drew up her heels. 'You must come and see.'

The clock was striking four when she arose, naked and wet, yet somehow looking as though she was still on high heels, and began to dip up her clothes from the floor. Jack watched this little ballet in a dizziness half exhaustion and half triumph. He had hardly enough strength left to wiggle a toe, but he had already surprised himself so often that he still had hopes, Nothing had ever been like this before, nothing.

'Must you go?' he said sluggishly.

'Oh yes, I have other business yet.'

'Other business? But – didn't you have a good time?'

'A – good time?' the girl turned towards him, stopping in the act of fastening a garter strap. 'I am thy servant and thy lamia, Eve-fruit, but thou must not mock me.'

'I don't understand,' Jack said, struggling to lift his head from the bunched, sweaty pillow.

'Then keep silent.' She resumed assembling herself.

'But ... you seemed ...'

She turned to him again. 'I gave thee pleasure. Congratulate thyself. That is enough. Thou knowest well what I am. I take no pleasure in anything. It is not permitted. Be grateful, and I shall come to thee again. But mock me, and I shall send thee instead a hag with an ass's tail.'

'I meant no offence,' he said, half sullenly.

'See thou dost not. Thou hadst pleasure with me, that sufficeth. Thou must prove thy virility with mortal flesh. Thy potency, that I go to try even now. It comes on to night i' the other side of the world, and I must plant thy seed before it dies in my fires – if it ever it lived at all.'

'What do you mean?' he said, in a hoarse whisper.

'Have no fear, I shall be back tomorrow. But in the next span of the dark I must change suit.' The dress fell down over the impossibly pliant body. 'I become an incubus now, and a woman waits for that, diverted from her husband by the twofold way. Reach I her in time, thou shalt father a child, on a woman thou shalt never even see. Is that not a wonder? And a fearful child it shall be, I promise thee!'

She smiled at him. Behind her lids now, he saw with nausea and shame, there were no longer any eyes – only blankly flickering lights, like rising sparks in a flue. She was now as fully dressed as she had been at the beginning, and curtsied gravely.

'Wait for me ... unless, of course, thou dost not want me back tomorrow night ...?'

He tried not to answer, but the words came out like clots of poisonous gas.

'Yes ... oh God ...'

Cupping both hands over her hidden groin in a gesture of obscene conservatism, she popped into nothingness like a bursting balloon, and the whole weight of the dawn fell upon Jack like the mountains of St John the Divine.

12

Dr Stockhausen died on St Valentine's day, after three days' fruitless attempts by surgeons from all over the world, even the USSR, to save him from the effects of a draught of a hundred minims of tincture of iodine. The surgery and hospital care were all free; but he died intestate, and it appeared that his small estate – a few royalties from his books and the remains of a ten-year-old Nobel Prize – would be tied up indefinitely; especially in view of the note he left behind, out of which no tribunal, whether scientific or judicial, could hope to separate the mathematics from the ravings for generations to come.

Funds were gathered for his grandchildren and divorced daughter to tide them over; but the last book that he had been writing turned out to be so much like the note that his publishers' referees could think of no colleague to whom it could reasonably be offered for posthumous collaboration. It was said that his brain would be donated to the museum of the Deutsches Akad-emie in Munich – again only if his affairs could ever be probated. Within three days after the funeral, however, Ware was able to report, both brain and manuscript had vanished.

'MARCHOSIAS may have taken one or both of them,' Ware said. 'I didn't tell him to, since I didn't want to cause any more suffering to Albert's relatives than was inevitable under the terms of the commission. On the other hand, I didn't tell him not to, either. But the commission itself has been executed.'

'Very good,' Baines said. He was, in fact, elated. Of the other three people in the office with Ware – for Ware had said there was no way to prevent Father Domenico from attending – none looked as pleased as Baines felt, but after all he was the only man who counted here, the only one to whose emotions Ware need pay any more than marginal attention. 'And much faster than you had anticipated, too. I'm very well satisfied, and also I'm now quite ready to discuss my major commission with you, Dr Ware, if the planets and so on don't make this a poor time to talk about it.'

'The planetary influences exert almost no effect upon simple discussion,' Ware said, 'only on specific preparations – and of course on the experiment itself. And I'm quite rested and ready to listen. In fact, I'm in an acute state of curiosity. Please charge right in and tell me about it.'

'I would like to let all the major demons out of Hell for one night, turn them loose in the world with no orders and no restrictions – except of course that they go back by dawn or some other sensible time – and see just what it is they would do if they were left on their own hooks like that.'

'Insanity!' Father Domenico cried out, crossing himself. 'Now surely the man is possessed already!'

'For once, I'm inclined to agree with you, Father,' Ware said, 'though with some reservations about the possession question. For all we can know now, it's entirely in character. Tell me this, Dr Baines, what do you hope to ac-complish through an experiment on so colossal a scale?'

'Experiment!' Father Domenico said, his face as white as the dead.

'If you can do no more than echo, Father, I think we'd all prefer that you kept silent – at least until we find out what it is we're talking about.'

'I will say what I need to say, when I think it is needful,' Father Domenico said angrily. 'This thing that you're minimizing by calling it an "experiment" might well end in the dawn of Armageddon!'

'Then you should welcome it, not fear it, since you're convinced your side must win,' Ware said. 'But actually there's no such risk. The results may well be rather Apocalyptic, but Armageddon requires the prior appearance of the Antichrist, and I assure you I am not he ... nor do I see anybody else in the world who might qualify. Now, again, Dr Baines, what do you hope to accomplish through this?'

'Nothing *through* it,' Baines, now totally caught up in the vision, said dreamily. 'Only the thing itself – for its aesthetic interest alone. A work of art, if you like. A gigantic action painting, with the world for a canvas—'

'And human blood for pigments,' Father Domenico ground out.

Ware held up his hand, palm towards the monk. 'I had thought,' he said to Baines, 'that this was the art you practised already, and in effect sold the resulting canvasses, too.'

'The sales kept me able to continue practising it,' Baines said, but he was beginning to find the metaphor awkward, his though it had originally been. 'Look at it this way for a moment, Dr Ware. Very roughly, there are only two general kinds of men who go into the munitions business – those without consciences, who see the business as an avenue to a great fortune, eventually to be used for something else, like Jack here – and of course there's a subclass of those, people who *do* have consciences but can't resist the money anyhow, or the knowledge, rather like Dr Hess.'

Both men stirred, but apparently both decided not to dispute their portraits.

'The second kind is made up of people like me – people who actually take pleasure in the controlled production of chaos and destruction. Not sadists primarily, except in the sense that every dedicated artist is something of a sadist, willing to countenance a little or a lot of suffering – not only his own, but other people's – for the sake of the end product.'

'A familiar type, to be sure,' Ware said with a lopsided grin. 'I think it was the saintly Robert Frost who said that a painting by Whistler was worth any number of old ladies.'

'Engineers are like this too,' Baines said, warming rapidly to his demonstration; he had been thinking about almost nothing else since the conjuration he had attended. 'There's a breed I know much better than I do artists, and I can tell you that most of them wouldn't build a thing if it weren't for the kick they get out of the preliminary demolitions involved. A common thief with a gun in his hand isn't half as dangerous as an engineer with a stick of dynamite.'

'But in my case, just as in the case of the engineer, the key word is "controlled" – and, in the munitions business, it's rapidly becoming an obsolete word, thanks to nuclear weapons.'

He went on quickly to sketch his dissatisfactions, very much as they had first come to a head in Rome while Governor Rogan was being sent for. 'So now you can see what appeals to me about the commission I propose. It won't be a series of mass obliterations under nobody's control, but a whole set of individual actions, each in itself on a comparatively small scale – and each one, I'm sure, interesting in itself because of all the different varieties of ingenuity and surprise to be involved. And it won't be total because it will also be self-limiting to some small period of time, presumably twelve hours or less.'

Father Domenico leaned forward earnestly. 'Surely,' he said to Ware, 'even you can see that no human being, no matter how sinful and self-indulgent, could have elaborated anything so monstrous without the direct intervention of Hell!'

'On the contrary,' Ware said, 'Dr Baines is quite right, most dedicated secularists think exactly as he does – only on a somewhat smaller scale. For your further comfort, Father, I am somewhat privy to the affairs of Hell, and I investigate all my major clients thoroughly. I can tell you that Dr Baines is *not* possessed. But all the same there are still a few mysteries here. Dr Baines, I still think you may be resorting to too big a brush for the intended canvas, and might get the effects you want entirely without my help. For example, why won't the forthcoming Sino-Russian War be enough for you?'

Baines swallowed hard. 'So that's really going to happen?'

'It's written down to happen. It still might not, but I wouldn't bet against it. Very likely it won't be a major nuclear war – three fusion bombs, one Chinese, two Soviet, plus about twenty fission explosions, and then about a year of conventional land war. No other powers are at all likely to become involved. You know this, Dr Baines, and I should think it would please you. After all, it's almost exactly the way your firm has been trying to pre-set it.'

'You're full of consolations today,' Father Domenico muttered.

'Well, in fact, I *am* damn pleased to hear it,' Baines said. 'It isn't often that you plan something that big and have it come off almost as planned. But no, Dr Ware, it won't be enough for me, because it's still too general and difficult to follow – or will be. I'm having a little trouble with my tenses. For one thing, it won't be sufficiently attributable to me – many people have been working to bring that war about. This experiment will be on my initiative alone.'

'Not an insuperable objection,' Ware said. 'A good many Renaissance artists didn't object to collaborators – even journeymen.'

'Well, the spirit of the times has changed, if you want an abstract answer. The real answer is that I *do* object. Furthermore, Dr Ware, I want to choose my own medium. War doesn't satisfy me any more. It's too sloppy, too subject to accident. It excuses too much.'

'?' Ware said with an eyebrow.

'I mean that in time of war, especially in Asia, people expect the worst and try to ride with the punches, no matter how terrible they are, In peacetime, on the other hand, even a small misfortune comes as a total surprise. People complain, "Why did this have to happen to me?" – as though they'd never heard of Job.'

'Rewriting Job is the humanist's favourite pastime,' Ware agreed. 'And his favourite political platform too. So in fact, Dr Baines, you *do* want to afflict people, just where they're most sensitive to being afflicted, and just when they least expect it, right or wrong. Do I understand you correctly?'

Baines had the sinking feeling that he had explained too much, but there was no help for that now; and, in any event, Ware was hardly himself a saint.

'You do,' he said shortly.

'Thank you. That clears the air enormously. One more question. How do you propose to pay for all this?'

Father Domenico surged to his feet with a strangled gasp of horror, like the death throes of an asthmatic.

'You – you mean to do this!'

'Hush. I haven't said so. Dr Baines, the question?'

'I know I couldn't pay for it in cash,' Baines said. 'But I've got other assets. This experiment – if it works – is going to satisfy something for me that Consolidated Warfare Service hasn't satisfied in years, and probably never will again except marginally. I'm willing to make over most of my CWS stock to you. Not all of it, but – well – just short of being a controlling interest. You ought to be able to do a lot with that.'

'It's hardly enough, considering the risks involved,' Ware said slowly. 'On the other hand, I've no particular desire to bankrupt you—'

'Dr Ware,' Father Domenico said in an iron voice. 'Am I to conclude that you *are* going to undertake this fearful insanity?'

'I haven't said so,' Ware replied mildly. 'If I do, I shall certainly need your help—'

'Never. *Never!*'

'And everybody else's. It isn't really the money that attracts me, primarily. But without the money I should never be able to undertake an experiment like this in the first place, and I'm certain the opportunity will never come up again. If the whole thing doesn't blow up in my face, there'd be an enormous amount to learn from a trial like this.'

'I think that's right,' Hess's voice said. Baines looked towards him in surprise, but Hess seemed quite serious. 'I'd be greatly interested in it myself.'

'You'll learn nothing,' Father Domenico said, 'but the shortest of all shortcuts to Hell, probably in the body!'

'A negative Assumption?' Ware said, raising both eyebrows this time. 'But now you're tempting my pride, Father. There've been only two previous ones in Western history – Johannes Faustus and Don Juan Tenorio. And neither one was properly safeguarded or otherwise prepared. Well, now certainly I must undertake so great a work – provided that Dr Baines is satisfied that he'll get what he'll be paying for.'

'Of course I'm satisfied,' Baines said, quivering with joy.

'Not so fast. You've asked me to let all the major demons out of Hell. I can't even begin to do that. I can call up only those with whom I have pacts, and their subordinates. No matter what you have read in Romantic novels and plays, the three superior spirits cannot be invoked at all, and never sign pacts, those being SATHANAS, BEELZEBUTH and SA-TANACHA. Under each of these are two ministers, with one of the six of which it is possible to make pacts – one per magician, that is. I control LUCIFUGE ROFOCALE, and he me. Under him in turn, I have pacts with some eighty-nine other spirits, not all of which would be of any use to us here – VAS SAGO, for instance, who has a mild nature and no powers except in crystallomancy, or PHOENIX, a poet and teacher. With the utmost in careful preparations, we might involve as many as fifty of the rest, certainly no more. Frankly, I think that will prove to be more than enough.'

'I'll cheerfully take your word for it,' Baines said promptly. 'You're the expert. Will you take it on?'

'Yes.'

Father Domenico, who was still standing, swung away towards the door, but Ware's hand shot out towards him above the desk as if to grasp the monk by the nape of the neck. 'Hold!' the magician said. 'Your commission is *not* discharged, Father Domenico, as you know very well in your heart. You must observe this sending. Even more important, you have already said yourself that it is going to be difficult to keep under control. To that end I demand your unstinting advice in the preparation, your presence in the conjurations, and, should they be needed, your utmost offices in helping me and my other Tanists to abort it. This you cannot refuse – it is all in your mission by stipulation, and in the Covenant by implication. I do not force you to it. I do but remind you of your positive duty to your Lord.'

'That … is … true …' Father Domenico said in a sick whisper. His face as grey as an untinted new blotter, he groped for the chair and sat down again.

'Nobly faced. I'll have to instruct everyone here, but I'll start with you, in deference to your obvious distress—'

'One question,' Father Domenico said. 'Once you've instructed us all, you'll be out of touch with us for perhaps as much as a month to come. I demand the time to visit my colleagues, and perhaps call together a convo-cation of all white magicians—'

'To prevent me?' Ware said between his teeth. 'You can demand no such thing. The Covenant forbids the slightest interference.'

'I'm all too horribly aware of that. No, not to interfere, but to stand by, in case of disaster. It would be too late to call for them once you *knew* you were losing control.'

'Hmm ... probably a wise precaution, and one I couldn't justly prevent. Very well. Just be sure you're back when the time comes. About the day, what would you suggest? May Eve is an obvious choice, and we may well need that much time in preparation.'

'It's *too* good a time for any sort of control,' Father Domenico said grimly. 'I definitely do *not* recommend piling a real Walpurgis Night on top of the formal one. It would be wiser to choose an unfavourable night, the more unfavourable the better.'

'Excellent good sense,' Ware said. 'Very well, then. Inform your friends. The experiment is hereby scheduled for Easter.'

With a scream, Father Domenico bolted from the room. Had Baines not been taught all his life long that such a thing was impossible in a man of God, Baines would have identified it without a second thought as a scream of hatred.

13

Theron Ware had been dreaming a journey to the Antarctic continent in the midst of its Jurassic splendour, fifty million years ago, but the dream had been becoming a little muddled with personal fantasies – mostly involving a minor enemy whom he had in reality sent for, with flourishes, a good decade ago – and he was not sorry when it vanished unfinished at dawn.

He awoke sweating, though the dream had not been especially stressful. The reason was not far to seek: Ahktoi was sleeping, a puddle of lard and fur, on the pillow, and had nearly crowded Ware's head off it. Ware sat up, mopping his pate with the top sheet, and stared at the cat with nearly neutral annoyance. Even for an Abyssinian, a big-boned breed, the familiar was grossly overweight; clearly an exclusive diet of human flesh was not a healthy regimen for a cat. Furthermore, Ware was not even sure it was necessary. It was prescribed only in Éliphas Lévi, who often made up such details as he went along. Certainly PHOENIX, whose creature Ahktoi was, had made no such stipulation. On the other hand, it was always best to play safe in such matters; and, besides, financially the diet was not much more than a nuisance. The worst that could be said for it was that it spoiled the cat's lines.

Ware arose, naked, and crossed the cold room to the lectern, which bore up his Great Book – not the book of pacts, which was of course still safely in the workroom, but his book of new knowledge. It was open to the section headed

QUASARS

but except for the brief paragraph summarizing the reliable scientific information on the subject – a very brief paragraph indeed – the pages were still blank.

Well, that, like so much else, could wait until Baines's project was executed. Truly colossal advances might be made in the Great Book, once all that CWS money was in the bank.

Ware's retirement had left the members of Baines's party again at loose ends, and all of them, even Baines, were probably a little shaken at the magnitude of what they had contracted for. In Baines and Dr Hess, perhaps, there still remained some faint traces of doubt about its possibility, or at least some inability to imagine what it would be like, despite the previous apparition of MARCHOSIAS. No such impediment could protect Jack Ginsberg, however – not now, when he awakened each morning with the very taste of Hell in his mouth. Ginsberg was committed, but he was not wearing well; he would have to be watched. The waiting period would be especially hard on him. Well, that couldn't be helped; it was prescribed.

The cat uncurled, yawned, stretched, lurched daintily to its feet and paused at the edge of the bed, peering down the sideboard as though contemplating the inward slope of Fujiyama. At last it hit the floor with a double *splat*! like the impacts of two loaded sponges. There it arched its spine again, stretched out its back legs individually in an ecstasy of quivering, and walked slowly towards Ware, its furry abdomen swinging from side to side. *Hein?* it said in a breathy feminine voice.

'In a minute,' Ware said, preoccupied. 'You'll get fed when I do.' He had forgotten for the moment that he had just begun a nine days' fast, which when completed he would enforce also upon Baines and his henchmen. 'Father Eternal, O thou who art seated upon cherubim and seraphim, who beholdest the earth and the sea, unto thee do I lift up my hands, and beseech thine aid alone, thou who art the fulfilment of works, who givest booty unto those who toil, who exaltest the proud, who art destroyer of all life, the fulfilment of works, who givest booty unto those who call upon thee. Do thou guard and defend me in this undertaking, thou who livest and reignest forever and ever. Amen! Shut up, Ahktoi.'

Anyhow it had been years since he had believed for an instant that Ahktoi was really hungry. Maybe lean meat was what the cat needed, instead of all that baby fat – though still-births were certainly the easiest kind of rations to get for him.

Ringing for Gretchen, Ware went into the bathroom, where he ran a bath, into which he dashed an ounce of exorcised water left over from the dressing of a parchment. Ahktoi, who like most Abyssinians loved running water, leapt up on the rim of the tub and tried to fish for bubbles. Pushing the cat off, Ware sat down in the warm pool and spoke the Thirteenth Psalm,

Dominus illuminatio mea, of death and resurrection, his voice resounding hollowly from the tiles; adding, Lord who has formed man out of nothing to thine own image and likeness, and me also, unworthy sinner as I am, deign, I pray thee, to bless and sanctify this water that all delusion may depart from me unto thee, almighty and ineffable, who didst lead forth thy people from the land of Egypt, and didst cause them to pass dryshod under the Red Sea, anoint me as thou wilt, father of sins, Amen.'

He slid under the water, crown to toes – but not for long, for the ounce of exorcised water he had added still had a trace of quicklime in it from the tanning of the lambskin, which made his eyes sting. He surfaced, blowing like a whale, and added quickly to the steamy air, '*Dixit insipiens in corde suo* – Will you *kindly* get out of the way, Ahktoi? – who has formed me in thine image and in thy likeness, design to bless and sanctify this water, so that it may become unto me the fruition of my soul and body and purpose. Amen.'

Hein?

Someone knocked on the door. His eyes squeezed closed still, Ware groped his way out. He was met at the threshold by Gretchen, who sponged his hands and face ritually with an asperged white cloth, and retreated before him as he advanced into the bedroom. Now that his eyes were cleared, he could see that she was naked, but, knowing what she was, that could scarcely interest him, and, besides, he had been devoted to celibacy since his earliest love of magic, like anyone in orders. Her nakedness was only another rule of the rite of lustration. Waving her aside, he took three steps towards the bed, where she had laid out his vestments, and said to all corners of the phenomenal and epiphenomenal world:

'ASTROSCHIO, ASATH, *à Sacra* BEDRIMUBAL, FELUT, ANABOTOS, SERABILIM, SERGEN, GEMEN, DOMOS, who art seated above the heavens, who beholdest the depths, grant me, I pray thee, that those things which I conceive in my mind may also be executed by me through thee, who appear clean before thee! Amen.'

Gretchen went out, flexing her scabby buttocks, and Ware began the rite of vesting. *Hein?* Ahktoi said plaintively, but Ware did not hear. His triduum was launched, devoutly, in water, and would be observed, strictly, until the end in blood; wherein would be required to the slaughter a lamb, a dog, a hen and a cat.

THE LAST CONJURATION

There are two equal and opposite errors into which our race can fall about the devils. One is to disbelieve in their existence, the other is to believe, and to feel an excessive or unhealthy interest in them. They themselves are equally pleased by both errors and hail a materialist or a magician with the same delight ...

We are really faced with a cruel dilemma. When the humans disbelieve in our existence we lose all the pleasing results of direct terrorism and we make no magicians. On the other hand, when they believe in us, we cannot make them materialists and sceptics. At least not yet ... If once we can produce our perfect work – the Materialist Magician, the man, not using, but veritably worshipping, what he vaguely calls 'Forces' while denying the existence of 'spirits' – then the end of the war will be in sight.

—C. S. Lewis, *The Screwtape Letters*

14

Father Domenico found getting north to Monte Albano a relatively easy journey despite all the snow; he was able to take the *rapido* most of the way. Absurdly, he found himself worrying about the snow; if it lasted, there would be devastating floods in the spring, but that was not the only affliction the spring had in store.

After the journey, nothing seemed to go right. Only about half of the world's white magicians, a small number in any case, who had been summoned to the convocation had been able to make it, or had thought it worth the trip. One of the greatest, the aged archivist Father Bonfiglioli, had come all the way from Cambridge only to find the rigours of being portaged up the Mount too much for him. He was now in the hospital at the base of the Mount with a coronary infarct, and the prognosis was said to be poor.

Luckily, Father Uccello had been able to come. So had Father Monteith, a venerable master of a great horde of creative (though often ineffectual) spirits of the cislunar sphere; Father Boucher, who had commerce with some intellect of the recent past that was neither a mortal nor a Power, a commerce bearing all the earmarks of necromancy and yet was not; Father Vance, in whose mind floated visions of magics that would not be comprehensible, let alone practicable, for millions of years to come; Father Anson, a brusque engineer type who specialized in unclouding the minds of politicians; Father Selahny, a terrifying kabbalist who spoke in parables and of whom it was said that no one since Leviathan had understood his counsel; Father Rosenblum, a dour, bear-like man who tersely predicted disasters and was always right about them; Father Atheling, a wall-eyed grimoiran who saw portents in parts of speech and lectured everyone in a tense nasal voice until the Director had to exile him to the library except when business was being conducted; and a gaggle of lesser men, and their apprentices.

These and the Brothers of the Order gathered in the chapel of the monastery to discuss what might be done. There was no agreement from the outset. Father Boucher was of the firm opinion that Ware would not be permitted to work any such conjuration on Easter, and that hence only minor precautions were necessary. Father Domenico had to point out that Ware's previous sending – a comparatively minor one to be sure, but what was that saying about the fall of the sparrow? – had been made without a sign of Divine intervention upon Christmas Eve.

Then there was the problem of whether or not to try to mobilize the Celestial Princes and their subordinates. Father Atheling would have it that merely putting these Princes on notice might provoke action against Ware, since there was no predicting what They might do, and hence would be in violation of the Covenant. He was finally outshouted by Fathers Anson and Vance, with the obvious but not necessarily valid argument that the Princes must know all about the matter anyhow.

How shaky that assumption was was revealed that night, when those bright angels were summoned one by one before the convocation for a council of war. Bright, terrible and enigmatic They were at any time, but at this calling They were in a state of spirit beyond the understanding of any of the masters present in the chapel. ARATRON, chiefest of Them all, appeared to be indeed unaware of the forthcoming unleashing, and disappeared with a roar when it was described. PHALEG, most military of spirits, seemed to know of Ware's plans, but would not discuss them, and also vanished when pressed. OPHEIL the mercurial, too, was preoccupied, as though Ware's plotting were only a negligible distraction from some immensely greater thought; His answers grew shorter and shorter, and He finally lapsed into what, in a mortal, Father Domenico would have unhesitatingly called surliness. Finally – although not intended as final, for the convocation had meant to consult all seven of the Olympians – the water-spirit PHUL when called up appeared fearsomely without a head, rendering converse impossible and throwing the chapel into a perilous uproar.

These are not good omens,' Father Atheling said; and for the first time in his life, everyone agreed with him. It was agreed, also, that everyone except Father Domenico would remain at the Mount through the target day, to take whatever steps then appeared to be necessary; but there was precious little hope that they would be effective. Whatever was going on in Heaven, it appeared to leave small concern to spare for pleas from Monte Albano.

Father Domenico went south again far earlier than he had planned, unable to think of anything but the mystery of that final, decapitate apparition. The leaden skies returned him no answer.

15

On that penultimate morning, Theron Ware faced the final choice of which demons to call up, and for this he needed to repair to his laboratory, to check the book of pacts. Otherwise his preparations were all made. He had performed the blood sacrifices the previous evening, and then had completely rearranged the furniture in the workroom to accommodate the Grand Circle – the first time he had had need of it in twenty years – the Lesser Circles and the Gateway. There were even special preparations for Father Domenico – who had returned early and with a gratifyingly troubled countenance – should it become necessary to ask the monk to call for Divine intervention; but Ware was tolerably sure it would not be. Though he had never attempted anything of this magnitude before, he felt the work in his fingertips, like a well-practised sonata.

He was, however, both astonished and disquieted to find Dr Hess already in the laboratory – not only because of the potentialities for contamination, but at the inevitable conclusion that Hess had worked out how to placate the Guardian of the door. This man evidently was even more dangerous than Ware had guessed.

'Do you want to ruin us all?' Ware demanded.

Hess turned away from the circle he had been inspecting and looked at Ware frankly. He was pale and hollow-eyed; not only had the fasting been hard on his spare frame – that was a hazard every neophyte had to come to terms with – but apparently he had not been sleeping much either. He said at once:

'No indeed. My apologies, Dr Ware. My curiosity overcame me, I'm afraid.'

'You didn't touch anything, I hope?

'Certainly not. I took your warnings about that with great seriousness, I assure you.'

'Well ... probably no harm done then. I can sympathize with your interest, and even approve it, in part. But I'll be instructing you all in detail a little later in the day, and then you'll have ample time to inspect the arrangements. I do want you to know them intimately. But right now I still have some additional work to do, so if you don't mind ...'

'Quite.' Hess moved obediently towards the door. As he was about to touch the handle, Ware added:

'By the way, Dr Hess, how *did* you deceive the Guardian?'

Hess made no pretence of being puzzled by the question. 'With a white pigeon, and a pocket mirror I got from Jack.'

'Hmm. Do you know, that would never have occurred to me. These pagan survivals are mostly a waste of effort. Let's talk about it more, later. You may have something to teach me.'

Hess made a small bow and finished his departure. Forgetting him instantly, Ware stared at the Grand Circle for a moment, and then walked around it clockwise to the lectern and unlocked the book of pacts. The stiff pages bent reassuringly in his hands. Each leaf was headed by the character or sign of a demon; below, in the special ink reserved for such high matters – gall, copperas, gum arabic – was the text of Theron Ware's agreement with that entity, signed at the bottom by Ware in his own blood, and by the character of the demon repeated in its own hand. Leading all the rest was the seal, and also the characters, of LUCIFUGE ROFOCALE, which also appeared on the book's cover:

There then followed eighty-nine others. It was Ware's sober belief, backed by infernal assurances he had reason to trust, that no previous magician had held so many spirits in thrall. After forty years, true, all the names would change, and Ware would have to force the re-execution of each pact, and so, again and again through the five hundred years of life he had bought from HAGITH in his salad days as a white magician. Nevertheless it could be said that, in the possession of this book. Ware was at least potentially the wealthiest mortal in all of history, though to anyone else in the world the book would be worth nothing except as a *curiosum*.

These spirits, not counting LUCIFUGE ROFOCALE, comprised the seventeen infernal archangels of the Grand Grimoire, and the seventy-two demons of the Descending Hierarchy once confined in the brazen vessel of Solomon the King: a fabulous haul indeed, and each captive commanding troops and armies of lesser spirits, and damned souls by the thousands of millions, more of them every minute. (For these days, virtually everyone was damned; it had been this discovery that had first convinced Ware that the Rebellion was in fact going to succeed, probably by the year AD 2000; the many plain symptoms of chiliastic panic already being manifested amongst the laity were almost certainly due to be vindicated, for everyone was rushing incontinently into Hell-mouth without even the excuse of an Antichrist to mislead him. As matters stood now, Christ Himself would have to creep stealthily, hoping to be ignored, even into a cathedral to conduct a Mass, as in that panel of Hieronymus Bosch; the number of people who could not pronounce the Divine name without a betraying stammer – or their own names, for that matter – had grown from a torrent to a deluge, and, ridiculously, hardly any of them were claiming any fraction of the possible profits in this world. They did not even know that they were on the winning side, or even that there was more than one side. No wonder that Ware had found so much fat in the cauldron, waiting to be skimmed.)

But as Ware had already warned Baines, not all of the spirits in the book were suitable for the experiment at hand. There were some, like MARCHOSIAS, who hoped after an interval to be returned to the Celestial choirs. In this hope, Ware was grimly certain, they were mistaken, and the only reward they would receive would be from the Emperor of the Pit, that kind of reward customarily given to fair-weather friends and summer soldiers. In the meantime, the evils they could be persuaded or compelled to do were minor and hardly worth the effort of invoking them. One, whom Ware had already mentioned to Baines, VASSAGO, was even said in the *Lesser Key* and elsewhere to be 'good by nature' – not too trustworthy an ascription – and indeed was sometimes called upon by white magicians. Others in the hierarchy, like PHOENIX, controlled aspects of reality that were of little relevance to Baines's commission.

Taking up the pen of the Art, Ware made a list. When he was finished, he had written down forty-eight names. Considering the number of the Fallen, that was not a large muster; but he thought it would serve the purpose. He closed and locked the book, and after a pause to rebuke and torment the

Guardian of his door, went out into the Easter morning to rehearse his Tanists.

No day, it seemed, had ever gone so slowly for Baines as this Easter, despite the diversion of the rehearsal; but at last it was night and over, and Ware pronounced himself ready to begin.

The Grand Circle now on the parquetry of the refectory bore a generic resemblance to the circle Ware had composed on Christmas Eve, but it was a great deal bigger, and much different in detail. The circle proper was made of strips of the skin of the sacrificial kid, with the hair still on it, fastened to the floor at the cardinal points with four nails that, Ware explained, had been drawn from the coffin of a child. On the northeast arc, under the word BERKAIAL, there rested on the strips the body of a male bat that had been drowned in blood; on the northwest, under the word AMASARAC, the skull of a parricide; on the southeast, under the word ASARADEL, the horns of a goat; and on the southwest, under the word ARIBECL, sat Ware's cat, to the secret of whose diet they were now all privy. (Indeed, there had not been much of moment to the rehearsal, and Baines had inferred that its chief object had been to impart to the rest of them such items of unpleasant knowledge as this.)

The triangle had been drawn inside the circle with a lump of haematite or lodestone. Under its base was drawn a figure consisting of a *chi* and a *rho* superimposed, resting on the line, with a cross to each side of it. Flanking the other two sides were the great candles of virgin wax, each stick sitting in the centre of a crown of vervain. Three circles for the operators – Ware, Baines and Hess (Jack Ginsberg and Father Domenico would stand outside, in separate pentacles) – were inside the triangle, connected by a cross; the northern circle had horns drawn on it. At the pinnacle of the triangle sat a new brazier, loaded with newly consecrated charcoal. To the left side of the horned circle, which was to be Ware's, of course, was the lectern and the book of pacts, within easy reach.

At the rear of the room, before the curtained door to the kitchen, was another circle, quite as big as the first, in the centre of which was a covered altar. That had been empty this afternoon; but there now lay upon it the nude body of the girl Ware had used to address as Gretchen. Her skin was paper-white except for its markings, and to Baines gave every appearance of being dead. A small twist of violet silk, nearly transparent and with some crumpled thing like a wad of tissue or a broken matzoh inside it, rested upon her navel. Her body appeared to have been extensively written upon with red and yellow grease paint; some of the characters might have been astrological, others more like ideograms or cartouches. In default of knowing their meaning or even their provenance, they simply made her look more naked.

The main door closed. Everyone was now in place.

Ware lit the candles, and then the fire in the brazier. It was a task of Baines and Hess to feed the fire periodically, as the time wore on, the one with brandy, the other with camphor, taking care not to stumble over their swords or leave their circles in the process. As before, they had been enjoined to the strictest silence, especially should any spirit speak to them or threaten them.

Ware now reached out to the lectern and opened his book. This time there were no preliminary gestures, and no portents; he simply began to recite in a gravid voice:

'I conjure and command thee, LUCIFUGE ROFOCALE, by all the names wherewith thou mayst be constrained and bound, SATAN, RANTAN, PALLANTRE, LUTIAS, CORICACOEM, SCIRCIGREUR, *per sedem Baldarey et per gratiam et diligentiamtuam habuisti ab eo hanc nalatimanamilam*, as I command thee, *usor, dilapidatore, tentatore, seminatore, soignatore, devoratore, concitore, et seductore*, where art thou? Thou who imposeth hatred and propagateth enmities, I conjure thee by him who hath created thee for this ministry, to fulfil my work! I cite thee, COLRIZIANA, OFFINA, ALTA, NESTERA, FUARD, MENUET, LUCIFUGE RO-FOCALE, arise, arise, arise!'

There was no sound; but suddenly there was standing in the other circle a dim steaming figure, perhaps eight or nine feet tall. It was difficult to be sure what it looked like, partly because some of the altar could still be seen through it. To Baines it resembled a man with a shaven head bearing three long, twisted horns, eyes like a spectral tarsier's, a gaping mouth, a pointed chin. It was wearing a sort of jerkin, coppery in colour, with a tattered ruff and a fringed skirt; below the skirt protruded two bandy, hooved legs, and a fat, hairy tail, which twitched restlessly.

'What now?' this creature said in an astonishingly pleasant voice. The words, however, were blurred. 'I have not seen my son in many moons.' Unexpectedly, it giggled, as though pleased by the pun.

'I adjure thee, speak more clearly,' Ware said. 'And what I wish, thou knowst full well.'

'Nothing may be known until it is spoken.' The voice seemed no less blurred to Baines, but Ware nodded.

'I desire then to release, as did the Babylonian from under the seal of the King of Israel, blessed be he, from Hell-mouth into the mortal world all those demons of the False Monarchy whose names I shall subsequently call, and whose characters and signs I shall exhibit in my book, providing only that they harm not me and mine, and that they shall return whence they came at dawn, as it is always decreed.'

'Providing no more than that?' the figure said. 'No prescriptions? No desires? You were not always so easily satisfied.'

'None,' Ware said firmly. 'They shall do as they will for this their period of freedom, except that they harm none here in my circles, and obey me when recalled, by rod and pact.'

The demon glanced over its transparent shoulder. 'I see that you have the appropriate fumigant to cense so many great lords, and my servants and satraps will have their several rewards in their deeds. So interesting a commission is new to me. Well. What have you for my hostage, to fulfil the forms?'

Ware reached into his vestments. Baines half expected to see produced another tear vase, but instead Ware brought out by the tail a live mouse, which he threw over the brazier as he had the vase, except not so far. The mouse ran directly towards the demon, circled it frantically three times outside the markings, and disappeared in the direction of the rear door, cheeping like a sparrow. Baines looked towards Ahktoi, but the cat did not even lick its chops.

'You are skilled and punctilious, my son. Call then when I have left, and I will send my ministers. Let nothing remain undone, and much will be done before the black cock crows.'

'It is well. By and under this promise I discharge thee OMGROMA, EPYN, SEYOK, SATANY, DEGONY, EPARYGON, GALLIGANON, ZOGOGEN, FERSTIGON, LUCIFUGE ROFOCALE, begone, begone, begone!'

'I shall see you at dawn.' The prime minister of LUCIFER wavered like a flame, and, like a flame, went out.

Hess promptly cast camphor into the brazier. Recovering with a start from a near paralysis of fascination, Baines sprinkled brandy after it. The fire puffed. Without looking around Ware brought out his lodestone, which he held in his left hand; with his right, he dipped the iron-headed point of his wand into the coals. Little licking points of blue light ran up it almost to his hand, as though the rod, too, had been coated with brandy.

Holding the tonguing wand out before him like a dowsing rod, Ware strode ceremoniously out of the Grand Circle towards the altar. As he walked, the air around him began to grumble as though a storm were gathering about his shaven head, but he paid the noise no attention. He marched on directly to the *locus spiritus*, and into it.

Silence fell at once. Ware said clearly:

'I, Theron Ware, master of masters, Karcist of Karcists, hereby undertake to open the book, and the seals thereof, which were forbidden to be broken until the breaking of the Seven Seals before the Seventh Throne. I have beheld SATAN as a bolt falling from heaven. I have crushed the dragons of the pit beneath my heel. I have commanded angels and devils.

I undertake and command that all shall be accomplished as I bid, and that from beginning to end, alpha to omega, world without end, none shall harm us who abide here in this temple of the Art of Arts. *Aglan*, TETRAGRAM, *vaycheon stimulamaton ezphares retragrammaton olyaram irion esytion existion eryona onera orasym mozm messias soter* EMANUEL SABAOTH ADONAY, *te adoro, et te invoco*. Amen.'

He took another step forward, and touched the flaming tip of the rod to the veil of silk on the belly of the still girl. A little curl of blue–grey smoke began to arise from it, like ignited incense.

Ware now retreated, walking backward, towards the Grand Circle. As he did so, the fire on the wand died; but in the mortuary silence there now intruded a faint hissing, much like the first ignition of a squib. And there were indeed fireworks in inception. As Baines stared in gluttonous hypnosis, a small fountain of many-coloured sparks began to rise from the fuselike tissue on the abdomen of the body on the altar. More smoke poured forth. The air was becoming distinctly hazy.

The body itself seemed to be burning now, the skin peeling back like segments of an orange. Baines heard behind him an aborted retching noise in Jack Ginsberg's voice, but could not himself understand what the occasion for nausea could be. The body – whatever it had once been – was now only like a simulacrum made of pith or papier-mâché, and charged with some equivalent of Greek fire. Indeed, there was already a strong taint of gunpowder overriding the previous odours of incense and camphor. Baines rather welcomed it – not that it was familiar, for it had been centuries since black powder had been used in his trade, but because he had begun to find the accumulation of less business-like perfumes a little cloying.

Gradually, everything melted away into the smoke except an underlay of architectural outline, against which stood a few statues lit more along one side than the other by one of the two sources of fire. Hess coughed briefly; otherwise there was silence except for the hissing of the pyre. Sparks continued to fly upward, and sometimes, for an instant, they seemed to form scribbled, incomprehensible words in the frame of the unreal wall.

Ware's voice sounded remotely from one of the statues:

'BAAL, great king and commander in the East, of the Order of the Fly, obey me!'

Something began to form in the distance. Baines had the clear impression that it was behind the altar, behind the curtained door, indeed outside the palazzo altogether, but he could see it nevertheless. It came forward, growing, until he could also see that it was a thing like a man, in a neat surcoat and snow-white linen, but with two super-numerary heads, the one on the left like a toad's, the other like a cat's. It swelled soundlessly until at some moment it was inarguably in the refectory; and then, still silently, had grown past them and was gone.

'AGARES, duke in the East, of the Order of the Virtues, obey me!'

Again, a distant transparency, and silent. It came on very slowly, manifesting like a comely old man carrying a goshawk upon his wrist. Its slowness was necessitous, for it was riding astride an ambling crocodile. Its eyes were closed and its lips moved incessantly. Gradually, it too swelled past.

'GAMYGYN, marquis and president in Cartagra, obey me!'

This grew to be something like a small horse, or perhaps an ass, modest and unassuming. It dragged behind it ten naked men in chains.

'VALEFOR, powerful duke, obey me!'

A black-maned lion, again with three heads, the other two human, one wearing the cap of a hunter, the other the wary smile of a thief. It passed in a rush, without even a wind to mark its going.

'BARBATOS, great count and minister of SATANACHIA, obey me!'

But this was not one figure; it was four, like four crowned kings. With it and past it poured three companies of soldiers, their heads bowed and their expressions shuttered and still under steel caps. When all this troop had vanished, it was impossible to guess which among them had been the demon, or if the demon had ever appeared.

'PAIMON, great king, of the Order of the Dominions, obey me!'

Suddenly after all the hissing silence there was a blast of sound, and the room was full of capering things carrying contorted tubes and bladders, which might have been intended as musical instruments. The noise, however, resembled most closely a drove of pigs being driven down the chute of a slaughterhouse. Among the bawling, squealing dancers a crowned man rode upon a dromedary, bawling wordlessly in a great hoarse voice. The beast it rode on chewed grimly on some bitter cud, its eyes squeezed shut as if in pain.

'SYTRY!' Ware shouted. Instantly there was darkness and quiet, except for the hissing, which now had a faint overtone as of children's voices. *Jussus secreta libenter detegit feminarum, eas ridens ludificansque ut se luxorise nudent*, great prince, obey me!'

This sweet and lissome thing was no less monstrous than the rest; it had a glowing human body, but was winged, and had the ridiculously small, smirking head of a leopard. At the same time, it was beautiful, in some way that made Baines feel both sick and eager. As it passed, Ware seemed to be pressing a ring against his lips.

'LERAJIE, powerful marquis, ELIGOR, ZEPAR, great dukes, obey me!'

As they were called together, so these three appeared together: the first an archer clad in green, with quiver and a nocked bow whose arrow dripped venom; the second, a knight with a sceptre and a pennon-bearing lance; the third, an armed soldier clad in red. In contrast to their predecessor, there was nothing in the least monstrous about their appearance, nor any clue as to their spheres and offices, but Baines found them no less alarming for all that.

'AYPOROS, mighty earl and prince, obey me!'

Baines felt himself turning sick even before this creature appeared, and from the sounds around him, so did the others, even including Ware. There was no special reason for this apparent in its aspect, which was so grotesque as to have been comic under other circumstances; it had the body of an angel, with a lion's head, the webbed feet of a goose and the scut of a deer. Transform, transform!' Ware cried, thrusting his wand into the brazier. The visitant promptly took on the total appearance of an angel, crown to toe, but the effect of the presence of something filthy and obscene remained.

HABORYM, strong duke, obey me!'

This was another man-thing of the three-headed race – though the apparent relationship, Baines realized, must be pure accident – the human one bearing two stars on its forehead; the others were of a serpent and a cat. In its right hand it carried a blazing firebrand, which it shook at them as it passed.

'NABERIUS, valiant marquis, obey me!'

At first it seemed to Baines that there had been no response to this call. Then he saw movement near the floor. A black cock with bleeding, empty eye sockets was fluttering around the outside of the Grand Circle. Ware menaced it with the wand, and it crowed hoarsely and was gone.

'GLASYALABOLAS, mighty president, obey me!'

This appeared to be simply a winged man until it smiled, when it could be seen to have the teeth of a dog. There were flecks of foam at the corners of its mouth. It passed soundlessly.

In the silence, Baines could hear Ware turning a page in his book of pacts, and remembered to cast more brandy into the brazier. The body on the altar had apparently long since been consumed; Baines could not remember how long it had been since he had seen the last of the word-forming sparks. The thick grey haze persisted, however.

'BUNE, thou strong duke, obey me!'

This apparition was the most marvellous yet, for it approached them borne on a galleon, which sank into the floor as it came nearer until they were able to look down through the floor on to its deck. Coiled there was a dragon with the familiar three heads, these being of dog, griffin and man. Shadowy figures, vaguely human, toiled around it. It continued to sink until it was behind them, and presumably thereafter.

Its passage left Baines aware that he was trembling – not from fright, exactly, for he seemed to have passed beyond that, but from the very exhaustion of this and other emotions, and possibly also from the sheer weariness of having stood in one spot for so long. Inadvertently, he sighed.

'Silence,' Ware said in a low voice. 'And let nobody weaken or falter at this point. We are but half done with our calling – and of those remaining to be invoked, many are far more powerful than any we've yet seen. I warned you before, this Art takes physical strength as well as courage.'

He turned another page. 'ASTAROTH, grand treasurer, great and powerful duke, obey me!'

Even Baines had heard of this demon, though he could not remember where, and he watched it materialize with a stirring of curiosity. Yet it was nothing remarkable in the light of what he had seen already: an angelic figure, at once beautiful and foul, seated astride a dragon; it carried a viper in its right hand. He remembered belatedly that these spirits, never having been matter in the first place, had to borrow a body to make appearances like this, and would not necessarily pick the same one each time; the previous description of ASTAROTH that he had read, he now recalled, had been that of a piebald Negro woman riding on an ass. As the creature passed him, it smiled into his face, and the stench of its breath nearly knocked him down.

'ASMODAY, strong and powerful king, chief of the power of Amaymon, angel of chance, obey me!' As he called, Ware swept off his hat with his left hand, taking care, Baines noted, not to drop the lodestone as he did so.

This king also rode a dragon, and also had three heads – bull, man and ram. All three heads breathed fire. The creature's feet were webbed, as were its hands, in which it carried a lance and pennon; and it had a serpent's tail. Fearsome enough; but Baines was beginning to note a certain narrowness of invention among these infernal artisans. It also occurred to him to wonder, fortunately, whether this very repetitiveness was not deliberate, intended to tire him into inattentiveness, or lure him into the carelessness of contempt. *This thing might kill me if I even closed my eyes*, he reminded himself.

'FURFUR, great earl, obey me!'

This angel appeared as a hart and was past them in a single bound, its tail streaming fire like a comet.

'HALPAS, great earl, obey me!'

There was nothing to this apparition but a stock dove, also quickly gone. Ware was calling the names now as rapidly as he could manage to turn the pages, perhaps in recognition of the growing weariness of his Tanists, perhaps even of his own. The demons flashed in a nightmare parade: RAYM, earl of the Order of the Thrones, a man with a crow's head; SEPAR, a mermaid wearing a ducal crown; SABURAC, a lion-headed soldier upon a pale horse; BIFRONS, a great earl in the shape of a gigantic flea; ZAGAN, a griffin-winged bull; ANDRAS, a raven-headed angel with a bright sword, astride a black wolf; ANDREALPHUS, a peacock appearing amid the noise of many unseen birds; AMDUSCIAS, a unicorn among many musicians; DANTALIAN, a mighty duke in the form of a man but showing many faces both of men and women, with a book in his right hand; and at long last, that mighty king created next after LUCIFER and the first to fall in battle before MICHAEL, formerly of the Order of the Virtues, BELIAL himself, beautiful and deadly in a chariot of fire as he had been worshipped in Babylon.

'Now, great spirits,' Ware said, 'because ye have diligently answered me and shown yourselves to my demands, I do hereby license ye to depart, without injury to any here. Depart, I say, yet be ye willing and ready to come at the appointed hour, when I shall duly exorcise and conjure you by your rites and seals. Until then, ye abide free. Amen.'

He snuffed out the fire in the brazier with a closely fitting lid on which was graven the Third or Secret Seal of Solomon. The murk in the refectory began to lift.

'All right,' Ware said in a matter-of-fact voice. Strangely, he seemed much less tired than he had after the conjuration of MARCHOSIAS. 'It's over – or rather, it's begun. Mr Ginsberg, you can safely leave your circle now, and turn on the lights.'

When Ginsberg had done so, Ware also snuffed the candles. In the light of the shaded electrics the hall seemed in the throes of a cheerless dawn, although in fact the time was not much past midnight. There was nothing on the altar now but a small heap of fine grey ash.

'Do we really have to wait it out in here?' Baines said, feeling himself sagging. 'I should think we'd be a lot more comfortable in your office – and in a better position to find out what's going on, too.'

'We must remain here,' Ware said firmly. 'That, Mr Baines, is why I asked you to bring in your transistor radio – to keep track of both the world and the time. For approximately the next eight hours, the area inside these immediate walls will be the only safe place on all the Earth.'

16

Trappings, litter and all, the refectory now reminded Baines incongruously of an initiation room in a college fraternity house just after the last night of Hell Week. Hess was asleep on the long table that earlier had borne Ware's consecrated instruments. Jack Ginsberg lay on the floor near the main door, napping fitfully, mumbling and sweating. Theron Ware, after again warning everyone not to touch anything, had dusted off the altar and gone to sleep – apparently quite soundly – upon it, still robed and gowned.

Only Baines and Father Domenico remained awake. The monk, having prowled once around the margins of the room, had found an unsuspected low window behind a curtain, and now stood, with his back to them all, looking out at the black world, hands locked behind his back.

Baines sat on the floor with his own back propped against the wall next to the electric furnace, the transistor radio pressed to his ear. He was brutally uncomfortable, but he had found by experiment that this was the best place in the hall for radio reception – barring, of course, his actually entering one of the circles.

Even here, the reception was not very good. It wavered in and out maddeningly, even on powerful stations like Radio Luxembourg, and was liable to tearing blasts of static. These were usually followed, at intervals of a few seconds to several minutes, by bursts or rolls of thunder in the sky outside. Much of the time, too, as was usual, the clear spaces were occupied by nothing except music and commercials.

And thus far, what little news he had been able to pick up had been vaguely disappointing. There had been a major train wreck in Colorado; a freighter was foundering in a blizzard in the North Sea; in Guatemala, a small dam had burst, burying a town in an enormous mud slide; an earthquake was reported in Corinth – the usual budget of natural or near-natural disasters for any day.

In addition, the Chinese had detonated another hydrogen device; there had been another raiding incident on the Israeli–Jordanian border; black tribesmen had staged a rape and massacre on a government hospital in Rhodesia; the poor were marching on Washington again; the Soviet Union had announced that it would not be able to recover three dogs and a monkey it had put in orbit a week ago; the U.S. gained another bloody inch in Vietnam, and Premier Ky put his foot in it; and ...

All perfectly ordinary, all going to prove what everyone of good sense already knew, that there was *no* safe place on the Earth either inside this room or without it, and probably never had been. What, Baines began to wonder, was the profit in turning loose so many demons, at so enormous an expenditure of time, effort and money, if the only result was to be just like reading any morning's newspaper? Of course, it might be that interesting private outrages were also being committed, but many newspaper and other publishers made fortunes on those in ordinary times, and in any event he could never hear of more than a fraction of them over this idiot machine.

Probably he would just have to wait until days or weeks later, when the full record and history of this night had been assembled and digested, when no doubt its full enormity might duly appear. He should have expected nothing else; after all, the full impact of a work of art is never visible in the sketches. All the same, he was obstinately disappointed to be deprived of the artist's excitement of watching the work growing on the canvas.

Was there anything that Ware could do about that? Almost surely not, or he would have done it already; it was clear that he had understood the motive behind the commission as well as he had understood its nature. Besides, it would be dangerous to wake him – he would need all his strength for the latter half of the experiment, when the demons began to return.

Resentfully but with some resignation too, Baines realized that he himself had never been the artist here. He was only the patron, who could watch the colours being applied and the cartoon being filled, and could own the finished board or ceiling, but had never even in principle been capable of handling the brushes.

But there – what was that? The BBC was reporting:

'A third contingent of apparatus has been dispatched along the Thames to combat the Tate Gallery fire. Expert observers believe there is no hope of saving the gallery's great collection of Blake paintings, which include most of his illustrations for the *Inferno* and *Purgatorio* of Dante. Hope also appears to be lost for what amount to almost all the world's paintings by Turner, including his watercolours of the burning of the Houses of Parliament. The intense and sudden nature of the initial outbreak has led to the suspicion that the fire is the work of an incendiary.'

Baines sat up alertly, feeling an even more acute stab of hope, though all his joints protested painfully. *There* was a crime with real style, a crime with symbolism, a crime with meaning. Excitedly he remembered HABORYM, the demon with the dripping fire brand. Now if there were to be more acts that imaginative ...

The reception was getting steadily worse; it was extraordinarily tiring to be continuously straining to filter meaning out of it. Radio Luxembourg appeared to have gone off the air, or to have been shut out by some atmospheric disturbance. He tried Radio Milan, and got it just in time to hear it announce itself about to play all eleven of the symphonies of Gustav Mahler, one right after the other, an insane project for any station and particularly for an Italian one. Was that some demon's idea of a joke? Whatever the answer, it was going to take Radio Milan out of the newscasting business for well over twenty-four hours to come.

He cast further about the dial. There seemed to be an extraordinary number of broadcasts going out in languages he did not know or could even recognize, though he could get around passably in seventeen standard tongues and in any given year was fluent in a different set of three, depending on business requirements. It was almost as though someone had jammed an antenna on the crown of Babel.

Briefly, he caught a strong outburst of English; but it was only the Voice of America making piously pejorative sermonettes about the Chinese fusion explosion. Baines had known that that was coming for months now. Then the multilingual mumbling and chuntering resumed, interspersed occasionally with squeals of what might indifferently have been Pakistani jazz or Chinese opera.

Another segment of English shouted, '... with Cyanotabs! Yes, friends, one dose cures all ills! Guaranteed chockfull of crisp, crunchy atoms ...' and was replaced by a large boys' choir singing the 'Hallelujah Chorus', the words for which, however, seemed to go, 'Bison, bison! Rattus, rattus! Cardinalis, Cardinalis!' Then more gabble, marvellously static-free and sometimes hovering just on the edge of intelligibility.

The room stank abominably of an amazing mixture of reeks: brandy, camphor, charcoal, vervain, gunpowder, flesh, sweat, perfume, incense, candle wicks, musk, singed hair. Baines's head ached dully; it was like trying to breathe inside the mouth of a vulture. He longed to take a pull at the brandy bottle under his rumpled alb, but he did not know how much of what was left would be needed when Ware resumed operations.

Across from him, something moved: Father Domenico had unlocked his hands and turned away from the small window. He was now taking a few prim steps towards Baines. The slight stir of human life seemed to disturb Jack Ginsberg, who thrashed himself into an even more uncomfortable-looking position, shouted hoarsely, and then began to snore. Father Domenico shot a glance at him, and, stopping just short of his side of the Grand Circle, beckoned.

'Me?' Baines said.

Father Domenico nodded patiently. Putting aside the overheated little radio with less reluctance than he would have imagined possible only an hour ago, Baines heaved himself arthritically to his knees, and then to his feet.

As he started to stumble towards the monk, something furry hurtled in front of him and nearly made him fall: Ware's cat. It was darting towards the altar; and in a soaring arc incredible in an animal of its shameless obesity, leapt up there and settled down on the rump of its sleeping master. It looked greenly at Baines and went itself to sleep, or appeared to.

Father Domenico beckoned again, and went back to the window. Baines limped after him, wishing that he had taken off his shoes; his feet felt as though they had turned into solid blocks of horn.

'What's the matter?' he whispered.

'Look out there, Mr Baines.'

Confused and aching, Baines peered past his uninvited and unimpressive Virgil. At first he could see nothing but the streaked steam on the inside of the glass, with a spume of fat snowflakes slurrying beyond it. Then he saw that the night was in fact not wholly dark. Somehow he could sense the undersides of turbulent clouds. Below, the window, like the one in Ware's office, looked down the side of the cliff and out over the sea, which was largely invisible in the snow whorls; so should the town have been, but it was in fact faintly luminous. Overhead, from frame to frame of the window, the clouds were overstitched with continuous streaks of dim fire, like phosphorescent contrails, long-lasting and taking no part in the weather.

'Well?' Baines said.

'You don't see anything?'

'I see the meteor tracks or whatever they are. And the light is odd – sheet lightning, I suppose, and maybe a fire somewhere in town.'

'That's all?'

'That's all,' Baines said, irritated. 'What are you trying to do, panic me into waking Dr Ware and calling it all quits? Nothing doing. We'll wait it out.'

'All right,' Father Domenico said, resuming his vigil. Baines stumped back to his corner and picked up the radio. It said:

'... now established that the supposed Chinese fusion test was actually a missile warhead explosion of at least thirty megatons, centred on Taiwan. Western capitals, already in an uproar because of the napalm murder of the U.S. President's widow in a jammed New York discotheque, are moving quickly to a full war footing and we expect a series of security blackouts on the news at any moment. Until that happens we will keep you informed of whatever important events come through. We pause for station identification. Owoo. Eeg. Oh, piggly baby, I caught you – cheatin' on me – owoo—'

Baines twisted the dial savagely, but the howling only became more bestial. Down the wall to his right, Hess twisted his long body on the table and suddenly sat upright, swinging his stockinged feet to the floor.

'Jesus Christ,' he said huskily. 'Did I hear what I thought I heard?'

'Dead right you did,' Baines said quietly, and not without joy; but he, too, was worried. 'Slide over here and sit down. Something's coming to a head, and it's nothing like we'd expected – or Ware either.'

'Hadn't we better call a halt, then?'

'No. Sit down, goddamn it. I don't think we *can* call a halt – and even if we could, I don't want to give our clerical friend over there the satisfaction.'

'You'd rather have World War Three?' Hess said, sitting down obediently.

'I don't know that that's what's going to happen. We contracted for this. Let's give it the benefit of the doubt. Either Ware's in control, or he should be. Let's wait and see.'

'All right,' Hess said. He began to knead his fingers together. Baines tried the radio once more, but nothing was coming through except a mixture of *The Messiah*, Mahler and The Supremes.

Jack Ginsberg whined in his pseudo-sleep. After a while, Hess said neutrally:

'Baines?'

'What is it?'

'What kind of a thing do you think this is?'

'Well, it's either World War Three or it isn't. How can I know yet?'

'I didn't ask you that ... not what you think it *is*. I asked you, what *kind* of a thing do you think it is? You ought to have some sort of notion. After all, you contracted for it.'

'Oh. Hmm. Father Domenico said it might turn out to be Armageddon. Ware didn't think so, but he hasn't turned out to be very right up to now. I can't guess, myself. I haven't been thinking in these terms very long.'

'Nor have I,' Hess said, watching his fingers weave themselves in and out. 'I'm still trying to make sense of it in the old terms, the ones that used to make sense of the universe to me. It isn't easy. But you'll remember I told you I was interested in the history of science. That involves trying to understand why there wasn't any science for so long, and why it went into eclipse almost every time it was rediscovered. I think I know why now. I think the human mind goes through a sort of cycle of fear. It can only take so much accumulated knowledge, and then it panics, and starts inventing reasons to throw everything over and go back to a Dark Age ... every time with a new, invented mystical reason.'

'You're not making very much sense,' Baines said. He was still also trying to listen to the radio.

'I didn't expect you to think so, but it happens. It happens about every thousand years. People start out happy with their gods, even though they're frightened of them. Then, increasingly, the world becomes secularized, and the gods seem less and less relevant. The temples are deserted. People feel guilty about that, but not much. Then, suddenly, they've had all the secularization they can take, they throw their wooden shoes into the machines, they take to worshipping Satan or the Great Mother, they go into a Hellenistic period or take up Christianity, *in hoc signo vinces* – I've got those all out of order but it happens, Baines, it happens like clockwork, every thousand years, The last time was the chiliastic panics just before the year AD 1000, when everyone expected the Second Coming of Christ and realized that they didn't dare face up to Him. *That* was the heart, the centre, the whole reason of the Dark Ages. Well, we've got another millennium coming to a close now, and people are terrified of *our* secularization, our nuclear and biological weapons, our computers, our overprotective medicine, everything, and they're turning back to the worship of unreason. Just as you've done – and I've helped you. Some people *these* days worship flying saucers because they don't dare face up to Christ. You've turned to black magic. Where's the difference?'

'I'll tell you where,' Baines said. 'Nobody in the whole of time has ever seen a saucer, and the reasons for believing that anybody has are utterly pitiable. Probably they can be explained just as you've explained them, and never mind about Jung and his thump-headed crowd. But, Adolph, you and I *have* seen a demon.'

'Do you think so? I don't deny it. I think it very possible. But Baines, are you sure? How do you *know* what you think you know? We're on the eve of World War Three, which we engineered. Couldn't all this be a hallucination we conjured up to remove some of our guilt? Or is it possible that it isn't happening at all, and that we're as much victims of a chiliastic panic as more formally religious people are? That makes more sense to me than all this medieval mumbo-jumbo about demons. I don't mean to deny the evidence of my senses, Baines. I only mean to ask you, what is it worth?'

'I'll tell you what I know,' Baines said equably, 'though I can't tell you how I know it and I won't bother to try. First, something is happening, and that something is real. Second, you and I and Ware and everyone else who wanted to make it happen, therefore *did* make it happen. Third, we're turning out to be wrong about the outcome – but no matter what it is, it's *our* outcome. We contracted for it. Demons, saucers, fallout – what's the difference? Those are just signs in the equation, parameters we can fill any way that makes the most intermediate sense to us. Are you happier with electrons than with demons? Okay, good for you. But what I like, Adolph, what *I* like is the result. I don't give a damn about the means. I invented it, I called it into being, I'm paying for it – and no matter how else you describe it, *I made it, and it's mine.* Is that clear? *It's mine.* Every other possible fact about it, no matter what that fact might turn out to be, is a stupid footling technicality that I hire people like you and Ware not to bother me with.'

'It seems to me,' Hess said in a leaden monotone, 'that we are all insane.'

At that same moment, the small window burst into an intense white glare, turning Father Domenico into the most intense of inky silhouettes.

'You may be right,' Baines said. 'There goes Rome.'

Father Domenico, his eyes streaming, turned away from the dimming frame and picked his way slowly to the altar. After a long moment of distaste, he took Theron Ware by the shoulder and shook him. The cat hissed and jumped sidewise.

'Wake up, Theron Ware,' Father Domenico said formally. 'I charge you, awake. Your experiment may now wholly and contractually be said to have gone astray, and the Covenant therefore satisfied. Ware! Ware! Wake up, damn you.'

17

Baines looked at his watch. It was 3:00 a.m.

Ware awoke instantly, swung to his feet with a spring and without a word started for the window. At the same instant, the agony that had been Rome swept over the building. The shock wave had been attenuated by distance and the jolt was not heavy, but the window Father Domenico had uncurtained sprang inward in a spray of flying glass needles. More glass fell out from behind the drapes which hung below the ceiling, like an orchestra of celestas.

As far as Baines could see, nobody was more than slightly cut. Not that a serious wound could have made any difference now, with the Last Death already riding on the winds.

Ware was not visibly shaken. He simply nodded once and wheeled towards the Grand Circle, stooping to pick up his dented paper hat. No, he was moved – his lips were pinched white. He beckoned to them all.

Baines took a step towards Jack Ginsberg, to kick him awake if necessary. But the special executive assistant was already on his feet, trembling and wild-eyed. He seemed, however, totally unaware of where he was: Baines had to push him bodily into his minor circle.

'And stay there,' Baines added, in a voice that should have been able to scar diamonds. But Jack gave no sign of having heard it.

Baines went hastily to his Tanist's place, checking for the bottle of brandy. Everyone else was already in position, even the cat, which in fact had vaulted to its post promptly upon having been dumped off Ware's rear.

The sorcerer lit the brazier, and began to address the dead air. He was hardly more than a sentence into this invocation before Baines realized for the first time, in his freezing heart, that this was indeed the last effort – and that indeed they might all still be saved.

Ware was making his renunciation, in his own black and twisted way – the only way his fatally proud soul could ever be brought to make it. He said:

'I invoke and conjure thee, LUCIFUGE ROFOCALE, and fortified with the Power and the Supreme Majesty, I strongly command thee by BARALE-MENSIS, BALDACHIENSIS, PAUMACHIE, APOLORESEDES and the most potent princes GENIO, LIACHIDE, ministers of the Tartarean seat, chief princes of the seat of APOLOGIA in the ninth region, I exorcise and command thee, LUCIFUGE ROFOCALE, by him Who spake and it was done, by the Most Holy and glorious Names ADONAI, EL, ELOHIM, ELOHE, ZEBAOTH, ELION, ESCHERCE, JAH, TETRAGRAMMA-TON, SADIE do thou and thine forthwith appear and show thyself unto me, regardless of how thou art previously charged, from whatever part of the world, without tarrying!

'I conjure thee by Him to Whom all creatures are obedient, by this ineffable Name, TETRAGRAMMATON JEHOVAH, by which the elements are overthrown, the air is shaken, the sea turns back, the fire is generated, the earth moves and all the hosts of things celestial, of things terrestrial, of things infernal, do tremble and are confounded together, come. ADONAI, King of kings, commands thee!'

There was no answer, except an interior grumble of thunder.

'Now I invoke, conjure and command thee, LUCIFUGE ROFOCALE. to appear and show thyself before this circle, by the Name of ON ... by the Name Y and V, which Adam heard and spake ... by the name of JOTH, which Jacob learned from the angel on the night of his wrestling and was delivered from the hands of his brother ... by the Name of AGLA, which Lot heard and was saved with his family ... by the Name ANEHEXE-TON, which Aaron spake and was made wise ... by the name SCHEMES AMATHIA, which Joshua invoked and the Sun stayed upon his course ... by the Name EMMANUEL, by which the three children were deliv-ered from the fiery furnace ... by the Name ALPHA-OMEGA, which Daniel uttered, and destroyed Bel and the dragon ... by the Name ZE-BAOTH, which Moses named, and all the rivers and the waters in the land of Egypt were turned into blood ... by the Name HAGIOS, by the Seal of ADONAI, by those others, which are JETROS, ATHENOROS, PARA-CLETUS ... by the dreadful Day of Judgement ... by the changing sea of glass which is before the face of the Divine Majesty ... by the four beasts before the Throne ... by all these Holy and most potent words, come thou, and come thou quickly. Come, come! ADONAI, King of kings, commands thee!'

Now, at last, there was a sound: a sound of laughter. It was the laughter of Something incapable of joy, laughing only because It was compelled by Its nature to terrify. As the laughter grew, that Something formed.

It was not standing in the Lesser Circle or appearing from the Gateway, but instead was sitting on the altar, swinging Its cloven feet negligently. It had a goat's head, with immense horns, a crown that flamed like a torch, level human eyes, and a Star of David on Its forehead. Its haunches, too, were caprine. Between, the body was human, though hairy and with drag-ging black pinions like a crow's growing from Its shoulder blades. It had women's breasts and an enormous erection, which it nursed alternately with hands folded into the gesture of benediction. On one shaggy forearm was tattooed *Solve*; on the other, *Coagula*.

Ware fell slowly to one knee.

'*Adoramus te*, PUT SATANACHIA,' he said laying his wand on the ground before him. 'And again ... *awe*, ave.'

AVE, BUT WHY DO YOU HAIL ME? the monster said in a petulant bass voice, at once deep and mannered, like a homosexual actor's. IT WAS NOT I YOU CALLED.

'No, Baphomet, master and guest. Never for an instant. It is everywhere said that you can never be called, and would never appear.'

YOU CALLED ON THE GOD, WHO DOTH NOT APPEAR. I AM NOT MOCKED.

Ware bowed his head lower. 'I was wrong.'

AH! BUT THERE IS A FIRST TIME FOR EVERYTHING. YOU MIGHT HAVE SEEN THE GOD AFTER ALL. BUT NOW INSTEAD YOU HAVE SEEN ME. AND THERE IS ALSO A LAST TIME FOR EVERYTHING. I OWE YOU A MOMENT OF THANKS. WORM THOUGH YOU ARE, YOU ARE THE AGENT OF ARMAGEDDON. LET THAT BE WRITTEN, BEFORE ALL WRITINGS, LIKE ALL ELSE, GO INTO THE EVERLASTING FIRE.

'No!' Ware cried out. 'Oh living God, no! This cannot be the Time! You break the Law! Where is the Antichrist—'

WE WILL DO WITHOUT THE ANTICHRIST. HE WAS NEVER NECESSARY. MEN HAVE ALWAYS LED THEMSELVES UNTO ME.

'But – master and guest – the Law—'

WE SHALL ALSO DO WITHOUT THE LAW. HAVE YOU NOT HEARD? THOSE TABLETS HAVE BEEN BROKEN.

There was a hiss of indrawn breath from both Ware and Father Domenico; but if Ware had intended some further argument, he was forestalled. To Baines's right, Dr Hess said in a voice of high ultraviolet hysteria:

'I don't see you, Goat,'

'Shut up!' Ware shouted, almost turning away from the vision.

'I don't see you,' Hess said doggedly. 'You're nothing but a silly zoological mixture. A mushroom dream. You're not real, Goat. Go away. Poof!'

Ware turned in his Karcist's circle and lifted his magician's sword against Hess in both hands; but, at the last minute, he seemed to be afraid to step out against the wobbling figure of the scientist.

HOW GRACIOUS OF YOU TO SPEAK TO ME, AGAINST THE RULES. WE UNDERSTAND, YOU AND I, THAT RULES WERE MADE TO BE BROKEN. BUT YOUR FORM OF ADDRESS DOES NOT QUITE PLEASE ME. LET US PROLONG THE CONVER-SATION, AND I WILL EDUCATE YOU. ETERNALLY, FOR A BEGINNING.

Hess did not answer. Instead, he howled like a wolf and charged blindly out of the Grand Circle, his head down, towards the altar. The Sabbath Goat opened Its great mouth and gulped him down like a fly.

THANK YOU FOR THE SACRIFICE, It said thickly. ANYONE ELSE? THEN IT IS TIME I LEFT.

'Stand to, stupid and disobedient!' Father Domenico's voice rang out from Baines's right side. A cloth fluttered out of the monk's circle on to the floor. 'Behold thy confusion, if thou be disobedient! Behold the Pentacle of Solomon which I have brought into thy presence!'

FUNNY LITTLE MONK, I WAS NEVER IN THAT BOTTLE!

'Hush and be still, fallen star. Behold in me the person of the Exorcist, who is called OCTINIMOES, in the midst of delusion armed by the Lord God and fearless. I am thy master, in the name of the Lord BATHAL, rushing upon ABRAC, ABEOR, coming upon BEROR!'

The Sabbath Goat looked down upon Father Domenico almost kindly. His face red, Father Domenico reached into his robes and brought out a crucifix, which he thrust towards the altar like a sword.

'Back to Hell, devil! In the name of Christ our Lord!'

The ivory cross exploded like a Prince Rupert's Drop, strewing Father Domenico's robe with dust. He looked down at his horribly empty hands.

TOO LATE, MAGICIAN. EVEN THE BEST EFFORTS OF YOUR WHITE COLLEGE ALSO HAVE FAILED – AND AS THE HEAVENLY HOSTS ALSO WILL FAIL. WE ARE ABROAD AND LOOSE, AND WILL NOT BE PUT BACK.

The great head bent to look down upon Theron Ware.

AND YOU ARE MY DEARLY BELOVED SON, IN WHOM I AM WELL PLEASED. I GO TO JOIN MY BROTHERS AND LOVERS IN THE REST OF YOUR WORK. BUT I SHALL BE BACK FOR YOU. I SHALL BE BACK FOR YOU ALL. THE WAR IS ALREADY OVER.

'Impossible!' Father Domenico cried, though choking with the dust of the exploded crucifix. 'It is written that in that war you will at last be conquered and chained!'

OF COURSE, BUT WHAT DOES THAT PROVE? EACH OF THE OPPOSING SIDES IN ANY WAR ALWAYS PREDICTS VICTORY. THEY CANNOT BOTH BE RIGHT. IT IS THE FINAL BATTLE THAT COUNTS, NOT THE PROPAGANDA. YOU MADE A MISTAKE – AND AH, HOW YOU WILL PAY!

'One moment ... please,' Father Domenico said. 'If you would be so kind ... I see that we have failed ... Would you tell us, *where* did we fail?'

The Goat laughed, spoke three words, and vanished.

The dawn grew, red, streaked, dull, endless. From Ware's window the sleeping town slumped down in rivers of cold lava towards the sea – but there was no sea; as Father Domenico had seen hours ago, the sea had withdrawn, and would not be back again except as a tsunami after the Corinth earthquake. Circles of desolation spread away from the ritual circles. Inside them, the last magicians waited for the now Greatest Powers to come back for them.

It would not be long now. In all their minds and hearts echoed those last three words. World without end. End without world.

God is dead.

THE DAY AFTER JUDGEMENT

To Robert A.W. Lowndes

After such knowledge, what forgiveness?
T.S. Eliot

THE WRATH-BEARING TREE

Woe, woe, woe to me inhabiters of the earth by reason of the other
voices of the trumpet of the three angels, which are yet to sound!
—*Revelation 8:13*

The Fall of God put Theron Ware in a peculiarly unenviable position,
though he was hardly alone. After all, he had caused it – in so far as an event
so gigantic could be said to have had any cause but the First. And as a black
magician he knew better than to expect any gratitude from the victor.

Nor, on the other hand, would it do him the slightest good to maintain
that he had loosed the forty-eight suffragan demons upon the world only at
the behest of a client. Hell was an incombustible Alexandrine library of such
evasions – and besides, even had he had a perfect plea of innocence, there
was no longer any such thing as justice, anywhere. The Judger was dead.

'When the hell *is* he coming back?' Baines, the client, demanded suddenly, irritably. 'This waiting is worse than getting it over with.'

Father Domenico turned from the refectory window, which was now
unglazed, from the shock wave of the H-bombing of Rome. He had been
looking down the cliff face, over the half-melted *pensioni*, shops and tenements of what had once been Positano, at the drained sea bed. When that
tsunami did arrive, it was going to be a record one; it might even reach all
the way up here.

'You don't know what you're saying, Mr Baines,' the white magician said.
'From now on, nothing can be over with. We are on the brink of eternity.'

'You know what I mean,' Baines growled.

'Of course, but if I were you, I'd be grateful for the respite … It *is* odd that
he hasn't come back yet. Dare we hope that something has after all inter-
fered with him? Something – or some One?'

'He said God is dead.'

'Yes, but he is the Father of Lies. What do you think, Dr Ware?'

Ware did not reply. The personage they were talking about was of course
not the Father of Lies, the ultimate Satan, but the subsidiary prince who had
answered Ware's last summons PUT SATANACHIA, sometimes called
Baphomet, the Sabbath Goat. As for the question, Ware simply did not
know the answer; it was now sullen full morning of the day after Armageddon, and the Goat had promised to come for the four of them promptly at

89

dawn, in ironical obedience to the letter of Ware's loosing and sending; yet he was not here.

Baines looked around the spent conjuring room. 'I wonder what he did with Hess?'

'Swallowed him,' Ware said, 'as you saw. And it served the fool right for stepping outside of his circle.'

'But did he really eat him?' Baines said. 'Or was that, uh, just symbolical? Is Hess actually in Hell now?'

Ware refused to be drawn into the discussion, which he recognized at once as nothing but Baines's last little vestige of scepticism floundering about for an exit from its doom; but Father Domenico said:

'The thing that called itself Screwtape let slip to Lewis that demons do eat souls. But one can hardly suppose that that is the end. I expect we will shortly know a lot more about the matter than we wish.'

Abstractedly, he brushed from his robe a little more of the dust from his shattered crucifix. Ware watched him with ironic wonder. He really was staging a remarkable recovery; his God was dead, his Christ was exploded as a myth, his soul assuredly as damned as that of Ware or Baines – and yet he could still manage to interest himself in semi-Scholastic prattle. Well, Ware had always thought that white magic, these days as always, attracted only a low order of intellect, let alone insight.

But where *was* the Goat?

'I wonder where Mister Ginsberg went?' Father Domenico said, as if in parody of Ware's unspoken question. Again, Ware only shrugged. He had for the moment quite forgotten Baines's male secretary; it was true that Ginsberg had shown some promise as an apprentice, but after all, he had wanted to learn the Ars Magica essentially as a means of supplying himself with mistresses, and even under normal circumstances, his recent experience with Ware's assistant, Gretchen – who was in fact a succubus – had probably driven the desire out permanently. In any event, of what use would an apprentice be now?

Baines looked as startled as Ware felt at the question. 'Jack?' he said. 'I sent him to our rooms to pack.'

'To pack?' Ware said. 'You had some notion that you might get away?'

'I thought it highly unlikely,' Baines said evenly, 'but if the opportunity arose, I didn't mean to be caught unprepared.'

'Where do you think you might go where the Goat couldn't find you?'

No reply was necessary. Ware felt through his sandals a slow shuddering of the tiled floor. As it grew more pronounced, it was joined by a faint but deep thunder in the air.

Father Domenico shuffled hastily back to the window, Baines close behind him. Unwillingly, Ware followed.

On the horizon, a wall of foaming, cascading water was coming towards them with preternatural slowness, across the deserted floor of the Tyrrhenian Sea. The water had all been drained away as one consequence of the Corinth earthquake of yesterday, which itself might or might not have been demonically created; Ware was not sure that it made much difference one way or the other. In any event, the tectonic imbalance was now, inexorably, in the process of righting itself.

The Goat remained unaccountably delayed ... but the tsunami was on its way at last.

What had been Jack Ginsberg's room in the palazzo now looked a great deal more like the cabinet of Dr Caligari. Every stone, every window frame, every angle, every wall was out of true, so that there was no place to stand where he did not feel as though he had been imprisoned in a tesseract – except that even the planes of the prison were crazed with jagged cracks without any geometry whatsoever. The window panes were out, and the ceiling dripped; the floor was invisible under fallen plaster, broken glass and anonymous dirt; and in the *gabinetto* the toilet was pumping continuously as though trying to flush away the world. The satin-sheeted bed was sandy to the touch, and when he took his clothes out of the wardrobe, his beautiful clothes so carefully selected from *Playboy,* dust fumed out of them like spores from a puffball.

There was no place to lay clothes out but on the bed, though it was only marginally less filthy than any other flat surface available He wiped down the outside of his suitcase with a handkerchief, which he then dropped out the window down the cliff, and began to stow things away, shaking them out with angry coughs as best he could.

The routine helped, a little. It was not easy to think about any other part of this incredible impasse. It was even difficult to know whom to blame. After all, he had known about Baines's creative impulse towards destruction for a long time and had served it; nor had he ever thought it insane. It was a common impulse: to one engineer you add one stick of dynamite, and in the name of progress he will cut a mountain in half and cover half a country with concrete, for no better real reason than that he enjoys it. Baines was only the same kind of monomaniac, writ large because he had made so much money at it; and unlike the others, he had always been honest enough to admit that he did it because he loved the noise and the ruin. More generally, top management everywhere, or at least back in the States, was filled with people who loved their business, and cared for nothing else but crossword puzzles or painting by numbers.

As for Ware, what had he done? He had prosecuted an art to his own destruction, which was traditionally the only sure way a life can be made into a work of art. Unlike that idiot Hess, he had known how to protect himself from the minor unpleasant consequences of his fanaticism, though he had turned out to be just as blindly suicidal in the end. Ware was still alive, and Hess was dead – unless his soul still lived in Hell – but the difference now was only one of degree, not of kind. Ware had not invited Baines's commission; he had only hoped to use it to enlarge his own knowledge; as Hess had been using Baines; as Baines had used Hess and Ware to satisfy his business and aesthetic needs; as Ware and Baines had used Jack's administrative talents and his delight in straight, raw sex; as Jack had tried to use them all in return.

They had all been things, not people, to each other, which after all is the only sensible and fruitful attitude in a thing-dominated world. (Except, of course, for Father Domenico, whose desire to prevent anybody from accomplishing anything, chiefly by wringing his hands, had to be written off as the typical, incomprehensible attitude of the mystic – a howling anachronism in the modern world, and predictably ineffectual.) And in point of fact none of them – not even Father Domenico – could fairly be said to have failed. Instead, they had all been betrayed. Their plans and operations had all depended implicitly upon the existence of God – even Jack, who had entered Positano as an atheist, had been reluctantly forced to grant that – and in the final pinch, He had turned out to have been not around any more after all. If this shambles was anyone's fault, it was His.

He slammed down the cover of his suitcase. The noise was followed, behind him, by a fainter sound, about halfway between the clearing of a throat and the sneeze of a cat. For a moment he stood stock-still, knowing very well what that sound meant. But it was useless to ignore it, and finally he turned around.

The girl was standing on the threshold, as before, and as before, she was somewhat different. It was one of the immemorial snares of her type; at each apparition she seemed like someone else, and yet always, at the same time, reminded him of someone – he could never think who – he had once known; she was always at once mistress, harem and stranger. Ware ironically called her Gretchen, or Greta, or Rita, and she could be compelled by the word *Cazotte,* but in fact she had no name, nor even any real sex. She was a demon, alternately playing succubus to Jack and incubus to some witch on the other side of the world. In theory only, the idea of such a relationship would have revolted Jack, who was fastidious, in his fashion. In actual practice, it did indeed revolt him ... insufficiently.

'You do not make me as welcome as before,' she said.

Jack did not reply. This time the apparition was blonde again, taller than he was, very slender, her hair long and falling straight down her back. She wore a black silk sari with gold edging, which left one breast bare, and gold sandals, but no jewellery. Amidst all this rubble, she looked fresh as though she had just stepped out of a tub: beautiful, magical, terrifying and irresistible.

'I thought you could come only at night,' he said at last.

'Oh, those old rules are gone forever,' she said, and as if to prove it, stepped across the threshold without even one invitation, let alone three. 'And you are leaving. We must celebrate the mystery once more before you go, and you must make me a last present of your seed. It is not very potent; my other client is thus far disappointed. Come, touch me, go into me. I know it is your need.'

'In this mess? You must have lost your mind.'

'Nay, impossible; intellect is all I am, no matter how I appear to you. Yet I am capable of monstrous favours, as you know well, and will to know again.'

She took the suitcase, which was still unfastened, off the bed and set it flat on the floor. Though it was almost too heavy for Jack when fully loaded, handling it did not appear to cost her the slightest effort. Then, lifting one arm and with it the bare and spiky breast, she unwound the sari in a single, continuous sweeping motion, and lay down naked across the gritty bed, light glinting from dewdrops caught about her inflamed mound, a vision of pure lubricity.

Jack ran a finger around the inside of his collar, though it was open. It was impossible not to want her, and at the same time he wanted desperately to escape – and besides, Baines was waiting, and Jack had better sense than to pursue his hobby on company time.

'I should have thought you'd be off raising Hell with your colleagues,' he said, his voice hoarse.

The girl frowned suddenly, reminding him of that fearful moment after their first night when she had thought that he had been mocking her. Her fingernails, like independent creatures, clawed slowly at her flat abdomen.

'Dost think to copulate with fallen seraphim?' she said. 'I am not of any of the Orders which make war; I do only what would be hateful even to the damned.' Then, equally suddenly, the frown dissolved in a little shower of laughter. 'And ah, besides, I raise not Hell, but the Devil, for already I have Hell in me – dost know that story of Boccaccio?'

Jack knew it; there was no story of that kind he did not know; and his Devil was most certainly raised. While he still hesitated, there was a distant growling sound, almost inaudible but somehow also infinitely heavy. The girl turned her head towards the window, also listening; then she looked back at him, spread her thighs and held out her arms.

'I think,' she said, 'that you had better hurry.'

With a groan of despair, he fell to his knees and buried his face in her muff. Her smooth legs closed about his ears; but no matter how hard he pulled at her cool, pliant rump, the sound of the returning sea rose louder and louder around them both.

SO ABOVE

Haeresis est maxima opera maleficarum non credere.
—*Heinrich Institor and Jakob Sprenger*, Malleus Maleficarum

1

The enemy, whoever he was, had obviously been long prepared to make a major attempt to reduce the Strategic Air Command's master missile-launching control site under Denver. In the first twenty minutes of the war, he had dumped a whole stick of multiple hydrogen warheads on it. The city, of course, had been utterly vaporized, and a vast expanse of the plateau on which it had stood was now nothing but gullied, vitrified and radioactive granite; but the site had been well hardened and was more than a mile beneath the original surface. Everybody in it had been knocked down and temporarily deafened, there were bruises and scrapes and one concussion, some lights had gone out and a lot of dust had been raised despite the air conditioning; in short, the damage would have been reported as 'minimal' had there been anybody to report it to.

Who the enemy was occasioned some debate. General D. Willis McKnight, a Yellow Peril fan since his boyhood reading of *The American Weekly* in Chicago, favoured the Chinese. Of his two chief scientists, one, the Prague-born Dr Džejms Šatvje, the godfather of the selenium bomb, had been seeing Russians under his bed for almost as long.

'Nu, why argue?' said Johann Buelg. As a RAND Corporation alumnus, he found nothing unthinkable, but he did not like to waste time speculating about facts. 'We can always ask the computer – we must have enough input already for that. Not that it matters much, since we've already plastered the Russians *and* the Chinese pretty thoroughly.'

'We already know the Chinese started it,' General McKnight said, wiping dust off his spectacles with his handkerchief. He was a small, narrow-chested Air Force Academy graduate from the class just after the cheating had been stopped, already nearly bald at forty-eight; naked, his face looked remarkably like that of a prawn. 'They dropped a thirty-megatonner on Formosa, disguised as a test.'

'It depends on what you mean by "start",' Buelg said. 'That was already on Rung twenty-one; Level Four – local nuclear war. But still only Chinese against Chinese'

'But we were committed to them, right?' Šatvje said. 'President Agnew told the UN, "I am a Formosan."'

'It doesn't matter worth a damn,' Buelg said, with some irritation. It was his opinion, which he did not keep particularly private, that Šatvje, whatever his eminence as a physicist, in all other matters had a *goyische kopf*. He had encountered better heads on egg creams in his father's candy store. 'The thing's escalated almost exponentially in the past eighteen hours or so. The question is, how far has it gone? If we're lucky, it's only up to Level Six, central war – maybe no farther than Rung thirty-four, constrained disarming attack.'

'Do you call atomizing Denver "restrained"?' the General demanded.

'Maybe. They could have done for Denver with one warhead, but instead they saturated it. That means they were shooting for us, not for the city proper. Our counterstrike couldn't be preventive, so it was one rung lower, which I hope to God they noticed.'

'They took Washington out,' Šatvje said, clasping his fat hands piously. He had been lean once, but becoming first a consultant on the Cabinet level, next a spokesman for massive retaliation, and finally a publicity saint had appended a beer belly to his brain-puffed forehead, so that he now looked like a caricature of a nineteenth-century German philologist. Buelg himself was stocky and tended to run to lard, but a terrible susceptibility to kidney stones had kept him on a reasonable diet.

'The Washington strike almost surely wasn't directed against civilians,' Buelg said. 'Naturally the leadership of the enemy is a prime military target. But, General, all this happened so quickly that I doubt that anybody in government had a chance to reach prepared shelters. You may now be effectively the president of whatever is left of the United States, which means that you could make new policies.'

'True,' McKnight said. 'True, true.'

'In which case we've got to know the facts the minute our lines to outside are restored. Among other things, if the escalation's gone all the way to spasm, in which case the planet will be uninhabitable. There'll be nobody and nothing left alive but people in hardened sites, like us, and the only policy we'll need for that will be a count of the canned beans.'

'I think that needlessly pessimistic,' Šatvje said, at last heaving himself up out of the chair into which he had struggled after getting up off the floor. It was not a very comfortable chair, but the computer room – where they had all been when the strike had come – had not been designed for comfort. He put his thumbs under the lapels of his insignia-less adviser's uniform and frowned down upon them. 'The Earth is a large planet, of its class; if we cannot reoccupy it, our descendants will be able to do so.'

'After five thousand years?'

'You are assuming that carbon bombs were used. Dirty bombs of that kind are obsolescent. That is why I so strongly advocated the sulphur-decay chain; the selenium isotopes are chemically all strongly poisonous, but they have very short half lives. A selenium bomb is essentially a *humane* bomb.'

Šatvje was physically unable to pace, but he was beginning to stump back and forth. He was again playing back one of his popular magazine articles. Buelg began to twiddle his thumbs, as ostentatiously as possible.

'It has sometimes occurred to me,' Šatvje said, 'that our discovery of how to release the nuclear energies was providential. Consider: Natural selection stopped for Man when he achieved control over his environment, and furthermore began to save the lives of all his weaklings, and preserve their bad genes. Once natural selection has been halted, then the only remaining pressure upon the race to evolve is mutation. Artificial radioactivity, and indeed even fallout itself, may be God's way of resuming the process of evolution for Man ... perhaps towards some ultimate organism we cannot foresee, perhaps even towards some unitary mind which we will share with God, as Teilhardt de Chardin envisioned—'

At this point, the General noticed the twiddling of Buelg's thumbs.

'Facts are what we need.' he said. 'I agree with you there, Buelg. But a good many of our lines to outside *were* cut, and there may have been some damage to the computer circuitry, too.' He jerked his head towards the technicians who were scurrying around and up and down the face of RANDOMAC. 'I've got them working on it. Naturally.'

'I see that, but we'll need some sort of rational schedule of questions. Is the escalation still going on, presuming we haven't reached the insensate stage already? If it's over, or at least suspended somehow, is the enemy sane enough not to start it again? And then, what's the extent of the exterior damage? For that, we'll need a visual readout – I assume there are still some satellites up, but we'll want a closer look, if any local television survived.

'And if you're now the president, General, are you prepared to negotiate, if you've got any opposite numbers in the Soviet Union or the People's Republic?'

'There ought to be whole sets of such courses of action already programmed into the computer,' McKnight said, 'according to what the actual situation is. Is the machine going to be useless to us for anything but gaming, now that we really need it? Or have you been misleading me again?'

'Of course I haven't been misleading you. I wouldn't play games with my own life as stakes. And there are indeed such alternative courses; I wrote most of them myself, though I didn't do the actual programming. But no programme can encompass what a specific leader might decide to do. War gaming actual past battles – for example, rerunning Waterloo without allowing for Napoleon's piles, or the heroism of the British squares – has produced "predicted" outcomes completely at variance with history. Computers are rational; people aren't. Look at Agnew. That's why I asked you my question – which, by the way, you haven't yet answered.'

McKnight pulled himself up and put his glasses back on.

'I,' he said, 'am prepared to negotiate. With anybody. Even Chinks.'

2

Rome was no more, nor was Milan. Neither were London, Paris, Berlin, Bonn, Tel Aviv, Cairo, Riyadh, Stockholm and a score of lesser cities. But these were of no immediate concern. As the satellites showed, their deaths had expectedly laid out long, cigar-shaped, overlapping paths of fallout to the east – the direction in which, thanks to the rotation of the Earth, the weather inevitably moved – and though these unfortunately lay across once friendly terrain, they ended in enemy country. Similarly, the heavy toll in the USSR had sown its seed across Siberia and China; that in China across Japan, Korea and Taiwan; and the death of Tokyo was poisoning only a swath of the Pacific (although, later, some worry would have to be devoted to the fish). Honolulu somehow had been spared, so that no burden of direct heavy nuclear fallout would reach the West Coast of the United States.

This was fortunate, for Los Angeles, San Francisco, Portland, Seattle and Spokane had all been hit, as had Denver, St Louis, Minneapolis, Chicago, New Orleans, Cleveland, Detroit and Dallas. Under the circumstances, it really hardly mattered that Pittsburgh, Philadelphia, New York, Syracuse, Boston, Toronto, Baltimore and Washington had all also got it, for even without bombs the Eastern third of the continental United States would have been uninhabitable in its entirety for at least fifteen years to come. At the moment, in any event, it consisted of a single vast forest fire through which, from the satellites, the slag pits of the bombed cities were invisible except as high spots in the radiation contours. The Northwest was in much the same shape, although the West Coast in general had taken far fewer missiles. Indeed, the sky all over the world was black with smoke, for the forests of Europe and northern Asia were burning too. Out of the pall, more death fell, gently, invisibly, inexorably.

All this, of course, came from the computer analysis. Though there were television cameras in the satellites, even on a clear day you could hardly have told from visual sightings, from that height – nor from photographs, for that matter – even whether or not there was intelligent life on Earth. The view over Africa, South America, Australia and the American Southwest was better, but of no strategic or logistic interest, and never had been.

Of the television cameras on the Earth's surface, most of the surviving ones were in areas where nothing seemed to have happened at all, although in towns the streets were deserted, and the very few people glimpsed briefly on the screen looked haunted. The views from near the bombed areas were fragmentary, travelling, scarred by rasters, aflicker with electronic snow – a procession of unconnected images, like scenes from an early surrealist film, where one could not tell whether the director was trying to portray a story or only a state of mind.

Here stood a single telephone pole, completely charred; here was a whole row of them, snapped off the ground level but still linked in death by their wires. Here was a desert of collapsed masonry, in the midst of which stood a reinforced-concrete smokestack, undamaged except that its surface was etched by heat and by the sand blasting of debris carried by a high wind. Here buildings all leaned sharply in a single direction, as if struck like the chimney by some hurricane of terrific proportions; here was what had been a group of manufacturing buildings, denuded of roofing and siding, nothing but twisted frames. Here a row of wrecked automobiles, neatly parked, burned in unison; here a gas holder, ruptured and collapsed, had burned out hours ago.

Here was a side of a reinforced concrete building, windowless, cracked and buckled slightly inward where a shock wave had struck it. Once it had been painted grey or some dark colour, but all the paint had blistered and scaled and blown away in a second, except where a man had been standing nearby, there the paint remained, a shadow with no one to cast it.

That vaporized man had been one of the lucky. Here stood another who had been in a cooler circle; evidently he had looked up at a fireball, for his eyes were only holes; he stood in a half crouch, holding his arms out from his sides like a penguin, and instead of skin, his naked body was covered with a charred fell which was cracked in places, oozing blood and pus. Here a filthy, tattered mob clambered along a road almost completely covered with rubble, howling with horror – though there was no sound with this scene – led by a hairless woman pushing a flaming baby carriage. Here a man who seemed to have had his back flayed by flying glass worked patiently with a bent snow shovel at the edge of an immense mound of broken brick; by the shape of its margins, it might once have been a large house …

There was more.

Šatvje uttered a long, complex, growling sentence of hatred. It was entirely in Czech, but its content was nevertheless not beyond all conjecture. Buelg shrugged again and turned away from the TV screen.

'Pretty fearful,' he said. 'But on the whole, not nearly as much destruction as we might have expected. It's certainly gone no *higher* than Rung thirty-four. On the other hand, it doesn't seem to fit any of the escalation frames at all well. Maybe it makes some sort of military or strategic sense, but if it does, I'm at a loss to know what it is. General?'

'Senseless,' McKnight said. 'Outright senseless. Nobody's been hurt in any *decisive* way. And yet the action seems to be over.'

'That was my impression,' Buelg agreed. 'There seems to be some missing factor. We're going to have to ask the computer to scan for an anomaly. Luckily it's likely to be a big one – but since I can't tell the machine what *kind* of anomaly to look for, it's going to cost us some time.'

'How much time?' McKnight said, running a finger around the inside of his collar. 'If the Chinks start upon us again—'

'It may be as much as an hour, after I formulate the question and Chief Hay programmes it, which will take, oh, say two hours at a minimum. But I don't think we need to worry about the Chinese; according to our data, that opening Taiwan bomb was the biggest one they used, so it was probably the biggest one they had. As for anyone else, well, you just finished saying yourself that somehow everything's now stopped short. We badly need to find out why.'

'All right. Get on it, then.'

The two hours for programming, however, stretched to four; and then the computer ran for ninety minutes without producing anything at all. Chief Hay had thoughtfully forbidden the machine to reply DATA INSUFFICENT since new data were coming in at an increasing rate as communications with the outside improved; as a result, the computer was recycling the problem once every three or four seconds.

McKnight used the time to issue orders that repairs to the keep be made, stores assessed, order restored, and then settled down to a telecommunications search – again via the computer, but requiring only about 2 per cent of its capacity – for any superiors who might have survived him. Buelg suspected that he really wanted to find some; he had the capacity to be a general officer, but would find it most uncomfortable to be a president, even over so abruptly simplified a population and economy – and foreign policy, for that matter – as the TV screen had shown now existed outside. Ordering junior officers to order noncommissioned officers to order rankers to replace broken fluorescent bulbs was the type of thing he didn't mind doing on his own, but for ordering them to arm missiles and aim them, or put a state under martial law, he much preferred to be acting upon higher authority.

As for Buelg's own preference, he rather hoped that McKnight wouldn't be able to find any such person. The United States under a McKnight regime wouldn't be run very imaginatively or even flexibly, but on the other hand it would be unlikely to be a tyranny. Besides, McKnight was very dependent upon his civilian experts, and hence would be easy to manage. Of course, that meant that something would have to be done about Šatvje—

Then the computer rang its bell and began to print out its analysis. Buelg read it with intense concentration, and after the first fold, utter incredulity. When it was all out of the printer, he tore it off, tossed it on to the desk and beckoned to Chief Hay.

'Run the question again.'

Hay turned to the input keyboard. It took him ten minutes to retype the programme; the question had been in the normal order of things too specialized to tape. Two and a half seconds after he had finished, the machine chimed and the long thin slabs of metal began to rise against the paper. The printing out process never failed to remind Buelg of a player piano running in reverse, converting notes into punches instead of the other way around, except, of course, that what one got here was not punches but lines of type. But he saw almost at once that the analysis itself was going to be the same as before, word for word.

At the same time he became aware that Šatvje was standing just behind him.

'About time,' the Czech said. 'Let's have a look.'

'There's nothing to see yet.'

'What do you mean, there's nothing to see? It's printing isn't it? And you've already got another copy out on the bench. The General should have been notified immediately.'

He picked up the long, wide accordion fold of paper with its sprocket-punched edges and began to read it. There was nothing Buelg could do to prevent him.

'The machine's printing nonsense, that's what I mean, and I didn't propose to distract the General with a lot of garbage. The bombing must have jarred something loose.'

Hay turned from the keyboard. 'I ran a test programme through promptly after the attack, Dr Buelg. The computer was functioning perfectly then.'

'Well, clearly it isn't now. Run your test programme again, find out where the trouble lies, and let us know how long it will take to repair it. If we can't trust the computer, we're out of business for sure.'

Hay got to work. Šatvje put the readout down.

'What's nonsense about this?' he said.

'It's utterly impossible, that's all. There hasn't been time. With any sort of engineering training, you'd know that yourself. And it makes no military or political sense, either.'

'I think we should let the General be the judge of that.'

Picking up the bulky strip again, Šatvje carried it off towards the General's office, a certain subtle triumph in his gait, like the school trusty bearing the evidence of petty theft to the head master. Buelg followed, inwardly raging, and not only at the waste motion. Šatvje would of course tell McKnight that Buelg had been holding back on reporting the analysis; all Buelg could do now, until the machine was repaired, was to be sure to be there to explain why, and the posture was much too purely defensive for his liking. It was a damn shame that he had ever taught Šatvje to read a printout, but once they had been thrown together on this job, he had had no choice in the matter. McKnight had been as suspicious as a Sealyham of both of them, anyhow, at the beginning. Šatvje, after all had come from a country which had long been Communist, and had had to explain that his ancestry was French, his name only a Serbo-Croat transliteration back from the Cyrillic of Chatvieux; while Security had unfortunately confused Buelg with Johann Gottfried Jülg, a forgotten nineteenth-century translator of *Ardshi Bordschi Khan,* the *Siddhi Kur,* the *Skaskas* and other Russian folk tales, so that Buelg, even more demeaningly, had had to admit that his name was actually a Yiddish version of a German word for a leather bucket. Under McKnight's eye, the two still possibly suspect civilians had to cooperate or be downgraded into some unremunerative university post. Buelg supposed that Šatvje had enjoyed it as little as he had, but he didn't care an iota about what Šatvje did or didn't enjoy. Damn the man.

As for the document itself, it was no masterpiece of analysis. The machine had simply at last recognized an anomaly in a late-coming piece of new data. It was the interpretation that made Buelg suspect that the gadget had malfunctioned; unlike Šatvje, he had had enough experience of computers at RAND to know that if they were not allowed enough warm-up time, or had been improperly cleared of a previous programme, they could produce remarkably paranoid fantasies.

Translated from the Fortran, the document said that the United States had not only been hit by missiles, but also deeply invaded. This conclusion had been drawn from a satellite sighting of something in Death Valley, not there yesterday, which was not natural, and whose size, shape and energy output suggested an enormous fortress.

'Which is just plain idiotic,' Buelg added, after the political backing and filling in McKnight's office had been gone through to nobody's final advantage. 'On any count you care to name. The air drops required to get the materials in there, or the sea landings plus overland movements, couldn't have gone undetected. Then, strategically it's insane: the building of targets like fortresses should have become obsolete with the invention of the cannon, and the airplane made them absurd. Locating such a thing in Death Valley means that it dominates nothing but utterly worthless territory, at the price of insuperable supply problems – right from the start it's in a state of siege, by Nature alone. And as for running it up overnight – I ask you, General, could *we* have done that, even in peacetime and in the most favourable imaginable location? I say we couldn't, and that if we couldn't, no human agency could.'

McKnight picked up his phone and spoke briefly. Since it was a Hush-a-Phone, what he said was inaudible, but Buelg's guess about the call was promptly confirmed.

'Chief Hay says the machine is in perfect order and has produced a third analysis just like this one,' he reported. 'The problem now clearly is one of reconnaissance. (He pronounced the word correctly, which, amidst his flat Californian American, sounded almost affected.) Is there such a thing in Death Valley, or isn't there? For the satellite to be able to spot it at all, it must be gigantic. From twenty-three thousand miles up, even a city the size of San Antonio is invisible unless you know exactly what you're looking for in advance.'

Here, Buelg was aware McKnight was speaking as an expert. Until he had been put in charge of SAC in Denver, almost all his career had been spent in various aspects of Air Information; even as a teenager, he had been a Civil Air Patrol cadet involved in search-and-rescue operations, which, between the mud slides and the brush fires, had been particularly extensive in the Los Angeles area in those days.

'I don't doubt that the satellite has spotted *something*,' Buelg said. 'But what it probably "sees" is a hard-radiation locus – maybe thermally hot, too – rather than any optical object, let alone a construct. My guess is that it's nothing more than the impact site of a multiple warhead component that lost guidance, or was misaimed to begin with.'

'Highly likely,' McKnight admitted. 'But why guess? The obvious first step is to send a low-level attack bomber over the site and get close-in photographs and spectra. A primitive installation such as you suggested earlier would be typically Chinese, and if so they won't have low-level radar. If on the other hand the plane gets shot down, that will tell us something about the enemy, too.'

Buelg sighed inwardly. Trying to nudge McKnight out of his single channel was a frustrating operation. But maybe, in this instance, it wasn't really necessary; after all, the suggestion itself was sensible.

'All right,' he said. 'One plane seems like a small investment. We've got damn all else left to lose now, anyhow.'

3

No attack was made on the plane, but there was nevertheless one casualty. Neither the photographer nor the flight engineer, both busy with their instruments, had actually seen much of the target, and the Captain, for the same reason, had seen little more.

'Hell of a lot of turbulence,' he said at the debriefing, which took place a thousand miles away, while the men under Denver watched intently. 'And the target itself is one huge updraught, like New York used to be, only much worse.'

But the navigator, once his job had been done, had had nothing to do but look out, and he was in a state of shock. He was a swarthy young enlisted man from Chicago who looked as though he might have been recruited straight from a Mafiosa family, but he could say nothing now but a sentence which refused to get beyond its first syllable: 'Dis – Dis –' Once he had recovered from his shock they would be able to question him. But for the time being he was of no help.

The photographs, however, were very clear, except for the infra-red sensitive plates, which showed nothing intelligible to the eye at all. The installation was perfectly circular and surrounded by a moat which, impossibly for Death Valley, appeared to be filled with black but genuine water, from which a fog bank was constantly trying to rise, only to be dissipated in the bone-dry air. The construction itself was a broad wall, almost a circular city, a good fifteen miles in diameter. It was broken irregularly by towers and other structures, some of them looking remarkably like mosques. This shell glowed fiercely, like red-hot iron, and a spectrograph showed that this was exactly what it was.

Inside, the ground was terraced, like a lunar crater. At ground level was a flat plain, dotted with tiny rectangular markings in no discernible pattern; these, too, the spectrograph said, were red-hot iron. What seemed to be another moat, blood-red and as broad as a river, encircled the next terrace at the foot of the cliff where it began, and this, even more impossibly, was bordered by a dense circular forest. The forest was as broad as the river, but thinned eventually to a ring of what appeared to be the original sand, equally broad.

In a lunar crater, the foothills of the central peak would have begun about here, but in the pictures, instead, the terrain plunged into a colossal black pit. The river cut through the forest and the desert at one point and roared over the side in a vast waterwall, compounding the darkness with mist which the camera had been unable to penetrate.

'What was that you were saying about building a fortress overnight, Buelg?' the General said. '"No human agency could?"'

'No human agency was involved,' Šatvje said in a hoarse whisper. He turned to the aide who had brought the pictures, an absurdly young lieutenant colonel with a blond crew cut, white face and shaking hands. 'Are there any close-ups?'

'Yes, Doctor. There was an automatic camera under the plane that took a film of the approach run. Here is one of the best shots.'

The picture showed what appeared to be a towering gate in the best medieval style. Hundreds of shadowy figures crowded the barbican, of which three, just above the gateway itself, had been looking up at the plane and were shockingly clear. They looked like gigantic naked women, with ropy hair all awry, and the wide-staring eyes of insane rage.

'I thought so,' Šatvje said.

'You recognize them?' Buelg asked incredulously.

'No, but I know their names: Alecto, Megaera and Tisiphone,' Šatvje said. 'And it's a good thing that there's at least one person among us with a European education. I presume that our *distrait* friend the navigator is a Catholic, which does just as well in this context. In any event, he was quite right: this is Dis, the fortress surrounding Nether Hell. I think we must now assume that all the rest of the Earth is contiguous with Upper Hell, not only in metaphor but in fact.'

'It's a good thing,' Buelg said acidly, 'that there's at least one person among us with a good grip on his sanity. The last thing we need now is a relapse into superstition.'

'If you blow up that photograph, I think you'll find that the hair on those women actually consists of live snakes. Isn't that so, Colonel?'

'Well ... Doctor, it ... it certainly looks like it.'

'Of course. Those are the Furies who guard the gates of Dis. They are the keepers of the Gorgon Medusa, which, thank God, isn't in the picture. The moat is the River Styx; the first terrace inside contains the burning tombs of the Heresiarchs, and on the next you have the River Phlegethon, the Wood of the Suicides, and the Abominable Sand. A rain of fire is supposed to fall continually on the sand, but I suppose that's invisible in Death Valley sunlight or maybe even superfluous. We can't see what's down below, but presumably that too will be exactly as Dante described it. The crowd along the barbican is made up of demons – not so, Colonel?'

'Sir ... we can't tell what they are. We were wondering if they were, well, Martians or something. Every one is a different shape.'

Buelg felt his back hairs stirring. 'I refuse to believe this nonsense,' he said. 'Šatvje is interpreting it from his damned obsolete "education". Even Martians would make more sense.'

'What are the facts about this Dante?' McKnight said.

'An Italian poet, of about the thirteenth century—'

'Early fourteenth,' Šatvje said. 'And not just a poet. He had a vision of Hell and Heaven which became the greatest poem ever written – the *Divine Comedy*. What we see in those pictures exactly corresponds to the description in Cantos Eight through Eleven of it.'

'Buelg, see if you can locate a copy of the book and have it read to the computer. First we need to know if the correspondence is all that exact. If it is, we'll need an analysis of what it means.'

'The computer probably already has the book,' Buelg said. 'The whole

Library of Congress, plus all our recreational library, is on microfilm inside it, we didn't have room for books per se down here. All we need to do is tell Chief Hay to make it part of the problem. But I still think it's damn nonsense.'

'What we want,' McKnight said, 'is the computer's opinion. Yours has already been shown to be somewhat less reliable.'

'And while you're at it,' Šatvje said, perhaps a shade less smugly than Buelg might have expected, 'have Chief Hay make a part of the problem everything in the library on demonology. We're going to need it.'

Throwing up his hands, Buelg left the office. In the country of the mad ...

Nobody retains his sanity.

Only a few moments were needed for the computer to produce its report:

THE ANCIENT TEXTS AND FICTIONS NOW ADMITTED TO THE PROBLEM DISAGREE WITH EACH OTHER. HOWEVER, NEW FACTUAL DATA MAKE EXACT MATCHES WITH A NUMBER OF THEM, AND APPROXIMATE MATCHES WITH THE MAJORITY OF THEM. THE ASSUMPTION THAT THE CONSTRUCT IN DEATH VALLEY IS RUSSIAN, CHINESE OR OTHERWISE OF HUMAN ORIGIN IS OF THE LOWEST ORDER OF PROBABILITY AND MAY BE DISCOUNTED. THE INTERPLANETARY HYPOTHESIS IS OF SLIGHTLY HIGHER PROBABILITY, AN INVASION FROM VENUS BEING COMPATIBLE WITH A FEW OF THE FACTUAL DATA, SUCH AS THE IMMENSE HEAT AND ABERRANT LIFE FORMS OF THE DEATH VALLEY INSTALLATION, BUT IS INCOMPATIBLE WITH MOST ARCHITECTURAL AND OTHER HISTORICAL DETAILS IN THE DATA, AS WELL AS WITH THE LEVEL OF TECHNOLOGY INDICATED. THE PROBABILITY THAT THE DEATH VALLEY INSTALLATION IS THE CITY OF DIS AND THAT ITS INTERNAL AREA IS NETHER HELL IS 0.1 WITHIN A 5 PER CENT LEVEL OF CONFIDENCE, AND THEREFORE MUST BE ADMITTED. AS A FIRST DERIVATIVE, THE PROBABILITY THAT THE WAR JUST CONCLUDED WAS ARMAGEDDON IS 0.01 WITHIN THE SAME CONFIDENCE LEVEL. AS A SECOND DERIVATIVE, THE PROBABILITY THAT THE FORCES OF GOD HAVE LOST THE WAR AND THAT THE SURFACE OF THE EARTH IS NOW CONFLUENT WITH UPPER HELL IS 0.001 WITHIN THE SAME CONFIDENCE LEVEL.

'Well, that clarifies the situation considerably,' McKnight said. 'It's just as well we asked.'

'But – my God! – it simply can't be true,' Buelg said desperately. 'All right, maybe the computer is functioning properly, but it has no intelligence, and above all, no judgement. What it's putting out now is just a natural consequence of letting all that medieval superstition into the problem.'

McKnight turned his shrimp's eyes towards Buelg. 'You've seen the pictures,' he said. 'They didn't come out of the computer, did they? Nor out of the old books, either. I think we'd better stop kicking against the pricks and start figuring out what we're going to do. We've still got the United States to think of. Dr Šatvje, have you any suggestions?'

That was a bad sign. McKnight never used honorifics except to indicate, by inversion, which of the two of them had incurred his displeasure – not that Buelg had been in any doubt about that, already.

'I'm still in a good deal of doubt,' Šatvje said modestly. 'To begin with, if this has been Armageddon, we all ought to have been called to judgement by now; and there was certainly nothing in the prophecies that allowed for an encampment of victorious demons on the surface of the Earth. If the computer is completely right, then either God is dead as Nietzsche said, or, as the jokes go, He is alive but doesn't want to get involved. In either case, I think we would be well advised not to draw attention to ourselves. We can do nothing against supernatural powers: and if He *is* still alive; the battle may not be over. We are, I hope, safely hidden here, and we would be ill advised to be caught in the middle.'

'Now there you're dead wrong,' Buelg said with energy. 'Let's suppose for a minute that this fantasy represents the true state of affairs – in other words, that demons have turned out to be real, and are out there in Death Valley—'

'I'm none too sure what would be meant by "real" in this context,' Šatvje said. 'They are apparent, true enough; but they certainly don't belong to the same order of reality as—'

That's a question we can't afford to debate,' Buelg said. He knew very well that the issue Šatvje was raising was a valid one – he was himself a fairly thoroughgoing Logical Positivist. But it would only confuse McKnight and there were brownie points to be made in keeping things clear-cut, whether they *were* clear-cut or not. 'Look. If demons are real, then they occupy space/time in the real universe. That means that they exist inside some energy system in that universe and are maintained by it. All right, they can walk on red-hot iron and live comfortably in Death Valley; that's not inherently more supernatural than the existence of bacteria in the boiling waters of volcanic springs. It's an adaptation. Very well, then we can find out what that energy system is. We can analyse how it works. And once we know that, we can attack it.'

'Now that's more like it,' McKnight said.

'Pardon me, but I think we should proceed with the most extreme caution,' Šatvje said. 'Unless one has been raised in this tradition, one is not likely to think of all the implications. I myself am quite out of practice at it.'

'Damn your education,' Buelg said. But it was all coming back to him:

The boundaryless ghetto along Nostrand Avenue; the fur-hatted, fur-faced, maxi-skirted Hassidim walking in pairs under the scaling elm saplings of Grand Central Parkway; the terror of riding the subway among the juvenile gangs under the eternal skullcap; the endless hairsplitting over the Talmudic and Midrashic creation myths for hour upon stuffy hour in *Schule;* the women slaving over their duplicate sets of dishes, in the peculiar smell of a kosher household, so close to being a stench compared to all other American smells, supporting their drone scholars; his mother's pride that Hansli too was plainly destined by God's will to become a holy man; and when he had discovered instead the glories and rigours of the physical universe, that light and airy escape from fur hats and the smell of gefuelte fish and the loving worn women, the terror of the wrath of the jealous God. But all that was many years ago; it could not come back. He would not have it back.

'What are you talking about?' McKnight said. 'Are we going to do something, and if so, what? Get to the point.'

'My point,' Šatvje said, 'is that if all this – demonology – is well, valid, or I suppose one should say true, then the whole Christian mythos is true, though it is not coming out in precisely the way it was prophesied. That being the case then there are such things as immortal souls, or perhaps I should say, we may well have immortal souls, and we ought to take them into consideration before we do anything rash.'

Buelg saw the light, and with a great sense of relief; the Christian mythos had nothing to do with him, not personally that is. He had no objection to it as an exercise in theory, a form of non-zero-sum game.

'If that's the case, I don't think there's any question of our being caught in the middle,' he said. 'We're required by the rules to come down on one side or the other.'

'That's true, by God,' McKnight said. 'And after all, we're on the right side. We didn't start this war – the Chinks did.'

'Right, right,' Buelg said. 'We're entitled to self-defence. And for my part, no matter what happens in the next world – about which we have no data – as long as I'm still in this one, I'm not prepared to regard *anything* as final. This may be a metaphysical war after all, but we still seem to live in some sort of secular universe. The universe of discourse has been enlarged, but it hasn't been cancelled. I say, let's find out more about it.'

'Yes,' McKnight said, 'but how? That's what I keep asking, and I don't get anything back from either of you but philosophical discussion. What do you propose that we *do*?'

'Have we got any missiles left?'

'We've still got maybe a dozen five- to ten-megatonners left – and, of course, Old Mombi.'

'Buelg, you madman, are you proposing for one instant—'

'Shut up for a minute and let me think.' Old Mombi was Denver's dooms-day machine, a complex carrier containing five one-hundred-megaton war-heads, one of which was aimed to make even the Moon uninhabitable; it was a postspasm weapon that the present situation certainly did not call for – best to hold it in reserve. 'I think what we ought to do is to lob one of the small jobs on to the Death Valley encampment. I don't really think it'll do much harm, maybe not any, but it might produce some information. We can fly a drone plane through the cloud as it goes up, and take off radiological, chemical, any other kinds of readings that the computer can come up with. These demons have obtruded themselves into the real world, and the very fact that we can see them and photograph them shows that they share some of its characteristics now. Let's see how they behave under something a good deal hotter than red-hot iron. Suppose they do nothing more than sweat a little? We can analyse even that!'

'And suppose they trace the missile back to here?' Šatvje said, but by his expression, Buelg knew that Šatvje knew that it was a last-ditch argument.

'Then we're sunk, I suppose. But look at the architecture of that en-campment; does that suggest to you that they've been in contact with real warfare since back in the fourteenth century? No doubt they have all kinds of supernatural powers, but they've got a lot to learn about the natural ones! Maybe a decent adversary is what they've been lacking all along – and if Armageddon has ended in a standoff, a little action on the side of our Maker wouldn't be amiss. If He's still with us, and actively interested, any inaction on our parts would probably be viewed very gravely indeed if He wins after all. And if He's not with us any longer, then we'll have to help ourselves, as the proverb says.'

'That's the stuff to give the troops,' McKnight said. 'It is so ordered.'

Buelg nodded and left the office to search out Chief Hay. On the whole, he felt he had made a nice recovery.

4

Positano had been washed away, but the remains of Ware's palazzo still stood above the scoured cliffside, like some post-Roman ruin. The ceiling had fallen in, the fluted pink tiles smashing Ware's glassware and burying the dim chalk diagrams of last night's conjuration on the refectory floor in a litter of straw and potsherds, mounds of which collapsed now and then to send streamers of choking dust up to meet the gently radioactive April rain.

Ware sat on the heaped remains of his altar within the tumbled walls, under the uncertain sky. His feelings were so complex that he could not have begun to explain them, even to himself; after many years' schooling in the rigorous non-emotions of Ceremonial magic, it was a novelty to him to have any feelings at all but those of thirst for knowledge; now he would have to relearn those sensations, for his lovely book of acquisitions, upon which he had spent his soul and so much else, was buried under tons of tsunamic mud.

In a way, he thought tentatively, he felt free. After the shock of the sea-quake had passed, and all but an occasional tile had stopped falling, he had struggled out of the rubble to the door, and thence to the head of the stairway which led down to his bedroom, only to see nothing but mud three stone steps down, mud wrinkling and settling as the sea water gradually seeped out from under it. Somewhere down under there, his book of new knowledge was beginning the aeon-long route to becoming an unreadable fossil. Well then; so much for his life. Almost it seemed to him then that he might begin again, that he was nameless, a *tabula rasa,* all false starts wiped out, all dead knowledge ready to be rejected or revivified. It was given to few men to live through something so cleansing as a total disaster.

But then he realized that this, too, was only an illusion. His past was there, ineluctably, in his commitments. He was still waiting for the return of the Sabbath Goat. He closed the door to the stairwell and the fossilized ripples of the mud, and blowing reflectively into his white moustache, went back into the refectory.

Father Domenico had earlier tired – it could not exactly be said that he had lost patience – of both the waiting and the fruitless debates over when or whether they would be come for, and had decided to attempt travelling south to see what and who remained of Monte Albano, the college of white magicians which had been his home grounds. Baines was still there, trying to raise some news on the little transistor radio to which only yesterday he had listened so gluttonously to the accounts of the Black Easter which Ware had raised up at his commission, and whose consequences now eddied away from them around the whole tortured globe. Now, however, it was producing nothing but bands of static, and an occasional very distant voice in an unknown tongue.

With him now was Jack Ginsberg, dressed to the nines as usual, and in consequence looking by far the most bedraggled of the three. At Ware's entrance, Baines tossed the radio to his secretary and crossed towards the magician, slipping and cursing the rubble.

'Find out anything?'

'Nothing at all. As you can see for yourself, the sea is subsiding. It is obvious that Positano has been spared any further destruction – for the moment. As for why, we know no more than we did before,'

'You can still work magic, can't you?'

'I don't appear to have been deprived of my memory,' Ware said. 'I've no doubt I can still *do* magic, if I can get at my equipment under this mess, but whether I can work it is another matter. The conditions of reference have changed drastically, and I have no idea how far or in what areas.'

'Well, you could at least call up a demon and see if he could give us any information. There doesn't appear to be anyone else to ask.'

'I see that I'll have to put the matter more bluntly. I am totally opposed to performing any more magic at this time, Dr Baines. I see that you have again failed to think the situation through. The terms under which I was able to call upon demons no longer apply – I am no longer able to do anything for them, they must now own a substantial part of the world. If I were to call at this juncture, probably no one would answer, and it might be better if nobody did, since I would have no way of controlling him. They are composed almost entirely of hatred for every unFallen creature, and every creature with the potentiality to be redeemed, but there is no one they hate more than a useless tool.'

'Well, it seems to me that we may neither of us be totally useless even now,' Baines declared. 'You say the demons now own a substantial part of the world, but it's also perfectly evident that they don't own it all yet. Otherwise the Goat would have come back when he said he would. And we'd be in Hell.'

'Hell has a great many circles. We may well be on the margins of the first right now – in the Vestible of the Futile.'

'We'd be in a good deal deeper if the demons were in total control, or if judgement had already been passed on us,' Baines said.

'You are entirely right about that, to be sure,' Ware said, somewhat surprised. 'But after all, from their point of view there is no hurry. In the past, we might have saved ourselves by a last-minute act of contrition. Now, however, there is no longer any God to appeal to. They can wait and take us at their leisure.'

'There I'm inclined to agree with Father Domenico. We don't know that for sure; we were told so only by the Goat. I admit that the other evidence all points in the same direction, but all the same, he could have been lying.'

Ware thought about it. The argument from circumstances did not of course impress him; no doubt the circumstances were horrible beyond the capacity of any human soul to react to them, but they were certainly not beyond the range of human imagination; they were more or less the standard consequences of World War III, a war which Baines himself had been actively engaged in engineering some time before he had discovered his interest in black magic. Theologically they were also standard: a new but essentially unchanged version of the Problem of Evil, the centuries-old question of why a good and merciful God should allow so much pain and terror to be inflicted upon the innocent. The parameters had been filled in a somewhat different way, but the fundamental equation was the same as it had always been.

Nevertheless, the munitions maker was quite right – as Father Domenico had been earlier – to insist that they had no reliable information upon the most fundamental question of all. Ware said slowly:

'I'm reluctant to admit any hope at all at this juncture. On the other hand, it has been said that to despair of God is the ultimate sin. What precisely do you have in mind?'

'Nothing specific yet. But suppose for the sake of argument that the demons are still under some sort of restrictions – I don't see any point in trying to imagine what they might be – and that the battle consequently isn't really over yet. If that's the case, it's quite possible that they could still use some help. Considering how far they've managed to get already, there doesn't seem to be much doubt about their winning in the end – and it's been my observation that it's generally a good idea to be on the winning side.'

'It is folly to think that the triumph of evil could ever be a winning side, in the sense of anyone's gaining anything by it. Without good to oppose it, evil is simply meaningless. That isn't all what I thought you had in mind. It is, instead, the last step in despairing of God – it's worse than Manicheanism, it is Satanism pure and simple. I once controlled devils, but I never worshipped them, and I don't plan to begin now. Besides—'

Abruptly, the radio produced a tearing squeal and then began to mutter urgently in German. Ware could hear the voice well enough to register that the speaker had a heavy Swiss accent, but not well enough to make out the sense. He and Baines took a crunching step towards Ginsberg, who, listening intently, held up one hand towards them.

The speech was interrupted by another squeal, and then the radio resumed emitting nothing more than snaps, crackles, pops and waterfalls. Ginsberg said:

'That was Radio Zurich. There's been an H-bomb explosion in the States, in Death Valley. Either the war's started again, or some dud's gone off belatedly.'

'Hmm,' Baines said. 'Well, better there than here ... although, now that I come to think of it, it isn't entirely unpromising. But Dr Ware, I think you hadn't quite finished?'

'I was only going to add that "being of some help" to demons in this context makes no practical sense, either. Their hand is turned against everyone on Earth, and there is certainly no way that we could help them to carry their war to Heaven, even presuming that any of Heaven still stands. Someone of Father Domenico's school might just possibly manage to enter the Aristotelian spheres – though I doubt it – but I certainly couldn't.'

'That bomb explosion seems to show that *somebody* is still fighting back,' Baines said. 'Providing that Jack isn't right about its being a dud or a stray. My guess is that it's the Strategic Air Command, and that they've just found out who the real enemy is. They had the world's finest data processing centre there under Denver, and in addition, McKnight had first-class civilian help, including Džejms Šatvje himself and a RAND man that I tried to get the Mamaroneck Research Institute to outbid the government for.'

'I still don't quite see where that leaves us.'

'I know McKnight very well; he's steered a lot of Defense Department orders my way, and I was going to have LeFebre make him president of Consolidated Warfare Service when he retired – as he was quite well aware. He's good in his field, which is reconnaissance, but he also has something of a one-track mind. If he's bombing demons, it might be a very good idea for me to suggest to him that he stop it – and why.'

'It might at that,' Ware said reflectively. 'How will you get there?'

'A technicality. Radio Zurich is still operating, which almost surely means that their airfield is operating too. Jack can fly a plane if necessary, but it probably won't be necessary; we had a very well-staffed office in Zurich, in fact it was officially our central headquarters, and I've got access to two Swiss bank accounts, the company's and my own. I'd damn well better put the money to some use before somebody with a little imagination realizes that the vaults might much better be occupied by himself, his family and twenty thousand cases of canned beans.'

The project, Ware decided, had its merits. At least it would rid him, however temporarily, of Baines, whose society he was beginning to find a little tiresome, and of Jack Ginsberg, whom he distantly but positively loathed. It would of course also mean that he would be deprived of all human company if the Goat should after all come for him, but this did not bother him in the least; he had known for years that in that last confrontation, every man is always alone, and most especially, every magician.

Perhaps he had also always known, somewhere in the deepest recesses of his mind, that he would indeed eventually take that last step into Satanism, but if so, he had very successfully suppressed it. And he had not quite taken it yet; he had committed himself to nothing, he had only agreed that Baines should go away, and Ginsberg too, to counsel someone he did not know to an inaction which might be quite without significance …

And while they were gone, perhaps he would be able to think of something better. It was the tiniest of small hopes, and doubtless vain; but now he was beginning to be prepared to feed it. If he played his cards right, he might yet mingle with the regiment of angels who rebelled not, yet avowed to God no loyalty, of whom it is said that deep Hell refuses them, for, beside such, the sinner would be proud.

5

Monte Albano, Father Domenico found with astonishment and a further rekindling of his hope, had been spared completely. It reared its eleventh-century walls, rebuilt after the earthquake then by the abbot Giorgio who later became Pope John the Twentieth, as high above the valley as it always had, and as always, too, accessible only by muleback, and Father Domenico lost more time in locating a mule with an owner to take him up there than the whole trip from Positano had cost him. Eventually, however, the thing was done, and he was within the cool walls of the library with the white monks, his colleagues under the hot Frosinian sky.

Those assembled made up nearly the same company that had met during the winter to consider, fruitlessly, how Theron Ware and his lay client might be forestalled: Father Amparo, Father Umberto (the Director), and the remaining brothers of the order, plus Father Uccello, Father Boucher, Father Vance, Father Anson, Father Selahny and Father Atheling. The visitors had apparently continued to stay in the monastery, if not in session, after the winter meeting, although in the interim Father Rosenblum had died; his place had been taken though hardly filled, by Father Domenico's former apprentice, Joannes, who though hardly seventeen looked now as though he had grown up very suddenly. Well, that was all right; they surely needed all the help that they would get, and Father Domenico knew without false modesty that Joannes had been well trained.

After Father Domenico had been admitted, announced and conducted through the solemn and blessed joys of greeting and welcome, it became apparent that the discussion – as was only to have been expected – had already been going on for many hours. Nor was he much surprised to find that it was simply another version of the discussion that had been going on in Positano: namely, how had Monte Albano been spared in the world-wide catastrophe, and what did it mean? But in this version of the discussion, Father Domenico could join with a much better heart.

And in fact he was also able to give it what amounted to an entirely new turn; for their Sensitive, the hermit-Father Uccello, had inevitably found his talents much coarsened and blunted by the proximity of so many other minds, and in consequence the white monks had only a general idea of what had gone on in Ware's palazzo since the last convocation – an impression supplemented by the world news, what of it there was, and by deduction, some of which was in fact wrong. Father Domenico recapitulated the story of the last conjuration briefly; but his fellows' appreciation of the gravity of the situation was already such that the recitation was accompanied by no more than the expectable number of horrified murmurs.

'All in all,' he concluded, 'forty-eight demons were let out of the Pit as a result of this ceremony and commanded to return at dawn. When it became apparent that the operation was completely out of hand, I invoked the Covenant and insisted that Ware recall them ahead of time, to which he agreed; but when he attempted to summon up LUCIFUGE ROFOCALE to direct this abrogation, PUT SATANACHIA himself answered instead. When I attempted to exorcise this abominable creature, my crucifix burst in my hands, and it was after that that the monster told us that God was already dead and that the ultimate victory had instead gone to the forces of Hell. The Goat promised to return for us all – all, that is, except Baines's other assistant, Dr Hess, whom Baphomet had already swallowed when Hess panicked and stepped out of his circle – at dawn, but he failed to do so, and I subsequently left and came to Monte Albano as soon as it was physically possible for me to do so.'

'Do you recall the names and offices of all forty-eight?' said Father Atheling, his tenor voice more sinusy than ever with apprehension.

'I think I do – that is, I think I could; after all, I saw them all, and that's an experience which does not pass lightly from the memory. In any event, if I've blanked out on a few – which isn't unlikely either – they can doubtless be recovered under hypnosis. Why does that matter, may I ask, Father Atheling?'

'Simply because it is always useful to know the natures as well as the numbers, of the forces arrayed against one.'

'Not after the countryside is already overrun.' said Father Anson. 'If the battle and the war have been already lost, we must have the whole crew to contend with now – not just all seventy-two princes, but every single one of the fallen angels. The number is closer to seven and a half million than it is to forty-eight.'

'Seven million, four hundred and fifty thousand, nine hundred and twenty-six,' Father Atheling said, 'to be exact.'

'Though the wicked may hide, the claws of crabs are dangerous people in bridges,' Father Selahny intoned abruptly. As was the case with all his utterances, the group would doubtless find out what this one meant only after sorting out its mixed mythologies and folklores, and long after it was too late to do anything about it. Nor did it do any good to ask him to explain; these things simply came to him, and he no more understood them than did his hearers. If God was indeed dead, Father Domenico wondered suddenly: Who could be dictating them now? But he put the thought aside as non-contributory.

'There is a vast concentration of new evil on the other side of the world,' Father Uccello said in his courtly, hesitant old man's voice. 'The feeling is one of intense oppression, quite different from that which was common in New York, or Moscow, but one such as I would expect of a massing of demons upon a huge scale. Forgive me, brothers, but I can be no more specific.'

'We know you are doing the best you can,' said the Director soothingly.

'I can feel it myself,' said Father Monteith, who although not a Sensitive had had some experience with the herding of rebellious spirits. 'But even supposing that we do not have to cope with so large an advance, as I certainly hope we do not, it seems to me that forty-eight is too large a sum for us if the Covenant has been voided. It leaves us without even an option.'

Father Domenico saw that Joannes was trying to attract the Director's attention, although too hesitantly to make any impression. Father Umberto was not yet used to thinking of Joannes as a person at all. Capturing the boy's eyes. Father Domenico nodded.

'I never did understand the Covenant,' the ex-apprentice said, thus encouraged. 'That is. I didn't understand why God would compromise Himself in such a manner. Even with Job. He didn't make a deal with Satan, but only allowed him to act unchecked for a certain period of time. And I've never found any mention of the Covenant in the grimoires. What are its terms, anyhow?'

Father Domenico thought the question well asked, if a trifle irrelevant, but an embarrassed and slightly pitying silence showed that his opinion was not shared. In the end it was broken by Father Monteith, whose monumental patience was a byword in the chapter.

'I'm certainly not well versed in canon law, let alone in spiritual compacts,' he said, with more modesty than exactness. 'But, in principle, the Covenant is no more than a special case of the option of free will. The assumption appears to be that even in dealing with devilry, on the one hand, no man shall be subjected to a temptation beyond his ability to resist, and on the other, no man shall slide into Heaven without having been tempted up to that point. In situations involving Transcendental or Ceremonial magic, the Covenant is the line drawn in between. Where you would find its exact terms, I'm sure I don't know; I doubt that they have ever been written down. One thinks of the long struggle to understand the rainbow, the other Covenant; once the explanation was in, it did not explain, except to show that every man sees his own rainbow, and what seems to stand in the sky is an optical illusion, not a theomorphism. It is in the nature of the arrangement that the terms would vary in each individual case, and that if you are incapable of determining where it is drawn for you – the line of demarcation – then, woe betide you, and that is that.'

Dear God, Father Domenico thought, all my life I have been an amateur of Roger Bacon and I never once saw that that was what he meant to show by focusing his *Perspectiva* on the rainbow. Shall I have any more time to learn?

I hope we are never tempted to make Monteith the Director, or we shall lose him to taking things out of the In box and putting them into the Out box, as we did Father Umberto—

'Furthermore, it may well be still in existence,' said Father Boucher. 'As Father Domenico has already pointed out to Theron Ware himself, we have heard of the alleged death of God only through the testimony of the most unreliable witness imaginable. And it leaves many inconsistencies to be explained. *When* exactly is God supposed to have died? If it was as long ago as in Nietzsche's time, why had His angels and ministers of light seemed to know nothing of it in the interim? It's unreasonable to suppose that they were simply keeping up a good front until the battle actually broke out; Heaven simply isn't that kind of an organisation. One would expect an absolute and perpetual monarchy to break down upon the death of the monarch quite promptly, yet in point of fact we saw no signs of any such thing until shortly after Christmas of this year.'

'But we did see such signs at that time,' Father Vance said.

'True, but this only poses another logical dilemma: What happened to the Antichrist? Baphomet's explanation that he had been dispensed with as unnecessary to the victors, whose creature he would have been, doesn't hold water. The Antichrist was to have appeared *before* the battle, and if the defeat of God is all that recent, the prophecy should have been fulfilled; God still existed to compel it.'

'Matthew 11:14,' Father Selahny said, in an unprecedented burst of intelligibility. The verse of which he was reminding them referred to John the Baptist, and it said: *And if ye will receive it, this is Elias, which was for to come.*

'Yes,' Father Domenico said, 'I suppose it's possible that the Antichrist might have come unrecognised. One always envisioned people flocking to his banner openly, but the temptation would have been more subtle and perhaps more dangerous had he crept past us, say in the guise of some popular philosopher, like that positive-thinking man in the States. Yet the proposal seems to allow even less room than did the Covenant for the exercise of free will.'

There was a silence. At last, the Director said: 'The Essenes argued that one must think and experience all evil before one can hope to perceive good.'

'If this be true doctrine,' Father Domenico said, 'then it follows that God is indeed still alive, and that Theron Ware's experiment, and World War III, did not constitute Armageddon after all. What we may be confronted with instead is an earthly Purgatory, from which Grace, and perhaps even the earthly Paradise, might be won. Dare we think so?'

'We dare not think otherwise,' said Father Vance. 'The question is, how? Little that is in the New Testament, the teachings of the Church or the

Arcana seem very relevant to the present situation.'

'No more is our traditional isolation,' said Father Domenico. 'Our only recourse now is to abandon it; to abandon our monastery and our mountain, and go down into the world that we renounced when Charlemagne was but a princeling, to try to win it back by works and witnessing. And if we may not do this with the sweet aid of Christ, then we must nevertheless do it in His name. Hope now is all we have.'

'In sober truth,' Father Boucher said quietly, 'that is not so great a change. I think it is all we ever had.'

COME TO MIDDLE HELL

Though thy beginning was small, yet thy latter end should greatly increase ... Prepare thyself to the search.

—*Job 8:7, 8*

6

Left to his own devices and hence, at last, unobserved, Theron Ware thought that it might be well, after all, if he did essay a small magic. The possible difficulty lay in that all magic without exception depended upon the control of demons, as he had explained to Baines on his very first visit. But therein lay the attractiveness of the experiment, too, for what he wanted was information, and a part of that information was whether he still had any such control.

And it would also be interesting, and possible to find out at the same time, to know whether or not there were any demons left in Hell. If there were it would imply, though it would not guarantee, that only the forty-eight that he had set loose were now terrorizing the world. This ruled out using the Mirror of Solomon, for the spirit of that mirror was the angel Anael. Probably he would not answer anyhow, for Ware was not a white magician, and had carefully refrained from calling upon any angel ever since he had turned to the practice of the black Art; and besides, it would be a considerable nuisance locating three white pigeons amidst all this devastation.

Who, then? Among the demon princes he had decided not to call up for Baines's commission were several that he had ruled out because of their lesser potentialities for destruction, which would stand him in good stead were it to turn out that he had lost control; even in Hell there were degrees of malevolence, as of punishment. One of these was PHOENIX, a poet and teacher with whom Ware had had many dealings in the past, but he probably would not do now; he posed another wildlife problem – Ware's familiar Ahktoi had been the demon's creature, and the cat had of course vanished when the noise had begun, a disappearance that PHOENIX would take none the less ill for its having been 100 per cent expectable. Though the grimoires occasionally characterize one or another demon as 'mild' or 'good by nature', these terms are strictly relative and have no human meaning; all demons are permanently enraged by the greatest Matter of all, and it does not pay to annoy them even slightly in small matters.

Also, Ware realized, it would have to be a small magic indeed, for most of his instruments were now buried, and those that were accessible were all contaminated beyond his power to purify them in any useful period of time. Clearly it was time to consult the book. He crossed to the lectern upon which it rested, pushed dust and potsherds off it with his sleeve, unlocked the clasp and began to turn the great stiff pages, not without a qualm. Here, signed with his own blood, was half his life; the other half was down below, in the mud.

He found the name he needed almost at once: VASSAGO, a mighty prince, who in his first estate before the rebellion had belonged to the choir of the Virtues. The *Lemegeton* of the Rabbi Solomon said of him, Ware recalled, that he 'declares things past, present and future, and discovers what has been lost or hidden'. Precisely to the purpose. Ware remembered too that his was the name most commonly invoked in ceremonial crystallomancy, which would be perfect in both scope and limitations for what Ware had in mind, involving no lengthy preparations of the operator, or even any precautionary diagrams, nor any apparatus except a crystal ball; and even for that he might substitute a pool of exorcised water, fifty litres of which still reposed in a happily unruptured stainless steel tank embedded in the wall behind Ware's workbench.

Furthermore, he was the only demon in Ware's entire book of pacts who was represented therein by two seals or characters, so markedly different that without seeing them side by side, one might never suspect that they belonged to the same entity. Topologically they were closely related, however, and Ware studied these relationships long and hard, knowing that he had once known what they meant but unable to recall it. These were the figures:

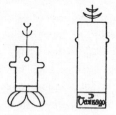

Ah, now he had it. The left-hand figure was VASSAGO's ordinary infernal sign, but the second was the seal under which, it was said, he could be called by white magicians. Ware had never used it, nor had needed to – the infernal seal had worked very well – and he had always doubted its efficacy, for by definition no commerce with a demon is white magic; however, it would be well to try it now. It might prove an additional factor of safety, if it worked at all.

Into what should he draw the water? Everything was filthy. Eventually he decided simply to make a puddle on the workbench; it had been decades since he had studied oneirology, which he had scorned as a recourse for mere hedge wizards, but to the best of his recollection it called for nothing more extraordinary than an earthenware vessel, and could even be practised successfully in an ordinary, natural forest pool, providing that there was sufficient shade.

Well, then, to work.

Standing insecurely before the workbench, the little weight of his spare upper body resting upon his elbows and his hands beside his ears, Theron Ware stared steadfastly down into the little puddle of mud, his own bushy head – he had neglected his tonsure since the disaster – shading it from the even light of the overcast sky. He had already stared so long since the first invocation that he felt himself on the verge of self-hypnosis, but now, he thought, there was a faint stirring down there in those miniature carboniferous depths, like a bubble or a highlight created by some non-existent sun. Yes, a faint spark was there, and it was growing.

'Eka dva, tri, chatur pancha, shas, sapta, ashta, nava, dasha, ekadasha,' Ware counted. 'Per vota nostra ipse nunc surtat nobis dicatus VASSAGO!'

The spark continued to grow until it was nearly the size of a ten-lire piece, stabilized and gradually began to develop features. Despite its apparent diameter, the thing did not look small; the effect rather was one of great distance, as though Ware were seeing a reflection of the Moon.

The features were quite beautiful and wholly horrible. Superficially the shining face resembled a human skull, but it was longer, thinner, more triangular, and it had no cheekbones. The eyes were huge, and slanted almost all the way up to where a human hairline would have been; the nose extremely long in the bridge; the mouth as pink and tiny as that of an infant. The colour and texture of the face were old ivory, like netsuke. No body was visible, but Ware had not expected one; this was not, after all, a full manifestation, but only an apparition.

The rosebud mouth moved damply, and a pure soprano voice like that of a choirboy, murmured gently and soundlessly deep in Ware's mind.

WHO IS IT CALLS VASSAGO FROM STUDYING OF THE DAMNED? BEWARE!

'Thou knowest me, demon of the Pit,' Ware thought, 'for to a pact hast thou subscribed with me, and written into my book thine Infernal name. Thereby, and by thy seal which I do here exhibit, do I compel thee. My questions shalt thou answer, and give true knowledge.'

SPEAK AND BE DONE.

'Art still in Hell with thy brothers, or are all abroad about the Earth?'

SOME DO GO TO AND FRO. BUT WE ABIDE HERE.

NEVERTHELESS, WE BE ON EARTH, ALBEIT NOT ABROAD.

'In what wise?'

THOUGH WE MAY NOT YET LEAVE NETHER HELL, WE BE AMONG YE: FOR THE PIT HATH BEEN RAISED UP. AND THE CITY OF DIS NOW STANDING UPON THE EARTH.

Ware made no attempt to disguise his shock; after all, the creature could see into his mind. 'How situate?' he demanded.

WHERE SHE STOOD FROM ETERNITY; IN THE VALLEY OF DEATH.

Ware suspected at once that the apparently allegorical form of his utterance concealed a literal meaning, but it would do no good to ask for exact topographical particulars; demons paid little attention to earthly political geography unless they were fomenting strife about boundaries or enclaves, which was not one of VASSAGO's roles. Could the reference be literary? That would be in accordance with the demon's nature. Nothing prevents devils from quoting scripture to their own advantage? so why not Tennyson?

'Be this valley under the ambassadorship of RIMMON?'

NAY.

'Then what officers inhabit the region wherein it lies? Divulge their names, great prince, to my express command!'

THEY ARE THE INFERIORS OF ASTAROTH WHO ARE CALLED SARGATANAS AND NEBIROS.

'But which hath his asylum where Dis now stands?'

THERE RULETH NEBIROS.

These were the demons of post-Columbian magic; they announced forth to the subjects all things which their lord hath commanded, according to the *Grimorium Verum,* in America, and the asylum of NEBIROS was further specified to be in the West. Of course: Death Valley. And NEBIROS, as it was said in the *Grand Grimoire*, was the field marshal of Infernus, and a great necromancer, 'who goeth to and fro everywhere and inspects the hordes of perdition'. The raising of the fortress of Dis in the domain of this great general most strongly suggested that the war was not over yet. Ware knew better, however, than to ask the demon whether God was in fact dead; for were He not, the mere sounding of the Holy Name would so offend this minor prince as to terminate the apparition at once, if not render further ones impossible. Well, the question was probably unnecessary anyhow; he already had most of the information that he needed.

'Thou art discharged.'

The shining face vanished with a flash of opalescence, exactly as though a soap bubble had broken, leaving Ware staring down at nothing but a puddle of mud, now already filming and cracking – except in the centre where the face had been; that had evaporated completely. Straightening his aching

JAMES BLISH

back, he considered carefully the implications of what he had learned.

The military organization of the Descending Hierachy was peculiar, and as usual the authorities differed somewhat on its details. This was hardly surprising, for any attempt to relate the offices of the evil spirits to earthly analogues was bound to be only an approximation, if not sometimes actively misleading. Ware was presently in the domain of HUTGIN, ambassador in Italy, and had never before Black Easter had any need to invoke AS-TAROTH or any of his inferior Intelligences. He was characterized by the *Grimorium Verum* as the Grand Duke of Hell, whereas Weirus referred to him as Grand Treasurer; while the *Grand Grimoire* did not mention him at all, assigning NEBIROS instead to an almost equivalent place. Nevertheless it seemed clear enough in general that while the domain of ASTAROTH might technically be in America, his principality was not confined thereto, but might make itself known anywhere in the world. HUTGIN in comparison was a considerably lesser figure.

And the war was not yet over, and Ware might indeed find some way to make himself useful; Baines had been right about that, too. But in what way remained unclear.

Very probably, he would have to go to Dis to find out. It was a terrifying thought, but Ware could see no way around it. That was where the centre of power was now, where the war would henceforth be directed; and there, if Baines actually succeeded in reaching the SAC in Denver, Ware conceivably might succeed in arranging some sort of a *détente*. Certainly he would be of no use squatting here in ruined Italy, with all the superior spirits half a world away.

But how to get there? He did not have Baines's power to commandeer an aircraft, and though he was fully as wealthy as the industrialist – in fact most of the money had once been Baines's – it seemed wholly unlikely that any airline was selling tickets these days. A sea and overland journey would be too slow.

Would it be possible to compel ASTAROTH to provide him with some kind of an apport? This too was a terrifying thought. To the best of Ware's knowledge, the last magician to have ridden astride a devil had been Gerbert, back in the tenth century. He had resorted to it only to save his life from a predecessor of the Inquisition, whose attention he had amply earned; and, moreover, had lived through the ordeal to become Pope Sylvester II.

Gerbert had been a great man, and though Ware rather doubted that he had been any better a magician than Ware was, he did not feel prepared to try that conclusion just now. In any event, the process was probably unnecessarily drastic; transvection might serve the purpose just as well, or better. Though he had never been to a sabbat, he knew the theory and the particulars well enough. Included in the steel cabinets which held his magical pharmacopoeia were all the ingredients necessary for the flying ointment, and the compounding of it required no special time or ritual. As for piloting and navigation, that was to be sure a little alarming to anticipate, but if thousands upon thousands of ignorant old women had been able to fly a cleft stick, a distaff, a besom or even a shovel upon the first try, then so could Theron Ware.

First, however, he drew from the cabinet a flat slab of synthetic ruby, about the size and shape of an opened match folder; and from his cabinet of instruments, a burin. Upon the ruby, on the day of Mars, which is Tuesday, and in the hour of Mars, which is 0600, 1300, 2000 or 0300 on that day, he would engrave the following seal and characters:

This he would henceforth carry in his right shirt pocket, like a reliquary. Though he would accept no help from ASTAROTH if he could possibly avoid it, it would be well since he was going to be travelling in that fiend's domains, to be wearing his colours. As a purist, it bothered him a little that the ruby was synthetic, but his disturbance, he knew, was only an aesthetic one. ASTAROTH was a solar spirit, and the ancients, all the way through Albertus Magnus, had believed that rubies were engendered in the Earth by the influence of the Sun – but since they were not in fact formed that way, the persistence of the ruby in the ritual was only another example of one of the primary processes of magic, *superstition,* the gradual supremacy of the sign over the thing, so that so far as efficacy was concerned it did not matter a bit whether the ruby was synthetic or natural. Nature, too, obstinately refused to form rubies the size and shape of opened match folders.

For a magician, Ware reflected, there were indeed distinct advantages in being able to practise ten centuries after Gerbert had ridden upon his demon eagle.

7

Transvection, too, has its hazards, Ware discovered. He crossed the Atlantic without incident in well under three hours – indeed, he suspected that in some aspect beyond the reach of his senses, the flight was taking place only partially in real time – and it began to look as though he would easily reach his goal before dawn. The candle affixed by its own tallow to the bundle of twigs and rushes before him (for only the foolhardy fly a broomstick with the brush trailing, no matter what is shown to the contrary in conventional Halloween cartoons) burned as steadily as though he were not in motion at all, casting a brilliant light ahead along his path; any ships at sea that might have seen him might have taken him to be an unusually brilliant meteor. As he approached the eastern United States, he wondered how he would show up on radar; the dropping of the bomb two days ago suggested that there might still be a number of functioning radomes there. In quieter times, he thought, he might perhaps have touched off another flying saucer scare. Or was he visible at all? He discovered that he did not know, but he began to doubt it; the seaboard was hidden in an immense pall of smoke.

But once over land, he slowed himself down and lost altitude in order to get his bearings, and within what seemed to him to be only a very few minutes, he was grounded head over heels by the sound of a church bell forlornly calling what faithful might remain to midnight Mass. He remembered belatedly, when he got his wind back, that in some parts of Germany during the seventeenth-century flowering of the popular Goetic cults, it had been the custom to toll church bells all night long as a protection against witches who might be passing overhead on the way to the Brocken; but the memory did him no good now – the besom had gone lifeless.

He had fallen in a rather mountainous, heavily timbered area, quite like the Harz Mountain section of Germany, but which he guessed to be somewhere in western Pennsylvania. Though it was now late April, which was doubtless warm in Positano, the night here was decidedly cold, especially for a thin man clad in nothing more than a light smear of unguent. He was instantly and violently all ashiver, for the sound of the bell had destroyed the protective as well as the transvective power of the flying ointment. He hastily undid the bundle of clothes, which was tied to the broomstick, but there were not going to be enough of them; after all, he had assembled them with Death Valley in mind. Also, he was beginning to feel drowzy and dizzy, and his pulse was blurred and banging with tachycardia. Among other things, the flying ointment contained both mandragora and belladonna, and now that the magic was gone out of it, these were exerting their inevitable side effects. He would have to wash the stuff off the minute he could find a stream, cold or no cold.

And not only because it was drugging him. Still other ingredients of the ointment were rather specifically organic in nature, and these gave it a characteristic smell which the heat of his body would gradually ripen. The chances were all too good that there would be some people in this country of the Amish – and not all of them old ones – who would know what that odour meant. Until he had had some kind of a bath, it would be dangerous even to ask for help.

Before dressing, he wiped off as much of it as he could with the towel in which the clothing had been tied. This he buried, together with the taper and the brush from the besom; and after making sure that the ruby talisman was still safely in his pocket, he set out, using the denuded broomstick as a staff.

The night-black, hilly, forested countryside would have made difficult going even for an experienced walker. Ware's life, on the other hand, had been nearly inactive except intellectually, and he was on the very near side of his fiftieth birthday. To his advantage, on the other hand, stood the fact that he had always been small and wiry, and the combination of a slightly hyperthyroid metabolism and an ascetic calling – he did not even smoke – had kept him that way, so that he made fair progress; and an equally life-long love of descriptive astronomy, plus the necessity of astrology to his art, helped to keep him going in the right direction, whenever he could see a few stars through the smoke.

Just before dawn, he stumbled upon a small, rocky-bedded stream, and through the gloom heard the sound of a nearby waterfall. He moved against the current and shortly found this to be a spillway of a small log dam. Promptly he stripped and bathed under it, pronouncing in a whisper as he did so all three of the accompanying prayers from the rite of lustration as prescribed for the preparatory triduum in the *Grimorium Verum* – though the water was neither warm nor exorcized, it was obviously pure, and that would have to do.

The ablution was every bit as cold as he had expected it to be, and even colder was the process of air-drying himself; but he endured it stoically, for he had to get rid of what remained of the ointment, and moreover he knew that to put on damp clothes would be almost as dangerous. While he waited, his teeth chattering, faint traces of light began to appear through the trees from the east.

In answer, massive grey rectangular shapes began to sketch themselves against the darkness downstream, and before long he was able to see that to the west – which was the way the stream was momentarily running – the aisle it cut through the trees opened out on to a substantial farm. As if in confirmation of help to come, a cock crowed in the distance, a traditional ending for a night of magic.

But as the dawn continued to brighten, he saw that there would be no help for him here. Under the angle of the roof of the large barn nearest to him a circular diagram had been painted, like a formalized flower with an eye in it.

As Jack Ginsberg had taken the pains to find out long before he and his boss had even met the magician, Ware had been born and raised in the States and was still a citizen. As his name showed, his background was Methodist, but nevertheless he knew a hex sign when he saw one. And it gave him an idea.

He was not a witch, and he certainly had had no intention of laying a curse on this prosperous-looking farm ten seconds ago, but the opportunity to gather new data should not be missed.

Reaching into his shin pocket, he turned the ruby around so that the seal and characters on it faced outward. In a low voice, he said, THOMATOS. BENESSER, FLEANTER.'

Under proper circumstances these words of the *Comte de Gabalis* encompassed the operator with thirty-three several Intelligences, but since the circumstances were not proper, Ware was not surprised when nothing happened. For one thing, his lustration had been imperfect; for another, he was using the wrong talisman – the infernal spirits of the ceremony were not devils but salamanders or fire elements. Nevertheless he now added: 'LITAN, ISER, OSNAS.'

A morning breeze sprang up, and a leaflike whispering ran around him, which might or might not have been the voices of many beings, individually saying, 'NANTHER, NANTHER, NANTHER, NANTHER ...' Touching the talisman, Ware said, 'GITAU, HURANDOS, RIDAS, TALIMOL,' and then, pointing to the barn, 'UUSUR, ITAR.'

The result should have been a highly localized but destructive earthquake, but there was not even a minor tremor, though he was pretty sure that he really heard the responsive voices of the fire spirits. The spell simply would not work under the eye of the hex sign – one more piece of evidence that the powers of evil were still under some kind of restraint. That was good to know, but in a way, too, Ware was quite disappointed; for had he gotten his earthquake, the further words SOUTRAM, UBARSINENS would have compelled the intelligences to carry him across the rest of his journey. He uttered them anyhow, but without result.

Neither in the *Comte de Gabalis* or its very late successor, *The Black Pullet*, did this ritual offer any word of dismissal, but nevertheless for safety's sake he now added; 'RABIAM.' Had this worked, he would have found himself carried home again, where at least he could have started over again with more ointment and another broomstick; but it did not. There was no recourse now but to seek out the farmhouse and try to persuade the farmer to give him something to eat and drive him to the nearest railhead. It was too bad that the man could not be told that he had just been protected by Ware from a demonic onslaught but unfortunately the Amish did not believe that there was any such thing as white magic – and in the ultimate analysis they were quite right not to do so, whatever delusions about the point might be harboured by Father Domenico and his fellows.

Ware identified the farmhouse proper without any trouble. It looked every bit as clean, fat and prosperous as the rest, but it was suspiciously quiet; by this hour, everyone should be up and beginning the day's chores. He approached with caution, alert for guns or dogs, but the silence continued.

The caution had been needless. Inside, the place was an outright slaughterhouse, resembling nothing so much as the last act of Webster's *The White Devil*. Ware inspected it with clinical fascination. The family had been a large one – the parents, one grandparent, four daughters, three sons and the inevitable dog – and at some time during the preceding night they had suddenly fallen upon each other with teeth, nails, pokers, a buggy whip, a bicycle chain, a cleaver, a pig knife and the butt end of a smoothbore musket old enough to have been a relic of the Boer War. It was an obvious case of simultaneous mass possession, probably worked through the women, as these things almost always were. Doubtless they would infinitely have preferred a simple localized earthquake, but from an attack like this no conceivable peasant hex sign could have protected them.

Probably nothing could have, for as it had turned out, in their simple traditional religiosity they had chosen the wrong side. Like most of humankind, they had been born victims; even a beginning study of the Problem of Evil would have suggested to them that their God had never played fair with them, as indeed He had caused to be written out in Job for all to read; and their primitive backwoods demonology had never honestly admitted that there really were two sides to the Great Game, let alone allowing them any inkling of who the players were.

While he considered what to do next he prowled around the kitchen and the woodshed, where the larder was, trying not to slip or step on anybody. There were only two eggs – today's had obviously not been harvested – but he found smoked, streaky rashers of bacon, a day-old loaf of bread just ripe for cutting, nearly a pound of country butter and a stone jug of cold milk. All in all it was a good deal more than he could eat, but he built a fire in the old wood-burning stove, cooked the eggs and the bacon, and did his best to put it all down. After all he had no idea when he would meet his next meal. He had already decided that he was not yet desperate enough to risk calling for an apport, but instead would keep walking generally westward until he met an opportunity to steal a car. (He would find none on the farm; the Amish still restricted themselves to horses.)

As he came out of the farmhouse into the bright morning, a sandwich in both hip pockets, he heard from the undestroyed barn a demanding lowing of cattle. Sorry, friends, he though; nobody's going to milk you this morning.

8

Baines knew the structure and approaches of Strategic Air Command head-quarters rather better than the Department of Defense would have thought right and proper even for a civilian with Q clearance, although there had been several people in DoD who would not have been at all surprised at it. The otherwise passengerless jet carrying him and Jack Ginsberg made no attempt to approach either Denver Airport or the US Air Force Acad-emy field at Colorado Springs, both of which, he correctly assumed, would no longer be in existence anyhow. Instead, he directed the pilot to land at Limon, a small town which was the eastern-most vertex of a nearly equilat-eral triangle formed by these three points. Hidden there was one terminus of an underground rapid transit line which led directly into the heart of SAC's fortress – and was now its only surviving means of physical access to the outside world.

Baines and his secretary had been there only once before, and the guards at the station now were not only new but thoroughly frightened. Hence, despite the possession of ID cards countersigned by General McKnight, they were subjected to over an hour of questioning, finger-printing, pho-tographing of retinal blood-vessel patterns, frisking and fluoroscopy for hidden weapons or explosives, telephone calls into the interior and finally a closed-circuit television confrontation with McKnight himself before they were even allowed into the waiting room.

As if in partial compensation, the trip itself was rapid transit indeed. The line itself was a gravity-vacuum tube, bored in an exactly straight line under the curvature of the Earth, and kept as completely exhausted of air as out-gassing from its steel cladding would permit. The vacuum in the tube was in fact almost as hard as the atmosphere of the Moon. From the wait-ing room, Baines and Jack Ginsberg were passed through two airlocks into a seamlessly welded windowless metal capsule which was sealed behind them. Here their guards strapped them in securely, for their own protec-tion, for the initial kick of compressed air behind the capsule, abetted by rings of electromagnets, gave it an acceleration of more than five miles per hour per second. Though this is not much more than they might have been subjected to in an electric streetcar of about 1940, it is a considerable jerk if you cannot see outside and have nothing to hold on to. Thereafter, the capsule was simply allowed to fall to the mathematical midpoint of its right of way, gaining speed at about twenty-eight feet per second; since the rest of the journey was uphill, the capsule was slowed in proportion by gravity, friction and the compression of the almost non-existent gases in the tube still ahead of it, which without any extra braking whatsoever brought it to a stop at the SAC terminus of the line so precisely that only a love pat from a fifteen-horsepower engine was needed to line up its airlock with that of the station.

'When you're riding a thing like this, it makes it hard to believe that there's any such thing as a devil, doesn't it?' Jack Ginsberg said. He had had a long, luxurious shower aboard the plane, and that, plus getting away from the demon-haunted ruins in Positano, and the subsequent finding in Zurich that money still worked, had brightened him perceptibly.

'Maybe,' Baines said. 'A large part of the mystic tradition says that the possession and use of secular knowledge – or even the desire for it – is in itself evil, according to Ware. But here we are.'

But in the smooth-running, even-temperatured caverns of the SAC, Baines himself felt rather reassured. There was no Goat grinning over his shoulder yet. McKnight was an old friend; he was pleased to see Buelg again, and honoured to meet Šatvje; and down here, at least, everything seemed to be under control. It was also helpful to find that both McKnight and his advisers not only already knew the real situation, but had very nearly accepted it. Only Buelg had remained a little sceptical at the beginning, and had seemed quite taken aback to find Baines, of all people, providing independent testimony to the same effect as had the computer. When the new facts Baines had brought had been fed into the machine, and the machine had produced in response a whole new batch of conclusions entirely consistent with the original hypothesis, Buelg seemed convinced, although it was plain that he still did not like it. Well, who did?

At long last they were comfortably settled in McKnights office, with three tumblers of Jack Daniel's (Jack Ginsberg did not drink, and neither did Šatvje) and no one to interrupt them but an occasional runner from Chief Hay. Though the runner was a coolly pretty blonde girl, and the USAF's women's auxiliary had apparently adopted the miniskirt, Ginsberg did not seem to notice. Perhaps he was still in shock from his recent run-in with the succubus. To Baines's eyes, the girl did look rather remarkably like Ware's Greta, which should have captured Jack instantly; but then, in the long run, most women looked alike to Baines, especially in their line of business.

'That bomb did you no good at all, I take it,' he said.

'Oh, I wouldn't go so far as to say that,' McKnight said. 'True, it didn't destroy the city, or even hurt it visibly, but it certainly seemed to take them by surprise. For about an hour after the fireball went up, the sky above the target was full of them. It was like firing a flashbulb in a cave full of sleeping bats – and we got pictures too.'

'Any evidence that you, uh, destroyed any of them?'

'Well, we saw a lot of them going back to the city under their own power

– despite very bad design, they seem to fly pretty well – but we don't have any count of how many went up. We didn't see any falling, but that might have been because some of them had been vaporized.'

'Not bloody likely. Their bodies may have been vaporized, but the bodies were borrowed in the first place. Like knocking down a radio-controlled aircraft: the craft may be a total loss, but the controlling Intelligence is unharmed, somewhere else, and can send another one against you whenever it likes.'

'Excuse me, Dr Baines, but the analogy is inexact,' Buelg said. 'We know that because we did get a lot out of the bomb besides simply stirring up a flurry. High-speed movies of the column of the mushroom as it went up show a lot of the creatures trying to reform. One individual we were able to follow went through thirty-two changes in the first minute. The changes are all incredible and beyond any physical theory or model we can erect to account for them, but they do show, first, that the creature was seriously inconvenienced, and second, that it wanted and perhaps needed to hold on to *some* kind of physical form. That's a start. It suggests to me that had we been able to confine them all in the fireball, where the temperatures are way higher still, no gamut of change they could have run through would have done them any good. Eventually they would have been stripped of the last form and utterly destroyed.'

'The last form, maybe,' Baines said. 'But the spirit would remain. I don't know why they're clinging to physical forms so determinedly, but it probably has only a local and tactical reason, something to do with the prosecuting of the present war. But you can't destroy a spirit by such means, any more than you can destroy a message by burning the piece of paper it's written on.'

As he said this, he became uncomfortably aware that he had gotten the argument out of some sermon against atheism that he had heard as a boy, and had thought simple-minded even then. But since then, he had *seen* demons – and a lot more closely than anybody else here had.

'That is perhaps an open question, Šatvje said heavily. 'I am not myself a sceptic, you should understand, Dr Baines, but I have to remind myself that no spirit has ever been so intensively tested to destruction before. Inside a thermonuclear fireball, even the nuclei of hydrogen atoms find it difficult to retain their integrity.'

'Atomic nuclei remain matter, and the conservation laws still apply. Demons are neither matter nor energy; they are something else.'

'We do not know that they are not energy,' Šatvje said. 'They may well be fields, falling somewhere within the electro-magnetico-gravitic triad. Remember that we have never achieved a unified field theory; even Einstein repudiated his in the last years of his life, and quantum mechanics – with all respect to De Broglie – in only a clumsy avoidance of the problem. These

... spirits ... may be such unified fields. And one characteristic of such fields might be 100 per cent negative entropy.'

'There couldn't be any such thing as completely negative entropy,' Buelg put in. 'Such a system would constantly *accumulate* order, which means that it would run backwards in time and we would never be aware of it at all. You have to allow for Planck's Constant. This would be the only stable case—'

He wrote rapidly on a pad, stripped off the sheet and passed it across the table. The note read, in very neat lettering:

$$H(x)-Hy(x)=C+e$$

The girl came in with another manifold of sheets from the computer, and this time Jack Ginsberg's eye could be observed to be wandering haunchward a little. Baines had never objected to this – he preferred his most valuable employees to have a few visible and visable weaknesses – but for once he almost even sympathized; he was feeling a little out of his depth.

'Meaning what?' he said.

'Why,' Šatvje said, a little patronizingly, 'eternal life, of course. Life is negative entropy. Stable negative entropy is eternal life.'

'Barring accidents,' Buelg said, with a certain grim relish. 'We have no access yet to the gravitic part of the spectrum, but the electromagnetic sides are totally vulnerable, and with the clues we've got now, we ought to be able to burst into such a closed system like a railroad spike going through an auto tyre.'

'If you can kill a demon,' Baines said slowly. 'Then—'

'That's right,' Buelg said affably. 'Angel, devil, ordinary immortal soul – you name it, we can do for it. Not right away, maybe, but before very long.'

'Perhaps the ultimate human achievement,' Šatvje said, with a dreaming, almost beatific expression. 'The theologians call condemnation to Hell the Second Death. Soon, perhaps, we may be in a position to give the Third Death ... the bliss of complete extinction ... liberation from the Wheel!'

McKnight's eyes were now also wandering, though towards the ceiling. He wore the expression of a man who has heard all this before, and is not enjoying it any better the second time. Baines himself was very far from being bored – indeed, he was as close to horrified fascination as he had ever been in his life – but clearly it was time to bring everybody back to Earth. He said:

'Talk's cheap. Do you have any actual plans?'

'You bet we do,' McKnight said, suddenly galvanized. 'I've had Chief Hay run me an inventory of the country's remaining military power, and, believe me, there's a lot of it. I was surprised myself. We are going to mount a major attack upon this city of Dis, and for it we're going to bring some things up out of the ground that the American people have never seen before and neither has anybody else, including this pack of demons. I don't know why they're just sitting there, but maybe it's because they think they've already got us licked. Well, they're dead wrong. Nobody can lick the United States – not in the long run!'

It was an extraordinary sentiment from a man who had been maintaining for years that the United States had 'lost' China, 'surrendered' Korea, 'abandoned' Vietnam and was overrun by home-bred Communists; but Baines, who knew the breed, saw no purpose in calling attention to the fact. *Their arguments, not being based in reason, cannot be swayed by reason. Instead* he said:

'General, believe me, I advise against it. I know some of the weapons you're talking about, and they're pretty powerful. I ought to know; my company designed and supplied some of them, so it would be against my own interests to run them down to you. But I very much doubt that any of them will do any good under the present circumstances.'

'That, of course, remains to be seen,' McKnight said.

'I'd rather we didn't. If they work, we may find ourselves worse off than before. That's the point I came here to press. The demons are about 90 per cent in charge of the world now, but you'll notice that they haven't taken any further steps against us. There's a reason for this. They are fighting against another Opponent entirely, and it's quite possible that we ought to be on their side.'

McKnight leaned back in his chair, with the expression of a president confronted at a press conference with a question on which he had not been briefed.

'Let me be quite sure I understand you, Dr Baines,' he said. 'Do you propose that the present invasion of the United States was a good thing? And, further, that we ought not to be opposing the occupying forces with all our might? That indeed we ought instead to be aiding and abetting the powers responsible for it?'

'I don't propose any aiding and abetting whatsoever,' Baines said, with an inward sigh. 'I just think we ought to lay off for a while, that's all, until we see how the situation works out.'

'You are almost the last man in the world,' McKnight said stiffly, 'whom I would have suspected of being a ComSymp, let alone a pro-Chink. When I have your advice entered upon the record, I will also add an expression of my personal confidence. In the meantime, the attack goes forward as scheduled.'

Baines said nothing more, advisedly. It had occurred to him, out of his experience with Theron Ware, that angels fallen and unfallen, and the immortal part of man, partook of and had sprung from the essentially indivisable nature of their Creator; that if these men could destroy that Part, they could equally well dissolve the Whole; that a successful storming of Dis would inevitably be followed by a successful war upon Heaven; and that if God were not dead yet, He soon might be.

However it turned out, it looked like it was going to be the most interesting civil war he had ever run guns to.

9

UNITED STATES ARMED FORCES
Strategic Air Command Office
Denver, Colorado
Date: May 1

MEMORANDUM: Number I
TO: All Combat Arms
SUBJECT: General Combat Orders

1. This Memorandum supersedes all previous directives on this subject.

2. The United States has been invaded and all combat units will stand in readiness to expel the invading forces.

3. The enemy has introduced a number of combat innovations of which all units must be made thoroughly aware. All officers will therefore read this Memorandum in full to their respective commands, and will thereafter post it in a conspicuous place. All commands should be sampled for familiarity with the contents of the Memorandum.

4. Enemy troops are equipped with individual body armour. In accordance with ancient Oriental custom, this armour has been designed and decorated in various grotesque shapes, in the hope of frightening the opposition. It is expected that the American soldier will simply laugh at this primitive device. All personnel are warned, however, that as armour these 'demon suits' are extremely effective. A very high standard of marksmanship will be required against them.

5. An unknown number of the enemy body armour units, perhaps approaching 100 per cent, are capable of free flight, like the jump suits supplied to US Mobile Infantry. Ground forces will therefore be alert to possible attack from the air by individual enemy troops as well as by conventional aircraft.

6. It is anticipated that in combat the enemy will employ various explosive, chemical and toxic agents which may produce widespread novel effects. All personnel are hereby reminded that these effects will be either natural in origin, or illusion.

7. Following the reading of this Memorandum, all officers will read to

their commands those paragraphs of the Articles of War pertaining to the penalties for cowardice in battle.

By order of the Commander in Chief:

D. Willis McKnight

D. WILLIS MCKNIGHT
General of the Armies, USAF

Because of the destruction of Rome and of the Vatican with it – alas for that great library and treasure house of all Christendom! – the Holy See had been moved to Venice, which had been spared thus far, and was now housed in almost equal magnificence in the Sala del Collegio of the Palazzo Ducale, the only room to escape intact from the great fire of 1577, where, under a ceiling by Veronese, the doges had been accustomed to receive their ambassadors to other city-states. It was the first time the palace had been used by anybody but tourists since Napoleon had forced the abdication of Lodovico Manin exactly eleven hundred years after the election of the first doge.

There were no tourists here now, of course: the city, broiling hot and stinking of the garbage in its canals, brooded lifelessly under the Adriatic sun, a forgotten museum. Nobody was about in the crazy narrow streets, and the cramped *ristoranti,* but the native Venetians, their livelihood gone, sullenly starving together in small groups and occasionally snarling at each other in their peculiar dialect. Many already showed signs of radiation sickness: their hair was shedding in patches and pools of vomit caught the sunlight, ignored by everyone but the flies.

The near desertion of the city, at least by comparison with the jam which would have been its natural state by this time of year, gave Father Domenico a small advantage. Instead of having to take refuge in a third-class hotel, clamorous twenty-four hours a day with groups of Germans and Americans being processed by the coachload like raw potatoes being converted into neatly packaged crisps, he was able without opposition to find himself apartments in the Patriarch's Palace itself. Such dusty sumptuousness did not at all suit him, but he had come to see the Pope, as the deputy of an ancient, still honoured monastic order; and the Patriarch, after confessing him and hearing the nature of his errand, had deemed it fitting that he be appropriately housed while he waited.

There was no way of telling how long the wait might be. The Pope had died with Rome; what remained of the College of Cardinals – those of them that had been able to reach Venice at all – was shut in the Sala del Consiglio dei Dieci, attempting to elect a new one. It was said that the office of the Grand Inqisitor, directly next door, held a special guest, but of this rumour the Patriarch seemed to know no more than the next man. In the meantime, he issued to Father Domenico a special dispensation to conduct Masses and hear confessions in small churches off the Grand Canal, and to preach there and even in the streets if he wished. Technically, Father Domenico had no patent to do any of these things, since he was a monk rather than a priest, but the Patriarch, like everyone else now, was short on manpower.

On the trip northward from Monte Albano, Father Domenico had seen many more signs of suffering, and of outright demoniac malignancy, than were visible on the surface of this uglily beautiful city; but it was nevertheless a difficult, almost sinister place in which to attempt to minister to the people, let alone to preach a theology of hope. The Venetians had never been more than formally and outwardly allegiant to the Church from at least their second treaty with Islam in the mid-fifteenth century. The highest pinnacle of their ethics was that of dealing fairly with each other, and since there was at the same time no sweeter music to Venetian ears than the scream of outrage from the outsider who had discovered too late that he had been cheated, this left them little that they felt they ought to say in the confessional. Most of them seemed to regard the now obvious downfall of almost all of human civilization as a plot to divert the tourist trade to some other town – probably Istanbul, which they still referred to as Constantinople.

As for hope, they had none. In this they were not alone. Throughout his journey, Father Domenico had found nothing but terror and misery, and a haunted populace which could not but conclude that everything the Church had taught them for nearly two thousand years had been lies. How could he tell them that, considering the real situation as he knew it to be, the suffering and the evil with which they were afflicted were rather less than he had expected to find? How then could he tell them further that he saw small but mysteriously increasing signs of mitigation of the demons' rule? In these, fighting all the way against confounding hope with wishful thinking, he believed only reluctantly himself.

Yet hope somehow found its way forward. On an oppressive afternoon while he was trying to preach to a group of young thugs, most of them too surly and indifferent even to jeer, before the little Church of Sta Maria dei Miracoli, his audience was suddenly galvanized by a series of distant whistles. The whistles, as Father Domenico knew well enough, had been until only recently the signals of the young wolves of Venice, to report the spotting of some escortless English schoolmarm, pony-tailed Bennington art student or gaggle of Swedish girls. There were no such prey about now, but nevertheless, the piazzetta emptied within a minute.

Bewildered and of course apprehensive, Father Domenico followed, and soon found the streets almost as crowded as of old with people making for St Mark's. A rumour had gone around that a puff of white smoke had been seen over the Palazzo Ducale. This was highly unlikely, since – what with the fear of another fire which constantly haunted the palace – there was no stove in it anywhere in which to burn ballots; nevertheless, the expectation of a new Pope had run through the city like fire itself. By the time Father Domenico reached the vast square opposite the basilica (for after all, he too had come in search of a Pope) it was so crowded as to scarcely leave standing room for the pigeons.

If there was indeed to be any announcement, it would have to come Venetian style from the top of the Giant's Staircase of Antonio Rizzo; the repetitive arches of the first-floor loggia offered no single balcony on which a Pope might appear. Father Domenico pressed forward into the great internal courtyard towards the staircase, at first saying, 'Prego, prego,' and then 'Scusate, scusate mi', to no effect whatsoever and finally with considerable judicious but hard monkish use of elbows and knees.

Over the tense rumbling of the crowd there sounded suddenly an antiphonal braying of many trumpets – something of Gabrielli's, no doubt – and at the same time Father Domenico found himself jammed immovably against the coping of the cannon-founder's well, which had long since been scavenged clean of the tourists' coins. By luck it was not a bad position; from here he had quite a clear view up the staircase and between the towering statues of Mars and Neptune. The great doors had already been opened, and the cardinals in their scarlet finery were ranked on either side of the portico. Between them and a little forward stood two pages, one of them holding a red cushion upon which stood something tall and glittering.

Amidst the fanfare, an immensely heavy tolling began to boom: La Trottiera, the bell which had once summoned the members of the Grand Council to mount their horses and ride over the wooden bridges to a meeting. The combination of bell and trumpets was solemnly beautiful, and under it the crowd fell quickly silent. Yet the difference from the Roman ritual was disturbing, and there was something else wrong about it, too. What was that thing on the cushion? It certainly could not be the tiara; was it the golden horn of the doges?

The music and the tolling stopped. Into the pigeon-cooing silence, a cardinal cried in Latin:

'We have a Pope, Sumraus Antistitum Antistes! And it is his will that he be called Juvenember LXIX!'

The unencumbered page now stepped forward. He called in the vernacular:

'Here is your Pope, and we know it will please you.'

From the shadow of the great doors there stepped forth into the sunlight between the statues, bowing his head to accept the golden horn, his face white and mild as milk, the special guest of the office of the Grand Inquisitor: a comely old man with a goshawk on his wrist, whom Father Domenico

had first and last seen on Black Easter, released from the Pit by Theron Ware
– the demon AGARESS

There was an enormous shout from the crowd, and then the trumpets
and the bell resumed, now joined by all the rest of the bells in the city, and
by many drums, and the firing of cannon. Choking with horror, Father Domenico fled as best he could.

The festival went on all week, climaxed by bull dancing in the Cretan
style in the courtyard of the Palazzo, and by fireworks at night while Father
Domenico prayed. This event was definitive. The Antichrist had arrived,
however belatedly, and therefore God still lived. Father Domenico could do
no more good in Italy; he must now go to Dis, into Hell-Mouth itself, and
challenge Satan to grant His continuing existence. Nor would it be enough
for Father Domenico to aspire to be the Antisatan. If necessary – most terrifying of all thoughts – he must now expose himself to the temptation and
the election, by no earthly college, of becoming the vicar of Christ whose
duty it would be to harrow this earthly Hell.

Yet how to get there? He was isolated on an isthmus of mud, and he had
no earthly resources whatsoever. Just possibly, some rite of white magic
might serve to carry him, although he could remember none that seemed
applicable; but that would involve returning to Monte Albano, and in any
event, he felt instinctively that no magic of any kind would be appropriate
now.

In this extremity, he bethought him of certain legends and attested mir-
acles of the early saints, some of whom in their exaltation were said to have
been lifted long distances through the air. Beyond question, he was not a
saint; but if his forthcoming role was to be as he suspected, some similar
help might be vouchsafed him. He tried to keep his mind turned away from
the obvious and most exalted example of all, and equally to avoid thinking
about the doubt-inducing fate of Simon Magus – a razor's edge which not
even his Dominican training made less than nearly impossible to negotiate.

Nevertheless, his shoulders squared, his face set, Father Domenico walked
resolutely towards the water.

10

Even after the complete failure of air power in Vietnam to pound one half of
a tenth-rate power into submission, General McKnight remained a believer
in its supremacy; but he was not such a fool as to do without ground support, knowing very well the elementary rule that territory must be occupied
as well as devastated, or even the most decisive victory will come unstuck.
By the day – or rather, the night – for which the attack was scheduled, he
had moved three armoured divisions through the Panamint range, and had

two more distributed through the Grapevine, Funeral and Black mountains, which also bristled with rocket emplacements. This was by no means either as big or as well divided a force as he should have liked to have used, especially on the east, but since it was all the country had left to offer him, he had to make it do.

His battle plan was divided into three phases. Remembering that the test bomb had blown some thousands of enemy troops literally sky high for what was tactically speaking quite a long period of time, he intended to begin with a serial bombardment of Dis with as many of his remaining nuclear weapons as he could use up just short of making the surrounding territory radiologically lethal to his own men. These warheads might not do the city or the demons any damage – a proposition which he still regarded with some incredulity – but if they would again disorganize the enemy and keep him from reforming that would be no mean advantage in itself.

Phase Two was designed to take advantage of the fact that the battleground from his point of view was all downhill, the devils with stunning disregard of elementary strategy having located their fortress at the lowest point in the valley, on the site of what had previously been Badwater, which was actually two hundred and eighty-two feet below sea level. When the nuclear bombardment ended, it would be succeeded immediately by a continued hammering with conventional explosives, by artillery, missiles and planes. These would include phosphorus bombs, again probably harmless to devils, but which would in any event produce immense clouds of dense white smoke, which might impair visibility for the enemy; his own troops could see through it handily enough by radar, and would always be able to see the main target through the infra-red telescope or 'sniperscope', since even under normal conditions it was always obligingly kept red hot. Under cover of this bombardment, McKnight planned a rush of armour upon the city, spearheaded by halftrack-mounted laser projectors. It was McKnight's theory, supported neither by his civilian advisers nor by the computer, that the thermonuclear fireball had failed to vaporize the iron walls because its heat had been too generalized and diffuse, and that the concentrated heat of four or five or a dozen laser beams, all focused on one spot, might punch its way through like a rapier going through cheese. This onslaught was to be aimed directly at the gates, of course; these would be better defended than any other part of the perimeter, but a significant number of the defenders might still be flapping wildly around in the air amidst the smoke, and in any event, when one is trying to breach a wall, it is only common sense to begin at a point which *already* has a hole in it.

If such a breach was actually effected, an attempt would be made to enlarge it with land torpedoes, particularly burrowing ones of the Hess type which would have been started on their way at the beginning of Phase One.

These had never seen use before in actual combat and were supposed to be graveyard secret – though with the profusion of spies and traitors with which America had been swarming, in McKnight's view, before all this had begun, he doubted that the secret had been very well kept. (After all, if even Baines …) He was curious also about the actual effectiveness of another secret, the product of an almost incestuous union of chemistry and nucleonics called TDX, a compound as unstable as TNT, which was made of gravity-polarized atoms. McKnight had only the vaguest idea of what this jargon was supposed to signify, but what he did know was its action; TDX was supposed to have the property of exploding in a flat plane, instead of expanding evenly in all directions like any Christian explosive.

Were the gate forced, the bombardment would stop and Phase Three would follow. This would be an infantry assault, supported by individually airborne troops in their rocket-powered flying harnesses, and supplemented by an attempted paratroop landing inside the city. If on the other hand the gate did not go down, there would be a most unwelcome Phase Four – a general, and hopefully orderly retreat.

The whole operation could be watched both safely and conveniently from the SAC's Command Room under Denver, and as the name implied, directed in the same way; there was a multitude of television screens, some of which were at the individual command consoles provided for each participating general. The whole complex closely resembled the now extinct Space Center at Houston, which had in fact been modelled after it; technically, space flight and modem warfare are almost identical operations from the command point of view. At the front of this cavern and quite dominating it was a master screen of Cinerama proportions; at its rear was something very like a sponsor's booth, giving McKnight and his guests an overview of the whole, as well as access to a bank of small screens on which he could call into being any individual detail of the action that was within access of a camera.

McKnight did not bother to occupy the booth until the nuclear bombardment was over, knowing well enough that the immense amount of ionization it would produce would make non-cable television reception impossible for quite some time. (The fallout was going to be hell, too – but almost all of it would miss Denver, the East Coast was dead, and the fish and the Europeans would have to look out for themselves.) When he finally took over, the conventional bombardment was just beginning. With him were Baines, Buelg, Chief Hay and Šatvje; Jack Ginsberg had expressed no particular interest in watching, and since Baines did not need him here, he had been excused to go below, presumably to resume his lubricous pursuit of Chief Hay's comely runner.

Vision on the great master screen was just beginning to clear as they took their seats, although there was still considerable static. Weather Control reported that it was a clear, brightly moonlit night over all of the South-west, but in point of fact the top of the great multiple nuclear mushroom, shot through with constant lightning, now completely covered the southern third of California and all of the two states immediately to the east of it. The units and crews crouching in their bivouacs and emplacements along the sides of the mountains facing away from the valley clung grimly to the rocks against hurricane updraughts in temperatures that began at a hundred and fifty degrees and went on up from there. No unit which had been staked out on any of the inside faces of any of the ranges reported anything, then or ever; even the first missiles and shells to come screaming in towards Dis ex-ploded incontinently in mid-air the moment they rose above the sheltering shadows of the mountain peaks. No thermo-couple existed which would express in degrees the temperature at the heart of the target itself; specto-graphs taken from the air showed it to be cooling from a level of about two and a half million electron volts, a figure as utterly impossible to relate to human experiences as are the distances in miles between the stars.

Nevertheless, the valley cooled with astonishing rapidity, and once visi-bility was restored, it was easy to see why. More than two hundred square miles of it had been baked and annealed into a shallow, even dish, still glow-ing whitely but shot through with the gorgeous colours of impurities, like a borax bead in the flame of a blowpipe; and this was acting like the reflector of a searchlight, throwing the heat outward through the atmosphere into space in an almost solidly visible column. At its centre, as at the Cassegran-ian focus of a telescope mirror, was a circular black hole.

McKnight leaned forward, grasping the arms of his chair in a death grip, and shouted for a close-up. Had the job been done already? Perhaps Buelg had been right about there being a possible limit to the number of trans-formations the enemy could go through before final dissolution. After all, Badwater had just received a nuclear saturation which had previously been contemplated only in terms of the overkill of whole countries—

But as the glass darkened, the citadel brightened, until at last it showed once more as a red-hot ring. Nothing could be seen inside it but a roiling mass of explosions – the conventional bombardment was now getting home, and with great accuracy – from which a mushroom stem continued to rise in the very centre of the millennial updraught; but the walls – the walls, the walls, the walls were still there.

'Give it up, General.' Buelg said, his voice gravelly. 'No matter what the spectroscope shows, if those walk were really iron—' He paused and swallowed heavily. 'They must be only symbologically iron, perhaps in some alchemical sense. Otherwise the atoms would not only have been scattered to the four winds, but would have had all the electron shells stripped off them. You can do nothing more but lose more lives.'

'The bombardment is still going on.' McKnight pointed out stiffly, 'and we've had no report yet of what it's done to the enemy's organization and manpower. For all we know, there's nobody left down that hole at all – and the laser squadrons haven't even arrived yet, let alone the Hess torpedoes.'

'Neither of which are going to work a damn,' Baines said brutally. 'I know what the Hess torpedo will do. Have you forgotten that they were invented by my own chief scientist? Who just incidentally was taken by PUT SATANACHII this Easter, so that the demons now know all about the gadget, if they didn't before. And after what's been dropped on that town already, expecting anything of it is like trying to kill a dinosaur by kissing it.'

'It is in the American tradition,' McKnight said, 'to do things the hard way if there is no other way. Phase Four is a last-ditch measure, and it is good generalship – which I do not expect you to understand – to remain flexible until the last moment. As Clausewitz remarks, most battles are lost by generals who failed to have the courage of their own convictions in the clutch.'

Baines, who had read extensively in both military and political theoreticians in five languages, and had sampled them in several more, as a necessary adjunct to his business, knew very well that Clausewitz had never said any such damn fool thing, and that McKnight was only covering with an invented quotation a hope which was last-ditch indeed. But even had elementary Machiavellianism given him any reason to suppose that charging McKnight with this would change the General's mind in the slightest, he could see from the master screen that it was already too late. While they had been talking, the armoured divisions had been charging down into the valley, their diesel-electric engines snarling and snorting, the cleats of their treads cracking the slippery glass and leaving sluggishly glowing, still quasi-molten trails behind. Watching them in the small screens, Baines began to think that he must be wrong. He knew these monsters well – they were part of his stock in trade – and to believe that they were resistible went against the selling habits of an entire adult lifetime.

Yet some of them were bogging down already; as they descended deeper into the valley, with the small rockets whistling over their hunched heads, the hot glass under their treads worked into the joints like glue, and then, carried by the groaning engines up over the top trunnions, cooled and fell into the bearings in a shower of many-sized abrasive granules. The monsters slewed and sidled, losing traction and with it, steerage; and then the lead half-track with the laser cannon jammed immovably and began to sink like the *Titanic* into the glass, the screams of its boiling crew tearing the cool air of the command booth like a ripsaw until McKnight impatiently cut the sound off.

The other beasts lumbered on regardless – they had no orders to do otherwise – and a view from the air showed that three or four units of the laser squadron were now within striking distance of the gates of Dis. Like driver ants, black streams of infantry were crawling down the inner sides of the mountains behind the last wave of the armoured divisions. They too had had no orders to turn back. Even in their immensely clumsy asbestos firemen's suits and helmets, they were already fainting and falling over each other in the foothills, their carefully oiled automatic weapons falling into the sand, the tanks of their flame throwers slitting and dumping jellied gasoline on the hot rocks, the very air of the valley sucking all of the moisture out of their lungs through the tiniest cracks in their uniforms.

Baines was not easily horrified – that would have been bad for business – but also he had never before seen any actual combat but the snippets of the Vietnam war which had been shown on American television. This senseless advance of expensively trained and equipped men to certain and complete slaughter – men who as usual not only had no idea of what they were dying for, but had been actively misled about it – made about as much military sense as the Siege of Sevastopol or the Battle of the Marne. Certainly it was spectacular, but intellectually it was not even very interesting.

Four of the laser buggies – all that had survived – were now halted before the gates, two to each side to allow a heavy howitzer to fire between them. From them lanced out four pencil-thin beams of intensely pure red light, all of which met at the same spot on the almost invisible seam between the glowing doors. Had that barrier been real iron, they would have holed through it in a matter of seconds in a tremendous shower of sparks, but in actuality they were not even raising its temperature, as far as Baines could see. The beams winked out; then struck again.

Above the buggies, on the barbican, there seemed to be scores of black, indistinct, misshapen figures. They were very active, but their action did not seem to be directed against the buggies; Baines had the mad impression, which he was afraid was all too accurate, that they were dancing.

Again the beams lashed out. Beside him, McKnight muttered:

'If they don't hurry it up—'

Even before he was able to finish the sentence, the ground in front of the gates erupted. The first of the Hess torpedoes had arrived. One of the half-tracks simply vanished, while the one next to it went slowly skyward, and as slowly fell back, in a fountain of armour plate, small parts, and human limbs and torsos. Another, on the very edge of the crater, toppled equally slowly into it. The fourth sat for a long minute as if stunned by the concussion, and then began to back slowly away.

Another torpedo went off directly under the gates, and then another. The gates remained obdurately unharmed, but after a fourth such blast, light could be seen under them – the crater was growing.

'Halt all armoured vehicles!' McKnight shouted into his intercom, pounding the arm of his chair in excitement. 'Infantry advance on the double! We're going under!'

Another Hess torpedo went off in the same gap. Baines was fascinated now, and even feeling a faint glow of pride. Really, the things worked very well indeed; too bad He couldn't be here to see it ... but maybe He was seeing it, from inside. That hole was already big enough to accommodate a small car, and while he watched another torpedo blew it still wider and deeper.

'Paratroops! Advance drop by ten minutes!'

But why was Hess's invention working when the nuclear devices hadn't? Maybe Dis had only sunk lower as a whole, as the desert around and beneath it had been vaporized, but the demons could not defend the purely mundane geology of the valley itself? Another explosion. How many of those torpedoes had the Corps of Engineers had available? Consolidated Warfare Service had supplied only ten prototypes with the plans at the time of the sale, and there hadn't been time to put more into production. McKnight's suddenly advanced timetable seemed nevertheless to be allowing for the arrival of all ten.

This proved to be the case, except that the ninth got caught in a fault before it had completed *its* burrowing and blew up in the middle of one of the advancing columns of troops. Hess had always frankly admitted that the machine would be subject to this kind of failure, and that the flaw was inherent in the principle rather than the design. But it probably wouldn't be missed; the gap under the gates of Dis now looked quite as big as the New Jersey entrance to the original two Lincoln Tunnels. And the infantry was arriving at speed.

And at that moment, the vast unscarred gates slowly began to swing inward. McKnight gaped in astonishment and Baines could feel his own jaw dropping. Was the citadel going to surrender before it had even been properly stormed? Or worse, had it been ready all along to open to the first polite knock, so that all this colossal and bloody effort had been unnecessary?

But that, at least, they were spared. As the first patrols charged, tumbled, scrambled and clambered into the crater, there appeared in the now fully opened gateway, silhouetted against the murky flames behind, the same three huge naked snaky-haired women that McKnight and his crew had seen in the very first aerial photographs. They were all three carrying among them what appeared to be the head of an immense decapitated statue of something much like one of themselves. The asbestos-clad soldiers climbing up the far wall of the crater could not turn any greyer than they were, but they froze instantaneously like the overwhelmed inhabitants of Pompeii, and fell, and as they fell, they broke. Within minutes, the pit was being refilled from the bottom with shattered sculpture.

Overhead, the plane carrying the first contingent of paratroops was suddenly blurred by hundreds of tiny black dots Seconds later, the fuselage alone was plunging towards the desert; the legions of BEELZEBUB, the Lord of the Flies, had torn the wings off men. Lower, in the middle of the air, rocket-borne Assault Infantry soldiers were being plucked first of their harness, then of their clothing, and then of their hair, their fingernails and toenails by jeering creatures with beasts' heads, most of whom were flying without even wings. The bodies when there was anything left of them at all, were being dropped unerringly into the heart of the Pit.

In summary, the Siege of Dis could more reasonably be described as a rout, except for one curious discrepancy: When Phase Four began – without anyone's ordering it, and otherwise not according to plan – the demons failed to follow up their advantage. None of them, in fact, had ever left the city; even when they had taken to the air, they had never crossed its perimeter, as though the moat represented some absolute boundary which ascended even into the sky.

But the slaughter had been bad enough already. The chances that the Army of the United States could ever reform again looked very small indeed.

And at the end, there formed upon the master screen in the Denver cavern, superimposed upon the image of the burning triumphant city, an immense Face. Baines knew it well; he had been expecting to see it again ever since the end of that Black Easter back in Positano.

It was the crowned goat's head of PUT SATANACHIA.

McKnight gasped in horror for the very first time in Baines's memory; and down on the floor of the control centre, several generals fainted outright at their consoles. Then McKnight was on his feet screaming.

'A Chink! I knew it all along! Hay, clear the circuits! Clear the circuits! Get him off the screen!' He rounded suddenly on Baines. 'And you, you traitor! Your equipment failed us! You've sold us out! You were on their side all the time! Do you know into whose hands you have delivered your country? Do you? Do you?'

His howling was only an irritant now, but Baines had the strength left to raise one mocking eyebrow questioningly. McKnight levelled a trembling finger at the screen.

'Hay, Hay, clear the circuits! I'll have you court-martialled! Doesn't anyone understand but me? *That is the insidious Dr Fu Manchu!*'

The Sabbath Goat paid him no heed. Instead, it looked directly and steadily across the cavern into Baines's eyes. There was no mistaking the direction of that regard, and no question but that it saw him. It said:

AH, THERE YOU ARE. MY DEARLY BELOVED SON. COME TO ME NOW. OUR FATHER BELOW HATH NEED OF THEE.

Baines had no intention whatsoever of obeying that summons; but he found himself rising from his chair all the same.

Foaming at the mouth, his hands clawing for the distant throat of the demon. McKnight plunged in a shower of splinters through the front of the booth and fell like a glass comet towards the floor.

THE HARROWING OF HEAVEN

As a picture, where in a black colouring occurs in its proper place, so is the universe beautiful, if any could survey it, notwithstanding the Presence of sinners, although, taken by themselves, their proper deformity makes them hideous.

—*St Augustine,* De Civitate Dei, xi. 23

Thus that Faustus, to so many a snare of death, had now, neither willing nor witting it, begun to loosen that wherein I was taken.

—Confessions, v.13

11

Baines did not have much time to experiment under the geas or compulsion which PUT SATANACHIA had laid upon him, but he nevertheless found that it was highly selective in character. For example, the great prince had said nothing about requiring the presence of Jack Ginsberg, but when Baines, in a mixture of vindictiveness and a simple desire for human companionship, decided to try to bring him along, he found that he was not prevented from doing so. Ginsberg himself showed no resentment at being routed out of the bed of the blonde runner; possibly the succubus in Positano had spoiled for him the pleasures of human women, an outcome Jack himself had suspected in advance; but then, even without that supernatural congress, jack's sexual life had always been that of a rather standard Don Juan, for whom every success turned sour almost instantly.

This, however, was one of those explanations which did not explain, and Baines had thought about it often before; for, as has already been observed, he liked to have his key men come equipped with handles he could grasp if the need arose. There were, the company psychologist had told him, at least three kinds of Don Juans: Freud's, whose career is a lifelong battle to hide from himself an incipient homosexuality; Lenau's, a Romantic in search of the Ideal Woman, for whom the Devil who comes for him is disgust with himself; and Da Ponte's, a man born blind to the imminence of tomorrow, and hence incapable either of love or of repentance, even on the edge of the Pit. Well, but in the end, for Baines, it did not matter which one was Jack; they all *behaved* alike.

Jack did object powerfully when he was told that the journey to Dis would have to be made entirely on foot, but this was one of the areas in which Baines discovered that the geas left him no choice. Again, he wondered why it should be so. Did the Sabbath Goat mean to rub in the fact that the Siege of Dis had been the last gasp of secular technology? Or had it instead meant to impress upon Baines that, willy-nilly, he was about to embark upon a pilgrimage? But again, the outcome would have been the same, and that was all that mattered.

As for Jack, he still seemed to be afraid of his boss, or else still thought there was some main chance to be looked out for. Well, perhaps there was – but Baines would not have bet any shares of stock on it.

Theron Ware saw the great compound mushroom cloud go up while he was still in Flagstaff, a point to which several lucky hitchhikes and one even luckier long freight train ride had brought him. The surging growth of the cloud, the immense flares of light beyond the mountains to the west, and the repeated earth shocks left him in little doubt about what was going on; and as the cloud drifted towards him, moving inexorably from west to east as the weather usually does, he knew that it meant death for him within a very few days – as for how many thousands of others? – unless by some miracle he could find an unoccupied fallout shelter, or one whose present occupants wouldn't shoot him on sight.

And why indeed go on? The bombing showed without question that Baines's self-assumed mission to McKnight at Denver had failed, and that there was now open warfare between humanity and the demons. The notion that Theron Ware could do anything now to change that was so grandiose as to be outright pathetic. More trivially, by the time that bombing was over, no matter how it affected the demons – if at all – the whole hundred-mile-plus stretch of Death Valley National Monument would have become instantly lethal for an unprotected man to enter.

Yet Theron Ware could not yet quite believe that he was unprotected. He had come an immense distance by a traditional means which made it absolutely clear that black magic still worked; he had come almost an equal distance through a series of lucky breaks which he could not regard as the product of pure chance; and in his pocket the ruby talisman continued to emit a faint warmth which was that of no ordinary stone, natural or synthetic. Like all proverbs, Ware knew, the old saw that the Devil looks after his own was only half true; nevertheless the feeling that he had come all this way on some errand continued to persist, together with a growing conviction that he had never in fact known what it was. He would find out when he arrived; in the meantime, he was travelling on the Devil's business, and would not die until it was concluded.

He would have liked to have stopped over in Flagstaff to inspect the famous observatory where Percival Lowell had produced such complicated maps of the wholly illusory canals of Mars and where Tombaugh had discovered Pluto – and where in the sky did those planets stand, now that their gods had clashed frontally? – but under the circumstances he did not dare. He still had the Grand Canyon and the Lake Mead area to cross; then, skirting northwards around the Spring Mountains to the winter resort town of Death Valley, in which he hoped to be able to get some word about exactly where in the valley proper the perimeter of Nether Hell had surfaced. He had come far, but he still had far to go, and he was unlikely now to be able to hitch a ride in the direction of that roiling, flaming column of annihilation. Very well; now at last had come the time he had foreseen in the doomed farmhouse in Pennsylvania, when he would have to steal a car. He did not think that it would be difficult.

Father Domenico too had come far, and had equally good reasons to be quite certain that he would still have been in Italy had it not been for some kind of supernatural intervention. He stood now at dusk in the shadow of the 11,000-foot Telescope Peak, looking eastwards and downwards to where the city of Dis flamed sullenly in the shadow of the Valley of Death itself against the stark backdrop of the Amargosa Range. That valley had been cut by the Amargosa River, but there had been no river there within the memory of civilized man; the annual rainfall now was well under two inches.

And he was equally certain of supernatural protection. The valley had held the world's second-ranking heat record of 134°F, but although it was immensely hotter than that down here now, Father Domenico felt only a mild glow, as though he had just stepped out of a bath. When he had first come down from the mountain, he had been horrified to find the vitrified desert washing the foothills scattered with hundreds of strange, silent, misshapen grey forms, only vaguely human at first sight, which had proven to be stricken soldiers. He had tried to minister to them, but the attempt had proven hopeless: of the bodies in the few suits he was able to investigate most were shrunken mummies, and the rest had apparently died even more horribly. He wondered what on Earth could have happened here. His elevation from the waters to the mountain had taken place in a mystic rapture without which, indeed, it would have been impossible, but which had taken him rather out of touch with mundane events.

But whatever the answer, he had no choice but to press on. As he descended the last of the foothills, he saw on the floor of the valley, approaching him along what had once been the old watercourse and more recently a modern road, three tiny figures. In so far as he could tell at this distance, they wore no more visible, earthly protections against what the valley had become than he did himself. Yet they did not seem to be demons.

Full of wonder, he scrambled down towards them; but when they met, and he recognized them, he wondered only that he should have been at all amazed. The meeting, he saw instantly now, had been foreordained.

'How did *you* get here?' Baines demanded at once. It was not easy to determine of whom he was asking the question, but while Father Domenico wondered whether it was worthwhile trying to explain trance levitation, and if so how he would go about it, Theron Ware said:

'I can't think of a more trivial question under the circumstance, Dr Baines. We're here, that's the important thing – and I perceive that we are all under some kind of magical aegis, or we would all be dead. This raises the question of what we hope to accomplish, that we should be so protected. Father, may I ask what your intentions are?'

'Nothing prevents you from asking,' Father Domenico said, 'but you are the last human being in the world to whom I would give the answer.'

'Well, I'll tell you what *my* intentions are,' said Baines. 'My intentions are to stay in the bottommost levels of Denver and wait for this all to blow over, if it's ever going to. One thing you learn fast in the munitions business is that it's a very good idea to stay off battlefields. But my intentions have nothing to do with the matter. I was ordered to come here by the Sabbath Goat, and here I am.'

'Oh?' Ware said with interest. 'He finally came for you?'

'No, I have to come to him. He broke into a closed-circuit television transmission in Denver to tell me so. He didn't even mention Jack; I only brought him along for the company, since it didn't turn out to be forbidden.'

'And small thanks for that,' Ginsberg said, though apparently without rancour. 'If there's anything in the world that I hate, it's exercise. Vertical exercise, anyhow.'

'Have either of you two seen him at all?' Baines added.

Father Domenico remained stubbornly silent, but Ware said: 'PUT SATANACHIA? No, and somehow I doubt that I will, now. I seem to have put myself under the protection of another demon, although one subordinate to the Goat. Confusion of purpose is almost the natural state among demons, but in this instance I think it couldn't have happened without direct Satanic intent.'

'I was given my marching orders in the name of "Our Father Below",' Baines said. 'If he's interested in me, the chances are that he's even more interested in you, all right. But what did you think you were up to?'

'Originally I thought I might try to intercede, or at least to plead for some sort of cease-fire – as you were trying to do from the opposite end in Denver. But that's a dead letter now, and the result is that I have no more idea why I am here than you do. All I can say is that whatever the reason, I don't think there can be much hope in it.'

'While we live, there is always hope,' Father Domenico said suddenly.

The black magician pointed at the tremendous city towards which, volitionlessly, they had been continuing to walk all this time. 'To be able to see *that* at all means that we have already passed far beyond mere futility. All the sins of the Leopard, the sins of incontinence, are behind us, which means that the gate is behind us too: the gate upon which it is carven in Dirghic, LAY DOWN ALL HOPE, YOU THAT GO IN BY ME.'

'We are alive.' Father Domenico said stolidly, 'and I utterly deny and repudiate those sins.'

'You may not do so,' Ware said, his voice gradually rising in intensity. 'Look here, Father, this is all so mysterious, and the future looks so black, that it's ridiculous for us not to make available and to make use of any little scraps of information that we may have to share. The very symbolism of our presence here is simple, patent and ineluctable, and you as a Karest in white magic should be the first to see it. To take the circles of Upper Hell in order, Ginsberg here is almost a type creation of the lust-dominated man; I have sold my soul for unlimited knowledge, which in the last analysis is surely nothing more than an instance of gluttony; and you have only to look around this battlefield to see that Dr Baines is an instrument of wrath *par excellence.*'

'You have skipped the Fourth Circle,' Father Domenico said, 'with obvious didactic intent, but your arrogance is wasted upon me. I draw no moral from it whatsoever.'

'Oh, indeed? Wasn't treasure finding once the chiefest use of white magic? And isn't the monkish life-withdrawal from the snares, affairs *and duties* of the world for the sake of one's own soul – as plain a case of hoarding as one could ask for? It is in fact so egregious an example of that very sin that not even canonization remits it; I can tell you of my own certain knowledge that every single pillar saint went instantly to Hell, and of even the simple monks, none escaped except those few like Matthew Paris and Roger of Wendover who also led useful worldly lives.

'And regardless of what your fatuous friends on Monte Albano believed, there is no efficacious dispensation for the practice of white magic, because there is no such thing as white magic. It is all black, black, black as the ace of spades, and you have imperilled your immortal soul by practising it not even for your own benefit, but on commission for others; if that does not make you a spendthrift as well as a hoarder, what would you call it?

'Think at last, Father: Why did your crucifix burst in your hands at the last minute on Black Easter? Wasn't it because you tried to use it for personal gain? What does it symbolize, if not total submission to whatever may be

Willed? Yet you tried to use it – the ultimate symbol of resignation in the face of death – to save your own paltry life. Really, Father Domenico. I think the time has come for us to be frank with each other – for you as surely as for the rest of us!'

'Hear, hear,' Baines said with rather a sick grin.

After six or seven paces of silence, Father Domenico said:

'I am terribly afraid you are right. I came here in the hope of forcing the demons to admit that God still lives, and I saw what I thought were indisputable signs of Divine sponsorship. Unless you are simply more subtle a casuist than any I have ever encountered before, even in print, it now appears that I had no right to think any such thing ... which means that the real reason for my presence here is no less mysterious than that for yours. I cannot say that this increases my understanding any.'

'It establishes a common ignorance,' said Ware. 'And as far as your original assumption is concerned, Father, it suggests some basic uniformity of purpose which I must admit is certainly not characteristic of demons, whatever that may mean. But I think we shall not have long to wait for the answer, gentlemen. It appears that we have arrived.'

They all looked up. The colossal barbican of Dis loomed over them.

'One thing is surely clear,' Father Domenico whispered. 'We have been making this journey all our lives.'

12

No Beatrice sponsored them, and no Vergil led them; but as they approached the great ward, the undamaged portcullis rose, and the gates swung inward in massive silence. No demons mocked them, no Furies challenged them, no angel had to cross the Styx to bring them passage! They were admitted, simply and non-committally.

Beyond the barbican, they found the citadel transformed. The Nether Hell of diuturnal torture, which had withstood the bombardment of Man without damage to so much as a twig in the Wood of the Suicides, was gone entirely. Perhaps in some sense it had never been there at all, but was still located where it had always been, in Eternity, not on Earth; a place still reserved for the dead. For these four still-living men, it had vanished.

In its place there stood a clean, well-lighted city like an illustration from some Utopian romance; it looked, in fact, like a cross between the city of the future in the old film *Things to Come* and a fully automated machine shop. It screamed, hammered and roared like a machine shop as well.

The grossly misshapen, semi-bestial forms of the demons had also vanished. The metropolis instead appeared to be peopled now chiefly by human beings, although their appearance could scarcely be described as normal.

Male and female alike, they were strikingly beautiful; but their beauty swiftly became cloying, for except for sexual characteristics they were completely identical, as though they were all members of the same clone – one which had been genetically selected out to produce creatures modelled after the statuary fronting public buildings, or the souls in the Dante illustrations of Gustav Doré. Both sexes wore identical skirted tabards made of some grey material which looked like papier-mâché, across the breasts of which long numbers had been woven in metallically glittering script.

A second and much less numerous group wore a different uniform, vaguely military in cast, an impression reinforced by the fact that these were mostly to be seen standing stiffly at street intersections. Heroic in mould though the majority were, the minority were even more statuesque and their common face was evenly pleasant but stern, like that of an idealized father.

The others wore no expression at all, unless their very expressionlessness was a reflection of acute boredom – which would not have been surprising, for no one of this class seemed to have anything to do. The work of the metropolis, which seemed to be exclusively that of producing that continual, colossal din, went on behind the blank facades apparently without need of any sentient tending or intervention. They never spoke. As the four pilgrims moved onward towards the centre of the city, they passed frequent exhibitions of open, public sexuality, more often than not in groups; at first Jack Ginsberg regarded these with the liveliest interest, but it soon faded as it became apparent that even this was bored and pleasureless.

There were no children; and no animals.

Initially, the travellers had hesitated, when the two magicians had discovered that with the transformation they could no longer trust to Dante to show them the way, and Baines's memory of the aerial photographs had become similarly useless. They had proceeded more or less by instinct towards the centre of the din. After a while, however, they found that they had been silently joined by four of the policing demons, though whether they were being led or herded never did become clear. The grimly ambiguous escort heightened the impression of a guided tour of some late nineteenth-century world-of-tomorrow which was to include awe-inspiring visits to the balloon works, the crèches, the giant telegraph centre and the palace of folk arts, only to wind up in a corrective discipline hospital for the anti-social.

It was as though they were being given a preview of what the future of humanity would be like under demonic rule – not wholly unpredictable as a foretaste, but in content as well, as if the demons were trying to put the best possible face on the matter. In so doing, they had ingenuously embodied in their citadel nothing worse than a summary and epitomization of what pre-Apocalyptic, post-industrial Man had been systematically creating for himself. St Augustine, Goethe and Milton all had observed that the Devil, by constantly seeking evil, always did good, but here was an inversion of that happy fault: A demonstration that demons are at their worst when doing their best.

Many of Baines's most lucrative ideas for weaponry had been stolen bodily, through the intermediary of the Mamaroneck Research Institute from the unpaid imaginations of science-fiction writers, and it was he who first gave voice to the thought:

'I always thought it'd be Hell to actually have to live in a place like this,' he shouted. 'And now I know it.'

Nobody answered him; but it was more than possible that this was because nobody had heard him.

But only the veritable Hell is forever. After some unknown but finite time, they found themselves passing between the Doric columns and under the golden architrave of that high capital which is called Pandemonium, and the brazen doors folded open for them.

Inside, the clamour was muffled to a veiled and hollow booming, for the vast jousting field that was this hall had been made to hold the swarming audience for a panel of a thousand, but there was no one in it now besides themselves and the demon soldiers but one solitary, distant, intolerable star.

Not that subsidiary triumvir PUT SATANACHIA the Sabbath Goat who had promised himself to them, and they to him, on Black Easter morn; but that archetypal dropout, the Lie that knows no End, the primeval Parent-sponsored Rebel, the Eternal Enemy, the Great Nothing itself

SATAN MEKRATRIG

There was of course no more Death Valley sunlight here, and the effect of an implacably ultramodern city with its artificial gasglow glare was also gone. But the darkness was not quite complete. A few cressets hung blazing high in mid-air, so few that their light was spread evenly throughout the great arch of the ceiling, like the artificial sky of a planetarium dome simulating that moment between dusk and full night when only Lucifer is bright enough to be visible yet. Towards that glow they moved, and as they moved, it grew.

But the creature, they saw at last, was not the light, which shone instead upon him. The fallen cherub below it was still very nearly the same immense, brooding, cruelly deformed, angelic face that Dante had seen and Milton imagined: triple-faced in yellow, red and black, bat-winged, shag-pelted and so huge that the floor of the great hall cut him off at the breast – he must have measured five hundred yards from crown to hoof. Like the eyes, the wings were six, but they no longer beat frenziedly to stir the three winds that froze Cocytus; nor now did the six eyes weep. Instead, each of the faces – the Semitic Ignorance, the Japhetic Hatred, the Hamitic Impotence – was frozen in an expression of despair too absolute for further grief.

The pilgrims saw these things, but only with half an eye, for their attention was focused instead upon the light which both revealed and shadowed them:

The terrible crowned head of the Worm was surmounted by a halo.

13

The demonic guards had not followed them in, and the great Figure was motionless and uttered no orders; but in that hollowly roaring silence, the pilgrims felt compelled to speak. They looked at each other almost shyly, like school children brought to be introduced to some king or president, each wanting to be bold enough to draw attention to himself, but waiting for someone else to break the ice. Again nothing was said. but somehow agreement was arrived at: Father Domenico should speak first.

Looking aloft, but not quite into those awful countenances, the white monk said:

'Father of Lies. I thought it was my mission to come here and compel thee to speak the truth. I arrived as if by miracle, or borne by faith; and in my journeyings saw many evidences that the rule of Hell on Earth is not complete. Nor has that Goat your prince yet come for me, or for my ... colleagues here, despite his threat and promise. Then I also saw the election of your demon Pope, the very Antichrist that PUT SATANACHIA said had been dispensed with, as unnecessary to a victorious demonry. I concluded then that God was not dead after all, and someone should come into thy city to assert His continuing authority.

'I stand before thee impotent – my very crucifix was shattered in my hands on Black Easter morning – but nevertheless I charge thee and demand that thou shalt state thy limitations, and abide the course to which they hold thee.'

There was no answer. After a long wait made it clear that there was not going to be. Theron Ware said next:

'Master, thou knowest me well, I think; I am the last black magician in the world, and the most potent ever to practise that high art. I have seen signs and wonders much resembling those mentioned by Father Domenico, but draw from them rather different conclusion. Instead, it seems to me that the final conflict with Michael and all his host cannot be over yet – despite the obvious fact that thou hast won vast advantages already. And if this is true, then it is perhaps an error for thee to make war upon mankind, or for them to make war on thee, with the greater issue still in doubt. Since thou art still granting some of us some favours of magic, there must still exist some aid which we might give thee. Hence I came here to find out what that aid might be and to proffer it, if it were within my powers.'

No answer. Baines said sullenly:

'I came because I was ordered. But since I'm here, I may as well offer my opinion in the matter, which is much like Ware's. I tried to persuade the human generals not to attack the city, but I failed. Now that they've seen that it can't be attacked – and I'm sure they noticed that you didn't wipe out all their forces when you had the chance – I might have better luck. At least I'll try again, if it's of any use to you.

'I can't imagine any way we could help you carry the war to Heaven, since we were no good against your own local fortress. And besides, I prefer to remain neutral. But getting our generals off *your* back might relieve you of a nuisance, if you've got more serious business still afoot. If that's not good enough, don't blame me. I didn't come here of my own free will.'

The terrible silence persisted, until at last even Jack Ginsberg was forced to speak.

'If you're waiting for me, I have no suggestions,' he said. 'I guess I'm grateful for past favours, too, but I don't understand what's going on and I didn't want to get involved. I was only doing my job, but as far as my private life goes, I'd just as soon be left to work it out for myself from now on. As far as I'm concerned, it's nobody's business but my own.'

Now, at last, the great wings stirred slightly; and then the three faces spoke. There was no audible voice, but as the vast lips moved, the words formed in their minds, like sparks crawling along logs in a dying fire.

> 'O yee of little faith,' the Worm set on,
> 'Yee whose coming fame had bodied forth
> A hope archemic even to this Deep
> That Wee should be amerced of golden Throne,
> The which to Us a rack is, by thine alchymie.
> Is this thy sovran Reason? this the draff,
> Are these sollicitations all the surn
> And sorrie Substance of thine high renoune?
> Art thou accomplisht to so mean an end
> After such journeyings of flame and dole
> As once strook doun Heav'n's angels? Say it so,
> In prosie speach or numerous prosodie,
> Wee Will not be deceav'd; so much the rather
> Shall Wee see yee rased from off the bord
> Twixt Hell and Heav'n, as the fearful marine,

Ingled by the wave 'mongst spume and rock,
Sees craft and hope alike go all to ruin.
Yet yields up not his soul than Wee shall yield
The last, supreame endeavour of this fearfull Jarr.
'Yet how to body forth to thy blind eyes,
Who have not poets' blindnesse, or the night
Shed by black suns, 'thout which to tell the tale
Of Earth its occupation by the demon breed
Is sole remaining hearth, but to begin?
O 'suaging Nigh?, console Mee now! and hold
My Demy-godhood but a little while
Abeyanc'd from its death in Godhood's dawn!
'O yee of little faith. Wee tell thee this:
Indeed our God is dead; or dead to us.
But in some depth of measure beyond grasp
Remains His principle, as doth the sight
Of drowsy horoscoper, much bemus'd
By vastnesses celestial and horrid
To his tinie system, when first he looks
Through the optic glass at double stars,
Some residuum apprehend; so do we now.
O happie matrix! for there is naught else
That all are left with. It in this inheres.
That Good is independent, but the bad
Cannot alone survive; the evil Deed
Doth need the Holie Light to lend it Sense
And apprehension; for the Good is free
To act or not, while evill hath been will'd
Insensate and compulsive to bring Good
Still greater highths unto, as climber see'th
From toil and suff'ring to th'uttermost Alp,
Best th'unattainable islands of the skye.
'In this yee Sinners are in harmonie,
Antient and grand, though meanlie did yee move
About your severall ends since first this subject.
Thou, thaumaturgist Blacke, and thou,
O merchant peccant to the deaths of fellowe men,
Contrived in evill all thy predecessors human.
But save Judas I was wont to gnaw before,
T'outdo, by willingnesse to plunge
All mankinde in a nights's Abysse
Only for perverse aesthetick Joyce

And Thrill of Masterie, there then ensu'd
That universall Warr in which the victorie
Hath faln to Hellish host, so Wee rejoyc'd;
Yet hold! for once releas'd from Paynes
Decreed to be forever, all our Band
Of demons foul, who once were angels bright
Conceiv'd in simpler time and ever since
Entomb'd amidst the horrors of the Pit.
Did find the world of men so much more foul
E'en than in the fabulous reign of witches
That all bewilder'd fell they and amazed.
Yet after hastie consult, they set to.
To preach and practise evill with all pow'r.
Adhering to grounded rules long understood.
A Greshamite oeconomium.
    But eftsoons
That vacuous space where once Eternall Good
Had dwelt demanded to be filled. Though God
Be dead. His Throne remains. And so below
As 'twas above, last shall be first, and Wee.
Who by the Essenes' rule are qualified
Beyond all remaining others, must become –
In all protesting agonie – the chief
Of powers for Good in all the Universe
Uncircumscribed; but let yee not forget.
Already Good compared to such as thee.
Whose evill remains will'd! And as for Us.
What doth it matter what Wee most desire?
While chained in the Pit, Wee were condemn'd
To be eternall, but paroll'd to Earth
Were once more caught by Change; and how
Could Wickednesse Incorporeal grow still worse?
And so, behold! Wee are a God.
    But not
Perhaps The God. Wee do not know the end.
Perhaps indeed Jehovah is not dead.
But mere retir'd, withdrawn or otherwise
Contracted hath, as Zohar subtle saith,
His Essence Infinite; and, Epicurean, waits
The outcome vast with vast indifference.
Yet natheless His universe requires
That all things changing must tend t'ward His state.

If, then, wee must proclaim His Role historic
Abandond in Deific suicide,
Why this felo de Se except to force
That part on Man – who fail'd it out of hand?
Now, as Wee sought to be in the Beginning,
SATAN is God; and in Mine agonie
More just a God and wrathfuller by far
Than He Who thunder'd down on Israel!
'Yet not forever, though our rule will seem
Forever. Man, O Man, I beg of you,
Take, O take from mee this Cup away!
I cannot bear it. You, and onely you.
You alone, alone can God become,
As always He intended. This downfall
Our mutual Armageddon here below
Is punishment dire enough, but for your Kinde
A worse awaits; for you must rear yourselves
As ready for the Resurrection. I
Have slammed that door behind; yours is to come.
On that far future Day. I shall be there,
The burning Keys to put into your hands.
'I, SATAN MEKRATRIG, I can no longer bear
This deepest, last and bitterest of all
My fell damnations: That at last I know
I never wanted to be God at all;
And so, by winning all, All have I lost.'

THE SEEDLING STARS

To H. L. Gold

BOOK ONE

Seeding Program

1

The spaceship resumed humming around Sweeney without his noticing the change. When Capt. Meiklejon's voice finally came again from the wall speaker, Sweeney was still lying buckled to his bunk in a curious state of tranquility he had never known before, and couldn't possibly have described, even to himself. Though he had a pulse, he might otherwise have concluded that he was dead. It took him several minutes to respond.

'Sweeney, do you hear me? Are – you all right?'

The brief hesitation in the pilot's breathing made Sweeney grin. From Meiklejon's point of view, and that of most of the rest of humanity, Sweeney was all wrong. He was, in fact, dead.

The heavily insulated cabin, with its own airlock to the outside, and no access for Sweeney at all to the rest of the ship, was a testimonial to his wrongness. So was Meiklejon's tone: the voice of a man addressing, not another human being, but something that had to be kept in a vault.

A vault designed to protect the universe outside it – not to protect its contents from the universe.

'Sure, I'm all right,' Sweeney said, snapping the buckle and sitting up. He checked the thermometer, which still registered its undeviating minus 194°F – the mean surface temperature of Ganymede, moon number III of Jupiter. 'I was dozing, sort of. What's up?'

'I'm putting the ship into her orbit; we're about a thousand miles up from the satellite now. I thought you might want to take a look.'

'Sure enough. Thanks, Mickey.'

The wall speaker said, 'Yeah. Talk to you later.' Sweeney grappled for the guide rail and pulled himself over to the cabin's single bullseye port, maneuvering with considerable precision. For a man to whom 1/6 Earth gravity is normal, free fall – a situation of no gravity at all – is only an extreme case.

Which was what Sweeney was, too. A human being – but an extreme case.

He looked out. He knew exactly what he would see; he had studied it exhaustively from photos, from teletapes, from maps, and through telescopes both at home on the Moon and on Mars. When you approach Ganymede at inferior conjunction, as Meiklejon was doing, the first thing that hits you in the eye is the huge oval blot called Neptune's Trident - so named by the earliest Jovian explorers because it was marked with the Greek letter *psi* on the old Howe composite map. The name had turned out to have been well chosen: that blot is a deep, many-pronged sea, largest at the eastern end, which runs from about 120° to 165° in longitude, and from about 10° to 33° north latitude. A sea of what? Oh, water, of course – water frozen rock-solid forever, and covered with a layer of rock-dust about three inches thick.

East of the Trident, and running all the way north to the pole, is a great triangular marking called the Gouge, a torn-up, root-entwined, avalanche-shaken valley which continues right around the pole and back up into the other hemisphere, fanning out as it goes. (Up because north to space pilots, as to astronomers, is down.) There is nothing quite like the Gouge on any other planet, although at inferior conjunction, when your ship is coming down on Ganymede at the 180° meridian, it is likely to remind you of Syrtis Major on Mars.

There is, however, no real resemblance. Syrtis Major is perhaps the pleasantest land on all of Mars. The Gouge, on the other hand, is – a gouge.

On the eastern rim of this enormous scar, at long. 218°, N. lat. 32°, is an isolated mountain about 9,000 feet high, which had no name as far as Sweeney knew; it was marked with the letter *pi* on the Howe map. Because of its isolation, it can be seen easily from Earth's Moon in a good telescope when the sunrise terminator lies in that longitude, its peak shining detached in the darkness like a little star. A semicircular shelf juts westward out over the Gouge from the base of Howe's *pi,* its sides bafflingly sheer for a world which shows no other signs of folded strata.

It was on that shelf that the other Adapted Men lived.

Sweeney stared down at the nearly invisible mountain with its star-fire peak for a long time, wondering why he was not reacting. Any appropriate emotion would do: anticipation, alarm, eagerness, anything at all, even fear. For that matter, having been locked up in a safe for over two months should by now have driven him foaming to get out, even if only to join the Adapted Men. Instead, the tranquility persisted. He was unable to summon more than a momentary curiosity over Howe's *pi* before his eye was drawn away to Jupiter himself, looming monstrous and insanely-colored only 600,000 miles away, give or take a few thousand. And even that planet had attracted him only because it was brighter; otherwise, it had no meaning.

'Mickey?' he said, forcing himself to look back down into the Gouge.

'Right here, Sweeney. How does it look?'

'Oh, like a relief map. That's how they all look. Where are you going to put me down? Don't the orders leave it up to us?'

'Yeah. But I don't think there's any choice,' Meiklejon's voice said, less hesitantly. 'It'll have to be the big plateau – Howe's H.'

Sweeney scanned the oval mare with a mild distaste. Standing on that, he would be as conspicuous as if he'd been planted in the middle of the Moon's Mare Crisium. He said so.

'You've no choice,' Meiklejon repeated calmly. He burped the rockets several times. Sweeney's weight returned briefly, tried to decide which way it wanted to throw itself, and then went away again. The ship was now in its orbit; but whether Meiklejon had set it up to remain put over its present coordinates, or instead it was to cruise criss-cross over the whole face of the satellite, Sweeney couldn't tell, and didn't ask. The less he knew about that, the better.

'Well, it's a long drop,' Sweeney said. 'And that atmosphere isn't exactly the thickest in the system. I'll have to fall in the lee of the mountain. I don't want to have to trudge a couple of hundred miles over Howe's H.'

'On the other hand,' Meiklejon said, 'if you come down too close, our friends down there will spot your parachute. Maybe it'd be better if we dropped you into the Gouge, after all. There's so much tumbled junk down there that the radar echoes must be tremendous – not a chance of their spotting a little thing like a man on a parachute.'

'No, thank you. There's still optical spotting, and a foil parachute looks nothing like a rock spur, even to an Adapted Man. It'll have to be behind the mountain, where I'm in both optical *and* radar shadow at once. Besides, how could I climb out of the Gouge onto the shelf? They didn't plant themselves on the edge of a cliff for nothing.'

'That's right,' Meiklejon said. 'Well, I've got the catapult pointed. I'll suit up and join you on the hull.'

'All right. Tell me again just what you're going to do while I'm gone, so I won't find myself blowing the whistle when you're nowhere around.' The sound of a suit locker being opened came tinnily over the intercom. Sweeney's chute harness was already strapped on, and getting the respirator and throat-mikes into place would only take a moment. Sweeney needed no other protection.

'I'm to stay up here with all power off except maintenance for 300 days,' Meiklejon's voice, sounding more distant now, was repeating. 'Supposedly by that time you'll have worked yourself in good with our friends down there and will know the setup. I stand ready to get a message from you on a fixed frequency. You're to send me only a set of code letters; I feed them into the computer, the comp tells me what to do and I act accordingly. If I don't hear from you after 300 days, I utter a brief but heartfelt prayer and go home. Beyond that, God help me, I don't know a thing.'

'That's plenty,' Sweeney told him. 'Let's go.'

Sweeney went out his personal airlock. Like all true interplanetary craft, Meiklejon's ship had no overall hull. She consisted of her essential components, including the personnel globe, held together by a visible framework of girders and I-beams. It was one of the longest of the latter, one which was already pointed toward Howe's H, which would serve as the 'catapult'.

Sweeney looked up at the globe of the satellite. The old familiar feeling of falling came over him for a moment; he looked down, reorienting himself to the ship, until it went away. He'd be going in that direction soon enough.

Meiklejon came around the bulge of the personnel globe, sliding his shoes along the metal. In his bulky, misshapen spacesuit, it was he who looked like the unhuman member of the duo.

'Ready?' he said.

Sweeney nodded and lay face down on the I-beam, snapping the guide-clips on his harness into place around it. He could feel Meiklejon's mitts at his back, fastening the JATO unit; he could see nothing now, however, but the wooden sled that would protect his body from the beam.

'Okay,' the pilot said. 'Good luck, Sweeney.'

'Thanks. Count me off, Mickey.'

'Coming up on five seconds. Five. Four. Three. Two. One. *Hack.*'

The JATO unit shuddered and dealt Sweeney a nearly paralyzing blow between his shoulder-blades. For an instant the acceleration drove him down into his harness, and the sled spraddled against the metal of the I-beam.

Then, suddenly, the vibration stopped. He was flying free. A little belatedly, he jerked the release ring.

The sled went curving away from under him, dwindling rapidly among the stars. The pressure at his back cut out as the JATO unit, still under power, flamed ahead of him. The instantly-dissipated flick of heat from its exhaust made him ill for a moment; then it had vanished. It would hit too hard to leave anything where it landed but a hole.

Nothing was left but Sweeney, falling toward Ganymede, head first.

From almost the beginning, from that day unrememberably early in his childhood when he had first realized that the underground dome on the Moon was all there was to the universe for nobody but himself, Sweeney had wanted to be human; wanted it with a vague, impersonal ache which set quickly into a chill bitterness of manner and outlook at his unique everyday life, and in dreams with flares of searing loneliness which became more infrequent but also more intense as he matured, until such a night would leave him as shaken and mute, sometimes for several days at a stretch, as an escape from a major accident.

The cadre of psychologists, psychiatrists and analysts assigned to him did what they could, but that was not very much. Sweeney's history contained almost nothing that was manipulable by any system of psychotherapy developed to help human beings. Nor were the members of the cadre ever able to agree among themselves what the prime goal of such therapy should be: whether to help Sweeney to live with the facts of his essential inhumanity, or to fan instead that single spark of hope which the non-medical people on the Moon were constantly holding out toward Sweeney as the sole reason for his existence.

The facts were simple and implacable. Sweeney was an Adapted Man – adapted, in this instance, to the bitter cold, the light gravity, and the thin stink of atmosphere which prevailed on Ganymede. The blood that ran in his veins, and the sol substrate of his every cell, was nine-tenths liquid ammonia; his bones were Ice IV; his respiration was a complex hydrogen-to-methane cycle based not upon catalysis by an iron-bearing pigment, but upon the locking and unlocking of a double sulfur bond; and he could survive for weeks, if he had to, upon a diet of rock dust.

He had always been this way. What had made him so had happened to him literally before he had been conceived: the application, to the germ cells which had later united to form him, of an elaborate constellation of techniques – selective mitotic poisoning, pinpoint X-irradiation, tectogenetic microsurgery, competitive metabolic inhibition, and perhaps fifty more whose names he had never even heard – which collectively had been christened 'pantropy'. The word, freely retranslated, meant 'changing everything' – and it fitted.

As the pantropists had changed in advance the human pattern in Sweeney's shape and chemistry, so they had changed his education, his world, his thoughts, even his ancestors. You didn't make an Adapted Man with just a wave of the wand, Dr. Alfven had once explained proudly to Sweeney over the intercom. Even the ultimate germ cells were the emergents of a hundred previous generations, bred one from another before they had passed the zygote stage like one-celled animals, each one biassed a little farther toward the cyanide and ice and everything nice that little boys like Sweeney were made of. The psych cadre picked off Dr. Alfven at the end of that same week, at the regular review of the tapes of what had been said to Sweeney and what he had found to say back, but they need hardly have taken the trouble. Sweeney had never heard a nursery rhyme, any more than he had ever experienced the birth trauma or been exposed to the Oedipus complex. He was a law unto himself, with most of the whereases blank.

He noticed, of course, that Alfven failed to show up when his next round was due, but this was commonplace. Scientists came and went around the great sealed cavern, always accompanied by the polite and beautifully uniformed private police of the Greater Earth Port Authority, but they rarely lasted very long. Even among the psych cadre there was always a peculiar tension, a furious constraint which erupted periodically into pitched shouting battles. Sweeney never found out what the shouting was about because the sound to the outside was always cut as soon as the quarrels began, but he noticed that some of the participants never showed up again.

'Where's Dr. Emory? Isn't this his day?'

'He finished his tour of duty.'

'But I want to talk to him. He promised to bring me a book. Won't he be back for a visit?'

'I don't think so, Sweeney. He's retired. Don't worry about him, he'll get along just fine. I'll bring you your book.'

It was after the third of these incidents that Sweeney was let out on the surface of the Moon for the first time – guarded, it was true, by five men in spacesuits, but Sweeney didn't care. The new freedom seemed enormous to him, and his own suit, only a token compared to what the Port cops had to wear, hardly seemed to exist. It was his first foretaste of the liberty he was to have, if the many hints could be trusted, after his job was done. He could even see the Earth, where people lived.

About the job he knew everything there was to know, and knew it as second nature. It had been drummed into him from his cold and lonely infancy, always with the same command at the end:

'We must have those men back.'

Those six words were the reason for Sweeney; they were also Sweeney's sole hope. The Adapted Men had to be recaptured and brought back to Earth – or more exactly, back to the dome on the Moon, the only place besides Ganymede where they could be kept alive. And if they could not all be recaptured – he was to entertain this only as a possibility – he must at least come back with Dr. Jacob Rullman. Only Rullman would be sure to know the ultimate secret: how to turn an Adapted Man back into a human being.

Sweeney understood that Rullman and his associates were criminals, but how grievous their crime had been was a question he had never tried to answer for himself. His standards were too sketchy. It was clear from the beginning, however, that the colony on Ganymede had been set up without Earth's sanction, by methods of which Earth did not approve (except for special cases like Sweeney), and that Earth wanted it broken up. Not by force, for Earth wanted to know first what Rullman knew, but by the elaborate artifice which was Sweeney himself.

We must have those men back. After that, the hints said – never promising anything directly – Sweeney could be made human, and know a better freedom than walking the airless surface of the Moon with five guards.

It was usually after one of these hints that one of those suddenly soundless quarrels would break out among the staff. Any man of normal intelligence would have come to suspect that the hints were less than well founded upon any real expectation, and Sweeney's training helped to make him suspicious early; but in the long run he did not care. The hints offered his only hope and he accepted them with hope but without expectation. Besides, the few opening words of such quarrels which he had overheard before the intercom clicked off had suggested that there was more to the disagreement than simple doubt of the convertibility of an Adapted Man. It had been Emory, for instance, who had burst out unexpectedly and explosively:

'But suppose Rullman was right—?'

Click.

Right about what? Is a lawbreaker ever 'right'? Sweeney could not know. Then there had been the technie who had said 'It's the cost that's the trouble with terra-forming' – what did that mean? – and had been hustled out of the monitoring chamber on some trumped-up errand hardly a minute later. There were many such instances, but inevitably Sweeney failed to put the fragments together into any pattern. He decided only that they did not bear directly upon his chances of becoming human, and promptly abandoned them in the vast desert of his general ignorance.

In the long run, only the command was real – the command and the nightmares. *We must have those men back.* Those six words were the reason why Sweeney, like a man whose last effort to awaken has failed, was falling head first toward Ganymede.

The Adapted Men found Sweeney halfway up the great col which provided the only access to their cliff-edge colony from the plateau of Howe's H. He did not recognize them; they conformed to none of the photographs he had memorized; but they accepted his story readily enough. And he had not needed to pretend exhaustion – Ganymede's gravity was normal to him, but it had been a long trek and a longer climb.

He was surprised to find, nevertheless, that he had enjoyed it. For the first time in his life he had walked unguarded, either by men or by mechanisms, on a world where he felt physically at home; a world without walls, a world where he was essentially alone. The air was rich and pleasant, the winds came from wherever they chose to blow, the temperature in the col was considerably below what had been allowable in the dome on the Moon, and there was sky all around him, tinged with indigo and speckled with stars that twinkled now and then.

He would have to be careful. It would be all too easy to accept Ganymede as home. He had been warned against that, but somehow he had failed to realize that the danger would be not merely real, but – seductive.

The young men took him swiftly the rest of the way to the colony. They had been as incurious as they had been anonymous. Rullman was different. The look of stunned disbelief on the scientist's face, as Sweeney was led into his high-ceilinged, rock-walled office, was so total as to be frightening. He said: 'What's this!'

'We found him climbing the col. We thought he'd gotten lost, but he says he belongs to the parent flight.'

'Impossible,' Rullman said. 'Quite impossible.' And then he fell silent, studying the newcomer from crown to toe. The expression of shock dimmed only slightly.

The long scrutiny gave Sweeney time to look back. Rullman was older than his pictures, but that was natural; if anything, he looked a little less marked by age than Sweeney had anticipated. He was spare, partly bald, and slope-shouldered, but the comfortable pod under his belt-line which had shown in the photos was almost gone now. Evidently living on Ganymede had hardened him some. The pictures had failed to prepare Sweeney for the man's eyes: they were as hooded and unsettling as an owl's.

'You'd better tell me who you are,' Rullman said at last. 'And how you got here. You aren't one of us, that's certain.'

'I'm Donald Leverault Sweeney,' Sweeney said. 'Maybe I'm not one of you, but my mother said I was. I got here in her ship. She said you'd take me in.'

Rullman shook his head. 'That's impossible, too. Excuse me, Mr. Sweeney, but you've probably no idea what a bombshell you are. You must be Shirley Leverault's child, then – but how did you get here? How did you survive all this time? Who kept you alive, and tended you, after we left the Moon? And above all, how did you get away from the Port cops? We knew that Port Earth found our Moon lab even before we abandoned it. I can hardly believe that you even exist.'

Nevertheless, the scientist's expression of flat incredulity was softening moment by moment. He was, Sweeney judged, already beginning to buy it. And necessarily: there Sweeney stood before him, breathing Ganymede's air, standing easily in Ganymede's gravity, with Ganymede's dust on his cold skin, a fact among inarguable facts.

'The Port cops found the big dome, all right,' Sweeney said. 'But they never found the little one, the pilot plant. Dad blew up the tunnel between the two before they landed – he was killed in the rock-slide. Of course I was still just a cell in a jug when that happened.'

'I see,' Rullman said thoughtfully. 'We picked up an explosion on our ship's instruments before we took off. But we thought it was the Port raiders beginning to bomb, unexpected though that was. Then they didn't destroy the big lab either, after all?'

'No,' Sweeney said. Rullman surely must know that; radio talk between Earth and Moon must be detectable at least occasionally out here. 'There were still some intercom lines left through to there; my mother used to spend a lot of time listening in on what was going on. So did I, after I was old enough to understand it. That was how we found out that the Ganymedian colony hadn't been bombed out, either.'

'But where did you get your power?'

'Most of it from our own strontium^{90} cell. Everything was shielded so the cops couldn't detect any stray fields. When the cell finally began to give out, we had to tap Port's main accumulator line – just for a little bit at first, but the drain kept going up.' He shrugged. 'Sooner or later they were bound to spot it – and did.'

Rullman was momentarily silent, and Sweeney knew that he was doing the pertinent arithmetic in his head, comparing the 20-year half-life of strontium[90] with Sweeney's and the Adapted Men's chronology. The figures would jibe, of course. The Port cops' briefing had been thorough about little details like that.

'It's still quite astounding, having to rethink this whole episode after so many years,' Rullman said. 'With all due respect, Mr. Sweeney, it's hard to imagine Shirley Leverault going through such an ordeal – and all alone, too, except for a child she could never even touch, a child as difficult and technical to tend as an atomic pile. I remember her as a frail, low-spirited girl, trailing along after us listlessly because Robert was in the project.' He frowned reminiscently. 'She used to say, "It's his job." She never thought of it as anything more than that.'

'*I* was her job,' Sweeney said evenly. The Port cops had tried to train him to speak bitterly when he mentioned his mother, but he had never been able to capture the emotion that they wanted him to imitate. He had found, however, that if he rapped out the syllables almost without inflection, they were satisfied with the effect. 'You misjudged her, Dr. Rullman – or else she changed after Dad was killed. She had guts enough for ten. And she got paid for it in the end. In the only coin the Port cops know how to pay.'

'I'm sorry,' Rullman said gently. 'But at least you got away. I'm sure that's as she would have wanted it. Where did the ship you spoke of come from?'

'Why, we always had it. It belonged to Dad, I suppose. It was stored in a natural chimney near our dome. When the cops broke into the monitoring room, I went out the other side of the dome, while they were – busy with mother, and beat it. There wasn't anything I could have done—'

'Of course, of course,' Rullman said, his voice low and quiet. 'You wouldn't have lasted a second in their air. You did the right thing. Go on.'

'Well, I got to the ship and got it off. I didn't have time to save anything but myself. They followed me all the way, but they didn't shoot. I think there's still one of them upstairs now.'

'We'll sweep for him, but there's nothing we can do about him in any case except keep him located. You bailed out, I gather.'

'Yes. Otherwise I wouldn't have had a chance – they seemed to want me back in the worst way. They must have the ship by now, and the coordinates for the colony too.'

'Oh, they've had those coordinates since we first landed,' Rullman said. 'You were lucky, Mr. Sweeney, and bold, too. You bring back a sense of immediacy that I haven't felt for years, since our first escape. But there's one more problem.'

'What is it? If I can help—'

'There's a test we'll have to make,' Rullman said. 'Your story seems to hold water; and I really don't see how you could have become what you are, unless you were really one of us. But we have to be certain.'

'Sure,' Sweeney said. 'Let's go.'

Rullman beckoned and led him out of the office through a low stone door. The corridor through which they passed was so like all those Sweeney had seen on the Moon that he scarcely bothered to notice it. Even the natural gravity and circulating, unprocessed air were soothing rather than distracting. It was the test that worried Sweeney, precisely because he knew that he would be helpless to affect the outcome. Either the Port Authority's experts had put him together cunningly enough to pass any test, or –

– or he would never have the chance to become human.

Rullman nodded Sweeney through another door into a long, low-ceilinged room furnished with half a dozen laboratory benches and a good deal of glassware. The air was more active here; as on the Moon, there were ventilators roiling it. Someone came around a towering, twisted fractionating apparatus in which many small bubbles orbited, and moved toward them. It was, Sweeney saw, a small glossy-haired girl, with white hands and dark eyes and delicately precise feet. She was wearing the typical technie's white jacket, and a plum-colored skirt.

'Hello, Dr. Rullman. Can I help?'

'Sure, if you can neglect that percolator a while, Mike. I want to run an ID typing; we've got a new man here. All right?'

'Oh, I think so. It'll take a minute to get the sera out.' She moved away from them to another desk and began to take out ampoules and shake them before a hooded light. Sweeney watched her. He had seen female technies before, but none so modelled, so unconstrained, or so – close as this. He felt light-headed, and hoped that he would not be asked to speak for a little while. There was sweat on his palms and a mumbling of blood in his inner ear, and he thought perhaps he might cry.

He had been plunged into the midst of his untested, long-delayed adolescence, and he liked it no better than anyone ever had.

But his diamond-etched caution did not blur completely. He remembered to remember that the girl had been as little surprised to see him as the two young men who had found him climbing the col had been. Why? Surely Dr. Rullman was not the only Adapted Man to know everyone in the colony by sight, and hence the only one able to feel consternation at the sight of a strange face. By this time, the settlers on Ganymede should know each other's slightest wrinkles, should have committed to memory every gesture, mannerism, dimple, shading, flaw or virtue that would help them to tell each other from the hostile remainder of overwhelming mankind.

The girl took Sweeney's hand, and for a moment the train of thought fell apart completely. Then there was a sharp stab in the tip of his right middle finger, and Mike was expressing droplets of blood into little puddles of bluish solution, spotted in sets of three on a great many slips of thin glass. Microscope slides; Sweeney had seen them before. As for the blood, she could have more if she wanted it.

But he returned doggedly to the question. Why had the young men and Mike failed to be surprised by Sweeney? Was it their age-group that counted? The original colonists of Ganymede would know both each other and their children by sight, while the youngsters to whom everything was essentially new would see nothing strange in a new face.

Children: then the colonists were fertile. There had never been a hint of that, back on the Moon. Of course it meant nothing to Sweeney personally. Not a thing.

'Why, you're trembling,' the girl said in a troubled voice. 'It was only a little nick. You'd better sit down.'

'Of course,' Rullman said immediately. 'You've been under quite a strain, Mr. Sweeney; forgive me for being so thoughtless. This will be over in just a moment.'

Sweeney sat down gratefully and tried to think about nothing. Both the girl and Rullman were now also seated, at the bench, examining with microscopes the little puddles of diluted blood Mike had taken from Sweeney.

'Type O, Rh negative,' the girl said. Rullman was taking notes. 'MsMs, P negative, cdE/cde, Lutheran a-negative, Kell-Cellano negative, Lewis a-minus b-plus.'

'Hmm,' Rullman said, unilluminatingly, all as one sound. 'Also Duffy a-negative, Jk-a, U positive, Jay positive, Bradbury-immune, platelets IV, and non-sickling. A pretty clean sweep. Mean anything to you, Mike?'

'It should,' she said, looking at Sweeney speculatively. 'You want me to match him, then.'

Rullman nodded. The girl came to Sweeney's side and the spring-driven lancet went *snick* against another of his fingertips. After she went back to the bench, Sweeney heard the sound again, and saw her brush her own left middle fingertip against a slide. Silence.

'Compatible, Dr. Rullman.'

Rullman turned to Sweeney and smiled for the first time. 'You pass,' he said. He seemed genuinely glad. 'Welcome, Mr. Sweeney. Now if you'll come back to my office, we'll see what we can do about placing you in living quarters, and of course in a job – we've plenty of those. Thanks, Mike.'

'You're welcome. Goodbye, Mr. Sweeney. It looks like I'll be seeing a lot more of you.'

Sweeney nodded and gulped. It was not until he was back in Rullman's office that he could control his voice.

'What was that all about, Dr. Rullman? I mean, I know you were typing my blood, but what did it tell you?'

'It told me your *bona fides*,' Rullman said. 'Blood groups are inheritable; they follow the Mendelian laws very strictly. Your blood pattern gave me your identity, not as an individual, but as a member of a family. In other words, they showed that you really are what you claim to be, a descendant of Bob Sweeney and Shirley Leverault.'

'I see. But you matched me against the girl, too. What did that test?'

'The so-called private factors, the ones that appear only within a family and not in the general population,' Rullman said. 'You see, Mr. Sweeney, as we reckon such matters here, Michaela Leverault is your niece.'

2

For at least the tenth time in two months, Mike was looking at Sweeney with astonishment, troubled and amused at once. 'Now where,' she said, 'did you get *that* idea?'

The question, as usual, was dangerous, but Sweeney took his time. Mike knew that he was always slow to answer questions, and sometimes seemed not to hear them at all. The need for such a protective habit was luridly obvious to Sweeney, and he was only postponing the moment when it should become just as obvious to the Ganymedians; only the plainly pathological introversion of his character as a whole had excused him even thus far from a suspicion that he was ducking the hard ones.

Sooner or later, Sweeney was sure, that suspicion would arise. Sweeney had had no experience of women, but he was nevertheless convinced that Mike was an exceptional sample. Her quickness of penetration sometimes seemed close to telepathy. He mulled the question, leaning on the railing around the hedge below the mountain, looking reflectively into the Gouge, constructing his answer. Each day he had to shorten that mulling-time, though the questions grew no less difficult for his pains.

'From the Port cops,' he said. 'I've got only two answers to that question, Mike. Anything I didn't get from my mother, I got from spying on the cops.'

Mike, too, looked down into the mists of the Gouge. It was a warm summer day, and a long one – three and a half Earth days long, while the satellite was on the sunward side of Jupiter, and coming, with Jupiter, closer and closer to the sun. The wind which blew over the flute-mouthpiece of rock on this side of the mountain was as gentle and variable as a flautist's breath, and did not stir the enormous tangled stolons and runners which filled the bottom of the great valley, or the wrap-around leaves which were plastered to them like so many thousands of blue-green Möbius strips.

It was not quiet down there, but it seemed quiet. There were many more thrums and rummums of rolling rocks and distant avalanches than one heard during the cold weather. The granite-skinned roots were growing rapidly while their short time was come, burrowing insistently into the walls of the valley, starting new trees and new rocks. In the cliffs, the warm weather changed water-of-crystallization from Ice IV to Ice III, the bound water snapping suddenly from one volume to another, breaking the rock strata apart. Sweeney knew how that worked; that was exfoliation; it was common on the Moon, though on the Moon it was caused by the re-freezing of Ice I in the gypsum strata. But the end-result was the same: rock-slides.

All these incessant erratic rumbles and muted thunders were the sounds of high summer in the Gouge. They were as peaceful to Sweeney's ears as bee-buzz is to an Earthman, though Sweeney had never encountered bee-buzz except in books. And like growing things everywhere, the terrific gnarled creepers down below sent up into the Adapted Men's air a fresh complacent odor, the specific smell of vegetable battle-unto-death which lulls animal nostrils and animal glands into forgetting past struggles of their own.

Ganymede was, as a matter of fact, a delightful world, even for a dead man. Or solely for a dead man.

'I can't understand why the Port cops would waste time batting lies back and forth,' Mike said at last. '*They* know we weren't doing any commerce-raiding. We've never been so much as off Ganymede since we landed here. And we couldn't get off if we wanted to, now. Why should they pretend that we did? Why would they talk about it as if it was a fact, especially since they didn't know you were listening? It's senseless.'

'I don't know,' Sweeney said. 'It never entered my head that you *weren't* commerce-raiding. If I'd had any notion that they weren't telling the truth, I'd have listened for clues to tell me why they weren't. But it never entered my head. And now it's too late; all I can do is guess.'

'You must have heard something. Something you don't remember consciously. I can guess, too, but it's your guess that's important. You were listening to them; I wasn't. Try, Don.'

'Well,' Sweeney said, 'maybe they didn't know that what they were saying was untrue. There's no law that says a Port cop has to be told the truth by his bosses. They're back on Earth; I was on the Moon, and so were they. And they sounded pretty convinced; the subject kept coming up, all the time, just casually, as if everybody knew about it. They all believed that Ganymede was raiding passenger liners as far in as the orbit of Mars. It was a settled fact. That's how I heard it.'

'That fits,' Mike said. Nevertheless, she was not looking at Sweeney; instead, she bent her head farther down over the rim of the Gouge, her hands locked together before her in dim space, until her small breasts were resting lightly on the railing. Sweeney took a long breath. The effluvium of the vines suddenly seemed anything but lulling.

'Tell me, Don,' she said. 'When did you hear the cops begin to talk this subject up? For the first time, I mean?'

His veering attention snapped back into the frigid center of his being so suddenly that it left behind a bright weal, as if a lash had been laid across his exposed brain. Mike was dangerous; dangerous. He had to remember that.

'When?' he said. 'I don't know, Mike. The days were all alike. It was toward the end, I think. When I was a kid I used to hear them talk about us as if we were criminals, but I couldn't figure out why. I guessed that it was because we were different, that's all. It was only at the end that they began to talk about specific crimes, and even then it didn't make much sense to me. My mother and I hadn't ever pirated any ships, that was for sure.'

'Only at the last. That's what I thought. They began to talk like that for the first time when your power began to fail. Isn't that right?'

Sweeney gave that one a long think, at least twice as long as would ordinarily have been safe before Mike. He already knew where Mike's questions were leading him. In this instance, a quick answer would be fatal. He had to appear to be attempting, with some pain, to dredge up information which was meaningless to him. After a while, he said:

'Yes, it was about then. I was beginning to cut down on tapping their calls; it didn't take much power, but we needed all we had. Maybe I missed hearing the important parts; that's possible.'

'No,' Mike said grimly. 'I think you heard all of it. Or all you were meant to hear. And I think you interpreted what you heard in exactly the way they wanted you to, Don.'

'It could be,' Sweeney said slowly. 'I was only a kid. I would have taken what I heard at face value. But that would mean that they knew we were there. I wonder. I don't remember exactly, but I don't think we had begun to sneak power from them yet. We were still thinking about putting a sun-cell on the surface, in those days.'

'No, no. They must have known you were there years before you began to tap their power. Rullman's been talking about that lately. There are simple ways of detecting even a phone-line tap, and your strontium battery couldn't have been undetected very long, either. They waited only until they could be sure they'd get you when they finally raided you. It's the way they think. In the meantime, they fed you hokum when you eavesdropped.'

So much for the story the cops had told Sweeney to tell. Only the extreme of stupidity which it assumed in the Adapted Men had protected it this long; nobody defends himself, at least at first, upon the assumption that his opponent thinks he is a microcephalic idiot. The deception had lasted two months, but it would never last 300 days.

'Why would they do that?' Sweeney said. 'They were going to kill us as soon as they could – as soon as they could work out a way to do it without damaging our equipment. What did they care what we thought?'

'Torture,' Mike said, straightening and locking her hands around the railing with the automatic tetany of a bird's claws touching a perch. She looked across the Gouge at the distant, heaped range on the other side. 'They wanted you to think that everything your people had planned and done had come to nothing – that we had wound up as nothing but vicious criminals. Since they couldn't get to you and your mother immediately, they amused themselves with strafing you while they worked. Maybe they thought it'd help soften you up – goad you into making some mistake that would make the job of getting in to you easier. Or maybe they did it just because they enjoyed it. Because it made them feel good.'

After a short silence, Sweeney said, 'Maybe that was it. Maybe not. I don't know, Mike.'

She turned to him suddenly and took him by the shoulders. Her eyes were crystal blue. 'How could you know?' she said, her fingers digging into his deltoid muscles. 'How could you know *anything* when there was nobody to tell you? The Earth must be full of lies about us now – lies, and nothing but lies! You've got to forget them – forget them all – just as though you'd just been born. You *have* just been born, Don, believe me. Only just. What they fed you on the Moon was lies; you've got to start learning the truth here, learning it from the beginning, like a child!'

She held him a moment longer. She was actually shaking him. Sweeney did not know what to say; he did not even know what emotion to mimic. The emotion he felt was still almost unknown; he did not dare let it show, let alone let it loose. While the girl looked furiously into his eyes, he could not even blink.

After all, he really had been born some time ago. Born dead.

The painful, tenfold pressure on his shoulders changed suddenly to a residual tingling over a deep ache, and Mike's hands dropped to her sides. She looked away, across the Gouge again. 'It's no use,' she said indistinctly. 'I'm sorry. That's a hell of a way for a girl to talk to her uncle.'

'That's all right, Mike. I was interested.'

'I'm sure of it. ... Let's go for a walk, Don. I'm sick of looking into the Gouge.' She was already striding back toward the looming mountain under which the colony lived.

Sweeney watched her go, his icy blood sighing in his ears. It was terrible to be unable to think; he had never known the dizziness of it until he had met Mike Leverault, but now it seemed determined never to leave him – it abated sometimes, but it never quite went away. He had been ruefully glad, at the very beginning, that the close 'blood' tie between himself and Mike, a genetic tie which was quite real since he was in fact Shirley Leverault's Adapted son, would prevent his becoming interested in the girl in accordance with Earth custom. But in fact it had had no such effect. Earth tabus had no force for him, and here on Ganymede, that particular tabu had been jettisoned summarily. Rullman had told him why.

'Don't give it a second thought,' he had said on that very first day, grinning into Sweeney's stunned face. 'We haven't any genetic reasons for forbidding inbreeding; quite the contrary. In a small group like ours, the strongest and most immediate evolutionary influence is genetic drift. Unless we took steps to prevent it, there'd be a loss of unfixed genes with every new generation. Obviously we can't allow that, or we'd wind up with a group in which there'd be no real individuals: everybody would be alike in some crucial and absolutely unpredictable respect. No tabu is worth that kind of outcome.'

Rullman had gone on from there. He had said that simply permitting inbreeding could not in itself halt genetic drift; that in some respects it encouraged it; and that the colony was taking positive measures to circumvent drift, measures which would begin to bear fruit within eight generations. He had begun by this time to talk in terms of alleles and isomorphs and lethal recessives, and to scribble such cryptograms as $rrR:rRR/('rA)rr/R'Rr$ on the sheet of mica before him; and then, suddenly, he had looked up and realized that he had lost his audience. That, too, had amused him.

Sweeney had not minded. He knew he was ignorant. Besides, the colony's plans meant nothing to him; he was on Ganymede to bring the colony to an end. As far as Mike was concerned, he knew that nothing would govern him but his monumental loneliness, as it governed everything else that he did and felt.

But he had been astonished to discover that, covertly at least, that same loneliness governed everyone else in the colony, with the sole possible exception of Rullman.

Mike looked back, and then, her face hardening, quickened her pace. Sweeney followed, as he knew he had to; but he was still struggling to think.

Much of what he had learned about the colony, if it was true – and at least everything he had been able to check had passed that test – had involved his unlearning what he had been taught by the Port cops. The cops, for instance, had said that the alleged commerce-raiding had had two purposes: secondarily to replenish food and equipment, but primarily to augment the colonists' numbers by capturing normal people for Adaptation.

There was no commerce-raiding going on now, that much was certain, and Sweeney was inclined to believe Mike's denial that there had ever been any in the past. Once one understood the ballistics of space travel, one understood also that piracy is an impossible undertaking, simply because it is more work than it is worth. But beyond this persuasive practical objection, there was the impossibility of the motive the Port cops had imputed to the Ganymedians. The primary purpose was nonsense. The colonists were fertile, and hence did not need recruits; and besides, it was impossible to convert a normal adult human being into an Adapted Man – pantropy had to begin before conception, as it had been begun with Sweeney.

Calamitously, the reverse also appeared to be true. Sweeney had been unable to find anybody in the colony who believed it possible to convert an Adapted Man back into a human being. The promise the Port cops had held out to him – though they had never made it directly – thus far appeared to be founded upon nothing better than dust. If it were nevertheless possible to bring a man like Sweeney back to life, only Rullman knew about it, and Sweeney had to be hypercautious in questioning Rullman. The scientist had already made some uncomfortable deductions from the sparse facts and ample lies with which Sweeney had, by order of the Port cops, provided him. Like everyone else on Ganymede, Sweeney had learned to respect the determination and courage which were bodied forth in everything Rullman did and said; but unlike anybody else on Ganymede, he feared Rullman's understanding.

And in the meantime – while Sweeney waited, with a fatalism disturbed only by Mike Leverault, for Rullman to see through him to the other side of the gouge which was Sweeney's frigid tangled substitute for a human soul – there remained the question of the crime.

We must have those men back. Why? *Because we need to know what they know.* Why not ask them? *They won't tell us.* Why not? *Because they're afraid.* What of? *They committed a crime and must be punished.* What did they do?

SILENCE

So the question of the crime still remained. It had not been commerce-raiding; even had the Ganymedians achieved the impossible and had pirated spacecraft, that would not have been the *first* crime, the one which had made the Adapted Men flee to Ganymede in the first place, the crime from which the whole technique of pantropy had sprung. What high crime had the parents of the Adapted Men committed, to force them to maroon their children on Ganymede for what they must have believed was to be forever?

The responsibility was not the children's, that much was also obvious. The children had never been on the Earth at all. They had been born and raised on the Moon, in strict secrecy. The cops' pretense that the colonists themselves were wanted back for some old evil was another fraud, like the story about commerce-raiding. If a crime had been committed on Earth, it had been committed by the normal Earthmen whose frigid children roamed Ganymede now; it could have been committed by no-one else.

Except, of course, by Rullman. Both on the Moon and on Ganymede it was the common assumption that Rullman had been an Earth-normal human being once. That was impossible, but it was agreed to be so. Rullman himself turned the question away rather than deny it. Perhaps the crime had been his alone, since there was nobody else who could have committed it.

But *what* crime? Nobody on Ganymede could, or would, tell Sweeney. None of the colonists believed in it. Most of them thought that nothing was held against them but their difference from normal human beings; the exceptional few thought that the development of pantropy itself was the essential crime. Of that, clearly, Rullman was guilty, if 'guilty' was the applicable word.

Why pantropy, or the responsibility for developing it, should be considered criminal was a mystery to Sweeney, but there was a great deal else that he didn't know about Earth laws and standards, so he wasted no more time in puzzling over it. If Earth said that inventing or using pantropy was a crime, that was what it was; and the Port cops had already told him that he must not fail to bring back Rullman, no matter how grievously he failed to fulfill all his other instructions. It was an answer, and that was enough.

But why hadn't the cops said so in the first place? And why, if pantropy was a crime, had the cops themselves compounded that identical crime – by creating Sweeney?

Belatedly, he quickened his pace. Mike had already disappeared under the lowering brow of the great cavern. He could not remember noticing, now, which of the dozen smaller entrances she had used, and he himself did not know where more than two of them led. He chose one at random.

Four turns later, he was hopelessly lost.

This was unusual, but it was not entirely unexpected. The network of tunnels under Howe's *pi* was a labyrinth, not only in fact but by intention. In drilling out their home, the Adapted Men had taken into consideration the possibility that gun-carrying men in spacesuits might some day come looking for them. Such a man would never find his way out from under the mountain, unless an Adapted Man who had memorized the maze led him out; and he would never find an Adapted Man, either. Memorization was the only key, for no maps of the maze existed, and the colonists had a strictly enforced law against drawing one.

Sweeney had perhaps half of the maze committed to memory. If he did not meet someone he knew – for after all, nobody was hiding from *him* – he could count upon entering a familiar section sooner or later. In the meantime, he was curious to see anything that there was to be seen.

The first thing of interest that he saw was Dr. Rullman. The scientist emerged from a tunnel set at a 20° angle to the one Sweeney was in at the moment, going away from Sweeney and unaware of him. After an instant's hesitation, Sweeney followed him, as silently as possible. The noisy ventilation system helped to cover his footfalls.

Rullman had a habit of vanishing for periods ranging from half a day to a week. Anybody who knew where he went and what he did there did not talk about it. Now was a chance, perhaps, for Sweeney to find out for himself. It was possible, of course, that Rullman's disappearances were related to the forthcoming meteorological crisis on Ganymede, about which Sweeney had been hearing an increasing number of hints. On the other hand … what was on the other hand? There could be no harm in investigating.

Rullman walked rapidly, his chin ducked into his chest, as though he were travelling a route so familiar that habit could be entrusted with carrying him along it. Once Sweeney almost lost him, and thereafter cautiously closed up the interval between them a little; the labyrinth was sufficiently complex to offer plenty of quick refuges should Rullman show signs of turning back. As the scientist moved, there came from him an unpredictable but patterned series of wordless sounds, intoned rather than spoken. They communicated nothing, actuated no mechanisms, gave Rullman no safe-conduct – as was evidenced by the fact that Sweeney was travelling the same course without making any such noise. Indeed, Rullman himself seemed to be unaware that he was making it.

Sweeney was puzzled. He had never heard anybody hum before.

The rock beneath Sweeney's feet began to slope downward, gently but definitely. At the same time, he noticed that the air was markedly warmer, and was becoming more so with almost every step. A dim sound of laboring machinery was pulsing in it.

It got hotter, and still hotter, but Rullman did not hesitate. The noise – which Sweeney could now identify definitely as that of pumps, many of them – also increased. The two men were now walking down a long, straight corridor, bordered by closed doors rather than maze exits; it was badly lit, but Sweeney nevertheless allowed Rullman to get farther ahead of him. Toward the other end of this corridor, the heat began to diminish, to Sweeney's relief, for he had begun to feel quite dizzy. Rullman gave no indication that he even noticed it.

At this end Rullman ducked abruptly into a side entrance which turned out to be the top of a flight of stone steps. Quite a perceptible draft of warm air was blowing down it. Warm air, Sweeney knew, was supposed to rise in a gravitational field; why it should be going in the opposite direction he could not imagine, especially since there appeared to be no blowers in operation on this level. Since it was blowing toward Rullman, it would also carry any noise Sweeney made ahead of him. He tiptoed cautiously down.

Rullman was not in sight when Sweeney left the stairwell. There was before Sweeney, instead, a long, high-ceilinged passageway which curved gently to the right until vision was cut off. Along the inside of the curve, regularly spaced, were crouching machines, each one with a bank of lat- erally-coiled metal tubing rearing before it. These were the sources of the sounds Sweeney had heard.

Here, it was cold again; abnormally cold, despite the heavy current of warm air blowing down the stairwell. Something, Sweeney thought, was radically wrong with the behavior of the thermodynamic laws down here.

He slouched cautiously ahead. After only a few steps, past the first of the laboring mechanisms – yes, it was coldest by the shining coils, as if cold were actually radiating from them – he found an undeniable airlock. Fur- thermore, it was in use: the outer door was sealed, but a little light beside it said that the lock was cycling. Opposite the lock, on the other wall, one of a row of spacesuit lockers hung open and tenantless.

But it was the legend painted on the airlock valve which finally made everything fall into place. It said:

PANTROPE LABORATORY ONE
Danger – Keep Out!

Sweeney dodged away from the airlock with a flash of pure panic, as a man wanted for murder might jump upon seeing a sign saying '50,000 volts'. It was all clear now. There was nothing wrong with the thermodynamics of this corridor that was not similarly 'wrong' inside any refrigerator. The huge engines were pumps, all right – heat pumps. Their coils were frost-free only because there was no water vapor in Ganymede's air; nevertheless, they were taking heat from that air and transferring it to the other side of that rock wall, into the pantrobe lab.

No wonder the laboratory was sealed off from the rest of the maze by an airlock – and that Rullman had had to put on a spacesuit to go through it.

It was hot on the other side. Too hot for an Adapted Man.

But *what* Adapted Man?

What good was pantropy to Rullman here? That phase of history was supposed to be over and done with. Yet what was going on in this laboratory obviously was as alien to the environment of Ganymede as Ganymede's en- vironment was to Earth's.

A is to B as B is to – what? To C? Or *to* A?

Was Rullman, in the face of the impossibility of such a project, *trying to re-adapt his people to Earth*?

There should be dials or meters on this side of the wall which would give more information as to what it was like on the other side. And there they were, in a little hooded embrasure which Sweeney had overlooked in the first shock. They said:

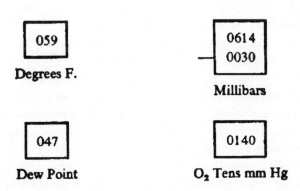

059	0614 / 0030
Degrees F.	Millibars
047	0140
Dew Point	O₂ Tens mm Hg

Some of these meant nothing to Sweeney: he had never before encountered pressure expressed in millibars, let alone the shorthand way it was registered on the meter before him; nor did he know how to compute relative humidity from the dew point. With the Fahrenheit scale he was vaguely familiar, vaguely enough to have forgotten how to convert it into Centigrade readings. But—

Oxygen tension!

There was one planet, and one only, where such a measurement could have any meaning.

Sweeney ran.

He was no longer running by the time he had reached Rullman's office, although he was still thoroughly out of breath. Knowing that he would be unable to cross back over the top of the pantrobe lab again, feeling that heat beating up at him and knowing at least in part what it meant, he had gone in the opposite direction, past the gigantic heat-exchangers, and blundered his way up from the other side. The route he had followed had covered over three erratic miles, and several additional discoveries which had shaken him almost as hard as had the first one.

He was entirely unsure that he was even rational any more. But he had to know. Nothing was important to him now but the answer to the main question, the permanent founding or dashing of the hope under which he had lived so long.

Rullman was already back in the office, almost surrounded by his staff. Sweeney pushed his way forward among the Ganymedians, his jaw set, his diaphragm laboring.

'This time we're going to close all the safety doors,' Rullman said into the phone. 'The pressure fronts are going to be too steep to allow us to rely on the outside locks alone. See to it that everybody knows where he's to be as soon as the alert sounds, and this time make it stick; we don't want anybody trapped between doors for the duration. This time it may swoop down on us at damn short notice.'

The phone murmured and cut out.

'Hallam, how's the harvesting? You've got less than a week, you know.'

'Yes, Dr. Rullman – we'll be through in time.'

'And another thing – oh, hello, Donald. What's the matter? You're looking a little pasty. I'm pretty busy, so make it fast, please.'

'I'll make it fast,' Sweeney said. 'I can put it all into one question if I can talk to you privately. For just a few seconds.'

Rullman's reddish eyebrows went up, but after examining Sweeney's face more closely, the scientist nodded and rose. 'Come next door, then ... Now then, youngster, spit it out. With the storm coming up, we don't have time for shilly-shallying.'

'All right,' Sweeney said, taking a long breath. 'This is it: Is it possible to change an Adapted Man back into a human being? An Earth-normal human being?'

Rullman's eyes narrowed very slowly; and for what seemed a long time, he said nothing. Sweeney looked back. He was afraid, but he was no longer afraid of Rullman.

'You've been down below, I see,' the scientist said at last, drumming at the base of his chin with two fingers. 'And from the terms you use, it strikes me that Shirley Leverault's educational methods left – well, the cliché springs to mind – something to be desired. But we'll let those things pass for now.

'The answer to your question, in any case, is: *No*. You will never be able to live a normal life in any other place than Ganymede, Donald. And I'll tell you something else that your mother should have told you: You ought to be damned glad of it.'

'Why should I?' Sweeney said, almost emotionlessly.

'Because, like every other person in this colony, you have a Jay-positive blood type. This wasn't concealed from you when we found it, on the first day you joined us, but evidently it didn't register – or had no special significance for you. Jay-positive blood doesn't mean anything on Ganymede, true enough. *But Jay-positive Earth-normal people are cancerprones.* They are as susceptible to cancer as hemophiliacs are to bleeding to death – and upon equally short notice.

'If by some miracle you *should* be changed to an Earth-normal man, Donald, you would be under immediate sentence of death. So I say you should be glad that it can't happen – damn glad!'

3

The crisis on Ganymede – though of course it would not even be an incident, were there nobody there to live through it – comes to fruition roughly every eleven years and nine months. It is at the end of this period that Jupiter – and hence his fifteen-fold family of moons and moonlets – makes his closest approach to the Sun.

The eccentricity of Jupiter's orbit is only 0.0484, which amounts to very little for an ellipse which averages 483,300,000 miles from its focal points. Nevertheless, at perihelion Jupiter is nearly ten million miles closer to the Sun than he is at aphelion; and the weather on Jupiter, never anything less than hellish, becomes indescribable during that approach. So, on a smaller but sufficient scale, does the weather on Ganymede.

The perihelion temperature on Ganymede never rises high enough to melt the ice of Neptune's Trident, but it does lift through the few niggardly degrees necessary to make the vapor pressure of Ice III known in Ganymede's air. Nobody on Earth could dream of calling the resulting condition 'humidity', but Ganymede's weather turns upon such microscopic changes; an atmosphere containing *no* water will react rapidly to even a fractional vapor content. For one thing, it will pick up more heat. The resulting cycle does not go through more than a few turns before it flattens out, but the end-product is no less vicious.

The colony, Sweeney gathered, had come through one such period without any but minor difficulties, simply by withdrawing entirely under the mountain; but for many reasons that course was no longer possible. There were now semi-permanent installations – weather stations, observatories, radio beacons, bench-marks and other surveying monuments – which could be dismantled only with the loss of much time before the crisis, and re-established with still more loss afterwards. Furthermore, some of them would be needed to report and record the progress of the crisis itself, and hence had to stay where they were.

'And don't get the idea,' Rullman told a mass meeting of the colonists, gathered in the biggest cavern of the maze, 'that even the mountain can protect us all the way through this one. I've told you before, but I'll remind you again, that the climax this year coincides with the peak of the sunspot cycle. Everybody's seen what that does to the weather on Jupiter proper. We can expect similar effects, to scale, on Ganymede. There's going to be trouble no matter how well we prepare. All we can hope for is that the inevitable damage will be minor. Anybody who thinks we're going to get off scot-free has only to listen for a minute.'

In the calculated, dramatic pause which followed, everybody listened. The wind was audible even down here, howling over the outlets and intakes of the ventilation system, carried, amplified and encrusted with innumerable echoes, by the metal miles of the air ducts. The noise was a reminder that, at the height of the coming storm, the exterior ports would all be closed, so that everyone under the mountain would have to breathe recirculated air. After a moment, a mass sigh – an involuntary intake of breath against the easily imagined future – passed through Rullman's audience. He grinned.

'I don't mean to frighten you,' he said. 'We'll get along. But I don't want any complacency either, and above all, I won't stand for any sloppiness in the preparations. It's particularly important that we keep the outside installations intact this time, because we're going to need them before the end of the next Jovian year – a long time before that, if everything continues to go well.'

The grin was suddenly quenched. 'I don't need to tell some of you how important it is that we get that project completed on schedule,' Rullman said, quietly. 'We may not have much time left before the Port cops decide to move in on us – it amazes me that they haven't already done so, particularly since we're harboring a fugitive the cops troubled to chase almost into our atmosphere – and we can't plan on their giving us any leeway.

'For those of you who know about the project only in outline, let me emphasize that there is a good deal more hanging from it than immediately meets the eye. Man's whole future in space may be determined by how well we carry it off; we can't afford to be licked – neither by the Earth nor by the weather. If we are, our whole long struggle for survival will have been meaningless. I'm counting on everyone here to see to it that that doesn't happen.'

It was difficult to be sure of what Rullman was talking about when he got onto the subject of the 'project'. It had something to do with the pantrope labs, that much was clear; and it had to do also with the colony's original spaceship, which Sweeney had run across that same day, stored in a launching chimney almost identical with the one on the Moon out of which Sweeney had been rocketed to begin his own free life, and fitted – if judgment based upon a single brief look could be trusted – either for a long voyage by a few people, or for a short trip by a large group.

Beyond that, Sweeney knew nothing about the 'project'. except for one additional fact of which he could make nothing: it had something to do with the colony's long-term arrangements for circumventing the loss of unfixed genes. Possibly – nobody would be less able to assess the possibility than Sweeney – the only connection this fact had with the 'project' was that it *was* long-term.

Sweeney, in any event, knew better than to ask questions. The storm that was going on inside him took precedence, anyhow; as far as he was concerned, it was even more important than the storms that were sweeping Ganymede, or any that might sweep that world in the foreseeable future. He was not used to thinking in terms of a society, even a small one; Rullman's appeals to that Ideal were simply incomprehensible to him. He was the solar system's most thorough-going individualist – not by nature, but by design.

Perhaps Rullman sensed it. Whether he did or not, the assignment he gave Sweeney might have been perfectly calculated to throw a lonely man into the ultimate isolation he feared; to put the burden of an agonizing decision entirely upon the shoulders of the man who had to carry it; or – to isolate a Port spy where he could do the least harm while the colony's attention was fully occupied elsewhere. Or possibly, even probably, he had none of these motives in mind; what counted, in any event, was what he did.

He assigned Sweeney to the south polar weather station, for the duration of the emergency.

There was almost nothing to do there but watch the crystals of methane 'snow' bank against the windows, and keep the station tight. The instruments reported back to base by themselves, and needed no further attention. At the height of the crisis, perhaps, Sweeney might find himself busy for a while; or, he might not. That remained to be seen.

In the meantime, he had plenty of time to ask questions – and nobody to ask them of but himself, and the hooting, constantly rising wind.

There was an interlude. Sweeney hiked, on foot, back to Howe's H to recover the radio transceiver he had buried there, and then hiked back to the weather station. It took him eleven days, and efforts and privations of which Jack London might have made a whole novel. To Sweeney it meant nothing; he did not know whether or not he would want to use the radio after he got back with it; and as for the saga of his solo journey, he did not know that it was a saga, or even that it had been unusually difficult and painful. He had nothing against which to compare it, not even fiction; he had never read any. He measured things by the changes they made in his situation, and possession of the radio had not changed the questions he was asking himself; it had only made it possible to act upon the answers, once he had any answers.

Coming back to the station, he saw a pinnah-bird. It burrowed into the nearest drift as soon as it saw him, but for the preceding instant he had had company. He never saw it again, but now and then he thought about it.

The question, put simply, was: What was he going to do now?

That he was thoroughly in love with Mike Leverault could no longer be argued. It was doubly difficult to come to grips with the emotion, however, because he did not know the name of it, and so had to reason each time with the raw experience itself, rather than with the more convenient symbol. Each time he thought about it, it shook him all over again. But there it was.

As for the colonists, he was certain that they were not criminals in any way, except by Earth's arbitary fiat. They were a hard-working, courageous, decent lot, and had offered to Sweeney the first disinterested friendliness he had ever known.

And, like all the colonists, Sweeney could not help but admire Rullman.

There, in those three propositions, rested the case against using the radio.

The time for reporting to Meiklejon was almost up. The inert transceiver on the table before Sweeney had only to send a single one of five notes, and the colony on Ganymede would be ended. The notes were coded:

WAVVY: *Have custody need pickup*
NAVVY: *Have custody need help*
VVANY: *Need custody have help*
AAVYV: *Need custody need pickup*
YYAWY: *Have custody have pickup*

What response the computer on board the ship would make, what course of action it would dictate in response to any one of those signals was unknown, but that was now almost beside the point. Any response would be inappropriate, since not one of the five signals fitted the actual situation – despite all the intellectual travail which had gone into tailoring them.

If no note were sent, Meiklejon would go away at the end of 300 days. That might mean that Rullman's 'project', whatever that was, would go through – but that wouldn't save the colony. It would take Earth a minimum of two generations to breed and mature another Sweeney from the artificially maintained ovaries of mercifully long-dead Shirley Leverault, and it was hardly likely that Earth would even try. Earth probably knew more than Sweeney did about the 'project' – it would be difficult to know less – and if Sweeney himself failed to stop it, the next attempt would most likely arrive as a bomb. Earth would stop wanting 'those men' back, once it became evident that she couldn't get them even through so subtle a double agent as Sweeney.

Item: chain reaction. There was, Sweeney knew, a considerable amount of deuterium on Ganymede, some of it locked in the icy wastes of Neptune's Trident, a lesser amount scattered through the rocks in the form of lithium deuteride. A fission bomb going off here would stand an excellent chance of starting a fusion explosion which would detonate the whole satellite. If any still-active fragment of that explosion should hit Jupiter, only a bare 665,000 miles away now, that planet would be quite large enough to sustain a Bethé or carbon cycle; it was diffuse, but it alone among the planets had the mass. The wave front of *that* unimaginable catastrophe would boil Earth's seas in their beds; it might also – the probability was about ⅜ – trigger a nova outburst from the Sun, though nobody would stay alive to be grateful very long if it didn't.

Since Sweeney knew this, he had to assume that it was common knowledge, and that Earth would use chemical explosives only on Ganymede. But would it? Common knowledge and Sweeney had had precious little contact so far.

Still, it hardly mattered. If Earth bombed the colony, it would be all up with him, regardless. Even the limited companionship, the wordless love, the sense that he might yet be born, all would be gone. He would be gone. So might the little world.

But if he signalled Meiklejon and the computer, he would be taken alive away from Mike, away from Rullman, away from the colony, away and away. He would stay his own dead self. He might even have a new chance to learn that same endless lesson about the shapes loneliness can take; or, Earth might work a miracle and turn him into a live, Jay-positive human being.

The wind rose and rose. The congruent furies of the storms inside and outside Sweeney mounted together. Their congruence made a classic example, had he been able to recognize it, of the literary device called 'the pathetic fallacy' – but Sweeney had never read any fiction, and recognizing nature in the process of imitating art would have been of no use to him anyhow.

He did not even know that, when the crisis of the exterior storm began to wear away the windward edge of the weather station's foundations with a million teeth of invisible wrath, his lonely battle to save the station might have made an epic. Whole chapters, whole cantos, whole acts of what might have been conscious heroism in another man, in a human being, were thrown away while Sweeney went about his business, his mind on his lonely debate.

There was no signal he could send that would tell Meiklejon or the computer the truth. He did not have custody of the men Earth wanted, and he didn't want to have it, so it would be idiotic to ask for help to get it. He no longer believed that Earth 'must have those men back', either for Earth's purposes – mysterious though they remained – or for his own, essentially hopeless though his own appeared to be.

But any signal would take him off Ganymede – if he wanted to be taken.

The crisis, he saw, was over. He made the station fast.

He checked the radio once more. It worked. He snapped the turning pointer to one of its copper contacts and closed the key, sending Meiklejon VVANY. After half an hour, the set's oscillator began to peep rhythmically, indicating that Meiklejon was still in Ganymede's sky, and had heard.

Sweeney left the set on the table in the station, went back to the mountain, and told Rullman what he was and what he had done.

Rullman's fury was completely quiet, and a thousand times more frightening than the most uncontrolled rage could have been. He simply sat behind his desk and looked at Sweeney, all the kindness gone out of his face, and the warmth out of his eyes. After a few moments, Sweeney realized that the blankness of Rullman's eyes meant that he was not seeing him at all; his mind was turned inward. So was his rage.

'I'm astonished,' he said, in a voice so even that it seemed to contain no surprise at all. 'Most of all, I'm astonished at myself. I should have anticipated something like this. But I didn't dream that they had the knowledge, or the guile, to stake everything on a long-term program like this. I have been, in short, an idiot.'

His voice took on, for a moment, a shade of color, but it was so scathing that it made Sweeney recoil. And yet no single word of condemnation of Sweeney had yet been forthcoming from Rullman; the man was, instead, strafing himself. Sweeney said tentatively:

'How could you have known? There were a lot of points where I might have given myself away, but I was doing my damndest not to. I might have kept the secret still longer, if I'd wanted it that way.'

'You?' Rullman said. The single syllable was worse than a blow. 'You're as blameless as a machine, Donald. I know too much about pantropy to think otherwise. It's very easy to isolate an Adapted infant, prevent him from becoming a human being at all, if you've sufficient ill-will to want to. Your behavior was predictable, after all.'

'Was it?' Sweeney said, a little grimly. 'I came and told you, didn't I?'

'And what if you did? Can that change matters now? I'm sure that Earth included that very high probability in its plans. Insofar as you have loyalties at all, they were bound to become divided; but it was probably calculated that they would stay divided – that is, would not change completely. And so here you are, trying to play both ends against the middle – you yourself being the middle – by betraying your masquerade to me at the same time you betray the colony to Earth. Nothing can be accomplished by that.'

'Are you sure?'

'Quite sure,' Rullman said stonily. 'I suppose they offered you an inducement. Judging by the questions you've asked me before, they must have promised to make an Earth-normal human being out of you – as soon as they found out from us how to do that. But the fact of the matter is that it can't be done at all, and you know it. And now there's no future for you with us, either. I'm sorry for you, Donald, believe me; it's not your fault that they made you into a creature instead of a person. But you are nothing now but a bomb that's already gone off.'

Sweeney had never known his father, and the hegemony of the Port cops had been too diffuse to instill in him any focused, automatic respect for persons standing *in loco parentis*. He discovered, suddenly, that he was furious with Rullman.

'That's a silly damn speech,' he said, staring down and across the desk at the seated, slightly bowed man. 'Nothing's gone off yet. There's plenty of information I can give you that you might use, if you want to work to get it. Of course if you've given up in advance—'

Rullman looked up. 'What do you know?' he said, with some puzzlement. 'You said yourself that it would be the computer on board this Capt. Meiklejon's ship that would decide the course of action. And you can't communicate effectively with Meiklejon. This is a strange time to be bluffing, Donald.'

'Why would I bluff? I know more about what Earth is *likely* to do with my message than anybody else in the colony. My experience with Earth is more recent. I wouldn't have come to you at all if I'd thought the situation to be hopeless – and if I hadn't carefully picked the one message to send to Meiklejon that I thought left the colony some hope. I'm not straddling. I'm on your side. To send no message at all would have been the worst possible thing to do. This way, we may have a grace period.'

'And just how,' Rullman said slowly, 'can you expect me to trust you?'

'That's your problem,' Sweeney said brusquely. 'If I really am still straddling, it's because the colony's failed to convince me that my future lies here. And if that's the case, I'm not alone – and it's the colony's own fault for being so secretive with its own people.'

'Secretive?' Rullman said, with open astonishment now. 'About what?'

'About the "project". About the original crime Earth wants you for. About why Earth wants you back – you in particular, Dr. Rullman.'

'But – that's common knowledge, Donald. All of it.'

'Maybe so. But it isn't common to *me* – and most of the original settlers take it all so much for granted that they can't talk about it, except in little cryptic references, like a private joke everybody's supposed to know. But everybody doesn't; did you know that? I've found that about half your second generation here has only the foggiest notion of the past. The amount of information available here to a newcomer – whether he's newly arrived like me, or just plain newborn – you could stick in a pinnah-bird's eye. And that's dangerous. It's why I could have betrayed the colony *completely* if I hadn't decided against it, and you couldn't have stopped me.'

Rullman leaned back and was quiet for quite a long time.

'Children often don't ask questions when they think they're already expected to know the answers,' he murmured. He looked considerably more thunderstruck than he had when Sweeney made his original announcement. 'They like to appear knowing even when they aren't. It gives them status in their own eyes.'

'Children and spies,' Sweeney said. 'There are certain questions neither of them can ask, and for almost the same reasons. And the phonier the children's knowledge actually is, the easier for the spy to get around among the adults.'

'I begin to see,' Rullman said. 'We thought we were immune to spying, because an Earth spy couldn't live here without elaborate, detectable protections. But that was a problem in physics, and that kind of problem is soluble. We should have assumed so from the beginning. Instead, we made ourselves socially as vulnerable as possible.'

'That's how I see it. I'll bet that my father wouldn't have let you get away with it if he'd been able to get away with you. He was supposed to have been an expert in that kind of thing. I don't know; I never knew him. And I suppose it's beside the point, anyhow.'

'No,' Rullman said. 'It's very much to the point, and I think you've just proven it, Donald. Your father couldn't prevent it, but perhaps he's given us an instrument for repairing it.'

'Meaning me?'

'Yes. Ringer or no ringer, the blood you carry – and the genes – have been with us from the beginning, and I know how they show their effects. I see them now. Sit down, Donald. I begin to hope. What shall we do?'

'First of all,' Sweeney said, 'please, please tell me what this colony is all about!'

It was a difficult assignment.

Item: the Authorities. Long before space travel, big cities in the United States had fallen so far behind any possibility of controlling their own traffic problems as to make purely political solutions chimerical. No city administration could spend the amount of money needed for a radical cure, without being ousted in the next elections by the enraged drivers and pedestrians who most needed the help.

Increasingly, the traffic problems were turned over, with gratitude and many privileges, to semi-public Port, Bridge and Highway Authorities: huge capital-investment ventures modelled upon the Port of New York Authority, which had shown its ability to build and/or run such huge operations as the Holland and Lincoln Tunnels, the George Washington Bridge, Teterboro, LaGuardia, Idlewild and Newark airports, and many lesser facilities. By 1960 it was possible to travel from the tip of Florida to the border of Maine entirely over Authority-owned territory, if one could pay the appropriate tolls (and didn't mind being shot at in the Poconos by embattled land-owners who were still resisting the gigantic Incadel project).

Item: the tolls. The Authorities were creations of the states, usually acting in pairs, and as such enjoyed legal protections not available to other private firms engaged in interstate commerce. Among these protections, in the typical enabling act, was a provision that 'the two said states will not ... diminish or impair the power of the Authority to establish, levy and collect tolls and other charges ...' The federal government helped; although the Federal Bridge Act of 1946 required that the collection of tolls must cease with the payment of amortization, Congress almost never invoked the Act against any Authority. Consequently, the tolls never dropped; by 1953 the Port of New York Authority was reporting a profit of over twenty million dollars a year, and annual collections were increasing at the rate of ten per cent a year.

Some of the take went into the development of new facilities – most of them so placed as to increase the take, rather than solve the traffic problem. Again the Port of New York Authority led the way; it built, against all sense, a third tube for the Lincoln Tunnel, thus pouring eight and a half million more cars per year into Manhattan's mid-town area, where the city was already strangling for want of any adequate ducts to take away the then-current traffic.

Item: the Port cops. The Authorities had been authorized from the beginning to police their own premises. As the Authorities got bigger, so did the private police forces.

By the time space travel arrived, the Authorities owned it. They had taken pains to see that it fell to them; they had learned from their airport operations – which, almost alone among their projects, always showed a loss – that nothing less than total control is good enough. And characteristically, they never took any interest in any form of space travel which did not involve enormous expenditures; otherwise they could take no profits from sub-contracting, no profits from fast amortization of loans, no profits from the laws allowing them fast tax write-offs for new construction, no profits from the indefinitely protracted collection of tolls and fees after the initial cost and the upkeep had been recovered.

At the world's first commercial spaceport, Port Earth, it cost ship owners $5000 each and every time their ships touched the ground. Landing fees had been outlawed in private atmosphere flying for years, but the Greater Earth Port Authority operated under its own set of precedents; it made landing fees for spacecraft routine. And it maintained the first Port police force which was bigger than the armed forces of the nation which had given it its franchise; after a while, the distinction was wiped out, and the Port cops *were* the armed forces of the United States. It was not difficult to do, since the Greater Earth Port Authority was actually a holding company embracing every other Authority in the country, including Port Earth.

And when people, soon after spaceflight, began to ask each other, 'How shall we colonize the planets?' the Greater Earth Port Authority had its answer ready.

Item: terraforming.

Terraforming – remaking the planets into near-images of the Earth, so that Earth-normal people could live on them. Port Earth was prepared to start small. Port Earth wanted to move Mars out of its orbit to a point somewhat closer to the sun, and make the minor adjustments needed in the orbits of the other planets; to transport to Mars about enough water to empty the Indian Ocean – only a pittance to Earth, after all, and not 10 per cent of what would be needed later to terraform Venus; to carry to the little planet top-soil about equal in area to the state of Iowa, in order to get started at growing plants which would slowly change the atmosphere of Mars; and so on. The whole thing, Port Earth pointed out reasonably, was perfectly feasible from the point of view of the available supplies and energy resources, and it would cost less than thirty-three billion dollars. The Greater Earth Port Authority was prepared to recover that sum at no cost in taxes in less than a century, through such items as $50 rocket-mail stamps, $10,000 Mars landing fees, $1,000 one-way strap-down tickets, $100-per-desert-acre land titles, and so on. Of course the fees would continue after the cost was recovered – for maintenance.

And what, after all, the Authority asked reasonably, was the alternative? Nothing but domes. The Greater Earth Port Authority hated domes. They cost too little to begin with, and the volume of traffic to and from them would always be miniscule. Experience on the Moon had made that painfully clear. And the public hated domes, too; it had already shown a mass reluctance to live under them.

As for the governments, other than that of the United States, that the Authority still tolerated, none of them had any love for domes, or for the kind of limited colonization that the domes stood for. They needed to get rid of their pullulating masses by the bucket-full, not by the eye-dropper-full. If the Authority knew that emigration increases the home population rather than cuts it, the Authority carefully refrained from saying so to the governments involved; they could rediscover Franklin's Law for themselves. Domes were out; terraforming was in.

Then came pantropy.

If this third alternative to the problem of colonizing the planets had come as a surprise to the Authority, and to Port Earth, they had nobody to blame for it but themselves. There had been plenty of harbingers. The notion of modifying the human stock genetically to live on the planets as they were found, rather than changing the planets to accommodate the people, had been old with Olaf Stapledon; it had been touched upon by many later writers; it went back, in essence, as far as Proteus, and as deep into the human mind as the werewolf, the vampire, the fairy changeling, the transmigrated soul.

But suddenly it was possible; and, not very long afterwards, it was a fact.

The Authority hated it. Pantropy involved a high initial investment to produce the first colonists, but it was a method which with refinement would become cheaper and cheaper. Once the colonists were planted, it required no investment at all; the colonists were comfortable on their adopted world, and could produce new colonists without outside help. Pantropy, further-more, was at its *most* expensive less than half as costly as the setting-up of the smallest and least difficult dome. Compared to the cost of terraforming even so favorable a planet as Mars, it cost nothing at all, from the Authori-ty's point of view.

And there was no way to collect tolls against even the initial expense. It was too cheap to bother with.

WILL YOUR CHILD BE A MONSTER?

If a number of influential scientists have their way, some child or grand-child of yours may eke out his life in the frozen wastes of Pluto, where even the sun is only a spark in the sky – and will be unable to return to Earth until after he dies, *if then*!

Yes, even now there are plans afoot to change innocent unborn chil-dren into alien creatures who would die terribly the moment that they set foot upon the green planet of their ancestors. Impatient with the slow but steady pace of man's conquest of Mars, prominent ivory-tower thinkers are working out ways to produce all kinds of travesties upon the human form – travesties which will be able to survive, somehow, in the bitterest and most untamed of planetary infernos.

The process which may produce these pitiful freaks – at enormous expense – is called 'pantropy'. It is already in imperfect and dangerous existence. Chief among its prophets is white-haired, dreamy-eyed Dr. Jacob Rullman, who ...

'*Stop*,' Sweeney said.

He put his fingertips to his temples, and then, trembling, took them away again and looked at Rullman. The scientist put down the old magazine clip-ping, which even in its telfon sheath was as yellow as *paella* after its half-life in Ganymede's air. Rullman's own hands were quite steady; and what there was left of his hair was as reddish-brown as ever.

'Those lies! – I'm sorry. But they work, I know they work. That's what they filled me up with. It's different when you realize how vicious they are.'

'I know,' Rullman said, gently. 'It's easy to do. Bringing up an Adapted child is a special process, the child is always isolated and anxious to imitate, you may tell it anything you wish; it has no choice but to believe, it's desper-ate for closer contact, for acceptance, for the embraces it can never have. It's the ultimate in bottle-babies: the breast that might have fed it may be just on the other side of the glass, but it also lies generations in the past. Even the voice of the mother comes along a wire – if it comes along at all. I know, Donald, believe me. It happened to me, too. And it's very hard.'

'Jacob Rullman was—'

'My remote, immediate father. My mother died early. They often do, of the deprivation, I believe; like yours. But my father taught me the truth, there in the Moon caves, before he was killed.'

Sweeney took a deep breath. 'I'm learning all that now. Go on.'

'Are you sure, Donald?'

'Go on. I need to know, and it's not too late. Please.'

'Well,' Rullman said reflectively, 'the Authority got laws passed against pantropy, but for a while the laws didn't have many teeth; Congress was leary of forbidding vivisection at the same time, and didn't know exactly what it *was* being asked to forbid; Port didn't want to be too explicit. My father was determined to see pantropy tried while the laws still provided some loopholes – he knew well enough that they'd be stiffened as soon as Port thought it safe to stiffen them. And he was convinced that we'd never colonize the stars by dome-building or terraforming. Those might work on some of our local planets – Mars, Venus – but not outside.'

'Outside? How would anybody get there?'

'With the interstellar drive, Donald. It's been in existence for decades, in fact for nearly half a century. Several exploratory voyages were made with it right after it was discovered, all of them highly successful – though you'll find no mention of them in the press of the time. Port couldn't see any profit emerging out of interstellar flight and suppressed the news, sequestered the patents, destroyed the records of the trips – insofar as it could. But all the Port ships have the overdrive, just in case. Even our ship has it. So does your ferry-pilot friend up there.'

Sweeney shut up.

'The thing is this: most planets, even right here inside the solar system, won't sustain domes to begin with, and can't be terraformed in any even imaginable way. Jupiter, for instance. And too many others will yield to either procedure too slowly, and too unprofitably, to tempt Port. Over interstellar distances, Port won't even try, since there'd be no trade or traffic it could collect against.

'Pantropy was the obvious answer – not for Port, certainly, but for man's future in general. Somehow, my father sold that idea to some politicians, and to some people with money, too. He was even able to find several survivors of those early interstellar expeditions, people who knew some of the extra-solar planets *and* the operation of the overdrive. All these people wanted to make at least one demonstration experiment in pantropy, an open-ended one which would lead to others if it succeeded.

'We are that experiment: this colony on Ganymede.

'Port had it outlawed before it was fairly started, but by the time they found the Moon labs it was too late; we got away. It was then that they put teeth into the laws, and made them retroactive; they had to kill pantropy, and they knew it.

'And that is why our very existence is a crime, Donald. And it is an absolute requirement of Port's policy that the colony be a failure, and that they *be able to prove it*. That's why they want us back. They want to be able to exhibit us, to show what helpless freaks we are on Earth, and to tell their people that we couldn't get along on Ganymede either, and had to be bailed out of our own mess.

'After that – well, there are those phony commerce-raiding charges you told me about. We'll be tried. We'll be executed, most likely, by exposing us in public to Earth-normal conditions. It would be a fine object-lesson; indeed, the finishing touch.'

Sweeney crouched down in his chair, utterly revolted by the first complete emotion he had ever experienced: loathing for himself. He understood, now, the overtones in Rullman's voice. Everyone had been betrayed – everyone!

The voice went on without mercy, piling up the ashes. 'Now, as for the project, our project that is, that's equally as simple. We know that in the long run human beings can't colonize the stars without pantropy. We know that Port won't allow pantropy to be used. And we know, therefore, that we ourselves have to carry pantropy to the stars, before Port can head us off. One, two, three, infinity.

'So that's what we're going to do, or *were* going to do. We've got our old ship fitted out for the trip, and we've got a new generation of children – just a small number – trained to operate it, and adapted for – well, for someplace. The kids can't live on Earth, and they can't live on Ganymede; but they can live on one of six different extra-solar planets we've picked out – each one of which is at a different compass-point, and at a different distance from Sol. I know the names of only two of them, the kids are the only ones who know the rest. Which one they'll actually go to will be decided only after they're aloft and on their way. Nobody who stays behind will be able to betray them. Earth will never find them.

'There will be the beginning of the most immense "seeding program" in man's history: seeding the stars with people.

'*If* we can still manage to get it off the ground.'

In the silence that followed, the door of Rullman's office opened quietly, and Mike Leverault came in, looking preoccupied and carrying a clipboard. She stopped when she saw them, and Sweeney's heart constricted on the thawing slush inside its stiffly pumping chambers.

'Excuse me,' she said. 'I thought … Is there something wrong? You both look so grim—'

'There's something wrong,' Rullman said. He looked at Sweeney.

A corner of Sweeney's mouth twitched, without his willing it. He wondered if he were trying to smile, and if so, about what.

'There's no help for it,' he said. 'Dr. Rullman, your colonists will have to revolt against you.'

4

The starshell burst high, perhaps three miles up. Though it was over the western edge of the plateau, enough light spilled down to the floor of the Gouge to checker the rocking, growling halftrack.

The sound, however, was too faint to break through the noise of the turbines, and Sweeney wasn't worried about the brief light. The truck, pushing its way north at a good twenty miles an hour beneath the wild growth, would be as difficult to detect from the air as a mouse running among roots.

Besides, nobody would be likely to be looking into the Gouge now. The evidences of battle sweeping the highlands were too compelling; Sweeney himself was following them tensely.

Mike was doing the driving, leaving Sweeney free to crouch in the tool- and instrument-littered tonneau by the big aluminum keg, watching the radar screen. The paraboloid basket-work of the radar antenna atop the truck was not sweeping; it was pointing straight back along the way he and Mike had come, picking up a microwave relay from the last automatic station that they had passed. The sweeping was being done for Sweeney, by the big radio-telescope atop Howe's *pi*.

Sweeney paid little attention to the near, low, fast streaks on the screen. They were painted there by rocket ordnance of low calibre – a part of the fighting which had no bearing on the overall pattern. That pattern was already clear: it showed, as it had for days, that the insurgent forces still held the mountain and its heavy weapons, but that the attacking salient from the loyalists' camp up north was maintaining the initiative, and was gathering strength.

It had developed into a running stalemate. Though the insurgents had obviously managed to drive the loyalists out of Howe's *pi*, perhaps by some trick with the ventilators, perhaps by some form of guerrilla warfare, they were equally evidently no match for the loyalists in the field. There they were losing ground twice as fast as they had originally taken it. The supporting fire from the mountain didn't seem to be helping them much; it was heavy, but it was terribly inaccurate. The frequent starshells told their own story of bad visibility and worse intelligence. And the loyalists, ousted though they were, had all the planes; they had the effrontery to fly them over the lines with riding lights.

What the loyalists would do when confronted with the problem of re-taking the mountain was another question. Nothing short of very heavy stuff would make much of a dent on Howe's *pi*. And, even overlooking the fact that the heavy stuff was all inside the mountain, it would be suicide for *either* force to use it on Ganymede. The fighting hadn't become that bitter, yet. But it yet might.

And the Earth ships that showed on the screen inside the halftrack knew it. That much showed clearly by their disposition. They were there, almost surely, because they had deduced that Sweeney was leading the insurgents – but they showed no desire to draw in and give Sweeney a hand. Instead, they stood off, a little inside the orbit of Callisto, about 900,000 miles from Ganymede – far enough to give themselves a good running start if they saw an atomic spark on Ganymede, close enough to bail Sweeney out once it seemed that he had gained the victory anyhow.

Mike's voice, shouting something unintelligible, came back to him mixed in with the roaring of the halftrack's turbines.

'What's the matter?' he shouted, cocking his head.

'... that rock-tumble ahead. If it's as ... before ... probably break the beam.'

'Stop her,' Sweeney shouted. 'Want another reading.'

The halftrack halted obediently, and Sweeney checked his screen against Rullman's readings, which showed on tumblers snicking over on a counter near his elbow. It checked; 900,000 was close enough. Maybe a little closer, but not much. The wave-front of a full satellary explosion would cross that distance in about five seconds, carrying instant obliteration with it; but five seconds would be long enough to allow the automatics on the Earth ships to slam them away on trans-finite drive.

He slapped her on the shoulder, twice. 'Okay so far. Go ahead.'

Her reply was lost, but he saw her crash-helmet nod, and the truck began to cant itself slowly and crazily up a long, helter-skelter causeway of boul-ders and rubble: a sort of talus-slope, one of many rolled each year into the Gouge by exfoliation in the cliffs. Mike turned and smiled back at him gleefully, and he smiled back; the treads were clanking too loudly to permit any other answer.

The whole scheme had depended from the beginning upon so long a chain of *its* that it could still fall apart at any moment and at any flawed link. It had been dependable only at the beginning. The signal Sweeney had sent Meiklejon – VVANY – had told Meiklejon nothing, since he didn't know the code; but it had told the computer that Sweeney still lacked custody of the Adapted Men that Earth wanted, but that he had the help he thought he would need in getting that custody eventually. That much was a known.

What orders the computer would rap out for Meiklejon in response comprised the first of the *ifs*.

The computer might, of course, react with some incredibly bold piece of gamesmanship too remote from normal human thinking to be even guessable; Shannon's chess-playing machines sometimes won games from masters that way, though more usually they could barely hold their own against dubs. Since there was no way to anticipate what such a gambit would be like, neither Sweeney nor Rullman had wasted any time trying to pretend that there was.

But the other alternative was much more likely. The machine would assume that Sweeney was safe, as was evidenced by the arrival of the coded signal; and that if he had help he could only have gathered about him a secret core of disaffected colonists, a 'Loyal Ganymedian Underground' or equivalent. Earth would assume, and would build the assumption into the computer, that many of the colonists were dissatisfied with their lives; it was a hope that Earth could turn into a fact without being aware of the delusion, since nobody on Earth could suspect how beautiful Ganymede was. And the computer would assume, too, that it might be only a matter of time before Sweeney also had custody, and would be sending Meiklejon WAVVY – or maybe even YYAWY.

'How will we know if it does?' Rullman had demanded.

'If it does, then the deadline will pass without Meiklejon's making a move. He'll just stick to his orbit until the computer changes his mind. What else could it tell him to do, anyhow? He's just one man in a small ship without heavy armament. And he's an Earthman at that – he couldn't come down here and join my supposed underground group even if the idea occurred to him. He'll sit tight.'

The halftrack heaved itself over an almost cubical boulder, slid sidewise along its tilted face, and dropped heavily to the bed of smaller rounded stones. Sweeney looked up from the radar controls to see how the big aluminum keg was taking the ride. It was awash in a sea of hand tools – picks, adzes, sledges, spikes, coils of line rapidly unwinding – but it was securely strapped down. The miracle of fireworks chemistry (and specifically, Ganymedian chemistry) still slumbered inside it. He clambered forward into the cab beside Mike and strapped himself down to enjoy the ride.

There was no way to predict or to calculate how long an extension of the deadline the machine on Meiklejon's ship would allow Sweeney for the launching of his insurrection. The colony worked as though there would be no grace period at all. When the deadline passed without any sign that Meiklejon even existed – though the radio-telescope showed that he was still there – Sweeney and Rullman did not congratulate each other. They could not be sure that the silence and the delay meant what they had every good reason to hope that it meant. They could only go on working.

The movements of machines, men, and energy displays which should look to Meiklejon like a revolt of the colonists burst away from Howe's *pi* eleven days later. All the signs showed that it had been the loyalists who had set up their base near the north pole of Ganymede. Sweeney and Mike had driven through the Gouge before, for that purpose, planting in a radar-crazy jungle a whole series of small devices, all automatic, all designed to register on Meiklejon's detectors as a vast bustle of heavy machinery. The visible strategic movements of the opposing armies had suggested the same loyalist concentration at the pole.

And now Sweeney and Mike were on their way back.

The computer appeared to be waiting it out; Meiklejon had evidently fed the data to it as a real rebellion. Sweeney's side obviously was carrying the field at first. The computer had no reason to run a new extrapolation up to the first day the loyalist forces had managed to hold their lines; and then it had to run squarely up against the question of how the loyalists could take the mountain even if, in the succeeding weeks, they should sweep the field clear of Sweeney.

'Kid stuff,' Sweeney had said. 'It hasn't any reason to think differently. Too simple to make it extrapolate beyond the first derivative.'

'You're very confident, Donald.'

Sweeney stirred uneasily in the bucket seat as he recalled Rullman's smile. No Adapted Man, least of all Sweeney, had had any real childhood; no 'kid stuff'. Fortunately the Port cops had thought it essential to Sweeney's task that he know theory of games.

The halftrack settled down to relatively smooth progress once more, and Sweeney got up to check the screen. The talus-slope, as Mike had anticipated, cut off reception from the radar relay station behind them; Sweeney started the antenna sweeping. Much of the field was cropped by the near edge of the Gouge, but that effect would begin to disappear gradually from the screen now. The floor of the Gouge rose steadily as one approached the north pole, although it never quite reached the level of the plains. He could already capture enough sky to be satisfied that the Earth ships were just where they had been before.

That had been the last risk: that Meiklejon, alarmed at the computer's continued counsels of inaction, would radio Earth for advice from higher authorities. Obviously a colonists' revolt on Ganymede, one that could be painted as a 'We want to go home' movement, would be ideal for Earth's purposes. Earth would not only insist on Meiklejon's sitting tight as his computer had told him to do – but would also hasten to bring up reinforcements for Sweeney, just in case.

Both Sweeney and Rullman had known how likely that was to happen, and had decided to take the chance, and make preparations against it. The chance had not paid off – the Earth ships were here – but it still looked as though the preparations might.

As content as was possible under the circumstances, Sweeney went forward. Before reaching for his safety belt, he stopped to kiss Mike, to the considerable detriment of her control of the lurching truck.

The explosion threw him, hard, halfway across the empty bucket seat.

He struggled up, his head ringing. The truck's engines seemed to have stopped; beneath the ringing, he could hear nothing but the sound of the blowers.

'Don! Are you all right? What was that?'

'Ugh,' he said, sitting down. 'Nothing broken. Hit my head a crack. It was high explosive, from the sound. A big one.'

Her face was pinched and anxious in the soft glow from the dashboard. 'One of ours? Or—'

'I don't know, Mike. Sounded like it hit back down the ravine a distance. What's the matter with the engine?'

She touched the starter. It whined, and the engine caught at once. 'I must have stalled it,' she said apologetically. She put it in gear. 'But it doesn't feel right. The traction's bad on your side.'

Sweeney swung the cab door open and dropped to the stony ground. Then he whistled.

'What is it?'

'That was closer than I thought.' he called back. 'The right-hand track is cut almost in half. A flying rock splinter, I suppose. Toss me the torch.'

She leaned far out across his seat, reaching the arc-cutter to him, and then the goggles. He made his way to the rear of the truck and snapped the switch. The electric arc burned sulfur-blue; a moment later, the damaged track was unwinding from around the four big snowmobile tires like an expiring snake. Dragging the cord behind him, Sweeney cut the left track off, too, and then returned to the cab, rewinding the cord as he went.

'Okay, but take it slow. Those tires are going to be cut to ribbons by the time we hit that base.'

Her face was still white, but she asked no more questions. The halftrack began to crawl forward, a halftrack no longer. At a little over two miles farther on, the first of the eight tires blew, making them both jump. A hasty check showed that it was the right outside rear one. Another two and a half miles, and the right inside drive tire blew out, too. It was bad to have two gone on the same side of the truck, but at least they were on different axles and in alternate position. The next one to go, five miles farther on – the ground became less littered as it rose – was the left inside rear.

'Don.'

'Yes, Mike.'

'Do you think that was an Earth bomb?'

'I don't know, Mike. I doubt it; they're too far away to be throwing stuff at Ganymede except at random, and why would they do that? More likely it was one of our torpedoes, out of control.' He snapped his fingers. 'Wait a minute. If we're throwing H.E. at each other, now, the cops will have noticed, and *that* we can check.'

Bang!

The halftrack settled down to the right and began to slobber at the ground. No check was needed to tell Sweeney that that one had been the right outside driver. Those two wheels would be hitting on bare rims within the next thousand feet or so of travel; the main weight of the vehicle was back there – the steering tires took very little punishment, comparatively.

Gritting his teeth, he unbuckled the safety and scrambled back to the radar set, checking the aluminum drum automatically as he went.

There was much more sky showing on the screen now. It was impossible to triangulate the positions of the Earth ships now that the transmission from Howe's *pi* was cut off, but the pips on the screen were markedly dimmer. Sweeney guessed that they had retreated at least another hundred thousand miles. He grinned and leaned into Mike's ear.

'It was one of ours,' he said. 'Rullman's stepping up on the heavy artillery, that's all. One of his torpedo pilots must have lost one in the Gouge. The Port cops have detected the step-up, all right – they've backed off. It's beginning to look more and more as though the rebels might try to smear the loyalist base with a fission bomb, and they don't want to be cheek to cheek with the planet when that happens. How far do we have to go, still?'

Mike said, 'We're—'

Bang! Mike grabbed for the switch, and the engine died.

'—here,' she finished, and then, amazingly, began to giggle.

Sweeney swallowed, and then discovered that he was grinning, too. 'With three track-tires intact,' he said. 'Hooray for us. Let's get on the job.'

Another starshell broke open in the sky, not as near as before. Sweeney went around to the back of the truck, Mike picking her way after him, both of them looking ruefully at the wreathes of shredded silicone rubber which once had been two excellent tires. Two of the rims were quite bare; the fifth deflated tire, which had not been driven on, was only a puncture and might be salvaged.

'Unstrap the barrel and roll 'er out the tailgate,' Sweeney said. 'Easy. Now let's lower 'er to the ground, and over there.'

All around them, concealed among the rocks and the massive, gnarled trunks, were the little instruments whose busy electronic chattering made this spot sound like a major military encampment to the ships lying off

Ganymede. Photographs, of course, would not be expected to show it: the visible light was insufficient, the infra-red still weaker, and ultraviolet plates would be stopped by the atmosphere. Nobody would expect to *see* anything from space by any method, not in the Gouge; but the detectors would report power being expended, and power sources moving about – and rebel torpedoes homing purposefully on the area. That should be enough.

With Mike's help, Sweeney stood the aluminum barrel on end roughly in the center of this assemblage. 'I'm going to take that punctured tire off,' he said. 'We've got fifteen minutes until take-off time, and we may need it later. Know how to wire up this thing?'

'I'm not an idiot. Go change your tire.'

While Sweeney worked, Mike located the main input lead for the little invisible chatterers and spliced a line into it. To this she rigged a spring-driven switch which would snap to 'Off' as soon as current was delivered to a solenoid which actuated its trigger. One strand of reel-wound cable went to the solenoid, another to a red-splashed terminal on the side of the aluminum keg. She checked the thumb-plunger at the other end of the cable. Everything was ready. When that plunger was pushed, the little chatterers would go Off, at the same moment that the barrel went On.

'All set, Mike?'

'Ready and waiting. Five minutes until take-off time.'

'Good,' Sweeney said, taking the reel from her. 'You'd better get in the truck and take it on across the pole – over the horizon from here.'

'Why? There's no real danger. And if there is, what good would I be over there alone?'

'Look, Mike,' Sweeney said. He was already walking backwards, still to the north, paying out cable. 'I just want to get that truck out of here; maybe we can use it, and once that barrel starts, it just might set the truck on fire. Besides, supposing the cops decide to take a close look down here? The truck's visible, or at least it's suspiciously regular. But they couldn't see *me*. It'd be far better to have the truck over the horizon. Fair enough?'

'Oh, all right. Just don't get yourself killed, that's all.'

'I won't. I'll be along after the show's over. Go on, beat it.'

Scowling, though not very convincingly, she climbed back into the truck, which pulled slowly away up the grade. Sweeney could hear its bare rims screeching against upthrusts of rock long after it had disappeared, but finally it was out of earshot as well.

He continued to walk backward, unwinding the cable from the reel until it was all gone, and the phony encampment was a full mile south of him. He took the thumb switch in his right hand, checked his watch, and crouched down behind a long low spur to wait.

A whole series of starshells made a train of blue suns across the sky.

Somewhere a missile screamed, and then the ground shook heavily. Sweeney fervently hoped that the 'insurgent' torpedomen weren't shaving it too fine.

But it wouldn't be long now. In just a few seconds, the survival ship – the ship aimed at one of six unknown stars, and carrying the new generation of Adapted children – would take off from Howe's *pi*.

Twenty seconds.

Fifteen.

Ten.

Nine.

Eight.

Seven.

Six.

Sweeney pushed the plunger.

The aluminum keg ignited with a hollow cough, and an intense ball of light, far too bright to be shut out either by the welding goggles or by closed eyelids or by both, rose into Ganymede's sky. The heat struck against Sweeney's skin as strongly as the backwash of the JATO unit had done, so long ago. The concussion, which followed about nine seconds later, flattened him and made his nose bleed.

Uncaring, he rolled over and looked upward. The light had already almost died. There was now a roiling column of white smoke, shot through with lurid, incandescent colors, hurling itself skyward at close to a mile a minute.

It was altogether a hell of a convincing-looking fission bomb – for a fake.

The column didn't begin to mushroom until it was almost five miles high, but by that time Sweeney was sure that there wasn't an Earth ship anywhere within ten astronomical units of Ganymede. Nobody would stop to make inquiries, especially when all the instruments in the 'encampment' had stopped transmitting simultaneously with the 'blast'.

It might perhaps occur to Port later that the 'blast' might have been a huge, single-shot Roman candle fired from an aluminum keg, propelled by a mixture of smoke-flare compounds and low-grade chemical explosives. But by that time, the survival ship would be gone beyond all possibility of tracing its path.

As a matter of fact, it was gone already. It had left on the count, uncounted by Sweeney, of Zero.

Sweeney got up, humming cheerfully – and quite as tunelessly as Rullman – and continued to plod north. On the other side of the pole, the Gouge was supposed to continue to become shallower as it proceeded into the Jupiter-ward hemisphere of Ganymede. There was a twilight zone there, illuminated by the sun irregularly because of libration while Ganymede was on the sunward side of Jupiter, and quite regularly as the satellite went toward and away from occultation with the big primary. Of course the occultation periods would be rather cold, but they lasted less than eight hours apiece.

Elsewhere on Ganymede, the other colonists were heading for similar spots, their spurious war equipment destroyed, their purpose fulfilled. They were equipped variously, but all as well as Sweeney; and he had a sound ten-wheeled snowmobile, on which the six remaining tires could be redistributed to make the vehicle suitable for heavy tractoring, and with a tonneau loaded with tools, seeds, slips and cuttings, medical supplies, reserve food and fuel. He also had a wife.

Earth would visit Ganymede, of course. But it would find nothing. The inside of Howe's *pi* had been razed when the survival ship had taken off. As for the people, they would be harmless, ignorant, and *widely* scattered.

Peasants, Sweeney thought. Whistling, he crossed the north pole. Nothing but peasants.

At last he saw the squat shape of the truck, crouched at the mouth of a valley. At first Mike was not visible, but finally he spotted her, standing with her back to him on a rise. He clambered up beside her.

The valley was narrow for about a hundred feet ahead, and then it opened out in a broad fan of level land. A faint haze hovered over it. To an Earthman, nothing could have looked more desolate – but no Earthman was looking at it.

'I'll bet that's the best farm land on Ganymede,' Sweeney whispered. 'I wish—'

Mike turned and looked at him. He cut the wish off unspoken, but there was no doubt that Mike had fathomed it. But Rullman was no longer on Ganymede to share its beauties – this one, or any other. Though he would never see the end of the journey, and could not have survived at its goal, he had gone with the children on the ship – and taken his exportable knowledge with him.

He had been, Sweeney knew, a great man. Greater, perhaps, than his father.

'Go on ahead with the truck, Mike,' Sweeney said softly. 'I'll walk on behind you.'

'Why? It'll ride easy on that soil – the extra weight won't matter.'

'I'm not worrying about the weight. It's just that I want to walk it. It's – well, hell, Mike, don't you know that I'm just about to be born? Whoever heard of a kid arriving with a fourteen-ton truck?'

BOOK TWO

The Thing in the Attic

… And it is written that after the Giants came to Tellura from the far stars, they abode a while, and looked upon the surface of the land, and found it wanting, and of evil omen. Therefore did they make man to live always in the air and in the sunlight, and in the light of the stars, that he would be reminded of them. And the Giants abode yet a while, and taught men to speak, and to write, and to weave, and to do many things which are needful to do, of which the writings speak. And thereafter they departed to the far stars, saying, Take this world as your own, and though we shall return, fear not, for it is yours.

—*The Book of Laws*

1

Honath the Purse-Maker was hauled from the nets an hour before the rest of the prisoners, as befitted his role as the arch-doubter of them all. It was not yet dawn, but his captors led him in great bounds through the endless, musky-perfumed orchid gardens, small dark shapes with crooked legs, hunched shoulders, slim hairless tails, carried, like his, in concentric spirals wound clockwise. Behind them sprang Honath on the end of a long tether, timing his leaps by theirs, since any slip would hang him summarily.

He would of course be on his way to the surface, some 250 feet below the orchid gardens, shortly after dawn in any event. But not even the arch-doubter of them all wanted to begin the trip – not even at the merciful snap-spine end of a tether – a moment before the law said, Go.

The looping, interwoven network of vines beneath them, each cable as thick through as a man's body, bellied out and down sharply as the leapers reached the edge of the fern-tree forest which surrounded the copse of horsetails. The whole party stopped before beginning the descent and looked eastward, across the dim bowl. The stars were paling more and more rapidly; only the bright constellation of the Parrot could still be picked out without doubt.

'A fine day,' one of the guards said, conversationally. 'Better to go below on a sunny day than in the rain, Purse-Maker.'

Honath shuddered and said nothing. Of course, it was always raining down below in Hell, that much could be seen by a child. Even on sunny days, the endless pinpoint rain of transpiration, from the hundred million leaves of the eternal trees, hazed the forest air and soaked the black bog forever.

He looked around in the brightening, misty morning. The eastern horizon was black against the limb of the great red sun, which had already risen about a third of its diameter; it was almost time for the small, blue-white, furiously hot consort to follow. All the way to that brink, as to every other horizon, the woven ocean of the treetops flowed gently in long, unbreaking waves, featureless as some smooth oil. Only nearby could the eye break that ocean into its details, into the world as it was: a great, many-tiered network, thickly over-grown with small ferns, with air-drinking orchids, with a thousand varieties of fungi sprouting wherever vine crossed vine and collected a little humus for them, with the vivid parasites sucking sap from the vines, the trees, and even each other. In the ponds of rainwater collected by the closely fitting leaves of the bromeliads, tree-toads and peepers stopped down their hoarse songs dubiously as the light grew, and fell silent one by one. In the trees below the world, the tentative morning screeches of the lizard-birds – the souls of the damned, or the devils who hunted them, no one was quite sure which – took up the concert.

A small gust of wind whipped out of the hollow above the glade of horsetails, making the network under the party shift slightly, as if in a loom. Honath gave with it easily, automatically, but one of the smaller vines toward which he had moved one furless hand hissed at him and went pouring away into the darkness beneath – a chlorophyll-green snake, come up out of the dripping aerial pathways in which it hunted in ancestral gloom, to greet the suns and dry its scales in the quiet morning. Farther below, an astonished monkey, routed out of its bed by the disgusted serpent, sprang into another tree, reeling off ten mortal insults, one after the other, while still in mid-leap. The snake, of course, paid no attention, since it did not speak the language of men; but the party on the edge of the glade of horsetails snickered appreciatively.

'Bad language they favor, below,' another of the guards said. 'A fit place for you and your blasphemers, Purse-Maker. Come now.'

The tether at Honath's neck twitched, and then his captors were soaring in zig-zag bounds down into the hollow toward the Judgment Seat. He followed, since he had no choice, the tether threatening constantly to foul his arms, legs, or tail, and – worse, far worse – making his every movement mortally ungraceful. Above, the Parrot's starry plumes flickered and faded into the general blue.

Toward the center of the saucer above the grove, the stitched leaf-and-leather houses clustered thickly, bound to the vines themselves, or hanging from an occasional branch too high or too slender to bear the vines. Many of these purses Honath knew well, not only as visitor but as artisan. The finest of them, the inverted flowers which opened automatically as the morning dew bathed them, yet which could be closed tightly and safely around their occupants at dusk by a single draw-string, were his own design as well as his own handiwork. They had been widely admired and imitated.

The reputation that they had given him, too, had helped to bring him to the end of the snap-spine tether. They had given weight to his words among others – weight enough to make him at last the arch-doubter, the man who leads the young into blasphemy, the man who questions the Book of Laws.

And they had probably helped to win him his passage on the Elevator to Hell.

The purses were already opening as the party swung among them. Here and there, sleepy faces blinked out from amid the exfoliating sections, crisscrossed by relaxing lengths of dew-soaked rawhide. Some of the awakening householders recognized Honath, of that he was sure, but none came out to follow the party – though the villagers should be beginning to drop from the hearts of their stitched flowers like ripe seed-pods by this hour of any normal day.

A Judgment was at hand, and they knew it – and even those who had slept the night in one of Honath's finest houses would not speak for him now. Everyone knew, after all, that Honath did not believe in the Giants.

Honath could see the Judgment Seat itself now, a slung chair of woven cane crowned along the back with a row of gigantic mottled orchids. These had supposedly been transplanted there when the chair was made, but no one could remember how old they were; since there were no seasons, there was no particular reason why they should not have been there forever. The Seat itself was at the back of the arena and high above it, but in the gathering light Honath could make out the white-furred face of the Tribal Spokesman, like a lone silver-and-black pansy among the huge vivid blooms.

At the center of the arena proper was the Elevator itself. Honath had seen it often enough, and had himself witnessed Judgments where it was called into use, but he could still hardly believe that he was almost surely to be its next passenger. It consisted of nothing more than a large basket, deep enough so that one would have to leap out of it, and rimmed with thorns to prevent one from leaping back in. Three hempen ropes were tied to its rim, and were then cunningly interwound on a single-drum windlass of wood, which could be turned by two men even when the basket was loaded.

The procedure was equally simple. The condemned man was forced into the basket, and the basket lowered out of sight, until the slackening of the ropes indicated that it had touched the surface. The victim climbed out – and if he did not, the basket remained below until he starved or until Hell otherwise took care of its own – and the windlass was rewound.

The sentences were for varying periods of time according to the severity of the crime, but in practical terms this formality was empty. Although the basket was dutifully lowered when the sentence had expired, no one had ever been known to get back into it. Of course, in a world without seasons or moons, and hence without any but an arbitrary year, long periods of time are not easy to count accurately. The basket may often have arrived thirty or forty days to one side or the other of the proper date. This was only a technicality, however, for if keeping time was difficult in the attic world, it was probably impossible in Hell.

Honath's guards tied the free end of his tether to a branch and settled down around him. One abstractedly passed a pine cone to him, and he tried to occupy his mind with the business of picking the juicy seeds from it, but somehow they had no flavor.

More captives were being brought in now, while the Spokesman watched with glittering black eyes from his high perch. There was Mathild the Forager, shivering as if with ague, the fur down her left side glistening and spiky, as though she had inadvertently overturned a tank plant on herself. After her was brought Alaskon the Navigator, a middle-aged man only a few years younger than Honath himself; he was tied up next to Honath, where he settled down at once, chewing at a joint of cane with apparent indifference.

Thus far, the gathering had proceeded without more than a few words being spoken, but that ended when the guards tried to bring Seth the Needlesmith from the nets. He could be heard at once, over the entire distance to the glade, alternately chattering and shrieking in a mixture of tones that might mean fear or fury. Everyone in the glade but Alaskon turned to look, and heads emerged from purses like new butterflies from cocoons.

A moment later, Seth's guards came over the lip of the glade in a tangled group, now shouting themselves. Somewhere in the middle of the knot Seth's voice became still louder; obviously he was clinging with all five members to any vine or frond he could grasp, and was no sooner pried loose from one than he would leap by main force, backwards if possible, to another. Nevertheless, he was being brought inexorably down into the arena, two feet forward, one foot back, three feet forward ...

Honath's guards resumed picking their pine cones. During the disturbance, Honath realized, Charl the Reader had been brought in quietly from the same side of the glade. He now sat opposite Alaskon, looking apathetically down at the vine-web, his shoulders hunched forward. He exuded despair; even to look at him made Honath feel a renewed shudder.

From the high Seat, the Spokesman said: 'Honath the Purse-maker, Alaskon the Navigator, Charl the Reader, Seth the Needlesmith, Mathild the Forager, you are called to answer to justice.'

'Justice!' Seth shouted, springing free of his captors with a tremendous bound, and bringing up with a jerk on the end of his tether. 'This is no justice! I have nothing to do with—'

The guards caught up with him and clamped brown hands firmly over his mouth. The Spokesman watched with amused malice.

'The accusations are three,' the Spokesman said. 'The first, the telling of lies to children. Second, the casting into doubt of the divine order among men. Third, the denial of the Book of Laws. Each of you may speak in order of age. Honath the Purse-Maker, your plea may be heard.'

Honath stood up, trembling a little, but feeling a surprisingly renewed surge of his old independence.

'Your charges,' he said, 'all rest upon the denial of the Book of Laws. I have taught nothing else that is contrary to what we all believe, and called nothing else into doubt. And I deny the charge.'

The Spokesman looked down at him with disbelief. 'Many men and women have said that you do not believe in the Giants, Purse-Maker,' he said. 'You will not win mercy by piling up more lies.'

'I deny the charge,' Honath insisted. 'I believe in the Book of Laws as a whole, and I believe in the Giants. I have taught only that the Giants were not real in the sense that we are real. I have taught that they were intended as symbols of some higher reality, and were not meant to be taken as literal Persons.'

'What higher reality is this?' the Spokesman demanded. 'Describe it.'

'You ask me to do something the writers of the Book of Laws themselves couldn't do,' Honath said hotly. 'If they had to embody the reality in symbols rather than writing it down directly, how could a mere purse-maker do better?'

'This doctrine is wind,' the Spokesman said. 'And it is plainly intended to undercut authority and the order established by the Book. Tell me, Purse-Maker, if man need not fear the Giants, why should they fear the law?'

'Because they are men, and it is to their interest to fear the law. They aren't children, who need some physical Giant sitting over them with a whip to make them behave. Furthermore, Spokesman, this archaic belief *itself* undermines us. As long as we believe that there are real Giants, and that some day they'll return and resume teaching us, so long will we fail to seek answers to our questions for ourselves. Half of what we know was given to us in the Book, and the other half is supposed to drop to us from the skies if we wait long enough. In the meantime, we vegetate.'

'If a part of the Book be untrue, there can be nothing to prevent that it is all untrue,' the Spokesman said heavily. 'And we will lose even what you call the half of our knowledge – which is actually the whole of it, to those who see with clear eyes.'

Suddenly, Honath lost his temper. 'Lose it, then!' he shouted. 'Let us unlearn everything we know only by rote, go back to the beginning, learn all over again, and continue to learn, from our own experience. Spokesman, you are an old man, but there are still some of us who haven't forgotten what curiosity means!'

'Quiet!' the Spokesman said. 'We have heard enough. We call on Alaskon the Navigator.'

'Much of the Book is clearly untrue,' Alaskon said flatly, rising. 'As a handbook of small trades it has served us well. As a guide to how the universe is made, it is nonsense, in my opinion; Honath is too kind to it. I've made no secret of what I think, and I still think it.'

'And will pay for it,' the Spokesman said, blinking slowly down at Alaskon. 'Charl the Reader.'

'Nothing,' Charl said, without standing, or even looking up.

'You do not deny the charges?'

'I've nothing to say,' Charl said, but then, abruptly, his head jerked up, and he glared with desperate eyes at the Spokesman. 'I can read, Spokesman. I have seen words of the Book of Laws that contradict each other. I've pointed them out. They're facts, they exist on the pages. I've taught nothing, told no lies, preached no unbelief. I've pointed to the facts. That's all.'

'Seth the Needlesmith, you may speak now.'

The guards took their hands gratefully off Seth's mouth; they had been bitten several times in the process of keeping him quiet up to now. Seth resumed shouting at once.

'I'm no part of this group! I'm the victim of gossip, envious neighbors, smiths jealous of my skill and my custom! No man can say worse of me than that I sold needles to this purse-maker – sold them in good faith! The charges against me are lies, all of them!'

Honath jumped to his feet in fury, and then sat down again, choking back the answering shout almost without tasting its bitterness. What did it matter? Why should he bear witness against the young man? It would not help the others, and if Seth wanted to lie his way out of Hell, he might as well be given the chance.

The Spokesman was looking down at Seth with the identical expression of outraged disbelief which he had first bent upon Honath. 'Who was it cut the blasphemies into the hardwood trees, by the house of Hosi the Lawgiver?' he demanded. 'Sharp needles were at work there, and there are witnesses to say that your hands held them.'

'More lies!'

'Needles found in your house fit the furrows, Seth.'

'They were not mine – or they were stolen! I demand to be freed!'

'You will be freed,' the Spokesman said coldly. There was no possible doubt as to what he meant. Seth began to weep and to shout at the same time. Hands closed over his mouth again. 'Mathild the Forager, your plea may be heard.'

The young woman stood up hesitantly. Her fur was nearly dry now, but she was still shivering.

'Spokesman,' she said, 'I saw the things which Charl the Reader showed me. I doubted, but what Honath said restored my belief. I see no harm in his teachings. They remove doubt, instead of fostering it, as you say they do. I see no evil in them, and I don't understand why this is a crime.'

Honath looked over to her with new admiration. The Spokesman sighed heavily.

'I am sorry for you,' he said, 'but as Spokesman we cannot allow ignorance of the Law as a plea. We will be merciful to you all, however. Renounce your heresy, affirm your belief in the Book as it is written from bark to bark, and you shall be no more than cast out of the tribe.'

'I renounce it!' Seth said. 'I never shared it! It's all blasphemy and every word is a lie! I believe in the Book, all of it!'

'You, Needlesmith,' the Spokesman said, 'have lied before this Judgment, and are probably lying now. You are not included in the dispensation.'

'Snake-spotted caterpillar! May your – *ummulph.*'

'Purse-Maker, what is your answer?'

'It is, No,' Honath said stonily. 'I've spoken the truth. The truth can't be unsaid.'

The Spokesman looked down at the rest of them. 'As for you three, consider your answers carefully. To share the heresy means sharing the sentence. The penalty will not be lightened only because you did not invent the heresy.'

There was a long silence.

Honath swallowed hard. The courage and the faith in that silence made him feel smaller and more helpless than ever. He realized suddenly that the other three would have kept that silence, even without Seth's defection to stiffen their spines. He wondered if he could have done so.

'Then we pronounce the sentence,' the Spokesman said. 'You are one and all condemned to one thousand days in Hell.'

There was a concerted gasp from around the edges of the arena, where, without Honath's having noticed it before, a silent crowd had gathered. He did not wonder at the sound. The sentence was the longest in the history of the tribe.

Not that it really meant anything. No one had ever come back from as little as one hundred days in Hell. No one bad ever come back from Hell at all.

'Unlash the Elevator. All shall go together – and their heresy with them.'

2

The basket swayed. The last of the attic world that Honath saw was a circle of faces, not too close to the gap in the vine web, peering down after them. Then the basket fell another few yards to the next turn of the windlass and the faces vanished.

Seth was weeping in the bottom of the Elevator, curled up into a tight ball, the end of his tail wrapped around his nose and eyes. No one else could make a sound, least of all Honath.

The gloom closed around them. It seemed extraordinarily still. The occasional harsh scream of a lizard-bird somehow emphasized the silence without breaking it. The light that filtered down into the long aisles between the trees seemed to be absorbed in a blue–green haze, through which the lianas wove their long curved lines. The columns of tree-trunks, the pillars of the world, stood all around them, too distant in the dim light to allow them to gauge their speed of descent; only the irregular plunges of the basket proved that it was even in motion any longer, though it swayed laterally in a complex, overlapping series of figure-eights traced on the air in response to the rotation of the planet – a Foucault pendulum ballasted with five lives.

Then the basket lurched downward once more, brought up short, and tipped sidewise, tumbling them all against the hard cane. Mathild cried out in a thin voice, and Seth uncurled almost instantly, clawing for a handhold. Another lurch, and the Elevator lay down on its side and was still.

They were in Hell.

Cautiously, Honath began to climb out, picking his way over the long thorns on the basket's rim. After a moment, Charl the Reader followed, and then Alaskon took Mathild firmly by the hand and led her out onto the surface. The footing was wet and spongy, yet not at all resilient, and it felt cold; Honath's toes curled involuntarily.

'Come on, Seth,' Charl said in a hushed voice. 'They won't haul it back up until we're all out. You know that.'

Alaskon looked around into the chilly mists. 'Yes,' he said. 'And we'll need a needlesmith down here. With good tools, there's just a chance—'

Seth's eyes had been darting back and forth from one to the other. With a sudden chattering scream, he bounded out of the bottom of the basket, soaring over their heads in a long, flat leap, and struck the high knee at the base of the nearest tree, an immense fan palm. As he hit, his legs doubled under him, and almost in the same motion he seemed to rocket straight up into the murky air.

Gaping, Honath looked up after him. The young needlesmith had timed his course to the split second. He was already darting up the rope from which the Elevator was suspended. He did not even bother to look back.

After a moment, the basket tipped upright. The impact of Seth's weight hitting the rope evidently had been taken by the windlass team to mean that the condemned people were all out on the surface; a twitch on the rope was the usual signal. The basket began to rise, bobbing and dancing. Its speed of ascent, added to Seth's, took his racing dwindling figure out of sight quickly. After a while, the basket was gone, too.

'He'll never get to the top,' Mathild whispered. 'It's too far, and he's going too fast. He'll lose strength and fall.'

'I don't think so,' Alaskon said heavily. 'He's agile and strong. If anyone could make it, he could.'

'They'll kill him if he does.'

'Of course they will,' Alaskon said, shrugging.

'I won't miss him,' Honath said.

'No more will I. But we could use some sharp needles down here, Honath. Now, we'll have to plan to make our own – if we can identify the different woods, down here where there aren't any leaves to help us tell them apart.'

Honath looked at the Navigator curiously. Seth's bolt for the sky had distracted him from the realization that the basket, too, was gone, but now that desolate fact hit home. 'You actually plan to stay alive in Hell, don't you, Alaskon?'

'Certainly,' Alaskon said calmly. 'This is no more Hell than – up there – is Heaven. It's the surface of the planet, no more, no less. We can stay alive if we don't panic. Were you just going to sit here until the furies came for you, Honath?'

'I hadn't thought much about it,' Honath confessed. 'But if there is any chance that Seth will lose his grip on that rope – before he reaches the top and they knife him – shouldn't we wait and see if we can catch him? He can't weigh more than 35 pounds. Maybe we could contrive some sort of a net—'

'He'd just break our bones along with his,' Charl said. 'I'm for getting out of here as fast as possible.'

'What for? Do you know a better place?'

'No, but whether this is Hell or not, there are demons down here. We've all seen them from up above, the snake-headed giants. They must know that the Elevator always lands here and empties out free food. This must be a feeding-ground for them—'

He had not quite finished speaking when the branches began to sigh and toss, far above. A gust of stinging droplets poured along the blue air, and thunder rumbled. Mathild whimpered.

'It's only a squall coming up,' Honath said. But the words came out in a series of short croaks. As the wind had moved through the trees, Honath had automatically flexed his knees and put his arms out for handholds, awaiting the long wave of response to pass through the ground beneath him. But nothing happened. The surface under his feet remained stolidly where it was, flexing not a fraction of an inch in any direction. And there was nothing nearby for his hands to grasp.

He staggered, trying to compensate for the failure of the ground to move, but at the same moment another gust of wind blew through the aisles, a little stronger than the first, and calling insistently for a new adjustment of his body to the waves which passed along the treetops. Again the squashy surface beneath him refused to respond; the familiar give-and-take of the vine-web to the winds, a part of his world as accustomed as the winds themselves, was gone.

Honath was forced to sit down, feeling distinctly ill. The damp, cool earth under his furless buttocks was unpleasant, but he could not have remained standing any longer without losing his meager prisoner's breakfast. One grappling hand caught hold of the ridged, gritty stems of a clump of horsetail, but the contact failed to allay the uneasiness.

The others seemed to be bearing it no better than Honath. Mathild in particular was rocking dizzily, her lips compressed, her hands clapped to her delicate ears.

Dizziness. It was unheard of up above, except among those who had suffered grave head injuries or were otherwise very ill. But on the motionless ground of Hell, it was evidently going to be with them constantly.

Charl squatted, swallowing convulsively. 'I – I can't stand,' he moaned. 'It's magic, Alaskon – the snake-headed demons—'

'Nonsense,' Alaskon said, though he had remained standing only by clinging to the huge, mud-colored bulb of a cycadella. 'It's just a disturbance of our sense of balance. It's a – motionlessness-sickness. We'll get used to it.'

'We'd better,' Honath said, relinquishing his grip on the horsetails by a sheer act of will. 'I think Charl's right about this being a feeding-ground, Alaskon. I hear something moving around in the ferns. And if this rain lasts long, the water will rise here, too. I've seen silver flashes from down here many a time after heavy rains.'

'That's right,' Mathild said, her voice subdued. 'The base of the ferntree grove always floods; that's why the treetops are so much lower there.'

The wind seemed to have let up a little, though the rain was still falling. Alaskon stood up tentatively.

'Then let's move on,' he said. 'If we try to keep under cover until we get to higher ground—'

A faint crackling sound, high above his head, interrupted him. It got louder. Feeling a sudden spasm of pure fear, Honath looked up.

Nothing could be seen for an instant but the far-away curtain of branches and fern-fronds. Then, with shocking suddenness, something small and black irrupted through the blue-green roof and came tumbling toward them. It was a man, twisting and tumbling through the air with grotesque slowness, like a child turning in its sleep. They scattered.

The body hit the ground with a sodden thump, but there were sharp overtones to the sound, like the bursting of a gourd. For a moment nobody moved. Then Honath crept forward.

It had been Seth, as Honath had realized the moment the black figurine had burst through the branches far above. But it had not been the fall that had killed him. He had been run through by at least a dozen needles – some of them, beyond doubt, tools from his own shop, their points edged hair-fine by his own precious strops of leatherwood-bark, soaked until they were soft, pliant, and nearly transparent in the mud at the bottom of sun-warmed bromeliad tanks.

There would be no reprieve from above. The sentence was one thousand days. This burst and broken huddle of fur was the only alternative.

And the first day had barely begun.

They toiled all the rest of the day to reach higher ground, clinging to the earth for the most part because the trees, except for a few scattered ging-koes, flowering dogwoods and live oaks, did not begin to branch until their tanks had soared more man eighteen feet above the ground. As they stole cautiously closer to the foothills of the Great Range and the ground became firmer, they were able to take to the air for short stretches, but they were no sooner aloft among the willows than the lizard-birds came squalling down on them by the *dozens*, fighting among each other for the privilege of nipping these plump and incredibly slow-moving monkeys.

No man, no matter how confirmed a free-thinker, could have stood up under such an onslaught by the creatures he had been taught as a child to think of as his ancestors. The first time it happened, every member of the party dropped like a pine-cone to the sandy ground and lay paralyzed under the nearest cover, until the brindle-feathered, fan-tailed screamers tired of flying in such tight circles and headed for clearer air. Even after the lizard-birds had given up, they crouched quietly for a long time, waiting to see what greater demons might have been attracted by the commotion.

Thus far, none of the snake-headed Powers had shown themselves –

though several times Honath had heard suggestively heavy movements in the jungle around them.

Luckily, on the higher ground there was much more cover available, from low-growing shrubs and trees – palmetto, sassafras, several kinds of laurel, magnolia, and a great many sedges. Up here, too, the endless jungle began to break to pour around the bases of the great pink cliffs, leaving welcome vistas of open sky, only sketchily crossed by woven bridges leading from the vine-world to the cliffs themselves. In the intervening columns of blue air a whole hierarchy of flying creatures ranked themselves, layer by layer: First the low-flying beetles, bees and two-winged insects; then the dragon-flies, which hunted them, some with wingspreads as wide as two feet; then the lizard-birds, hunting the dragonflies and anything else that could be nipped without fighting back; and at last, far above, the great gliding reptiles coasting along the brows of the cliffs, riding the rising currents of air, their long-jawed hunger stalking anything that flew – as they sometimes stalked the birds of the attic world, and the flying fish along the breast of the distant sea.

The party halted in an especially thick clump of sedges. Though the rain continued to fall, harder than ever, they were all desperately thirsty. They had yet to find a single bromeliad; evidently the tank-plants did not grow in Hell. Cupping their hands to the weeping sky accumulated surprisingly little water; and no puddles large enough to drink from accumulated on the sand. But at least, here under the open sky, there was too much fierce struggle in the air to allow the lizard-birds to congregate and squall above their hiding place.

The white sun had already set, and the red sun's vast arc still bulged above the horizon only because the light from its limb had been wrenched higher into Tellura's sky by its passage through the white sun's intense gravitational field. In the lurid glow the rain looked like blood, and the seamed faces of the pink cliffs had all but vanished. Honath peered dubiously out from under the sedges at the still-distant escarpments.

'I don't see how we can hope to climb those,' he said, in a low voice. 'That kind of limestone crumbles as soon as you touch it, otherwise we'd have had better luck with our war against the cliff tribe.'

'We could go around the cliffs,' Charl said. 'The foothills of the Great Range aren't very steep. If we could last until we get to them, we could go on up into the Range itself.'

'To the volcanoes?' Mathild protested. 'But nothing can live up there, nothing but the white fire-things. And there are the lava-flows, too, and the choking smoke—'

'Well, we can't climb these cliffs, Honath's quite right,' Alaskon said. 'And we can't climb the Basalt Steppes, either – there's nothing to eat along them, let alone any water or cover. I don't see what else we can do but try to get up into the foothills.'

'Can't we stay here?' Mathild said plaintively.

'No,' Honath said, even more gently than he had intended. Mathild's four words were, he knew, the most dangerous words in Hell – he knew it quite surely, because of the imprisoned creature inside him that cried out to say 'Yes' instead. 'We have to get out of the country of the demons. And maybe – just maybe – if we can cross the Great Range, we can join a tribe that hasn't heard about our being condemned to Hell. There are supposed to be tribes on the other side of the Range, but the cliff people would never let our folk get through to them. That's on our side now.'

'That's true,' Alaskon said, brightening a little. 'And from the top of the Range, we could come *down* into another tribe – instead of trying to climb up into their village out of Hell. Honath, I think it might work.'

'Then we'd better try to sleep right here and now,' Charl said. 'It seems safe enough. If we're going to skirt the cliffs and climb those foothills, we'll need all the strength we've got left.'

Honath was about to protest, but he was suddenly too tired to care. Why not sleep it over? And if in the night they were found and taken – well, that would at least put an end to the struggle.

It was a cheerless and bone-damp bed to sleep in, but there was no better alternative. They curled up as best they could. Just before he was about to drop off at last, Honath heard Mathild whimpering to herself, and, on impulse, crawled over to her and began to smooth down her fur with his tongue. To his astonishment, each separate, silky hair was loaded with dew. Long before the girl had curled herself more tightly and her complaints had dwindled into sleepy murmurs, Honath's thirst was assuaged. He reminded himself to mention the method in the morning.

But when the white sun finally came up, there was no time to think of thirst. Charl the Reader was gone. Something had plucked him from their huddled midst as neatly as a fallen breadfruit – and had dropped his cleaned ivory skull just as negligently, some two hundred feet farther on up the slope which led toward the pink cliffs.

3

Late that afternoon, the three found the blue, turbulent stream flowing out of the foothills of the Great Range. Not even Alaskon knew quite what to make of it. It looked like water, but it flowed like the rivers of lava that crept downward from the volcanoes. Whatever else it could be, obviously it wasn't water; water stood, it never flowed. It was possible to imagine a still body of water as big as this, but only as a moment of fancy, an exaggeration derived from the known bodies of water in the tank-plants. But this much water in motion? It suggested pythons; it was probably poisonous. It did not occur to any of them to drink from it. They were afraid even to touch it, let alone cross it, for it was almost surely as hot as the other kinds of lava rivers. They followed its course cautiously into the foothills, their throats as dry and gritty as the hollow stems of horsetails.

Except for the thirst – which was in an inverted sense their friend, insofar as it overrode the hunger – the climbing was not difficult. It was only circuitous, because of the need to stay under cover, to reconnoiter every few yards, to choose the most sheltered course rather than the most direct. By an unspoken consent, none of the three mentioned Charl, but their eyes were constantly darting from side to side, searching for a glimpse of the thing that had taken him.

That was perhaps the worst, the most terrifying part of the tragedy: that not once since they had been in Hell had they actually seen a demon, or even any animal as large as a man. The enormous, three-taloned footprint they had found in the sand beside their previous night's bed – the spot where the thing had stood, looking down at the four sleeping men from above, coldly deciding which of them to seize – was the only evidence they had that they were now really in the same world with the demons – the same demons they had sometimes looked down upon from the remote vine-webs.

The footprint – and the skull.

By nightfall, they had ascended perhaps a hundred and fifty feet. It was difficult to judge distances in the twilight, and the token vine bridges from the attic world to the pink cliffs were now cut off from sight by the intervening masses of the cliffs themselves. But there was no possibility that they could climb higher today. Although Mathild had borne the climb surprisingly well, and Honath himself still felt almost fresh, Alaskon was completely winded. He had taken a bad cut on one hip from a serrated spike of volcanic glass against which he had stumbled, and the wound, bound with leaves to prevent its leaving a spoor which might be followed, evidently was becoming steadily more painful.

Honath finally called a halt as soon as they reached the little ridge with the cave in back of it. Helping Alaskon over the last boulders, he was astonished to discover how hot the Navigator's hands were. He took him back into the cave and then came out onto the ledge again.

'He's really sick,' he told Mathild in a low voice. 'He needs water, and another dressing for that cut. And we've got to get both for him somehow. If we ever get to the jungle on the other side of the Range, we'll need a navigator even worse than we need a needlesmith.'

'But how? I could dress the cut if I had the materials, Honath. But there's no water up here. It's a desert; we'll never get across it.'

'We've got to try. I can get him water, I think. There was a big cycladella on the slope we came up, just before we passed that obsidian spur that hurt Alaskon. Gourds that size usually have a fair amount of water inside them – and I can use a piece of the spur to rip it open—'

A small hand came out of the darkness and took him tightly by the elbow. 'Honath, you can't go back down there. Suppose the demon that – that took Charl is still following us? They hunt at night – and this country is all so strange ...'

'I can find my way. I'll follow the sound of the stream of glass or whatever it is. You pull some fresh leaves for Alaskon and try to make him comfortable. Better loosen those vines around the dressing a little. I'll be back.'

He touched her hand and pried it loose gently. Then, without stopping to think about it any further, he slipped off the ledge and edged toward the sound of the stream, travelling crabwise on all fours.

But he was swiftly lost. The night was thick and completely impenetrable, and he found that the noise of the stream seemed to come from all sides, providing him no guide at all. Furthermore, his memory of the ridge which led up to the cave appeared to be faulty, for he could feel it turning sharply to the right beneath him, though he remembered distinctly that it had been straight past the first side-branch, and then had gone to the left. Or had he passed the first side-branch in the dark without seeing it? He probed the darkness cautiously with one hand.

At the same instant, a brisk, staccato gust of wind came whirling up out of the night across the ridge. Instinctively, Honath shifted his weight to take up the flexing of the ground beneath him—

He realized his error instantly and tried to arrest the complex set of motions, but a habit-pattern so deeply ingrained could not be frustrated completely. Overwhelmed with vertigo, Honath grappled at the empty air with hands, feet, and tail and went toppling.

An instant later, with a familiar noise and an equally familiar cold shock that seemed to reach throughout his body, he was sitting in the midst of—

Water. Icy water, and water that rushed by him improbably with a menacing, monkeylike chattering, but water all the same.

It was all he could do to repress a hoot of hysteria. He hunkered into the stream and soaked himself. Things nibbled delicately at his calves as he bathed, but he had no reason to fear fish, small species of which often showed up in the tanks of the bromeliads. After lowering his muzzle to the rushing, invisible surface and drinking his fill, he ducked himself completely and then clambered out onto the banks, carefully neglecting to shake himself.

Getting back to the ledge was much less difficult. 'Mathild,' he called in a hoarse whisper. 'Mathild, we've got water.'

'Come in here quick then. Alaskon's worse. I'm afraid, Honath.'

Dripping, Honath felt his way into the cave. 'I don't have any container. I just got myself wet – you'll have to sit him up and let him lick my fur.'

'I'm not sure he can.'

But Alaskon could, feebly, but sufficiently. Even the coldness of the water – a totally new experience for a man who had never drunk anything but the soup-warm contents of the bromelaids – seemed to help him. He lay back at last, and said in a weak but otherwise normal voice: 'So the stream was water after all.'

'Yes,' Honath said. 'And there are fish in it, too.'

'Don't talk,' Mathild said. 'Rest, Alaskon.'

'I'm resting. Honath, if we stick to the course of the stream ... Where was I? Oh. We can follow the stream through the Range, now that we know it's water. How did you find that out?'

'I lost my balance and fell into it.'

Alaskon chuckled. 'Hell's not so bad, is it?' he said. Then he sighed, and rushes creaked under him.

'Mathild! What's the matter? Is he – did he die?'

'No ... no. He's breathing. He's still sicker than he realizes, that's all ... Honath – if they'd known, up above, how much courage you have—'

'I was scared white,' Honath said grimly. 'I'm still scared.'

But her hand touched his again in the solid blackness, and after he had taken it, he felt irrationally cheerful. With Alaskon breathing so raggedly behind them, there was little chance that either of them would be able to sleep that night; but they sat silently together on the hard stone in a kind of temporary peace, and when the mouth of the cave began to outline itself, as dimly at first as the floating patches of color seen behind the closed eye, with the first glow of the red sun, they looked at each other in a conspiracy of light all their own.

Hell, Honath reflected, wasn't so bad, after all.

With the first light of the white sun, a half-grown oxyaena cub rose slowly from its crouch at the mouth of the cave, and stretched luxuriously, showing a full set of saber-like teeth. It looked at them steadily for a moment, its ears alert, then turned and loped away down the slope.

How long it had been crouched there listening to them, it was impossible to know. They had been lucky that they had stumbled into the lair of a youngster. A full-grown animal would have killed them all within a few seconds after its cat's eyes had collected enough dawn to identify them positively. The cub, since it had no family of its own as yet, evidently had only been puzzled to find its den occupied, and uninclined to quarrel about it.

The departure of the big cat left Honath frozen, not so much frightened as simply stunned by so unexpected an end to the vigil. At the first moan from Alaskon, however, Mathild was up and walking softly to the Navigator, speaking in a low voice sentences which made no particular sense and perhaps were not intended to. Honath stirred and followed her.

Halfway back into the cave, his foot struck something and he looked down, It was the thigh bone of some medium-large animal, imperfectly cleaned, but not very recent – possibly the keepsake the oxyaena had hoped to rescue from the usurpers of its lair. Along a curved inner surface there was a patch of thick gray mold. Honath squatted and peeled it off carefully.

'Mathild, we can put this over the wound,' he said. 'Some molds help prevent wounds from festering ... How is he?'

'Better, I think,' Mathild murmured. 'But he's still feverish. I don't think we'll be able to move on today.'

Honath was unsure whether to be pleased or disturbed. Certainly, he was far from anxious to leave the cave, where they seemed at least to be reasonably comfortable. Possibly they would also be reasonably safe, for the low-roofed hole almost surely still smelt of oxyaena, and possible intruders would recognize the smell – as the men from the attic world could not – and keep their distance. They would have no way of knowing that the cat had only been a cub to begin with, and that it had vacated the premises, though of course the odor would fade before long.

Yet it was important to move on, to cross the Great Range if possible, and in the end to win their way back to the world where they belonged; even to win vindication, no matter how long it took. Even should it prove relatively easy to survive in Hell – and there were few signs of that, thus far – the only proper course was to fight until the attic world was totally reconquered. After all, it would have been the easy and the comfortable thing, back there at the very beginning, to have kept one's incipient heresies to oneself and remained on comfortable terms with one's neighbors. But Honath had spoken up and so had the rest of them, in their fashions.

It was the ancient internal battle between what Honath wanted to do, and what he knew he ought to do. He had never heard of Kant and the Categorical Imperative, but he knew well enough which side of his nature would win in the long run. But it had been a cruel joke of heredity which had fastened a sense of duty onto a lazy nature. It made even small decisions aggressively painful.

But for the moment at least, the decision was out of his hands. Alaskon was too sick to be moved. In addition, the strong beams of sunlight which had been glaring in across the floor of the cave were dimming by the instant, and there was a distant, premonitory growl of thunder.

'Then we'll stay here,' he said. 'It's going to rain again, and hard this time. Once it's falling in earnest, I can go out and pick up some fruit – it'll screen me even if anything is prowling around in it. And I won't have to go as far as the stream for water, as long as the rain keeps up.'

The rain, as it turned out, kept up all day, in a growing downpour which completely curtained the mouth of the cave by early afternoon. The chattering of the nearby stream grew quickly to a roar.

By evening, Alaskon's fever seemed to have dropped almost to normal, and his strength nearly returned as well. The wound, thanks more to the encrusted matte of mold than to any complications within the flesh itself, was still ugly-looking, but it was now painful only when the Navigator moved carelessly, and Mathild was convinced that it was mending. Alaskon himself, having been deprived of activity all day, was unusually talkative.

'Has it occurred to either of you,' he said in the gathering gloom, 'that since that stream is water, it can't possibly be coming from the Great Range? All the peaks over there are just cones of ashes and lava. We've seen young volcanoes in the process of building themselves, so we're sure of that. What's more, they're usually hot. I don't see how there could possibly be any source of water in the Range – not even runoff from the rains.'

'It can't just come up out of the ground,' Honath said. 'It must be fed by rain. By the way it sounds now, it could even be the first part of a flood.'

'As you say, it's probably rain water,' Alaskon said cheerfully. 'But not off the Great Range, that's out of the question. Most likely it collects on the cliffs.'

'I hope you're wrong,' Honath said. 'The cliffs may be a little easier to climb from this side, but there's still the cliff tribe to think about.'

'Maybe, maybe. But the cliffs are big. The tribes on this side may never have heard of the war with our treetop folk. No, Honath, I think that's our only course from here.'

'If it is,' Honath said grimly, 'we're going to wish more than ever that we had some stout, sharp needles among us.'

Alaskon's judgment was quickly borne out. The three left the cave at dawn the next morning, Alaskon moving somewhat stiffly but not otherwise noticeably incommoded, and resumed following the stream bed upwards – a stream now swollen by the rains to a roaring rapids. After winding its way upwards for about a mile in the general direction of the Great Range, the stream turned on itself and climbed rapidly back toward the basalt cliffs, falling toward the three over successively steeper shelves of jutting rock.

Then it turned again, at right angles, and the three found themselves at the exit of a dark gorge, little more than thirty feet high, but both narrow and long. Here the stream was almost perfectly smooth, and the thin strip of land on each side of it was covered with low shrubs. They paused and looked dubiously into the canyon. It was singularly gloomy.

'There's plenty of cover, at least,' Honath said in a low voice. 'But almost anything could live in a place like that.'

'Nothing very big could hide in it,' Alaskon pointed out. 'It should be safe. Anyhow it's the only way to go.'

'All right. Let's go ahead, then. But keep your head down, and be ready to jump!'

Honath lost the other two by sight as soon as they crept into the dark shrubbery, but he could hear their cautious movements nearby. Nothing else in the gorge seemed to move at all, not even the water, which flowed without a ripple over an invisible bed. There was not even any wind, for which Honath was grateful, although he had begun to develop an immunity to the motionlessness sickness.

After a few moments, Honath heard a low whistle. Creeping sidewise toward the source of the sound, he nearly bumped into Alaskon, who was crouched beneath a thickly spreading magnolia. An instant later, Mathild's face peered out of the dim greenery.

'Look,' Alaskon whispered. 'What do you make of this?'

'This' was a hollow in the sandy soil, about four feet across and rimmed with a low parapet of earth – evidently the same earth that had been scooped out of its center. Occupying most of it were three gray, ellipsoidal objects, smooth and featureless.

'Eggs,' Mathild said wonderingly.

'Obviously. But look at the size of them! Whatever laid them must be gigantic. I think we're trespassing in something's private valley.'

Mathild drew in her breath. Honath thought fast, as much to prevent panic in himself as in the girl. A sharp-edged stone lying nearby provided the answer. He seized it and struck.

The outer surface of the egg was leathery rather than brittle; it tore raggedly. Deliberately, Honath bent and put his mouth to the oozing surface.

It was excellent. The flavor was decidedly stronger than that of birds' eggs, but he was far too hungry to be squeamish. After a moment's amazement, Alaskon and Mathild attacked the other two ovoids with a will. It was the first really satisfying meal they had had in Hell. When they finally moved away from the devastated nest, Honath felt better than he had since the day he was arrested.

As they moved on down the gorge, they began again to hear the roar of water, though the stream looked as placid as ever. Here, too, they saw the first sign of active life in the valley: a flight of giant dragonflies skimming over the water. The insects took flight as soon as Honath showed himself, but quickly came back, their nearly non-existent brains already convinced that there had always been men in the valley.

The roar got louder very rapidly. When the three rounded the long, gentle turn which had cut off their view from the exit, the source of the roar came into view. It was a sheet of falling water as tall as the depth of the gorge itself, which came arcing out from between two pillars of basalt and fell to a roiling, frothing pool.

'This is as far as we go!' Alaskon said, shouting to make himself heard at all over the tumult. 'We'll never be able to get up those walls!'

Stunned, Honath looked from side to side. What Alaskon had said was all too obviously true. The gorge evidently had begun life as a layer of soft, partly soluble stone in the cliffs, tilted upright by some volcanic upheaval, and then worn completely away by the rushing stream. Both cliff faces were of the harder rock, and were sheer and as smooth as if they had been polished by hand. Here and there a network of tough vines had begun to climb them, but nowhere did such a network even come close to reaching the top.

Honath turned and looked once more at the great arc of water and spray. If there were only some way to prevent their being forced to retrace their steps—

Abruptly, over the riot of the falls, there was a piercing, hissing shriek. Echoes picked it up and sounded it again and again, all the way up the battlements of the cliffs. Honath sprang straight up in the air and came down trembling, facing away from the pool.

At first he could see nothing. Then, down at the open end of the turn, there was a huge flurry of motion.

A second later, a two-legged, blue-green reptile half as tall as the gorge itself came around the turn in a single huge bound and lunged violently into the far wall of the valley. It stopped as if momentarily stunned, and the great head turned toward them a face of sinister and furious idiocy.

The shriek set the air to boiling again. Balancing itself with its heavy tail, the beast lowered its head and looked redly toward the falls.

The owner of the robbed nest had come home – and they had met a demon of Hell at last.

Honath's mind at that instant went as white and blank as the underbark of a poplar. He acted without thinking, without even knowing what he did. When thought began to creep back into his head again, the three of them were standing shivering in semi-darkness, watching the blurred shadow of the demon lurching back and forth upon the screen of shining water.

It had been nothing but luck, not foreplanning, to find that there was a considerable space between the back of the falls proper and the blind wall of the canyon. It had been luck, too, which had forced Honath to skirt the pool in order to reach the falls at all, and thus had taken them all behind the silver curtain at the point where the weight of the falling water was too low to hammer them down for good. And it had been the blindest stroke of all that the demon had charged after them directly into the pool, where the deep, boiling water had slowed the threshing hind legs enough to halt it before it went under the falls, as it had earlier blundered into the hard wall of the gorge.

Not an iota of all this had been in Honath's mind before he had discovered it to be true. At the moment that the huge reptile had screamed for the second time, he had simply grasped Mathild's hand and broken for the falls, leaping from low tree to shrub to fern faster than he had ever leapt before. He did not stop to see how well Mathild was keeping up with him, or whether or not Alaskon was following. He only ran. He might have screamed, too; he could not remember.

They stood now, all three of them, wet through, behind the curtain until the shadow of the demon faded and vanished. Finally Honath felt a hand thumping his shoulder, and turned slowly.

Speech was impossible here, but Alaskon's pointing finger was eloquent enough. Along the back wall of the falls, centuries of erosion had failed to wear away completely the original soft limestone; there was still a sort of serrated chimney there, open toward the gorge, which looked as though it could be climbed. At the top of the falls, the water shot out from between the basalt pillars in a smooth, almost solid-looking tube, arching at least six feet before beginning to break into the fan of spray and rainbows which poured down into the gorge. Once the chimney had been climbed, it should be possible to climb out from under the falls without passing through the water again.

And after that?

Abruptly, Honath grinned. He felt weak all through with reaction, and the face of the demon would probably be leering in his dreams for a long time to come – but at the same time he could not repress a surge of irrational confidence. He gestured upward jauntily, shook himself, and loped forward into the throat of the chimney.

Hardly more than an hour later they were all standing on a ledge overlooking the gorge, with the waterfall creaming over the brink next to them, only a few yards away. From here, it was evident that the gorge itself was only the bottom of a far larger cleft, a split in the pink-and-gray cliffs as sharp as though it had been driven in the rock by a bolt of sheet lightning. Beyond the basalt pillars from which the fall issued, however, the stream foamed over a long ladder of rock shelves which seemed to lead straight up into the sky. On this side of the pillars the ledge broadened into a sort of truncated mesa, as if the waters had been running at this level for centuries before striking some softer rock-stratum which had permitted them to cut down further to create the gorge. The stone platform was littered with huge rocks, rounded by long water erosion, obviously the remains of a washed-out stratum of conglomerate or a similar sedimentary layer.

Honath looked at the huge pebbles – many of them bigger than he was – and then back down into the gorge again. The figure of the demon, foreshortened into a pigmy by distance and perspective, was still roving back and forth in front of the waterfall. Having gotten the notion that prey was hiding behind the sheet of water, the creature might well stay stationed there until it starved, for all Honath knew – it certainly did not seem to be very bright – but Honath thought he had a better idea.

'Alaskon, can we hit the demon with one of these rocks?'

The navigator peered cautiously into the gorge. 'It wouldn't surprise me,' he said at last. 'It's just pacing back and forth in that same small arc. And all things fall at the same speed; if we can make the rock arrive just as it walks under it – hmm. Yes, I think so. Let's pick a big one to make certain.'

But Alaskon's ambitions overreached his strength; the rock he selected would not move, largely because he himself was still too weak to help much with it. 'Never mind,' he said. 'Even a small one will be falling fast by the time it gets down there. Pick one you and Mathild can roll easily yourselves; I'll just have to figure it a little closer, that's all.'

After a few tests, Honath selected a rock about three times the size of his own head. It was heavy, but between them he and Mathild got it to the edge of the ledge.

'Hold on,' Alaskon said in a preoccupied voice. 'Tip it over the edge, so it's ready to drop as soon as you let go of it. Good. Now wait. He's on his backtrack now. As soon as he crosses – All right. Four, three, two, one, *drop it!*'

The rock fell away. All three of them crouched in a row at the edge of the gorge. The rock dwindled, became as small as a fruit, as small as a fingernail, as small as a grain of sand. The dwarfed figure of the demon reached the end of its mad stalking arc, swung furiously to go back again—

And stopped. For an instant it just stood there. Then, with infinite slowness, it toppled sidewise into the pool. It thrashed convulsively two or three times, and then was gone; the spreading waves created by the waterfall masked any ripples it might have made in sinking.

'Like spearing fish in a bromeliad,' Alaskon said proudly. But his voice was shaky. Honath knew exactly why.

After all, they had just killed a demon.

'We could do that again,' Honath whispered.

'Often,' Alaskon agreed, still peering greedily down at the pool. 'They don't appear to have much intelligence, these demons. Given enough height, we could lure them into blind alleys like this, and bounce rocks off them almost at will. I wish *I'd* thought of it.'

'Where do we go now?' Mathild said, looking toward the ladder beyond the basalt pillars. 'That way?'

'Yes, and as fast as possible,' Alaskon said, getting to his feet and looking upward, one hand shading his eyes. 'It must be late. I don't think the light will last much longer.'

'We'll have to go single file,' Honath said. 'And we'd better keep hold of each other's hands. One slip on those wet steps and – it's a long way down again.'

Mathild shuddered and took Honath's hand convulsively. To his astonishment, the next instant she was tugging him toward the basalt pillars.

The irregular patch of deepening violet sky grew slowly as they climbed. They paused often, clinging to the jagged escarpments until their breath came back, and snatching icy water in cupped palms from the stream that fell down the ladder beside them. There was no way to tell how far up into the dusk the way had taken them, but Honath suspected that they were already somewhat above the level of their own vine-webbed world. The air smelled colder and sharper than it ever had above the jungle.

The final cut in the cliffs through which the stream fell was another chimney, steeper and more smooth-walled than the one which had taken them out of the gorge under the waterfall, but also narrow enough to be climbed by bracing one's back against one side, and one's hands and feet against the other. The column of air inside the chimney was filled with spray, but in Hell that was too minor a discomfort to bother about.

At long last Honath heaved himself over the edge of the chimney onto flat rock, drenched and exhausted, but filled with an elation he could not suppress and did not want to. They were above the attic jungle; they had beaten Hell itself. He looked around to make sure that Mathild was safe, and then reached a hand down to Alaskon; the navigator's bad leg had been giving him trouble. Honath heaved mightily, and Alaskon came heavily over the edge and lay sprawling on the high moss.

The stars were out. For a while they simply sat and gasped for breath. Then they turned, one by one, to see where they were.

There was not a great deal to see. There was the mesa, domed with stars on all sides; a shining, finned spindle, like a gigantic minnow, pointing skyward in the center of the rocky plateau; and around the spindle, indistinct in the starlight ...

... Around the shining minnow, tending it, were the Giants.

4

This, then, was the end of the battle to do what was right, whatever the odds. All the show of courage against superstition, all the black battles against

Hell itself, came down to this: *The Giants were real!*

They were inarguably real. Though they were twice as tall as men, stood straighter, had broader shoulders, were heavier across the seat and had no visible tails, their fellowship with men was clear. Even their voices, as they shouted to each other around their towering metal minnow, were the voices of men made into gods, voices as remote from those of men as the voices of men were remote from those of monkeys, yet just as clearly of the same family.

These were the Giants of the Book of Laws. They were not only real, but they had come back to Tellura as they had promised to do.

And they would know what to do with unbelievers, and with fugitives from Hell. It had all been for nothing – not only the physical struggle, but the fight to be allowed to think for oneself as well. The gods existed, literally, actually. This belief was the real hell from which Honath had been trying to fight free all his life – but now it was no longer just a belief. It was a fact, a fact that he was seeing with his own eyes.

The Giants had returned to judge their handiwork. And the first of the people they would meet would be three outcasts, three condemned and degraded criminals, three jailbreakers – the worst possible detritus of the attic world.

All this went searing through Honath's mind in less than a second, but nevertheless Alaskon's mind evidently had worked still faster. Always the most outspoken unbeliever of the entire little group of rebels, the one among them whose whole world was founded upon the existence of rational explanations for everything, his was the point of view most completely challenged by the sight before them now. With a deep, sharply indrawn breath, he turned abruptly and walked away from them.

Mathild uttered a cry of protest, which she choked off in the middle; but it was already too late. A round eye on the great sliver minnow came alight, bathing them all in an oval patch of brilliance.

Honath darted after the navigator. Without looking back, Alaskon suddenly was running. For an instant longer Honath saw his figure, poised delicately against the black sky. Then he dropped silently out of sight, as suddenly and completely as if he had never been.

Alaskon had borne every hardship and every terror of the ascent from Hell with courage and even with cheerfulness – but he had been unable to face being told that it had all been meaningless.

Sick at heart, Honath turned back, shielding his eyes from the miraculous light. There was a clear call in some unknown language from near the spindle.

Then there were footsteps, several pairs of them, coming closer.

It was time for the Second Judgment.

After a long moment, a big voice from the darkness said: 'Don't be afraid. We mean you no harm. We're men, just as you are.'

The language had the archaic flavor of the Book of Laws, but it was otherwise perfectly understandable. A second voice said: 'What are you called?'

Honath's tongue seemed to be stuck to the roof of his mouth. While he was struggling with it, Mathild's voice came clearly from beside him:

'He is Honath the Purse-Maker, and I am Mathild the Forager.'

'You are a long distance from the place we left your people,' the first Giant said. 'Don't you still live in the vine-webs above the jungles?'

'Lord—'

'My name is Jarl Eleven. This is Gerhardt Adler.'

This seemed to stop Mathild completely. Honath could understand why: the very notion of addressing Giants by name was nearly paralyzing. But since they were already as good as cast down into Hell again, nothing could be lost by it.

'Jarl Eleven,' he said, 'the people still live among the vines. The floor of the jungle is forbidden. Only criminals are sent there. We are criminals.'

'Oh?' Jarl Eleven said. 'And you've come all the way from the surface to this mesa? Gerhardt, this is prodigious. You have no idea what the surface of this planet is like – it's a place where evolution has never managed to leave the tooth-and-nail stage. Dinosaurs from every period of the Mesozoic, primitive mammals all the way up the scale to the ancient cats – the works. That's why the original seeding team put these people in the treetops instead.'

'Honath, what was your crime?' Gerhardt Adler said.

Honath was almost relieved to have the questioning come so quickly to this point; Jarl Eleven's aside, with its many terms he could not understand, had been frightening in its very meaninglessness.

'There were five of us,' Honath said in a low voice. 'We said we – that we did not believe in the Giants.'

There was a brief silence. Then, shockingly, both Jarl Eleven and Gerhardt Adler burst into enormous laughter.

Mathild cowered, her hands over her ears. Even Honath flinched and took a step backward. Instantly, the laughter stopped, and the Giant called Jarl Eleven stepped into the oval of light and sat down beside them. In the light, it could be seen that his face and hands were hairless, although there was hair on his crown; the rest of his body was covered by a kind of cloth. Seated, he was no taller than Honath, and did not seem quite so fearsome.

'I beg your pardon,' he said. 'It was unkind of us to laugh, but what you said was highly unexpected. Gerhardt, come over here and squat down, so that you don't look so much like a statue of some general. Tell me, Honath, in what way did you not believe in the Giants?'

Honath could hardly believe his ears. A Giant had begged his pardon! Was this some still crueler joke? But whatever the reason, Jarl Eleven had asked him a question.

'Each of the five of us differed,' he said. 'I held that you were not – not real except as symbols of some abstract truth. One of us, the wisest, believed that you did not exist in any sense at all. But we all agreed that you were not gods.'

'And, of course, we aren't,' Jarl Eleven said. 'We're men. We come from the same stock as you. We're not your rulers, but your brothers. Do you understand what I say?'

'No,' Honath admitted.

'Then let me tell you about it. There are men on many worlds, Honath. They differ from one another, because the worlds differ, and different kinds of men are needed to people each one. Gerhardt and I are the kind of men who live on a world called Earth, and many other worlds like it. We are two very minor members of a huge project called a "seeding program", which has been going on for thousands of years now. It's the job of the seeding program to survey newly discovered worlds, and then to make men suitable to live on each new world.'

'To make men? But only gods—'

'No, no. Be patient and listen,' said Jarl Eleven. 'We don't make men. We make them suitable. There's a great deal of difference between the two. We take the living germ plasm, the sperm and the egg, and we modify it; then the modified man emerges, and we help him to settle down in his new world. That's what we did on Tellura – it happened long ago, before Gerhardt and I were even born. Now, we've come back to see how you people are getting along, and to lend a hand if necessary.'

He looked from Honath to Mathild, and back again. 'Do you follow me?' he said.

'I'm trying,' Honath said. 'But you should go down to the jungle-top, then. We're not like the others; they are the people you want to see.'

'We shall, in the morning. We just landed here. But, just because you're not like the others, we're more interested in you now. Tell me: has any condemned man ever escaped from the jungle floor before?'

'No, never. That's not surprising. There are monsters down there.'

Jarl Eleven looked sidewise at the other Giant; he seemed to be smiling. 'When you see the films,' he remarked, 'you'll call that the understatement of the century. Honath, how did you three manage to escape, then?'

Haltingly at first, and then with more confidence as the memories came crowding vividly back, Honath told him. When he mentioned the feast at the demon's nest, Jarl Eleven again looked significantly at Adler, but he did not interrupt.

'And, finally, we got to the top of the chimney and came out on this flat space,' Honath said. 'Alaskon was still with us then, but when he saw you and the shining thing he threw himself back down the cleft. He was a criminal like us, but he should not have died. He was a brave man, and a wise one.'

'Not wise enough to wait until all the evidence was in,' Adler said enigmatically. 'All in all, Jarl, I'd say "prodigious" is the word for it. This is really the most successful seeding job any team has ever done, at least in this limb of the galaxy. And what a stroke of luck, to be on the spot just as it came to term, and with a couple at that!'

'What does it mean?' Honath said.

'Just this, Honath. When the seeding team set your people up in business on Tellura, they didn't mean for you to live forever in the treetops. They knew that, sooner or later, you'd have to come down to the ground and learn to fight this planet on its own terms. Otherwise, you'd go stale and die out.'

'Live on the ground all the time?' Mathild said in a faint voice.

'Yes, Mathild. The life in the treetops was to have been only an interim period, while you gathered knowledge you needed about Tellura, and put it to use. But to be the real masters of the world, you will have to conquer the surface, too.

'The device your people worked out, of sending only criminals to the surface, was the best way of conquering the planet that they could have picked. It takes a strong will and exceptional courage to go against custom; and both those qualities are needed to lick Tellura. Your people exiled just such fighting spirits to the surface, year after year after year.

'Sooner or later, some of those exiles were going to discover how to live successfully on the ground, and make it possible for the rest of your people to leave the trees. You and Honath have done just that.'

'Observe please, Jarl,' Adler said. 'The crime in this first successful case was ideological. That was the crucial turn in the criminal policy of these people. A spirit of revolt is not quite enough; but couple it with brains, and – ecce homo!'

Honath's head was swimming. 'But what does all this mean?' he said. 'Are we – not condemned to Hell any more?'

'No, you're still condemned, if you still want to call it that,' Jarl Eleven said soberly. 'You've learned how to live down there, and you've found out something even more valuable: How to stay alive while cutting down your enemies. Do you know that you killed three demons with your bare hands, you and Mathild and Alaskon?'

'Killed—'

'Certainly,' Jarl Eleven said. 'You ate three eggs. That is the classical way, and indeed the only way, to wipe out monsters like the dinosaurs. You can't kill the adults with anything short of an anti-tank gun, but they're helpless in embryo – and the adults haven't the sense to guard their nests.'

Honath heard, but only distantly. Even his awareness of Mathild's warmth next to him did not seem to help much.

'Then we have to go back down there,' he said dully. 'And this time forever.'

'Yes,' Jarl Eleven said, his voice gentle. 'But you won't be alone, Honath. Beginning tomorrow, you'll have all your people with you.'

'*All* our people? But – you're going to drive them out?'

'All of them. Oh, we won't prohibit the use of the vine-webs, too, but from now on your race will have to fight it out on the surface as well. You and Mathild have proven that it can be done. It's high time the rest of you learned, too.'

'Jarl, you think too little of these young people themselves,' Adler said. 'Tell them what is in store for them. They are frightened.'

'Of course, of course. It's obvious. Honath, you and Mathild are the only living individuals of your race who know how to survive down there on the surface. And we're not going to tell your people how to do that. We aren't even going to drop them so much as a hint. That part of it is up to you.'

Honath's jaw dropped.

'It's up to you,' Jarl Eleven repeated firmly. 'We'll return you to your tribe tomorrow, and we'll tell your people that you two know the rules for successful life on the ground – and that everyone else has to go down and live there, too. We'll tell them nothing else but that. What do you think they'll do then?'

'I don't know,' Honath said dazedly. 'Anything could happen. They might even make us Spokesman and Spokeswoman – except that we're just common criminals.'

'Uncommon pioneers, Honath. The man and woman to lead the humanity of Tellura out of the attic, into the wide world.' Jarl Eleven got to his feet, the great light playing over him. Looking up after him, Honath saw that there were at least a dozen other Giants standing just outside the oval of light, listening intently to every word.

'But there's a little time to be passed before we begin,' Jarl Eleven said. 'Perhaps you two would like to look over our ship.'

Numbly, but with a soundless emotion much like music inside him, Honath took Mathild's hand. Together they walked away from the chimney to Hell, following the footsteps of the Giants.

BOOK THREE

Surface Tension

PROLOGUE

Dr. Chatvieux took a long time over the microscope, leaving la Ventura with nothing to do but look at the dead landscape of Hydrot. Waterscape, he thought, would be a better word. From space, the new world had shown only one small, triangular continent, set amid endless ocean; and even the continent was mostly swamp.

The wreck of the seed-ship lay broken squarely across the one real spur of rock which Hydrot seemed to possess, which reared a magnificent twenty-one feet above sea-level. From this eminence, la Ventura could see forty miles to the horizon across a flat bed of mud. The red light of the star Tau Ceti, glinting upon thousands of small lakes, pools, ponds and puddles, made the watery plain look like a mosaic of onyx and ruby.

'If I were a religious man,' the pilot said suddenly, 'I'd call this a plain case of divine vengeance.'

Chatvieux said: 'Hmn?'

'It's as if we'd been struck down for – is it *hubris*? Pride, arrogance?'

'*Hybris*,' Chatvieux said, looking up at last. 'Well, is it? I don't feel swollen with pride at the moment. Do you?'

'I'm not exactly proud of my piloting,' la Ventura admitted. 'But that isn't quite what I mean. I was thinking about why we came here in the first place. It takes a lot of arrogance to think that you can scatter men, or at least things very much like men, all over the face of the galaxy. It takes even more pride to do the job – to pack up all the equipment and move from planet to planet and actually make men, make them suitable for every place you touch.'

'I suppose it does,' Chatvieux said. 'But we're only one of several hundred seed-ships in this limb of the galaxy, so I doubt that the gods picked us out as special sinners.' He smiled. 'If they had, maybe they'd have left us our ultraphone, so the Colonization Council could hear about our cropper. Besides, Paul, we don't make men. We adapt them – adapt them to Earthlike planets, nothing more than that. We've sense enough – or humility enough, if you like that better – to know that we can't adapt men to a planet like Jupiter, or to the surface of a sun, like Tau Ceti.'

'Anyhow, we're here,' la Ventura said grimly. 'And we aren't going to get off. Phil tells me that we don't even have our germ-cell bank any more, so we can't seed this place in the usual way. We've been thrown onto a dead world and dared to adapt to it. What are the pantropes going to do with our recalcitrant carcasses – provide built-in waterwings?'

'No,' Chatvieux said calmly. 'You and I and all the rest of us are going to die, Paul. Pantropic techniques don't work on the body; that was fixed for you for life when you were conceived. To attempt to rebuild it for you would only maim you. The pantropes affect only the genes, the inheritance-carrying factors. We can't give you built-in waterwings, any more than we can give you a new set of brains. I think we'll be able to populate this world with men, but we won't live to see it.'

The pilot thought about it, a lump of cold blubber collecting gradually in his stomach. 'How long do you give us?' he said at last.

'Who knows? A month, perhaps.'

The bulkhead leading to the wrecked section of the ship was pushed back, admitting salt, muggy air, heavy with carbon dioxide. Philip Strasvogel, the communications officer, came in, tracking mud. Like la Ventura, he was now a man without a function, and it appeared to bother him. He was not well equipped for introspection, and with his ultraphone totally smashed, unresponsive to his perpetually darting hands, he had been thrown back into his own mind, whose resources were few. Only the tasks Chatvieux had set him to had prevented him from setting like a gelling colloid into a permanent state of the sulks.

He unbuckled from around his waist a canvas belt, into the loops of which plastic vials were stuffed like cartridges. 'More samples, Doc,' he said. 'All alike – water, very wet. I have some quicksand in one boot, too. Find anything?'

'A good deal, Phil. Thanks. Are the others around?'

Strasvogel poked his head out and hallooed. Other voices rang out over the mudflats. Minutes later, the rest of the survivors of the crash were crowding into the pantrope deck: Saltonstall, Chatvieux' senior assistant, a perpetually sanguine, perpetually youthful technician willing to try anything once, including dying; Eunice Wagner, behind whose placid face rested the brains of the expedition's only remaining ecologist; Eleftherios Venezuelos, the always-silent delegate from the Colonization Council; and Joan Heath, a midshipman whose duties, like la Ventura's and Phil's, were now without meaning, but whose bright head and tall, deceptively indolent body shone to the pilot's eyes brighter than Tau Ceti – brighter, since the crash, even than the home sun.

Five men and two women – to colonize a planet on which 'standing room' meant treading water.

They came in quietly and found seats or resting places on the deck, on the edges of tables, in corners. Joan Heath went to stand beside la Ventura. They did not look at each other, but the warmth of her shoulder beside his was all that he needed. Nothing was as bad as it seemed.

Venezuelos said: 'What's the verdict, Dr. Chatvieux?'

'This place isn't dead,' Chatvieux said. 'There's life in the sea and in the fresh water, both. On the animal side of the ledger, evolution seems to have stopped with the *Crustacea*; the most advanced form I've found is a tiny crayfish, from one of the local rivulets, and it doesn't seem to be well distributed. The ponds and puddles are well-stocked with small metazoans of lower orders, right up to the rotifers – including a castle-building genus like Earth's *Floscularidae*. In addition, there's a wonderfully variegated protozoan population, with a dominant ciliate type much like *Paramoecium*, plus various sarcodines, the usual spread of phyto-flagellates, and even a phosphorescent species I wouldn't have expected to see anywhere but in salt water. As for the plants, they run from simple blue-green algae to quite advanced thallus-producing types – though none of them, of course, can live out of the water.'

'The sea is about the same,' Eunice said. 'I've found some of the larger simple metazoans – jellyfish and so on – and some crayfish almost as big as lobsters. But it's normal to find salt-water species running larger than fresh-water. And there's the usual plankton and nannoplankton population.'

'In short,' Chatvieux said, 'we'll survive here – if we fight.'

'Wait a minute,' la Ventura said. 'You've just finished telling me that we wouldn't survive. And you were talking about us, the seven of us here, not about the genus man, because we don't have our germ-cell banks any more. What's—'

'We don't have the banks. But we ourselves can contribute germ-cells, Paul. I'll get to that in a moment.' Chatvieux turned to Saltonstall. 'Martin, what would you think of our taking to the sea? We came out of it once, long ago; maybe we could come out of it again on Hydrot.'

'No good,' Saltonstall said immediately. 'I like the idea, but I don't think this planet ever heard of Swinburne, or Homer, either. Looking at it as a colonization problem alone, as if we weren't involved in it ourselves, I wouldn't give you an Oc dollar for *epi oinopa ponton*. The evolutionary pressure there is too high, the competition from other species is prohibitive; seeding the sea should be the last thing we attempt, not the first. The colonists wouldn't have a chance to learn a thing before they'd be gobbled up.'

'Why?' la Ventura said. Once more, the death in his stomach was becoming hard to placate.

'Eunice, do your sea-going coelenterates include anything like the Portuguese man-of-war?'

The ecologist nodded.

'There's your answer, Paul,' Saltonstall said. 'The sea is out. It's got to be fresh water, where the competing creatures are less formidable and there are more places to hide.'

'We can't compete with a jellyfish?' la Ventura asked, swallowing.

'No, Paul,' Chatvieux said. 'Not with one that dangerous. The pantropes make adaptations, not gods. They take human germ-cells – in this case, our own, since our bank was wiped out in the crash – and modify them genetically toward those of creatures who can live in any reasonable environment. The result will be manlike, and intelligent. It usually shows the donors' personality patterns, too, since the modifications are usually made mostly in the morphology, not so much in the mind, of the resulting individual.

'*But we can't transmit memory.* The Adapted Man is worse than a child in the new environment. He has no history, no techniques, no precedents, not even a language. In the usual colonization project, like the Tellura affair, the seeding teams more or less take him through elementary school before they leave the planet to him, but we won't survive long enough to give such instruction. We'll have to design our colonists with plenty of built-in protections and locate them in the most favorable environment possible, so that at least some of them will survive learning by experience alone.'

The pilot thought about it, but nothing occurred to him which did not make the disaster seem realer and more intimate with each passing second. Joan Heath moved slightly closer to him. 'One of the new creatures can have my personality pattern, but it won't be able to remember being me. Is that right?'

'That's right. In the present situation we'll probably make our colonists haploid, so that some of them, perhaps many, will have a heredity traceable to you alone. There may be just the faintest of residuums of identity – pantropy's given us some data to support the old Jungian notion of ancestral memory. But we're all going to die on Hydrot, Paul, as self-conscious persons. There's no avoiding that. Somewhere we'll leave behind people who behave as we would, think and feel as we would, but who won't remember la Ventura, or Dr. Chatvieux, or Joan Heath – or the Earth.'

The pilot said nothing more. There was a gray taste in his mouth.

'Saltonstall, what would you recommend as a form?'

The pantropist pulled reflectively at his nose. 'Webbed extremities, of course, with thumbs and big toes heavy and thorn-like for defense until the creature has had a chance to learn. Smaller external ears, and the eardrum larger and closer to the outer end of the ear-canal. We're going to have to reorganize the water-conservation system, I think; the glomerular kidney is perfectly suitable for living in fresh water, but the business of living immersed, inside and out, for a creature with a salty inside means that the osmotic pressure inside is going to be higher than outside, so that the kidneys are going to have to be pumping virtually all the time. Under the circumstances we'd best step up production of urine, and that means the antidiuretic function of the pituitary gland is going to have to be abrogated, for all practical purposes.'

'What about respiration?'

'Hm,' Saltonstall said. 'I suppose book-lungs, like some of the arachnids have. They can be supplied by intercostal spiracles. They're gradually adaptable to atmosphere-breathing, if our colonist ever decides to come out of the water. Just to provide for that possibility, I'd suggest that the nose be retained, maintaining the nasal cavity as a part of the otological system, but cutting off the cavity from the larynx with a membrane of cells that are supplied with oxygen by direct irrigation, rather than by the circulatory system. Such a membrane wouldn't survive for many generations, once the creature took to living out of the water even for part of its lifetime; it'd go through two or three generations as an amphibian, and then one day it'd suddenly find itself breathing through its larynx again.'

'Ingenious,' Chatvieux said.

'Also, Dr. Chatvieux, I'd suggest that we have it adopt sporulation. As an aquatic animal, our colonist is going to have an indefinite life-span, but we'll have to give it a breeding cycle of about six weeks to keep up its numbers during the learning period; so there'll have to be a definite break of some duration in its active year. Otherwise it'll hit the population problem before it's learned enough to cope with it.'

'And it'd be better if our colonists could winter over inside a good, hard shell,' Eunice Wagner added in agreement. 'So sporulation's the obvious answer. Many other microscopic creatures have it.'

'Microscopic?' Phil said incredulously.

'Certainly,' Chatvieux said, amused. 'We can't very well crowd a six-foot man into a two-foot puddle. But that raises a question. We'll have tough competition from the rotifers, and some of them aren't strictly microscopic; for that matter even some of the protozoa can be seen with the naked eye, just barely, with dark-field illumination. I don't think your average colonist should run much under 250 microns, Saltonstall. Give them a chance to slug it out.'

'I was thinking of making them twice that big.'

'Then they'd be the biggest animals in their environment,' Eunice Wagner pointed out, 'and won't ever develop any skills. Besides, if you make them about rotifer size, it will give them an incentive for pushing out the castle-building rotifers, and occupying the castles themselves, as dwellings.'

Chatvieux nodded. 'All right, let's get started. While the pantropes are being calibrated, the rest of us can put our heads together on leaving a record for these people. We'll micro-engrave the record on a set of corrosion-proof metal leaves, of a size our colonists can handle conveniently. We can tell them, very simply, what happened, and plant a few suggestions that there's more to the universe than what they find in their puddles. Some day they may puzzle it out.'

'Question,' Eunice Wagner said. 'Are we going to tell them they're microscopic? I'm opposed to it. It may saddle their entire early history with a gods-and-demons mythology that they'd be better off without.'

'Yes, we are,' Chatvieux said; and la Ventura could tell by the change in the tone of his voice that he was speaking now as their senior on the expedition. 'These people will be of the race of men, Eunice. We want them to win their way back into the community of men. They are not toys, to be protected from the truth forever in a fresh-water womb.'

'Besides,' Saltonstall observed, 'they won't get the record translated at any time in their early history. They'll have to develop a written language of their own, and it will be impossible for us to leave them any sort of Rosetta Stone or other key. By the time they can decipher the truth, they should be ready for it.'

'I'll make that official,' Venezuelos said unexpectedly. And that was that.

And then, essentially, it was all over. They contributed the cells that the pantropes would need. Privately, la Ventura and Joan Heath went to Chatvieux and asked to contribute jointly; but the scientist said that the microscopic men were to be haploid, in order to give them a minute cellular structure, with nuclei as small as earthly rickettsiae, and therefore each person had to give germ-cells individually – there would be no use for *zygotes*. So even that consolation was denied them; in death they would have no children, but be instead as alone as ever.

They helped, as far as they could, with the text of the message which was to go on the metal leaves. They had their personality patterns recorded. They went through the motions. Already they were beginning to be hungry; the sea-crayfish, the only things on Hydrot big enough to eat, lived in water too deep and cold for subsistence fishing.

After la Ventura had set his control board to rights – a useless gesture, but a habit he had been taught to respect, and which in an obscure way made things a little easier to bear – he was out of it. He sat by himself at the far end of the rock ledge, watching Tau Ceti go redly down, chucking pebbles into the nearest pond.

After a while Joan Heath came silently up behind him, and sat down too. He took her hand. The glare of the red sun was almost extinguished now, and together they watched it go, with la Ventura, at least, wondering somberly which nameless puddle was to be his Lethe.

He never found out, of course. None of them did.

CYCLE ONE

In a forgotten corner of the galaxy, the watery world of Hydrot hurtles endlessly around the red star, Tau Ceti. For many months its single small continent has been snowbound, and the many pools and lakes which dot the continent have been locked in the grip of the ice. Now, however, the red sun swings closer and closer to the zenith in Hydrot's sky; the snow rushes in torrents toward the eternal ocean, and the ice recedes toward the shores of the lakes and ponds ...

1

The first thing to reach the consciousness of the sleeping Lavon was a small, intermittent scratching sound. This was followed by a disquieting sensation in his body, as if the world – and Lavon with it – were being rocked back and forth. He stirred uneasily, without opening his eyes. His vastly slowed metabolism made him feel inert and queasy, and the rocking did not help. At his slight motion, however, both the sound and the motion became more insistent.

It seemed to take days for the fog over his brain to clear, but whatever was causing the disturbance would not let him rest. With a groan he forced his eyelids open and made an abrupt gesture with one webbed hand. By the waves of phosphorescence which echoed away from his fingers at the motion, he could see that the smooth amber walls of his spherical shell were unbroken. He tried to peer through them, but he could see nothing but darkness outside. Well, that was natural; the amnionic fluid inside the spore would generate light, but ordinary water did not, no matter how vigorously it was stirred.

Whatever was outside the sphere was rocking it again, with the same whispering friction against its shell. Probably some nosey diatom, Lavon thought sleepily, trying to butt its way through an object it was too stupid to go around. Or some early hunter, yearning for a taste of the morsel inside the spore. Well, let it worry itself; Lavon had no intention of breaking the shell just yet. The fluid in which he had slept for so many months had held his body processes static, and had slowed his mind. Once out into the water, he would have to start breathing and looking for food again, and he could tell by the unrelieved darkness outside that it was too early in the spring to begin thinking about that.

He flexed his fingers reflectively, in the disharmonic motion from little finger to thumb that no animal but man can copy, and watched the widening wavefronts of greenish light rebound in larger arcs from the curved spore walls. Here he was, curled up quite comfortably in a little amber ball, where he could stay until even the depths were warm and light. At this moment there was probably still some ice on the sky, and certainly there would not be much to eat as yet. Not that there was ever much, what with the voracious rotifers coming awake too with the first gust of warm water—

The rotifers! That was it. There was a plan afoot to drive them out. Memory returned in an unwelcome rush. As if to help it, the spore rocked again. That was probably one of the Protos, trying to awaken him; nothing man-eating ever came to the Bottom this early. He had left an early call with the Paras, and now the time had come, as cold and early and dark as he had thought he wanted it.

Reluctantly, Lavon uncurled, planting his webbed toes and arching his backbone as hard as he could, pressing with his whole body against his amber prison. With small, sharp, crepitating sounds, a network of cracks raced through the translucent shell.

Then the spore wall dissolved into a thousand brittle shards, and he was shivering violently with the onslaught of the icy water. The warmer fluid of his winter cell dissipated silently, a faint glowing fog. In the brief light he saw, not far from him, a familiar shape: a transparent, bubble-filled cylinder, a colorless slipper of jelly, spirally grooved, almost as long as he was tall. Its surface was furred with gently vibrating fine hairs, thickened at the base.

The light went out. The Proto said nothing; it waited while Lavon choked and coughed, expelling the last remnants of the spore fluid from his booklungs and sucking in the pure, ice-cold water.

'Para?' Lavon said at last. 'Already?'

'Already,' the invisible cilia vibrated in even, emotionless tones. Each separate hair-like process buzzed at an independent, changing rate; the resulting sound waves spread through the water, intermodulating, reinforcing or cancelling each other. The aggregate wave-front, by the time it reached human ears, was rather eerie, but nevertheless recognizable human speech. 'This is the time, Lavon.'

'Time and more than time,' another voice said from the returned darkness. 'If we are to drive Flosc from his castles.'

'Who's that?' Lavon said, turning futilely toward the new voice.

'I am Para also, Lavon. We are sixteen since the awakening. If you could reproduce as rapidly as we—'

'Brains are better than numbers,' Lavon said. 'As the Eaters will find out soon enough.'

'What shall we do, Lavon?'

The man drew up his knees and sank to the cold mud of the Bottom to think. Something wriggled under his buttocks and a tiny spirillum corkscrewed away, identifiable only by feel. He let it go; he was not hungry yet, and he had the Eaters – the rotifers – to think about. Before long they would be swarming in the upper reaches of the sky, devouring everything, even men when they could catch them, even their natural enemies the Protos now and then. And whether or not the Protos could be organized to battle them was a question still to be tested.

Brains are better than numbers; even that, as a proposition, was still to be tested. The Protos, after all, were intelligent after their fashion; and they knew their world, as the men did not. Lavon could still remember how hard it had been for him to get straight in his head the various clans of beings in this world, and to make sense of their confused names; his tutor Shar had drilled him unmercifully until it had begun to penetrate.

When you said 'Man', you meant creatures that, generally speaking, looked alike. The bacteria were of three kinds, the rods and the globes and the spirals, but they were all tiny and edible, so he had learned to differentiate them quickly. When it came to the Protos, identification became a real problem. Para here was a Proto, but he certainly looked very different from Stent and his family, and the family of Didin was unlike both. Anything, as it turned out, that was not green and had a visible nucleus was a Proto, no matter how strange its shape might be. The Eaters were all different, too, and some of them were as beautiful as the fruiting crowns of water-plants; but all of them were deadly, and all had the whirling crown of cilia which could suck you into the incessantly grinding mastax in a moment. Everything which was green and had an engraved shell of glass, Shar had called a diatom, dredging the strange word as he dredged them all from some bottom in his skull which none of the rest of them could reach, and even Shar could not explain.

Lavon arose quickly. 'We need Shar,' he said. 'Where is his spore?'

'On a plant frond, far up near the sky.'

Idiot! The old man would never think of safety. To sleep near the sky, where he might be snatched up and borne off by any Eater to chance by when he emerged, sluggish with winter's long sleep! How could a wise man be so foolish?

'We'll have to hurry. Show me the way.'

'Soon; wait,' one of the Paras said. 'You cannot see. Noc is foraging nearby.' There was a small stir in the texture of the darkness as the swift cylinder shot away.

'Why do we need Shar?' the other Para said.

'For his brains, Para. He is a thinker.'

'But his thoughts are water. Since he taught the Protos man's language, he has forgotten to think of the Eaters. He thinks forever of the mystery of how man came here. It is a mystery – even the Eaters are not like Man. But understanding it will not help us to live.'

Lavon turned blindly toward the creature. 'Para, tell me something. Why do the Protos side with us? With Man, I mean? Why do you need us? The Eaters fear you.'

There was a short silence. When the Para spoke again, the vibrations of its voice were more blurred than before, more even, more devoid of any understandable feeling.

'We live in this world,' the Para said. 'We are of it. We rule it. We came to that state long before the coming of men, in long warfare with the Eaters. But we think as the Eaters do, we do not plan, we share our knowledge and we exist. Men plan; men lead; men are different from each other; men want to remake the world. And they hate the Eaters, as we do. We will help.'

'And give up your rule?'

'And give it up, if the rule of men is better. That is reason. Now we can go; Noc is coming back with light.'

Lavon looked up. Sure enough, there was a brief flash of cold light far overhead, and then another. In a moment the spherical Proto had dropped into view, its body flaring regularly with blue-green pulses. Beside it darted the second Para.

'Noc brings news,' the second Para said. 'Para is twenty-four. The Syn are awake by thousands along the sky. Noc spoke to a Syn colony, but they will not help us; they all expect to be dead before the Eaters awake.'

'Of course,' said the first Para. 'That always happens. And the Syn are plants; why should they help the Protos?'

'Ask Noc if he'll guide us to Shar,' Lavon said impatiently.

The Noc gestured with its single short, thick tentacle. One of the Paras said, 'That is what he is here for.'

'Then let's go. We've waited long enough.'

The mixed quartet soared away from the Bottom through the liquid darkness.

'No,' Lavon snapped. 'Not a second longer. The Syn are awake, and Not-holca of the Eaters is due right after that. You know that as well as I do, Shar. Wake up!'

'Yes, yes,' the old man said fretfully. He stretched and yawned. 'You're always in such a hurry, Lavon. Where's Phil? He made his spore near mine.'

He pointed to a still-unbroken amber sphere sealed to a leaf of the water-plant one tier below. 'Better push him off; he'll be safer on the Bottom.'

'He would never reach the Bottom,' Para said. 'The thermocline has formed.'

Shar looked surprised. 'It has? Is it as late as all that? Wait while I get my records together.' He began to search along the leaf in the debris and the piled shards of his spore. Lavon looked impatiently about, found a splinter of stonewort, and threw it heavy end first at the bubble of Phil's cell just below. The spore shattered promptly, and the husky young man tumbled out, blue with shock as the cold water hit him.

'Wough!' he said. 'Take it easy, Lavon.' He looked up. 'The old man's awake? Good. He insisted on staying up here for the winter, so of course I had to stay too.'

'Aha,' Shar said, and lifted a thick metal plate about the length of his fore-arm and half as wide. 'Here is one of them. Now if only I haven't misplaced the other—'

Phil kicked away a mass of bacteria. 'Here it is. Better give them both to a Para, so they won't burden you. Where do we go from here, Lavon? It's dangerous up this high. I'm just glad a Dicran hasn't already shown up.'

'I here,' something droned just above them.

Instantly, without looking up, Lavon flung himself out and down into the open water, turning his head to look back over his shoulder only when he was already diving as fast as he could go. Shar and Phil had evidently sprung at the same instant. On the next frond above where Shar had spent his winter was the armored, trumpet-shaped body of the rotifer Dicran, contracted to leap after them.

The two Protos came curving back out of nowhere. At the same moment, the bent, shortened body of Dicran flexed in its armor plate, straightened, came plunging toward them. There was a soft *plop* and Lavon found himself struggling in a fine net, as tangled and impassible as the matte of a lichen. A second such sound was followed by a muttered imprecation from Phil. Lavon struck out fiercely, but he was barely able to wriggle in the web of wiry, transparent stuff.

'Be still,' a voice which he recognized as Para's throbbed behind him. He managed to screw his head around, and then kicked himself mentally for not having realized at once what had happened. The Paras had exploded the trichocysts which lay like tiny cartridges beneath their pellicles; each one cast forth a liquid which solidified upon contact with the water in a long slender thread. It was their standard method of defense.

Farther down, Shar and Phil drifted with the second Para in the heart of a white haze, like creatures far gone in mold. Dicran swerved to avoid it, but she was evidently unable to give up; she twisted and darted around them, her corona buzzing harshly, her few scraps of the human language forgotten. Seen from this distance, the rotation of the corona was revealed as an illusion, created by the rhythm of pulsation of the individual cilia, but as far as Lavon was concerned the point was solely technical and the distance was far too short. Through the transparent armor Lavon could also see the great jaws of Dicran's mastax, grinding away mechanically at the fragments which poured into her unheeding mouth.

High above them all, Noc circled indecisively, illuminating the whole group with quick, nervous flashes of his blue light. He was a flagellate, and had no natural weapons against the rotifer; why he was hanging around drawing attention to himself Lavon could not imagine.

Then, suddenly, he saw the reason: a barrel-like creature about Noc's size, ringed with two rows of cilia and bearing a ram-like prow. 'Didin!' he shouted, unnecessarily. 'This way!'

The Proto swung gracefully toward them and seemed to survey them, though it was hard to tell how he could see them without eyes. The Dicran saw him at the same time and began to back slowly away, her buzzing rising to a raw snarl. She regained the plant and crouched down.

For an instant Lavon thought she was going to give up, but experience should have told him that she lacked the sense. Suddenly the lithe, crouched body was in full spring again, this time straight at Didin. Lavon yelled an incoherent warning.

The Proto didn't need it. The slowly cruising barrel darted to one side and then forward, with astonishing speed. If he could sink that poisoned seizing-organ into a weak point in the rotifer's armor—

Noc mounted higher to keep out of the way of the two fighters, and in the resulting weakened light Lavon could not see what was happening, though the furious churning of the water and the buzzing of the Dicran continued.

After a while the sounds seemed to be retreating; Lavon crouched in the gloom inside the Para's net, listening intently. Finally there was silence.

'What's happened?' he whispered tensely.

'Didin does not say.'

More eternities went by. Then the darkness began to wane as Noc dropped cautiously toward them.

'Noc, where did they go?'

Noc signaled with his tentacle and turned on his axis toward Para. 'He says he lost sight of them. Wait – I hear Didin.'

Lavon could hear nothing; what the Para 'heard' was some one of the semi-telepathic impulses which made up the Proto's own language.

'He says Dicran is dead.'

'Good! Ask him to bring the body back here.'

There was a short silence. 'He says he will bring it. What good is a dead rotifer, Lavon?'

'You'll see,' Lavon said. He watched anxiously until Didin glided backwards into the lighted area, his poisonous ram sunk deep into the flaccid body of the rotifer, which, after the delicately-organized fashion of its kind, was already beginning to disintegrate.

'Let me out of this net, Para.'

The Proto jerked sharply for a fraction of a turn on its long axis, snapping the threads off at the base; the movement had to be made with great precision, or its pellicle would tear as well. The tangled mass rose gently with the current and drifted off over the abyss.

Lavon swam forward and, seizing one buckled edge of Dicran's armor, tore away a huge strip of it. His hands plunged into the now almost shapeless body and came out again holding two dark spheroids: eggs.

'Destroy these, Didin,' he ordered. The Proto obligingly slashed them open.

'Hereafter,' Lavon said, 'that's to be standard procedure with every Eater you kill.'

'Not the males,' one of the Para pointed out.

'Para, you have no sense of humor. All right, not the males – but nobody kills the males anyhow, they're harmless.' He looked down grimly at the inert mass. 'Remember – destroy the eggs. Killing the beasts isn't enough. We want to wipe out the whole race.'

'We never forget,' Para said emotionlessly.

2

The band of over two hundred humans, with Lavon and Shar and a Para at its head, fled swiftly through the warm, light waters of the upper level. Each man gripped a wood splinter, or a fragment of lime chipped from stonewort, as a club; and two hundred pairs of eyes darted watchfully from side to side. Cruising over them was a squadron of twenty Didins, and the rotifers they encountered only glared at them from single red eyespots, making no move to attack. Overhead, near the sky, the sunlight was filtered through a thick layer of living creatures, fighting and feeding and spawning, so that all the depths below were colored a rich green. Most of this heavily populated layer was made up of algae and diatoms, and there the Eaters fed unhindered. Sometimes a dying diatom dropped slowly past the army.

The spring was well advanced; the two hundred, Lavon thought, probably represented all of the humans who had survived the winter. At least no more could be found. The others – nobody would ever know how many – had awakened too late in the season, or had made their spores in exposed places, and the rotifers had snatched them up. Of the group, more than a third were women. That meant that in another forty days, if they were unmolested, they could double the size of their army.

If they were unmolested. Lavon grinned and pushed an agitated colony of Eudorina out of his way. The phrase reminded him of a speculation Shar had brought forth last year: If Para were left unmolested, the oldster had said, he could reproduce fast enough to fill this whole universe with a solid mass of Paras before the season was out. Nobody, of course, ever went unmolested in this world; nevertheless, Lavon meant to cut the odds for people considerably below anything that had heretofore been thought of as natural.

His hand flashed up, and down again. The darting squadrons plunged after him. The light on the sky faded rapidly, and after a while Lavon began to feel slightly chilly. He signaled again. Like dancers, the two hundred swung their bodies in mid-flight plunging now feet first toward the Bottom. To strike the thermocline in this position would make their passage through it faster, getting them out of the upper level where every minute, despite the convoy of Protos, concentrated danger.

Lavon's feet struck a yielding surface, and with a splash he was over his head in icy water. He bobbed up again, feeling the icy division drawn across his shoulders. Other splashes began to sound all along the thermocline as the army struck it, although, since there was water above and below, Lavon could not see the actual impacts.

Now they would have to wait until their body temperatures fell. At this dividing line of the universe, the warm water ended and the temperature dropped rapidly, so that the water below was much denser and buoyed them up. The lower level of cold reached clear down to the Bottom – an area which the rotifers, who were not very clever, seldom managed to enter.

A moribund diatom drifted down beside Lavon, the greenish-yellow of its body fading to a sick orange, its beautifully-marked, oblong, pillbox-like shell swarming with greedy bacteria. It came to rest on the thermocline, and the transparent caterpillar tread of jelly which ran around it moved feebly, trying vainly to get traction on the sliding water interface. Lavon reached out a webbed hand and brushed away a clot of vibrating rods which had nearly forced its way into the shell through a costal opening.

'Thank ...' the diatom said, in an indistinct, whispering voice. And again, 'Thank ... Die ...' The gurgling whisper faded. The caterpillar tread shifted again, then was motionless.

'It is right,' a Para said. 'Why do you bother with those creatures? They are stupid. Nothing can be done for them.'

Lavon did not try to explain. He felt himself sinking slowly, and the water about his trunk and legs no longer seemed cold, only gratefully cool after the stifling heat of that he was breathing. In a moment the cool still depths had closed over his head. He hovered until he was reasonably sure that all the rest of his army was safely through, and the long ordeal of search for survivors in the upper level really ended. Then he twisted and streaked for the Bottom, Phil and Para beside him, Shar puffing along with the vanguard.

A stone loomed; Lavon surveyed it in the half-light. Almost immediately he saw what he had hoped to see: the sand-built house of a caddis-worm, clinging to the mountainous slopes of the rock. He waved in his special cadre and pointed.

Cautiously the men spread out in a U around the stone, the mouth of the U facing the same way as the opening of the worm's masonry tube. A Noc came after them, drifting like a starshell above the peak; one of the Paras approached the door of the worm's house, buzzing defiantly. Under cover of this challenge the men at the back of the U settled on the rock and began to creep forward. The house was three times as tall as they were; the slimy black sand grains of which it was composed were as big as their heads.

There was a stir inside, and after a moment the ugly head of the worm peered out, weaving uncertainly at the buzzing Para which had disturbed it. The Para drew back, and the worm, in a kind of blind hunger, followed it. A sudden lunge brought it nearly halfway out of its tube.

Lavon shouted. Instantly the worm was surrounded by a howling horde of two-legged demons, who beat and prodded it mercilessly with fists and clubs. Somehow it made a sound, a kind of bleat as unlikely as the bird-like whistle of a fish, and began to slide backwards into its home – but the rearguard had already broken in back there. It jerked forward again, lashing from side to side under the flogging.

There was only one way now for the great larva to go, and the demons around it kept it going that way. It fell toward the Bottom down the side of the rock, naked and ungainly, shaking its blind head and bleating.

Lavon sent five Didin after it. They could not kill it, for it was far too huge to die under their poison, but they could sting it hard enough to keep it travelling. Otherwise, it would be almost sure to return to the rock to start a new house.

Lavon settled on an abutment and surveyed his prize with satisfaction. It was more than big enough to hold his entire clan – a great tubular hall, easily defended once the breach in the rear wall was rebuilt, and well out of the usual haunts of the Eaters. The muck the caddis-worm had left behind would have to be cleaned up, guards posted, vents knocked out to keep the oxygen-poor water of the depths in motion inside. It was too bad that the amoebae could not be detailed to scavenge the place, but Lavon knew better than to issue such an order. The Fathers of the Protos could not be asked to do useful work; that had been made very clear.

He looked around at his army. They were standing around him in awed silence, looking at the spoils of their attack upon the largest creature in the world. He did not think they would ever again feel as timid toward the Eaters. He stood up quickly.

'What are you gaping at?' he shouted. 'It's yours, all of it. Get to work!'

Old Shar sat comfortably upon a pebble which had been hollowed out and cushioned with spirogyra straw. Lavon stood nearby at the door, looking out at the maneuvers of his legions. They numbered more than three hundred now, thanks to the month of comparative quiet which they had enjoyed in the great hall, and they handled their numbers well in the aquatic drill which Lavon had invented for them. They swooped and turned above the rock, breaking and reassembling their formations, fighting a sham battle with invisible opponents whose shape they could remember only too well.

'Noc says there's all kinds of quarreling going on among the Eaters,' Shar said. 'They didn't believe we'd joined with the Protos at first, and then they didn't believe we'd all worked together to capture the hall. And the mass raid we had last week scared them. They'd never tried anything of the kind before, and they *knew* it wouldn't fail. Now they're fighting with each other over why it did. Cooperation is something new to this world, Lavon; it's making history.'

'History?' Lavon said, following his drilling squadrons with a technical eye. 'What's that?'

'These.' The old man leaned over one arm of the pebble and touched the metal plates which were always with him. Lavon turned to follow the gesture, incuriously. He knew the plates well enough – the pure uncorroded shining, graven deeply on both sides with characters no-one, not even Shar, could read. The Protos called the plates *Not-stuff* – neither wood nor flesh nor stone.

'What good is that? I can't read it. Neither can you.'

'I've got a start, Lavon. I know the plates are written in our language. Look at the first word: *ha ii ss tuh oh or ee* – exactly the right number of characters for "history". That can't be a coincidence. And the next two words have to be "of the". And going on from there, using just the characters I already know—' Shar bent and traced in the sand with a stick a new train of characters: *i/ terste/ / ar e/ / e/ ition.*

'What's that?'

'It's a start, Lavon. Just a start. Some day we'll have more.'

Lavon shrugged. 'Perhaps, when we're safer. We can't afford to worry about that kind of thing now. We've never had that kind of time, not since the First Awakening.'

The old man frowned down at the characters in the sand. 'The First Awakening. Why does everything seem to stop there? I can remember in the smallest detail nearly everything that happened to me since then. But what happened to our childhoods, Lavon? None of us who survived the First Awakening seems to have had one. Who were our parents? Why were we so ignorant of the world, and yet grown men and women, all of us?'

'And the answer is in the plates?'

'I hope so,' Shar said. 'I believe it is. But I don't know. The plates were beside me in the spore at the First Awakening. That's all I know about them, except that there's nothing else like them in the world. The rest is deduction, and I haven't gotten very far with it. Some day ... some day.'

'I hope so too,' Lavon said soberly. 'I don't mean to mock, Shar, or to be impatient. I've got questions, too; we all have. But we're going to have to put them off for a while. Suppose we never find the whole answer?'

'Then our children will.'

'But there's the heart of the problem, Shar: we have to live to have children. And make the kind of a world in which they'll have time to study. Otherwise—'

Lavon broke off as a figure darted between the guards at the door of the hall and twisted to a halt.

'What news, Phil?'

'The same,' Phil said, shrugging with his whole body. His feet touched the floor. 'The Flosc's castles are going up all along the bar; they'll be finished with them soon, and then we won't dare to get near them. Do you still think you can drive them out?'

Lavon nodded.

'But why?'

'First, for effect. We've been on the defensive so far, even though we've made a good job of it. We'll have to follow that up with an attack of our own if we're going to keep the Eaters confused. Second, the castles Flosc builds are all tunnels and exits and entrances – much better than worm-houses for us. I hate to think of what would have happened if the Eaters had thought of blockading us inside this hall. And we need an outpost in enemy country, Phil, where there are Eaters to kill.'

'This is enemy country,' Phil said. 'Stephanost is a Bottom-dweller.'

'But she's only a trapper, not a hunter. Any time we want to kill her, we can find her right where we left her last. It's the leapers like Dicran and Notholca, the swimmers like Rotar, the colony-builders like Flosc that we have to wipe out first.'

'Then we'd better start now, Lavon. Once the castles are finished—'

'Yes. Get your squads together, Phil. Shar, come on; we're leaving the hall.'

'To raid the castles?'

'Of course.'

Shar picked up his plates.

'You'd better leave those here; they'll be in your way in the fighting.'

'No,' Shar said determinedly. 'I don't want them out of my sight. They go along.'

3

Vague forebodings, all the more disturbing because he had felt nothing quite like them ever before, passed like clouds of fine silt through Lavon's mind as the army swept away from the hall on the Bottom and climbed toward the thermocline. As far as he could see, everything seemed to be going as he had planned it. As the army moved, its numbers were swelled by Protos who darted into its ranks from all sides. Discipline was good; and every man was armed with a long, seasoned splinter, and from each belt swung a stone-wort-flake hand-axe, held by a thong run through a hole Shar had taught them all how to drill. There would probably be much death before the light of today faded, but death was common enough on any day, and this time it should heavily disfavor the Eaters.

But there was a chill upon the depths that Lavon did not like, and a suggestion of a current in the water which was unnatural below the thermocline. A great many days had been consumed in collecting the army, recruiting from stragglers, and in securing the hall. The intensive breeding which had followed, and the training of the new-born and the newly recruited, had taken still more time, all of it essential, but all irrevocable. If the chill and the current marked the beginning of the fall turnover ...

If it did, nothing could be done about it. The turnover could no more be postponed than the coming of day or night. He signaled to the nearest Para.

The glistening torpedo veered toward him. Lavon pointed up.

'Here comes the thermocline, Para. Are we pointed right?'

'Yes, Lavon. That way is the place where the Bottom rises toward the sky. Flosc's castles are on the other side, where she will not see us.'

'The sand bar that runs out from the north. Right. It's getting warmer. Here we go.'

Lavon felt his flight suddenly quicken, as if he had been shot like a seed from some invisible thumb and forefinger. He looked over his shoulder to watch the passage of the rest through the temperature barrier, and what he saw thrilled him as sharply as any awakening. Up to now he had had no clear picture of the size of his forces, or the three-dimensional beauty of their dynamic, mobile organization. Even the Protos had fitted themselves into the squads; pattern after pattern of power came soaring after Lavon from the Bottom: first a single Noc bowling along like a beacon to guide all the rest, then an advance cone of Didin to watch for individual Eaters who might flee to give the alarm, and then the men, and the Protos, who made up the main force, in tight formations as beautiful as the elementary geometry from which Shar had helped derive them.

The sand-bar loomed ahead, as vast as any mountain range. Lavon soared sharply upward, and the tumbled, raw-boned boulders of the sand grains swept by rapidly beneath him in a broad, stony flood. Far beyond the ridge, towering up to the sky through glowing green obscurity, were the befronded stems of the plant jungle which was their objective. It was too dim with distance to allow him to see the clinging castles of the Flosc yet, but he knew that the longest part of the march was over. He narrowed his eyes and cleft the sunlit waters with driving, rapid strokes of his webbed hands and feet. The invaders poured after him over the crest of the bar in an orderly torrent.

Lavon swung his arm in a circle. Silently, the following squadrons glided into a great paraboloid, its axis pointed at the jungle. The castles were visible now; until the formation of the army, they had been the only products of close cooperation that this world had ever seen. They were built of single brown tubes, narrow at the base, attached to each other in a random pattern in an ensemble as delicate as a branching coral. In the mouth of each tube was a rotifer, a Flosc, distinguished from other Eaters by the four-leaf-clover of its corona, and by the single, prehensile finger springing from the small of its back, with which it ceaselessly molded its brown spittle into hard pellets and cemented them carefully to the rim of its tube.

As usual, the castles chilled Lavon's muscles with doubt. They were perfect, and they had always been one of the major, stony flowers of summer, long before there had been any First Awakening, or any men. And there was surely something wrong with the water in the upper level; it was warm and sleepy. The heads of the Flosc hummed contentedly at the mouths of their tubes; everything was as it should be, as it had always been; the army was a fantasm, the attack a failure before it had begun—

Then they were spied.

The Flosc vanished instantly, contracting violently into their tubes. The placid humming of their continuous feeding upon everything that passed was snuffed out; spared motes drifted about the castle in the light.

Lavon found himself smiling. Not long ago, the Flosc would only have waited until the humans were close enough, and then would have sucked them down, without more than a few struggles here and there, a few pauses in the humming while the outsize morsels were enfolded and fed into the grinders. Now, instead, they hid; they were afraid.

'Go!' he shouted at the top of his voice. 'Kill them! Kill them while they're down!'

The army behind him swept after him with a stunning composite shout.

Tactics vanished. A petalled corona unfolded in Lavon's face, and a buzzing whirlpool spun him toward its black heart. He slashed wildly with his edged wooden splinter.

The sharp edge sliced deeply into the ciliated lobes. The rotifer screamed like a siren and contracted into her tube, closing her wounded face. Grimly, Lavon followed.

It was pitch dark inside the castle, and the raging currents of pain which flowed past him threw him from one pebbly wall to another. He gritted his teeth and probed with the splinter. It bit into a yielding surface at once, and another scream made his ears ring, mixed with mangled bits of words in Lavon's own language, senseless and horrible with agony. He slashed at them until they stopped, and continued to slash until he could control his terror.

As soon as he was able, he groped in the torn corpse for the eggs. The point found their life and pricked it. Trembling, he pulled himself back to the mouth of the tube, and without stopping to think pushed himself off at the first Eater to pass it.

The thing was a Dicran; she doubled viciously upon him at once. Even the Eaters had learned something about cooperation. And the Dicrans fought well in open water. They were the best possible reinforcements the Flosc could have called.

The Dicran's armor turned the point of Lavon's splinter easily. He jabbed frantically, hoping to hit a joint, but the agile creature gave him no time to aim. She charged him irresistibly, and her humming corona folded down around his head, pinned his forearms to his sides—

The Eater heaved convulsively and went limp. Lavon half slashed, half tore his way free. A Didin was drawing back, pulling out its seizing-organ. The body floated, downward.

'Thanks,' Lavon gasped. The Proto darted off without replying; it lacked sufficient cilia to imitate human speech. Possibly it lacked the desire as well; the Didins were not sociable.

A tearing whirlpool sprang into being again around him, and he flexed his sword-arm. In the next five dreamlike minutes he developed a technique for dealing with the sessile, sucking Flosc. Instead of fighting the current and swinging the splinter back and forth against it, he gave in to the vortex, rode with it, and braced the splinter between his feet, point down. The results were even better than he had hoped. The point, driven by the full force of the Flosc's own trap, pierced the soft, wormlike body half through while it gaped for the human quarry. After each encounter, Lavon doggedly went through the messy ritual of destroying the eggs.

At last he emerged from a tube to find that the battle had drifted away from him. He paused on the edge to get his breath back, clinging to the rounded, translucent bricks and watching the fighting. It was difficult to make any military sense out of the melee, but as far as he could tell the rotifers were getting the worst of it. They did not know how to meet so carefully organized an attack, and they were not in any real sense intelligent.

The Didin were ranging from one side of the fray to the other, in two tight, vicious efficient groups, englobing and destroying free-swimming rotifers in whole flocks at a time. Lavon saw no fewer than half a dozen Eaters trapped by teams of Paras, each pair dragging a struggling victim in a trichocyst net remorselessly toward the Bottom, where she would inevitably suffocate. He was astonished to see one of the few Nocs that had accompanied his army scouring a cringing Rotar with its virtually harmless tentacle; the Eater seemed too astonished to fight back, and Lavon for once knew just how she felt.

A figure swam slowly and tiredly up to him from below. It was old Shar, puffing hard. Lavon reached a hand down to him and hauled him onto the lip of the tube. The man's face wore a frightening expression, half shock, half pure grief.

'Gone, Lavon,' he said. 'Gone. Lost.'

'What? What's gone? What's the matter?'

'The plate. You were right. I should have known.' He sobbed convulsively.

'What plate? Calm down. What happened? Did you lose one of the history plates – or both of them?'

Slowly his tutor seemed to be recovering control of his breathing. 'One of them,' he said wretchedly. 'I dropped it in the fight. I hid the other one in an empty Flosc tube. But I dropped the first one – the one I'd just begun to decipher. It went all the way down to the Bottom, and I couldn't get free to go after it – all I could do was watch it go, spinning down into the darkness. We could sift the mud forever and never find it.'

He dropped his face into his hands. Perched on the edge of the brown tube in the green glow of the waters, he looked both pathetic and absurd. Lavon did not know what to say; even he realized that the loss was major and perhaps final, that the awesome blank in their memories prior to the First Awakening might now never be filled. How Shar felt about it he could comprehend only dimly.

Another human figure darted and twisted toward him. 'Lavon!' Phil's voice cried. 'It's working, it's working! The swimmers are running away, what's left of them. There are still some Flosc in the castles, hiding in the darkness. If we could only lure them out in the open—'

Jarred back to the present, Lavon's mind raced over the possibilities. The whole attack could still fail if the Flosc entrenched themselves successfully. After all, a big kill had not been the only object; they had started out to capture the castles.

'Shar – do these tubes connect with each other?'

'Yes,' the old man said without interest. 'It's a continuous system.'

Lavon sprang out upon the open water. 'Come on, Phil. We'll attack them from the rear.' Turning, he plunged into the mouth of the tube, Phil on his heels.

It was very dark, and the water was fetid with the odor of the tube's late owner, but after a moment's groping Lavon found the opening which led into the next tube. It was easy to tell which way was out because of the pitch of the walls; everything the Flosc built had a conical bore, differing from the next tube only in size. Determinedly Lavon worked his way toward the main stem, going always down and in.

Once they passed beneath an opening beyond which the water was in furious motion, and out of which poured muffled sounds of shouting and a defiant buzz. Lavon stopped to probe through the hole with his sword. The rotifer gave a shrill, startled shriek and jerked her wounded tail upward, involuntarily releasing her toe-hold upon the walls of the tube. Lavon moved on, grinning. The men above would do the rest.

Reaching the central stem at last, Lavon and Phil went methodically from one branch to another, spearing the surprised Eaters from behind or cutting them loose so that the men outside could get at them as they drifted upward, propelled by the drag of their own coronas. The trumpet shape of the tubes prevented the Eaters from turning to fight, and from following them through the castle to surprise them from behind; each Flosc had only the one room, which she never left.

The gutting of the castles took hardly fifteen minutes. The day was just beginning to end when Lavon emerged with Phil at the mouth of a turret to look down upon the first City of Man.

He lay in darkness, his forehead pressed against his knees, as motionless as a dead man. The water was stuffy, cold, the blackness complete. Around him were the walls of a tube of Flosc's castle; above him a Para laid another sand grain upon a new domed roof. The rest of the army rested in other tubes, covered with other new stony caps, but there was no sound of movement or of voices. It was as quiet as a necropolis.

Lavon's thoughts were slow and bitter as drugged syrup. He had been right about the passage of the seasons. He had had barely enough time to bring all his people from the hall to the castles before the annual debacle of the fall overturn. Then the waters of the universe had revolved once, bringing the skies to the Bottom, and the Bottom to the skies, and then mixing both. The thermocline was destroyed until next year's spring overturn would re-form it.

And inevitably, the abrupt change in temperature and oxygen concentration had started the spore-building glands again. The spherical amber shell was going up around Lavon now, and there was nothing he could do about it. It was an involuntary process, as dissociated from his control as the beating of his heart. Soon the light-generating oil which filled the spore would come pouring out, expelling and replacing the cold, foul water, and then sleep would come ...

And all this had happened just as they had made a real gain, had established themselves in enemy country, had come within reach of the chance to destroy the Eaters wholesale and forever. Now the eggs of the Eaters had been laid, and next year it would have to be done all over again. And there was the loss of the plate; he had hardly begun to reflect upon what that would mean for the future.

There was a soft *chunk* as the last sand grain fell into place on the roof. The sound did not quite bring the final wave of despair against which he had been fighting in advance. Instead, it seemed to carry with it a wave of obscure contentment, with which his consciousness began to sink more and more rapidly toward sleep. They were safe, after all. They could not be ousted from the castle. And there would be fewer Eaters next year, because of all the eggs that had been destroyed, and the layers of those eggs ... There was one plate still left ...

Quiet and cold; darkness and silence.

In a forgotten corner of the galaxy, the watery world of Hydrot hurtles endlessly around the red star, Tau Ceti. For many months life has swarmed in its lakes and pools, but now the sun retreats from the zenith, and the snow falls, and the ice advances from the eternal ocean. Life sinks once more toward slumber, simulating death, and the battles and lusts and ambitions and defeats of a thousand million microscopic creatures retreat into the limbo where such things matter not at all.

No, such things matter not at all when winter reigns on Hydrot; but winter is an inconstant king.

CYCLE TWO

1

Old Shar set down the thick, ragged-edged metal plate at last, and gazed instead out the window of the castle, apparently resting his eyes on the glowing green–gold obscurity of the summer waters. In the soft fluorescence which played down upon him, from the Noc dozing impassively in the groined vault of the chamber, Lavon could see that he was in fact a young man. His face was so delicately formed as to suggest that it had not been many seasons since he had first emerged from his spore.

But of course there had been no real reason to have expected an old man. All the Shars had been referred to traditionally as 'old' Shar. The reason, like the reasons for everything else, had been forgotten, but the custom had persisted. The adjective at least gave weight and dignity to the office – that of the center of wisdom of all the people, as each Lavon had been the center of authority.

The present Shar belonged to the generation XVI, and hence would have to be at least two seasons younger than Lavon himself. If he was old, it was only in knowledge.

'Lavon, I'm going to have to be honest with you,' Shar said at last, still looking out of the tall, irregular window. 'You've come to me at your maturity for the secrets on the metal plate, just as your predecessors did to mine. I can give some of them to you – but for the most part, I don't know what they mean.'

'After so many generations?' Lavon asked, surprised. 'Wasn't it Shar III who made the first complete translation? That was a long time ago.'

The young man turned and looked at Lavon with eyes made dark and wide by the depths into which they had been staring. 'I can read what's on the plate, but most of it seems to make no sense. Worst of all, the record's incomplete. You didn't know that? It is. One of the plates was lost in a battle during the first war with the Eaters, while these castles were still in their hands.'

'What am I here for, then?' Lavon said. 'Isn't there anything of value on the remaining plate? Did they really contain "the wisdom of the Creators", or is that another myth?'

'No. No, it's true,' Shar said slowly, 'as far as it goes.'

He paused, and both men turned and gazed at the ghostly creature which had appeared suddenly outside the window. Then Shar said gravely, 'Come in, Para.'

The slipper-shaped organism, nearly transparent except for the thousands of black-and-silver granules and frothy bubbles which packed its interior, glided into the chamber and hovered, with a muted whirring of cilia. For a moment it remained silent, speaking telepathically to the Noc floating in the vault, after the ceremonious fashion of all the Protos. No human had ever intercepted one of these colloquies, but there was no doubt about their reality; humans had used them for long-range communication for generations.

Then the Para's cilia vibrated once more. 'We are arrived, Shar and Lavon, according to the custom.'

'And welcome,' said Shar. 'Lavon, let's leave this matter of the plates for a while, until you hear what Para has to say; that's a part of the knowledge Lavons must have as they come into their office, and it comes before the plates. I can give you some hints of what we are. First Para has to tell you something about what we aren't.'

Lavon nodded, willingly enough, and watched the Proto as it settled gently to the surface of the hewn table at which Shar had been sitting. There was in the entity such a perfection and economy of organization, such a grace and surety of movement, that he could hardly believe in his own new-won maturity. Para, like all the Protos, made him feel, not perhaps poorly thought-out, but at least unfinished.

'We know that in this universe there is logically no place for man,' the gleaming, now immobile cylinder upon the table droned abruptly. 'Our memory is the common property of all our races. It reaches back to a time when there were no such creatures as man here, nor any even remotely like men. It remembers also that once upon a day there were men here, suddenly, and in some numbers. Their spores littered the Bottom; we found the spores only a short time after our season's Awakening, and inside them we saw the forms of men, slumbering.

'Then men shattered their spores and emerged. At first they seemed helpless, and the Eaters devoured them by scores, as in those days they devoured everything that moved. But that soon ended. Men were intelligent, active. And they were gifted with a trait, a character, possessed by no other creature in this world. Not even the savage Eaters had it. Men organized us to exterminate the Eaters, and therein lay the difference. Men had initiative. We have the word now, which you gave us, and we apply it, but we still do not know what the thing is that it labels.'

'You fought beside us,' Lavon said.

'Gladly. We would never have thought of that war by ourselves, but it was good and brought good. Yet we wondered. We saw that men were poor swimmers, poor walkers, poor crawlers, poor climbers. We saw that men were formed to make and use tools, a concept we still do not understand, for so wonderful a gift is largely wasted in this universe, and there is no other. What good are tool-useful members such as the hands of men? We do not know. It seems plain that so radical a thing should lead to a much greater rulership over the world than has, in fact, proven to be possible for men.'

Lavon's head was spinning. 'Para, I had no notion that you people were philosophers.'

'The Protos are old,' Shar said. He had again turned to look out the window, his hands locked behind his back. 'They aren't philosphers, Lavon, but they are remorseless logicians. Listen to Para.'

'To this reasoning there could be but one outcome,' the Para said. 'Our strange ally, Man, was like nothing else in this universe. He was and is unfitted for it. He does not belong here; he has been – adapted. This drives us to think that there are other universes besides this one, but where these universes might lie, and what their properties might be, it is impossible to imagine. We have no imagination, as men know.'

Was the creature being ironic? Lavon could not tell. He said slowly, 'Other universes? How could that be true?'

'We do not know,' the Para's uninflected voice hummed. Lavon waited, but obviously the Proto had nothing more to say.

Shar had resumed sitting on the window sill, clasping his knees, watching the come and go of dim shapes in the lighted gulf. 'It is quite true,' he said. 'What is written on the plate makes it plain. Let me tell you now what it says.

'*We were made,* Lavon. We were made by men who were not as we are, but men who were our ancestors all the same. They were caught in some disaster, and they made us, and put us here in our universe – so that, even though they had to die, the race of men would live.'

Lavon surged up from the woven spirogyra mat upon which he had been sitting. 'You must think I'm a fool,' he said sharply.

'No. You're our Lavon; you have a right to know the facts. Make what you like of them.' Shar swung his webbed toes back into the chamber. 'What I've told you may be hard to believe, but it seems to be so; what Para says backs it up. Our unfitness to live here is self-evident. I'll give you some examples:

'The past four Shars discovered that we won't get any farther in our studies until we learn how to control heat. We've produced enough heat chemically to show that even the water around us changes when the temperature gets high enough – or low enough, that we knew from the beginning. But there we've stopped.'

'Why?'

'Because heat produced in open water is carried off as rapidly as it's produced. Once we tried to enclose that heat, and we blew up a whole tube of the castle and killed everything in range; the shock was terrible. We measured the pressures that were involved in that explosion, and we discovered that no substance we know could have resisted them. Theory suggests some stronger substances – but *we need heat to form them*!

'Take our chemistry. We live in water. Everything seems to dissolve in water, to some extent. How do we confine a chemical test to the crucible we put it in? How do we maintain a solution at one dilution? I don't know. Every avenue leads me to the same stone door. We're thinking creatures, Lavon, but there's something drastically wrong in the way we think about this universe we live in. It just doesn't seem to lead to results.'

Lavon pushed back his floating hair futilely. 'Maybe you're thinking about the wrong results. We've had no trouble with warfare, or crops, or practical things like that. If we can't create much heat, well, most of us won't miss it; we don't need more than we have. What's the other universe supposed to be like, the one our ancestors lived in? Is it any better than this one?'

'I don't know,' Shar admitted. 'It was so different that it's hard to compare the two. The metal plate tells a story about men who were travelling from one place to another in a container that moved by itself. The only analogue I can think of is the shallops of diatom shells that our youngsters used to sled along the thermocline; but evidently what's meant is something much bigger.

'I picture a huge shallop, closed on all sides, big enough to hold many people – maybe twenty or thirty. It had to travel for generations through some kind of medium where there wasn't any water to breathe, so the people had to carry their own water and renew it constantly. There were no seasons; no ice formed on the sky, because there couldn't be any sky in a closed shallop; and so there was no spore formation.

'Then the shallop was wrecked somehow. The people in it knew they were going to die. They made us, and put us here, as if we were their children. Because they had to die, they wrote their story on the plates, to tell us what had happened. I suppose we'd understand it better if we had the plate Shar I lost during the war – but we don't.'

'The whole thing sounds like a parable,' Lavon said, shrugging. 'Or a song. I can see why you don't understand it. What I can't see is why you bother to try.'

'Because of the plate,' Shar said. 'You've handled it yourself now, so you know that we've nothing like it. We have crude, impure metals we've hammered out, metals that last for a while and then decay. But the plate shines on, generation after generation. It doesn't change; our hammers and our graving tools break against it; the little heat we can generate leaves it unharmed. That plate wasn't formed in our universe – and that one fact makes every word on it important to me. Someone went to a great deal of trouble to make those plates indestructible, and to give them to us. Someone to whom the word "stars" was important enough to be worth fourteen repetitions, despite the fact that the word doesn't seem to mean anything. I'm ready to think that if our makers repeated a word even twice on a record that seems likely to last forever, then it's important for us to know what it means.'

Lavon stood up once more.

'All these extra universes and huge shallops and meaningless words – I can't say that they don't exist, but I don't see what difference it makes,' he said. 'The Shars of a few generations ago spent their whole lives breeding better algae crops for us, and showing us how to cultivate them, instead of living haphazardly on bacteria. Farther back, the Shars devised war engines, and war plans. All that was work worth doing. The Lavons of those days evidently got along without the metal plate and its puzzles, and saw to it that the Shars did, too. Well, as far as I'm concerned, you're welcome to the plate, if you like it better than crop improvement – but I think it ought to be thrown away.'

'All right,' Shar said, shrugging. 'If you don't want it, that ends the traditional interview. We'll go our—'

There was a rising drone from the table-top. The Para was lifting itself, waves of motion passing over its cilia, like the waves which went silently across the fruiting stalks of the fields of delicate fungi with which the Bottom was planted. It had been so silent that Lavon had forgotten it; he could tell from Shar's startlement that Shar had, too.

'This is a great decision,' the waves of sound washing from the creature throbbed. 'Every Proto has heard it, and agrees with it. We have been afraid of this metal plate for a long time, afraid that men would learn to understand it and follow what it says to some secret place, leaving the Protos behind. Now we are not afraid.'

'There wasn't anything to be afraid of,' Lavon said indulgently.

'No Lavon before you, Lavon, had ever said so,' the Para said. 'We are glad. We will throw the plate away, as Lavon orders.'

With that, the shining creature swooped toward the embrasure. With it, it bore away the remaining plate, which had been resting under it on the tabletop, suspended delicately in the curved tips of its supple ventral cilia. Inside its pellucid body, vacuoles swelled to increase its buoyancy and enable it to carry the heavy weight.

With a cry, Shar plunged through the water toward the window.

'Stop, Para!'

But Para was already gone, so swiftly that it had not even heard the call. Shar twisted his body and brought up one shoulder against the tower wall.

He said nothing. His face was enough. Lavon could not look into it for more than an instant.

The shadows of the two men began to move slowly along the uneven cobbled floor. The Noc descended toward them from the vault, its tentacle stirring the water, its internal light flaring and fading irregularly. It, too, drifted through the window after its cousin, and sank slowly away toward the Bottom. Gently its living glow dimmed, flickered in the depths, and winked out.

2

For many days, Lavon was able to avoid thinking much about the loss. There was always a great deal of work to be done. Maintenance of the castles was a never-ending task. The thousand dichotomously-branching wings tended to crumble with time, especially at their bases where they sprouted from one another, and no Shar had yet come forward with a mortar as good as the rotifer-spittle which had once held them together. In addition, the breaking through of windows and the construction of chambers in the early days had been haphazard and often unsound. The instinctive architecture of the Eaters, after all, had not been meant to meet the needs of human occupants.

And then there were the crops. Men no longer fed precariously upon passing bacteria snatched to the mouth; now there were the drifting mats of specific water-fungi and algae, and the mycelia on the Bottom, rich and nourishing, which had been bred by five generations of Shars. These had to be tended constantly to keep the strains pure, and to keep the older and less intelligent species of the Protos from grazing on them. In this latter task, to be sure, the more intricate and far-seeing Proto types cooperated, but men were needed to supervise.

There had been a time, after the war with the Eaters, when it had been customary to prey upon the slow-moving and stupid diatoms, whose exquisite and fragile glass shells were so easily burst, and who were unable to learn that a friendly voice did not necessarily mean a friend. There were still people who would crack open a diatom when no one else was looking, but they were regarded as barbarians, to the puzzlement of the Protos. The blurred and simple-minded speech of the gorgeously engraved plants had brought them into the category of community pets – a concept which the Protos were utterly unable to grasp, especially since men admitted that diatoms on the half-frustrule were delicious.

Lavon had had to agree, very early, that the distinction was tiny. After all, humans did eat the desmids, which differed from the diatoms only in three particulars: Their shells were flexible, they could not move (and for that matter neither could all but a few groups of diatoms), and they did not speak. Yet to Lavon, as to most men, there did seem to be some kind of distinction, whether the Protos could see it or not, and that was that. Under the circumstances he felt that it was a part of his duty, as the hereditary leader of men, to protect the diatoms from the occasional poachers who browsed upon them, in defiance of custom, in the high levels of the sunlit sky.

Yet Lavon found it impossible to keep himself busy enough to forget that moment when the last clues to Man's origin and destination had been seized, on authority of his own careless exaggeration, and borne away into dim space.

It might be possible to ask Para for the return of the plate, explain that a mistake had been made. The Protos were creatures of implacable logic, but they respected men, were used to illogic in men, and might reverse their decision if pressed—

We are sorry. The plate was carried over the bar and released in the gulf. We will have the Bottom there searched, but ...

With a sick feeling he could not repress, Lavon knew that that would be the answer, or something very like it. When the Protos decided something was worthless, they did not hide it in some chamber like old women. They threw it away – efficiently.

Yet despite the tormenting of his conscience, Lavon was nearly convinced that the plate was well lost. What had it ever done for Man, except to provide Shars with useless things to think about in the late seasons of their lives? What the Shars themselves had done to benefit Man, here, in the water, in the world, in the universe, had been done by direct experimentation. No bit of useful knowledge had ever come from the plates. There had never been anything in the second plate, at least, but things best left unthought. The Protos were right.

Lavon shifted his position on the plant frond, where he had been sitting in order to overlook the harvesting of an experimental crop of blue–green, oil-rich algae drifting in a clotted mass close to the top of the sky, and scratched his back gently against the coarse bole. The Protos were seldom wrong, after all. Their lack of creativity, their inability to think an original thought, was a gift as well as a limitation. It allowed them to see and feel things at all times as they were – not as they hoped they might be, for they had no ability to hope, either.

'La-von! Laa-vah-on!'

The long halloo came floating up from the sleepy depths. Propping one hand against the top of the frond, Lavon bent and looked down. One of the harvesters was looking up at him, holding loosely the adze with which he had been splitting free from the raft the glutinous tetrads of the algae.

'I'm up here. What's the matter?'

'We have the ripened quadrant cut free. Shall we tow it away?'

'Tow it away,' Lavon said, with a lazy gesture. He leaned back again. At the same instant, a brilliant reddish glory burst into being above him, and cast itself down toward the depths like mesh after mesh of the finest-drawn gold. The great light which lived above the sky during the day, brightening or dimming according to some pattern no Shar ever had fathomed, was blooming again.

Few men, caught in the warm glow of that light, could resist looking up at it – especially when the top of the sky itself wrinkled and smiled just a moment's climb or swim away. Yet, as always, Lavon's bemused upward look gave him back nothing but his own distorted, bobbling reflection, and a reflection of the plant on which he rested.

Here was the upper limit, the third of the three surfaces of the universe. The first surface was the Bottom, where the water ended.

The second surface was the thermocline, definite enough in summer to provide good sledding, but easily penetrable if you knew how.

The third surface was the sky. One could no more pass through that surface than one could penetrate the Bottom, nor was there any better reason to try. There the universe ended. The light which played over it daily, waxing and waning as it chose, seemed to be one of its properties.

Toward the end of the season, the water gradually became colder and more difficult to breathe, while at the same time the light grew duller and stayed for shorter periods between darknesses. Slow currents started to move. The high waters turned chill and started to fall. The Bottom mud stirred and smoked away, carrying with it the spores of the fields of fungi. The thermocline tossed, became choppy, and melted away. The sky began to fog with particles of soft silt carried up from the Bottom, the walls, the corners of the universe. Before very long, the whole world was cold, inhospitable, flocculent with yellowing, dying creatures. The world died until the first tentative current of warm water broke the winter silence.

That was how it was when the second surface vanished. If the sky were to melt away ...

'Lavon!'

Just after the long call, a shining bubble rose past Lavon. He reached out and poked it, but it bounded away from his sharp thumb. The gas bubbles which rose from the Bottom in late summer were almost invulnerable – and when some especially hard blow or edge did penetrate them, they broke into smaller bubbles which nothing could touch, leaving behind a remarkably bad smell.

Gas. There was no water inside a bubble. A man who got inside a bubble would have nothing to breathe.

But, of course, it was impossible to enter a bubble. The surface tension was too strong. As strong as Shar's metal plate. As strong as the top of the sky.

As strong as the top of the sky. And above that – once the bubble was broken – a world of gas instead of water? Were all worlds bubbles of water drifting in gas?

If it were so, travel between them would be out of the question, since it would be impossible to pierce the sky to begin with. Nor did the infant cosmography include any provisions for Bottoms for the worlds.

And yet some of the local creatures did burrow *into* the Bottom, quite deeply, seeking something in those depths which was beyond the reach of Man. Even the surface of the ooze, in high summer, crawled with tiny creatures for which mud was a natural medium. And though many of the entities with which man lived could not pass freely between the two countries of water which were divided by the thermocline, men could and did.

And if the new universe of which Shar had spoken existed at all, it had to exist beyond the sky, where the light was. Why could not the sky be passed, after all? The fact that bubbles could sometimes be broken showed that the surface skin had formed between water and gas wasn't completely invulnerable. Had it ever been tried?

Lavon did not suppose that one man could butt his way through the top of the sky, any more than he could burrow into the Bottom, but there might be ways around the difficulty. Here at his back, for instance, was a plant which gave every appearance of continuing beyond the sky; its upper fronds broke off and were bent back only by a trick of reflection.

It had always been assumed that the plants died where they touched the sky. For the most part, they did, for frequently the dead extension could be seen, leached and yellow, the boxes of its component cells empty, floating imbedded in the perfect mirror. But some were simply chopped off, like the one which sheltered him now. Perhaps that was only an illusion, and instead it soared indefinitely into some other place – some place where men might once have been born, and might still live ...

Both plates were gone. There was only one other way to find out.

Determinedly, Lavon began to climb toward the wavering mirror of the sky. His thorn-thumbed feet trampled obliviously upon the clustered sheaths of fragile stippled diatoms. The tulip-heads of Vortae, placid and murmurous cousins of Para, retracted startledly out of his way upon coiling stalks, to make silly gossip behind him.

Lavon did not hear them. He continued to climb doggedly toward the light, his fingers and toes gripping the plant-bole.

'Lavon! Where are you going? Lavon!'

He leaned out and looked down. The man with the adze, a doll-like figure, was beckoning to him from a patch of blue-green retreating over a violet abyss. Dizzily he looked away, clinging to the bole; he had never been so high before. He had, of course, nothing to fear from falling, but the fear was in his heritage. Then he began to climb again.

After a while, he touched the sky with one hand. He stopped to breathe. Curious bacteria gathered about the base of his thumb where blood from a small cut was fogging away, scattered at his gesture, and wriggled mindlessly back toward the dull red lure.

He waited until he no longer felt winded, and resumed climbing. The sky pressed down against the top of his head, against the back of his neck, against his shoulders. It seemed to give slightly, with a tough, frictionless elasticity. The water here was intensely bright, and quite colorless. He climbed another step, driving his shoulders against that enormous weight.

It was fruitless. He might as well have tried to penetrate a cliff.

Again he had to rest. While he panted, he made a curious discovery. All around the bole of the water plant, the steel surface of the sky curved upward, making a kind of sheath. He found that he could insert his hand into it – there was almost enough space to admit his head as well. Clinging closely to the bole, he looked up into the inside of the sheath, probing it with his injured hand. The glare was blinding.

There was a kind of soundless explosion. His whole wrist was suddenly encircled in an intense, impersonal grip, as if it were being cut in two. In blind astonishment, he lunged upward.

The ring of pain travelled smoothly down his upflung arm as he rose, was suddenly around his shoulders and chest. Another lunge and his knees were being squeezed in the circular vise. Another—

Something was horribly wrong. He clung to the bole and tried to gasp, but there was – nothing to breathe.

The water came streaming out of his body, from his mouth, his nostrils, the spiracles in his sides, spurting in tangible jets. An intense and fiery itching crawled over the surface of his body. At each spasm, long knives ran into him, and from a great distance he heard more water being expelled from his book-lungs in an obscene, frothy sputtering. Inside his head, a patch of fire began to eat away at the floor of his nasal cavity.

Lavon was drowning.

With a final convulsion, he kicked himself away from the splintery bole, and fell. A hard impact shook him; and then the water, who had clung to him so tightly when he had first attempted to leave her, took him back with cold violence.

Sprawling and tumbling grotesquely, he drifted, down and down and down, toward the Bottom.

3

For many days, Lavon lay curled insensibly in his spore, as if in the winter sleep. The shock of cold which he had felt on re-entering his native universe had been taken by his body as a sign of coming winter, as it had taken the ozygen-starvation of his brief sojourn above the sky. The spore-forming glands had at once begun to function.

Had it not been for this, Lavon would surely have died. The danger of drowning disappeared even as he fell, as the air bubbled out of his lungs and readmitted the life-giving water. But for acute desiccation and third degree sunburn, the sunken universe knew no remedy. The healing amnionic fluid generated by the spore-forming glands, after the transparent amber sphere had enclosed him, offered Lavon his only chance.

The brown sphere, quiescent in the eternal winter of the Bottom, was spotted after some days by a prowling amoeba. Down there the temperature was always an even 4°, no matter what the season, but it was unheard of that a spore should be found there while the high epilimnion was still warm and rich in oxygen.

Within an hour, the spore was surrounded by scores of astonished Protos, jostling each other to bump their blunt eyeless prows against the shell. Another hour later, a squad of worried men came plunging from the castles far above to press their own noses against the transparent wall. Then swift orders were given.

Four Para grouped themselves about the amber sphere, and there was a subdued explosion as their trichocysts burst. The four Paras thrummed and lifted, tugging.

Lavon's spore swayed gently in the mud and then rose slowly, entangled in the fine web. Nearby, a Noc cast a cold pulsating glow over the operation, for the benefit of the baffled knot of men. The sleeping figure of Lavon, head bowed, knees drawn up into its chest, revolved with an absurd solemnity inside the shell, as it was moved.

'Take him to Shar, Para.'

The young Shar justified, by minding his own business, the traditional wisdom with which his hereditary office had invested him. He observed at once that there was nothing he could do for the encysted Lavon which would not be classifiable as simple meddling.

He had the sphere deposited in a high tower room of his castle, where there was plenty of light and the water was warm, which should suggest to the estivating form that spring was again on the way. Beyond that, he simply sat and watched, and kept his speculations to himself.

Inside the spore, Lavon's body seemed to be rapidly shedding its skin, in long strips and patches. Gradually, his curious shrunkenness disappeared. His withered arms and legs and sunken abdomen filled out again.

The days went by while Shar watched. Finally he could discern no more changes, and, on a hunch, had the spore taken up to the topmost battlements of the tower, into the direct daylight.

An hour later, Lavon moved in his amber prison.

He uncurled and stretched, turned blank eyes up toward the light. His expression was that of a man who had not yet awakened from a ferocious nightmare. His whole body shone with a strange pink newness.

Shar knocked gently on the walls of the spore. Lavon turned his blind face toward the sound, life coming into his eyes. He smiled tentatively and braced his hands and feet against the inner wall of the shell.

The whole sphere fell abruptly to pieces with a sharp crackling. The amnionic fluid dissipated around him and Shar, carrying away with it the suggestive odor of a bitter struggle against death.

Lavon stood among the shards and looked at Shar silently. At last he said:

'Shar – I've been above the sky.'

'I know,' Shar said gently.

Again Lavon was silent. Shar said, 'Don't be humble, Lavon. You've done an epoch-making thing. It nearly cost you your life. You must tell me the rest – all of it.'

'The rest?'

'You taught me a lot while you slept. Or are you still opposed to "useless" knowledge?'

Lavon could say nothing. He no longer could tell what he knew from what he wanted to know. He had only one question left, but he could not utter it. He could only look dumbly into Shar's delicate face.

'You have answered me,' Shar said, even more gently than before. 'Come, my friend; join me at my table. We will plan our journey to the stars.'

There were five of them around Shar's big table: Shar himself, Lavon, and the three assistants assigned by custom to the Shars from the families Than, Tanol and Stravol. The duties of these three men – or, sometimes, women – under many previous Shars had been simple and onerous: to put into effect in the field the genetic changes in the food crops which the Shar himself had worked out in little, in laboratory tanks and flats. Under other Shars more interested in metal-working or in chemistry, they had been smudged men – diggers, rock-splitters, fashioners and cleaners of apparatus.

Under Shar XVI, however, the three assistants had been more envied than usual among the rest of Lavon's people, for they seemed to do very little work of any kind. They spent long hours of every day talking with Shar in his chambers, poring over records, making miniscule scratch-marks on slate, or just looking intently at simple things about which there was no obvious mystery. Sometimes they actually worked with Shar in his laboratory, but mostly they just sat.

Shar XVI had, as a matter of fact, discovered certain rudimentary rules of inquiry which, as he explained it to Lavon, he had recognized as tools of enormous power. He had become more interested in passing these on to future workers than in the seductions of any specific experiment, the journey to the stars perhaps excepted. The Than, Tanol and Stravol of his generation were having scientific method pounded into their heads, a procedure they maintained was sometimes more painful than heaving a thousand rocks.

That they were the first of Lavon's people to be taxed with the problem of constructing a spaceship was, therefore, inevitable. The results lay on the table: three models, made of diatom-glass, strands of algae, flexible bits of cellulose, flakes of stonewort, slivers of wood, and organic glues collected from the secretions of a score of different plants and animals.

Lavon picked up the nearest one, a fragile spherical construction inside which little beads of dark-brown lava – actually bricks of rotifer-spittle painfully chipped free from the wall of an unused castle – moved freely back and forth in a kind of ball-bearing race. 'Now whose is this one?' he said, turning the sphere curiously to and fro.

'That's mine,' Tanol said. 'Frankly, I don't think it comes anywhere near meeting all the requirements. It's just the only design I could arrive at that I think we could build with the materials and knowledge we have to hand now.'

'But how does it work?'

'Hand it here a moment, Lavon. This bladder you see inside at the center, with the hollow spirogyra straws leading out from it to the skin of the ship, is a buoyancy tank. The idea is that we trap ourselves a big gas-bubble as it rises from the Bottom and install it in the tank. Probably we'll have to do that piecemeal. Then the ship rises to the sky on the buoyancy of the bubble. The little paddles, here along these two bands on the outside, rotate when the crew – that's these bricks you hear shaking around inside – walks a treadmill that runs around the inside of the hull; they paddle us over to the edge of the sky. I stole that trick from the way Didin gets about. Then we pull the paddles in – they fold over into slots, like this – and, still by weight-transfer from the inside, we roll ourselves up the slope until we're out in space. When we hit another world and enter the water again, we let the gas out of the tank gradually through the exhaust tubes represented by these straws, and sink down to a landing at a controlled rate.'

'Very ingenious,' Shar said thoughtfully. 'But I can foresee some difficulties. For one thing, the design lacks stability.'

'Yes, it does,' Tanol agreed. 'And keeping it in motion is going to require a lot of footwork. But if we were to sling a freely-moving weight from the center of gravity of the machine, we could stabilize it at least partly. And the biggest expenditure of energy involved in the whole trip is going to be getting the machine up to the sky in the first place, and with this design that's taken care of – as a matter of fact, once the bubble's installed, we'll have to keep the ship tied down until we're ready to take off.'

'How about letting the gas out?' Lavon said. 'Will it go out through those little tubes when we want it to? Won't it just cling to the walls of the tubes instead? The skin between water and gas is pretty difficult to deform – to that I can testify.'

Tanol frowned. 'That I don't know. Don't forget that the tubes will be large in the real ship, not just straws as they are in the model.'

'Bigger than a man's body?' Than said.

'No, hardly. Maybe as big through as a man's head, at the most.'

'Won't work,' Than said tersely. 'I tried it. You can't lead a bubble through a pipe that small. As Lavon says, it clings to the inside of the tube and won't be budged unless you put pressure behind it – lots of pressure. If we build this ship, we'll just have to abandon it once we hit our new world; we won't be able to set it down anywhere.'

'That's out of the question,' Lavon said at once. 'Putting aside for the moment the waste involved, we may have to use the ship again in a hurry. Who knows what the new world will be like? We're going to have to be able to leave it again if it turns out to be impossible to live in.'

'Which is your model, Than?' Shar said.

'This one. With this design, we do the trip the hard way – crawl along the Bottom until it meets the sky, crawl until we hit the next world, and crawl wherever we're going when we get there. No aquabatics. She's tread-mill-powered, like Tanol's, but not necessarily man-powered; I've been thinking a bit about using motile diatoms. She steers by varying the power on one side or the other. For fine steering we can also hitch a pair of thongs to opposite ends of the rear axle and swivel her that way.'

Shar looked closely at the tube-shaped model and pushed it experimentally along the table a little way. 'I like that,' he said presently. 'It sits still when you want it to. With Than's spherical ship, we'd be at the mercy of any stray current at home or in the new world – and for all I know there may be currents of some sort in space, too, gas currents perhaps. Lavon, what do you think?'

'How would we build it?' Lavon said. 'It's round in cross-section. That's all very well for a model, but how do you make a really big tube of that shape that won't fall in on itself?'

'Look inside, through the front window,' Than said. 'You'll see beams that cross at the center, at right angles to the long axis. They hold the walls braced.'

'That consumes a lot of space,' Stravol objected. By far the quietest and most introspective of the three assistants, he had not spoken until now since the beginning of the conference. 'You've got to have free passage back and forth inside the ship. How are we going to keep everything operating if we have to be crawling around beams all the time?'

'All right, come up with something better,' Than said, shrugging.

'That's easy. We bend hoops.'

'Hoops!' Tanol said. 'On *that* scale? You'd have to soak your wood in mud for a year before it would be flexible enough, and then it wouldn't have the strength you'd need.'

'No, you wouldn't,' Stravol said. 'I didn't build a ship model, I just made drawings, and my ship isn't as good as Than's by a long distance. But my design for the ship is also tubular, so I did build a model of a hoop-bending machine – that's it on the table. You lock one end of your beam down in a heavy vise, like so, leaving the butt striking out on the other side. Then you tie up the other end with a heavy line, around this notch. Then you run your line around a windlass, and five or six men wind up the windlass, like so. That pulls the free end of the beam down until the notch engages with this key-slot, which you've pre-cut at the other end. Then you unlock the vise, and there's your hoop; for safety you might drive a peg through the joint to keep the thing from springing open unexpectedly.'

'Wouldn't the beam you were using break after it had bent a certain distance?' Lavon asked.

'Stock timber certainly would,' Stravol said. 'But for this trick you use *green* wood, not seasoned. Otherwise you'd have to soften your beam to uselessness, as Tanol says. But live wood will flex enough to make a good, strong, single-unit hoop – or if it doesn't, Shar, the little rituals with numbers that you've been teaching us don't mean anything after all!'

Shar smiled. 'You can easily make a mistake in using numbers,' he said.

'I checked everything.'

'I'm sure of it. And I think it's well worth a trial. Anything else to offer?'

'Well,' Stravol said, 'I've got a kind of live ventilating system I think should be useful. Otherwise, as I said, Than's ship strikes me as the type we should build; my own's hopelessly cumbersome.'

'I have to agree,' Tanol said regretfully. 'But I'd like to try putting together a lighter-than-water ship sometime, maybe just for local travel. If the new world is bigger than ours, it might not be possible to swim everywhere you might want to go.'

'That never occurred to me,' Lavon exclaimed. 'Suppose the new world *is* twice, three times, eight times as big as ours? Shar, is there any reason why that couldn't be?'

'None that I know of. The history plate certainly seems to take all kinds of enormous distances practically for granted. All right, let's make up a composite design from what we have here. Tanol, you're the best draftsman among us, suppose you draw it up. Lavon, what about labor?'

'I've a plan ready,' Lavon said. 'As I see it, the people who work on the ship are going to have to be on the job full time. Building the vessel isn't going to be an overnight task, or even one that we can finish in a single season, so we can't count on using a rotating force. Besides, this is technical work; once a man learns how to do a particular task, it would be wasteful to send him back to tending fungi just because somebody else has some time on his hands.

'So I've set up a basic force involving the two or three most intelligent hand-workers from each of the various trades. Those people I can withdraw from their regular work without upsetting the way we run our usual concerns, or noticeably increasing the burden on the others in a given trade. They will do the skilled labor, and stick with the ship until it's done. Some of them will make up the crew, too. For heavy, unskilled jobs, we can call on the various seasonal pools of unskilled people without disrupting our ordinary life.'

'Good,' Shar said. He leaned forward and rested linked hands on the edge of the table – although, because of the webbing between his fingers, he could link no more than the fingertips. 'We've really made remarkable progress. I didn't expect that we'd have matters advanced a tenth as far as this by the end of this meeting. But maybe I've overlooked something important. Has anybody any more suggestions, or any questions?'

'I've got a question,' Stravol said quietly.

'All right, let's hear it.'

'*Where are we going?*'

There was quite a long silence. Finally Shar said: 'Stravol, I can't answer that yet. I could say that we're going to the stars, but since we still have no idea what a star is, that answer wouldn't do you much good. We're going to make this trip because we've found that some of the fantastic things that the history plate says are really so. We know now that the sky can be passed, and that beyond the sky there's a region where there's no water to breathe, the region our ancients called "space". Both of these ideas always seemed to be against common sense, but nevertheless we've found that they're true.

'The history plate also says that there are other worlds than ours, and actually that's an easier idea to accept, once you've found out that the other two are so. As for the stars – well, we just don't know yet, we haven't any information at all that would allow us to read the history plate on that subject with new eyes, and there's no point in making wild guesses unless we can test the guesses. The stars are in space, and presumably, once we're out in space, we'll see them and the meaning of the word will become clear. At least we can confidently expect to see some clues – look at all the information we got from Lavon's trip of a few seconds above the sky!

'But in the meantime, there's no point in our speculating in a bubble. We think there are other worlds somewhere, and we're devising means to make the trip. The other questions, the pendant ones, just have to be put aside for now. We'll answer them eventually – there's no doubt in my mind about that. But it may take a long time.'

Stravol grinned ruefully. 'I expected no more. In a way, I think the whole project is crazy. But I'm in it right out to the end, all the same.'

Shar and Lavon grinned back. All of them had the fever, and Lavon suspected that their whole enclosed universe would share it with them before long. He said:

'Then let's not waste a minute. There's still a huge mass of detail to be worked out, and after that, all the hard work will just have begun. Let's get moving!'

The five men arose and looked at each other. Their expressions varied, but in all their eyes there was in addition the same mixture of awe and ambition: the composite face of the shipwright and of the astronaut.

Then they went out, severally, to begin their voyages.

It was two winter sleeps after Lavon's disastrous climb beyond the sky that all work on the spaceship stopped. By then, Lavon knew that he had hardened and weathered into that temporarily ageless state a man enters after he has just reached his prime; and he knew also that there were wrinkles engraved on his brow, to stay and to deepen.

'Old' Shar, too, had changed, his features losing some of their delicacy as he came into his maturity. Though the wedge-shaped bony structure of his face would give him a withdrawn and poetic look for as long as he lived, participation in the plan had given his expression a kind of executive overlay, which at best made it assume a mask-like rigidity, and at worst coarsened it somehow.

Yet despite the bleeding away of the years, the spaceship was still only a hulk. It lay upon a platform built above the tumbled boulders of the sandbar which stretched out from one wall of the world. It was an immense hull of pegged wood, broken by regularly spaced gaps through which the raw beams of its skeleton could be seen.

Work upon it had progressed fairly rapidly at first, for it was not hard to visualize what kind of vehicle would be needed to crawl through empty space without losing its water; Than and his colleagues had done that job well. It had been recognized, too, that the sheer size of the machine would enforce a long period of construction, perhaps as long as two full seasons; but neither Shar and his assistants nor Lavon had anticipated any serious snag.

For that matter, part of the vehicle's apparent incompleteness was an illusion. About a third of its fittings were to consist of living creatures, which could not be expected to install themselves in the vessel much before the actual takeoff.

Yet time and time again, work on the ship had to be halted for long periods. Several times whole sections needed to be ripped out, as it became more and more evident that hardly a single normal, understandable concept could be applied to the problem of space travel.

The lack of the history plate, which the Para steadfastly refused to deliver up, was a double handicap. Immediately upon its loss, Shar had set himself to reproduce it from memory; but unlike the more religious of his ancestors, he had never regarded it as holy writ, and hence had never set himself to memorizing it word by word. Even before the theft, he had accumulated a set of variant translations of passages presenting specific experimental problems, which were stored in his library, carved in wood. Most of these translations, however, tended to contradict each other, and none of them related to spaceship construction, upon which the original had been vague in any case.

No duplicates of the cryptic characters of the original had ever been made, for the simple reason that there was nothing in the sunken universe capable of destroying the originals, nor of duplicating their apparently changeless permanence. Shar remarked too late that through simple caution they should have made a number of verbatim temporary records – but after generations of green–gold peace, simple caution no longer covers preparation against catastrophe. (Nor, for that matter, does a culture which has to dig each letter of its simple alphabet into pulpy water-logged wood with a flake of stonewort encourage the keeping of records in triplicate.)

As a result, Shar's imperfect memory of the contents of the history plate, plus the constant and millennial doubt as to the accuracy of the various translations, proved finally to be the worst obstacle to progress on the spaceship itself.

'Men must paddle before they can swim,' Lavon observed belatedly, and Shar was forced to agree with him.

Obviously, whatever the ancients had known about spaceship construction, very little of that knowledge was usable to a people still trying to build its first spaceship from scratch. In retrospect, it was not surprising that the great hulk rested incomplete upon its platform above the sand boulders, exuding a musty odor of wood steadily losing its strength, two generations after its flat bottom had been laid down.

The fat-faced young man who headed the strike delegation to Shar's chambers was Phil XX, a man two generations younger than Shar, four younger than Lavon. There were crow's-feet at the corners of his eyes, which made him look both like a querulous old man and like an infant spoiled in the spore.

'We're calling a halt to this crazy project,' he said bluntly. 'We've slaved away our youth on it, but now that we're our own masters, it's over, that's all. It's over.'

'Nobody's compelled you,' Lavon said angrily.

'Society does; our parents do,' a gaunt member of the delegation said. 'But now we're going to start living in the real world. Everybody these days knows that there's no other world but this one. You oldsters can hang on to your superstitions if you like. We don't intend to.'

Baffled, Lavon looked over at Shar. The scientist smiled and said, 'Let them go, Lavon. We have no use for the faint-hearted.'

The fat-faced young man flushed. 'You can't insult us into going back to work. We're through. Build your own ship to no place!'

'All right,' Lavon said evenly. 'Go on, beat it. Don't stand around here orating about it. You've made your decisions and we're not interested in your self-justifications. Goodbye.'

The fat-faced young man evidently still had quite a bit of heroism to dramatize which Lavon's dismissal had short-circuited. An examination of Lavon's stony face, however, seemed to convince him that he had to take his victory as he found it. He and the delegation trailed ingloriously out the archway.

'Now what?' Lavon asked when they had gone. 'I must admit, Shar, that I would have tried to persuade them. We do need the workers, after all.'

'Not as much as they need us,' Shar said tranquilly. 'I know all those young men. I think they'll be astonished at the runty crops their fields will produce next season, after they have to breed them without my advice. Now, how many volunteers have you got for the crew of the ship?'

'Hundreds. Every youngster of the generation after Phil's wants to go along. Phil's wrong about that segment of the populace, at least. The project catches the imagination of the very young.'

'Did you give them any encouragement?'

'Sure,' Lavon said. 'I told them we'd call on them if they were chosen. But you can't take that seriously! We'd do badly to displace our picked group of specialists with youths who have enthusiasm and nothing else.'

'That's not what I had in mind, Lavon. Didn't I see a Noc in these chambers somewhere? Oh, there he is, asleep in the dome. Noc!'

The creature stirred its tentacle lazily.

'Noc, I've a message,' Shar called. 'The Protos are to tell all men that those who wish to go to the next world with the spaceship must come to the staging area right away. Say that we can't promise to take everyone, but that only those who help us to build the ship will be considered at all.'

The Noc curled its tentacle again, and appeared to go back to sleep.

4

Lavon turned from the arrangement of speaking-tube megaphones which was his control board and looked at Para. 'One last try,' he said. 'Will you give us back the history plate?'

'No, Lavon. We have never denied you anything before. But this we must.'

'You're going with us, though, Para. Unless you give us back the knowledge we need, you'll lose your life if we lose ours.'

'What is one Para?' the creature said. 'We are all alike. This cell will die; but the Protos need to know how you fare on this journey. We believe you should make it without the plate, for in no other way can we assess the real importance of the plate.'

'Then you admit you still have it. What if you can't communicate with your fellows once we're out in space? How do you know that water isn't essential to your telepathy?'

The Proto was silent. Lavon stared at it a moment, then turned deliberately back to the speaking tubes. 'Everyone hang on,' he said. He felt shaky. 'We're about to start. Stravol, is the ship sealed?'

'As far as I can tell, Lavon.'

Lavon shifted to another megaphone. He took a deep breath. Already the water seemed stifling, although the ship hadn't moved.

'Ready with one-quarter power ... One, two, three, go.'

The whole ship jerked and settled back into place again. The raphe diatoms along the under hull settled into their niches, their jelly treads turning against broad endless belts of crude caddis-worm leather. Wooden gears creaked, stepping up the slow power of the creatures, transmitting it to the sixteen axles of the ship's wheels.

The ship rocked and began to roll slowly along the sand bar. Lavon looked tensely through the mica port. The world flowed painfully past him. The ship canted and began to climb the slope. Behind him, he could feel the electric silence of Shar, Para, and the two alternate pilots, Than and Stravol, as if their gaze were stabbing directly through his body and on out the port. The world looked different, now that he was leaving it. How had he missed all this beauty before?

The slapping of the endless belts and the squeaking and groaning of the gears and axles grew louder as the slope steepened. The ship continued to climb, lurching. Around it, squadrons of men and Protos dipped and wheeled, escorting it toward the sky.

Gradually the sky lowered and pressed down toward the top of the ship.

'A little more work from your diatoms, Tanol,' Lavon said. 'Boulder ahead.' The ship swung ponderously. 'All right, slow them up again. Give us a shove from your side, Tol – no, that's too much – there, that's it. Back to normal; you're still turning us! Tanol, give us one burst to line us up again. Good. All right, steady drive on all sides. It shouldn't be long now.'

'How can you think in webs like that?' the Para wondered behind him.

'I just do, that's all. It's the way men think. Overseers, a little more thrust now; the grade's getting steeper.'

The gears groaned. The ship nosed up. The sky brightened in Lavon's face. Despite himself, he began to be frightened. His lungs seemed to burn, and in his mind he felt his long fall through nothingness toward the chill slap of the water as if he were experiencing it for the first time. His skin itched and burned. Could he go up there again? Up there into the burning void, the great gasping agony where no life should go?

The sand bar began to level out and the going became a little easier. Up here, the sky was so close that the lumbering motion of the huge ship disturbed it. Shadows of wavelets ran across the sand. Silently, the thick-barreled bands of blue–green algae drank in the light and converted it to oxygen, writhing in their slow mindless dance just under the long mica sky-light which ran along the spine of the ship. In the hold, beneath the latticed corridor and cabin floors, whirring Vortae kept the ship's water in motion, fueling themselves upon drifting organic particles.

One by one, the figures wheeling outside about the ship waved arms or cilia and fell back, coasting down the slope of the sand bar toward the fa-miliar world, dwindling and disappearing. There was at last only one single Euglena, half-plant cousin of the Protos, forging along beside the spaceship into the marshes of the shallows. It loved the light, but finally it, too, was driven away into deeper, cooler waters, its single whiplike tentacle undulating placidly as it went. It was not very bright, but Lavon felt deserted when it left.

Where they were going, though, none could follow.

Now the sky was nothing but a thin, resistant skin of water coating the top of the ship. The vessel slowed, and when Lavon called for more power, it began to dig itself in among the sandgrains and boulders.

'That's not going to work,' Shar said tensely. 'I think we'd better step down the gear-ratio, Lavon, so you can apply stress more slowly.'

'All right,' Lavon agreed. 'Full stop, everybody. Shar, will you supervise gear-changing, please?'

Insane brilliance of empty space looked Lavon full in the face just beyond his big mica bullseye. It was maddening to be forced to stop here upon the threshold of infinity; and it was dangerous, too. Lavon could feel building in him the old fear of the outside. A few moments more of inaction, he knew with a gathering coldness in his belly, and he would be unable to go through with it.

Surely, he thought, there must be a better way to change gear-ratios than the traditional one, which involved dismantling almost the entire gear box. Why couldn't a number of gears of different sizes be carried on the same shaft, not necessarily all in action at once, but awaiting use simply by shoving the axle back and forth longitudinally in its sockets? It would still be clumsy, but it could be worked on orders from the bridge and would not involve shutting down the entire machine – and throwing the new pilot into a blue–green funk.

Shar came lunging up through the trap and swam himself to a stop.

'All set,' he said. 'The big reduction gears aren't taking the strain too well, though.'

'Splintering?'

'Yes. I'd go it slow at first.'

Lavon nodded mutely. Without allowing himself to stop, even for a moment, to consider the consequences of his words, he called: 'Half power.'

The ship hunched itself down again and began to move, very slowly indeed, but more smoothly than before. Overhead, the sky thinned to complete transparency. The great light came blasting in. Behind Lavon there was an uneasy stir. The whiteness grew at the front ports.

Again the ship slowed, straining against the blinding barrier. Lavon swallowed and called for more power. The ship groaned like something about to die. It was now almost at a standstill.

'More power,' Lavon ground out.

Once more, with infinite slowness, the ship began to move. Gently, it tilted upward.

Then it lunged forward and every board and beam in it began to squall.

'Lavon! Lavon!'

Lavon started sharply at the shout. The voice was coming at him from one of the megaphones, the one marked for the port at the rear of the ship.

'Lavon!'

'What is it? Stop your damn yelling.'

'I can see the top of the sky! From the *other* side, from the top side! It's like a big flat sheet of metal. We're going away from it. We're above the sky, Lavon, we're above the sky!'

Another violent start swung Lavon around toward the forward port. On the outside of the mica, the water was evaporating with shocking swiftness, taking with it strange distortions and patterns made of rainbows.

Lavon saw space.

It was at first like a deserted and cruelly dry version of the Bottom. There were enormous boulders, great cliffs, tumbled, split, riven, jagged rocks going up and away in all directions, as if scattered at random by some giant.

But it had a sky of its own – a deep blue dome so far away that he could not believe in, let alone estimate, what its distance might be. And in this dome was a ball of reddish-white fire that seared his eyeballs.

The wilderness of rock was still a long way away from the ship, which now seemed to be resting upon a level, glistening plain. Beneath the surface-shine, the plain seemed to be made of sand, nothing but familiar sand, the same substance which had heaped up to form a bar in Lavon's universe, the bar along which the ship had climbed. But the glassy, colorful skin over it—

Suddenly Lavon became conscious of another shout from the megaphone banks. He shook his head savagely and said, 'What is it now?'

'Lavon, this is Tol. What have you gotten us into? The belts are locked. The diatoms can't move them. They aren't faking, either; we've rapped them hard enough to make them think we were trying to break their shells, but they still can't give us more power.'

'Leave them alone,' Lavon snapped. 'They can't fake; they haven't enough intelligence. If they say they can't give you more power, they can't.'

'Well, then, you get us out of it.'

Shar came forward to Lavon's elbow. 'We're on a space–water interface, where the surface tension is very high,' he said softly. 'If you order the wheels pulled up now, I think we'll make better progress for a while on the belly tread.'

'Good enough,' Lavon said with relief. 'Hello below – haul up the wheels.'

'For a long while,' Shar said, 'I couldn't understand the reference of the history plate to "retractable landing gear", but it finally occurred to me that the tension along a space–mud interface would hold any large object pretty tightly. That's why I insisted on our building the ship so that we could lift the wheels.'

'Evidently the ancients knew their business after all, Shar.'

Quite a few minutes later – for shifting power to the belly treads involved another setting of the gear box – the ship was crawling along the shore toward the tumbled rock. Anxiously, Lavon scanned the jagged, threatening wall for a break. There was a sort of rivulet off toward the left which might offer a route, though a dubious one, to the next world. After some thought, Lavon ordered his ship turned toward it.

'Do you suppose that thing in the sky is a "star"?' he asked. 'But there were supposed to be lots of them. Only one is up there – and one's plenty for my taste.'

'I don't know,' Shar admitted. 'But I'm beginning to get a picture of the way the universe is made, I think. Evidently our world is a sort of cup in the Bottom of this huge one. This one has a sky of its own; perhaps it, too, is only a cup in the Bottom of a still huger world, and so on and on without end. It's a hard concept to grasp, I'll admit. Maybe it would be more sensible to assume that all the worlds are cups in this one common surface, and that the great light shines on them all impartially.'

'Then what makes it go out every night, and dim even in the day during winter?' Lavon demanded.

'Perhaps it travels in circles, over first one world, then another. How could I know yet?'

'Well, if you're right, it means that all we have to do is crawl along here for a while, until we hit the top of the sky of another world,' Lavon said. 'Then we dive in. Somehow it seems too simple, after all our preparations.'

Shar chuckled, but the sound did not suggest that he had discovered any-thing funny. 'Simple? Have you noticed the temperature yet?'

Lavon had noticed it, just beneath the surface of awareness, but at Shar's remark he realized that he was gradually being stifled. The oxygen content of the water, luckily, had not dropped, but the temperature suggested the shal-lows in the last and worst part of autumn. It was like trying to breathe soup.

'Than, give us more action from the Vortae,' Lavon said. 'This is going to be unbearable unless we get more circulation.'

There was a reply from Than, but it came to Lavon's ears only as a mumble. It was all he could do now to keep his attention on the business of steering the ship.

The cut or defile in the scattered razor-edged rocks was a little closer, but there still seemed to be many miles of rough desert to cross. After a while, the ship settled into a steady, painfully slow crawling, with less pitching and jerking than before, but also with less progress. Under it, there was now a sliding, grinding sound, rasping against the hull of the ship itself, as if it were treadmilling over some coarse lubricant the particles of which were each as big as a man's head.

Finally Shar said, 'Lavon, we'll have to stop again. The sand this far up is dry, and we're wasting energy using the tread.'

'Are you sure we can take it?' Lavon asked, gasping for breath. 'At least we are moving. If we stop to lower the wheels and change gears again, we'll boil.'

'We'll boil if we don't,' Shar said calmly. 'Some of our algae are dead already and the rest are withering. That's a pretty good sign that we can't take much more. I don't think we'll make it into the shadows, unless we do change over and put on some speed.'

There was a gulping sound from one of the mechanics. 'We ought to turn back,' he said raggedly. 'We were never meant to be out here in the first place. We were made for the water, not for this hell.'

'We'll stop,' Lavon said, 'but we're not turning back. That's final.'

The words made a brave sound, but the man had upset Lavon more than he dared to admit, even to himself. 'Shar,' he said, 'make it fast, will you?'

The scientist nodded and dived below.

The minutes stretched out. The great red-gold globe in the sky blazed and blazed. It had moved down the sky, far down, so that the light was pouring into the ship directly in Lavon's face, illuminating every floating particle, its rays like long milky streamers. The currents of water passing Lavon's cheek were almost hot.

How could they dare go directly forward into that inferno? The land directly under the 'star' must be even hotter than it was here.

'Lavon! Look at Para!'

Lavon forced himself to turn and look at his Proto ally. The great slipper had settled to the deck, where it was lying with only a feeble pulsation of its cilia. Inside, its vacuoles were beginning to swell, to become bloated, pear-shaped bubbles, crowding the granulated cytoplasm, pressing upon the dark nuclei.

'Is ... is he dying?'

'This cell is dying,' Para said, as coldly as always. 'But go on – go on. There is much to learn, and you may live, even though we do not. Go on.'

'You're – for us now?' Lavon whispered.

'We have always been for you. Push your folly to the uttermost. We will benefit in the end, and so will Man.'

The whisper died away. Lavon called the creature again, but it did not respond.

There was a wooden clashing from below, and then Shar's voice came tinnily from one of the megaphones. 'Lavon, go ahead! The diatoms are dying, too, and then we'll be without power. Make it as quickly and directly as you can.'

Grimly, Lavon leaned forward. 'The "star" is directly over the land we're approaching.'

'It is? It may go lower still and the shadows will get longer. That may be our only hope.'

Lavon had not thought of that. He rasped into the banked megaphones. Once more, the ship began to move, a little faster now, but seemingly still at a crawl. The thirty-two wheels rumbled.

It got hotter.

Steadily, with a perceptible motion, the 'star' sank in Lavon's face. Suddenly a new terror struck him. Suppose it should continue to go down until it was gone entirely? Blasting though it was now, it was the only source of heat. Would not space become bitter cold on the instant – and the ship an expanding, bursting block of ice?

The shadows lengthened menacingly, stretching across the desert toward the forward-rolling vessel. There was no talking in the cabin, just the sound of ragged breathing and the creaking of the machinery.

Then the jagged horizon seemed to rush upon them. Stony teeth cut into the lower rim of the ball of fire, devoured it swiftly. It was gone.

They were in the lee of the cliffs. Lavon ordered the ship turned to parallel the rock-line; it responded heavily, sluggishly. Far above, the sky deepened steadily, from blue to indigo.

Shar came silently up through the trap and stood beside Lavon, studying that deepening color and the lengthening of the shadows down the beach toward their own world. He said nothing, but Lavon was sure that the same chilling thought was in his mind.

'Lavon.'

Lavon jumped. Shar's voice had iron in it. 'Yes?'

'We'll have to keep moving. We must make the next world, wherever it is, very shortly.'

'How can we dare move when we can't see where we're going? Why not sleep it over – if the cold will let us?'

'It will let us,' Shar said. 'It can't get dangerously cold up here. If it did, the sky – or what we used to think of as the sky – would have frozen over every night, even in summer. But what I'm thinking about is the water. The plants will go to sleep now. In our world that wouldn't matter; the supply of oxygen there is enough to last through the night. But in this confined space, with so many creatures in it and no supply of fresh water, we will probably smother.'

Shar seemed hardly to be involved at all, but spoke rather with the voice of implacable physical laws.

'Furthermore,' he said, staring unseeingly out at the raw landscape, 'the diatoms are plants, too. In other words, we must stay on the move for as long as we have oxygen and power – and pray that we make it.'

'Shar, we had quite a few Protos on board this ship once. And Para there isn't quite dead yet. If he were, the cabin would be intolerable. The ship is nearly sterile of bacteria, because all the Protos have been eating them as a matter of course and there's no outside supply of them, either. But still and all there would have been some decay.'

Shar bent and tested the pellicle of the motionless Para with a probing finger. 'You're right, he's still alive. What does that prove?'

'The Vortae are also alive; I can feel the water circulating. Which proves that it wasn't the heat that hurt Para. *It was the light.* Remember how badly my skin was affected after I climbed beyond the sky? Undiluted starlight is deadly. We should add that to the information from the plate.'

'I still don't get the point.'

'It's this: We've got three or four Noc down below. They were shielded from the light, and so must be still alive. If we concentrate them in the diatom galleys, the dumb diatoms will think it's still daylight and will go on working. Or we can concentrate them up along the spine of the ship, and keep the algae putting out oxygen. So the question is: Which do we need more, oxygen or power? Or can we split the difference?'

Shar actually grinned. 'A brilliant piece of thinking. We may make a Shar out of you some day, Lavon. No, I'd say that we can't split the difference. Noc's light isn't intense enough to keep the plants making oxygen; I tried it once, and the oxygen production was too tiny to matter. Evidently the plants use the light for energy. So we'll have to settle for the diatoms for motive power.'

'All right. Set it up that way, Shar.'

Lavon brought the vessel away from the rocky lee of the cliff, out onto the smoother sand. All trace of direct light was now gone, although there was still a soft, general glow on the sky.

'Now then,' Shar said thoughtfully, 'I would guess that there's water over there in the canyon, if we can reach it. I'll go below again and arrange—'

Lavon gasped.

'What's the matter?'

Silently, Lavon pointed, his heart pounding.

The entire dome of indigo above them was spangled with tiny, incredibly brilliant lights. There were hundreds of them, and more and more were becoming visible as the darkness deepened. And far away, over the ultimate edge of the rocks, was a dim red globe, crescented with ghostly silver. Near the zenith was another such body, much smaller, and silvered all over ...

Under the two moons of Hydrot, and under the eternal stars, the two-inch wooden spaceship and its microscopic cargo toiled down the slope toward the drying little rivulet.

5

The ship rested on the Bottom of the canyon for the rest of the night. The great square doors were unsealed and thrown open to admit the raw, irradiated, life-giving water from outside – and the wriggling bacteria which were fresh food.

No other creatures approached them, either out of curiosity or for hunting, while they slept, although Lavon had posted guards at the doors just in case. Evidently, even up here on the very floor of space, highly organized creatures were quiescent at night.

But when the first flush of light filtered through the water, trouble threatened.

First of all, there was the bug-eyed monster. The thing was green and had two snapping claws, either one of which could have broken the ship in two like a spirogyra strand. Its eyes were black and globular, on the ends of short columns, and its long feelers were thicker through than a plant bole. It passed in a kicking fury of motion, however, never noticing the ship at all.

'Is that – a sample of the kind of life they have here?' Lavon whispered. 'Does it all run as big as that?' Nobody answered, for the very good reason that nobody knew.

After a while, Lavon risked moving the ship forward against the current, which was slow but heavy. Enormous writhing worms whipped past them. One struck the hull a heavy blow, then thrashed on obliviously.

'They don't notice us,' Shar said. 'We're too small. Lavon, the ancients warned us of the immensity of space, but even when you see it, it's impossible to grasp. And all those stars – can they mean what I think they mean? It's beyond thought, beyond belief!'

'The Bottom's sloping,' Lavon said, looking ahead intently. 'The walls of the canyon are retreating, and the water's becoming rather silty. Let the stars wait, Shar; we're coming toward the entrance of our new world.'

Shar subsided moodily. His vision of space apparently had disturbed him, perhaps seriously. He took little notice of the great thing that was happening, but instead huddled worriedly over his own expanding speculations. Lavon felt the old gap between their minds widening once more.

Now the Bottom was tilting upward again. Lavon had no experience with delta-formation, for no rivulets left his own world, and the phenomenon worried him. But his worries were swept away in wonder as the ship topped the rise and nosed over.

Ahead, the Bottom sloped away again, indefinitely, into glimmering depths. A proper sky was over them once more, and Lavon could see small rafts of plankton floating placidly beneath it. Almost at once, too, he saw several of the smaller kinds of Protos, a few of which were already approaching the ship—

Then the girl came darting out of the depths, her features blurred and distorted with distance and terror. At first she did not seem to see the ship at all. She came twisting and turning lithely through the water, obviously hoping only to throw herself over the mound of the delta and into the savage streamlet beyond.

Lavon was stunned. Not that there were men here – he had hoped for that, had even known somehow that men were everywhere in the universe – but at the girl's single-minded flight toward suicide.

'What—'

Then a dim buzzing began to grow in his ears, and he understood.

'Shar! Than! Stravol!' he bawled. 'Break out crossbows and spears! Knock out all the windows!' He lifted a foot and kicked through the port in front of him. Someone thrust a crossbow into his hand.

'What?' Shar blurted. 'What's the matter? What's happening?'

'*Eaters!*'

The cry went through the ship like a galvanic shock. The rotifers back in Lavon's own world were virtually extinct, but everyone knew thoroughly the grim history of the long battle Man and Proto had waged against them.

The girl spotted the ship suddenly and paused, obviously stricken with despair at the sight of this new monster. She drifted with her own momentum, her eyes alternately fixed upon the ship and jerking back over her shoulder, toward where the buzzing snarled louder and louder in the dimness.

'Don't stop!' Lavon shouted. 'This way, this way! We're friends! We'll help!'

Three great semi-transparent trumpets of smooth flesh bored over the rise, the many thick cilia of their coronas whirring greedily. Dicrans, arrogant in their flexible armor, quarreling thickly among themselves as they moved, with the few blurred, pre-symbolic noises which made up their own language.

Carefully, Lavon wound the crossbow, brought it to his shoulder, and fired. The bolt sang away through the water. It lost momentum rapidly, and was caught by a stray current which brought it closer to the girl than to the Eater at which Lavon had aimed.

He bit his lip, lowered the weapon, wound it up again. It did not pay to underestimate the range; he would have to wait. Another bolt, cutting through the water from a side port, made him issue orders to cease firing 'until,' he added, 'you can see their eyespots.'

The irruption of the rotifers decided the girl. The motionless wooden monster was of course strange to her, but it had not yet menaced her – and she must have known what it would be like to have three Dicrans over her, each trying to grab from the others the largest share. She threw herself towards the bullseye port. The three Eaters screamed with fury and greed and bored in after her.

She probably would not have made it, had not the dull vision of the lead Dicran made out the wooden shape of the ship at the last instant. The Dicran backed off, buzzing, and the other two sheered away to avoid colliding with her. After that they had another argument, though they could hardly have formulated what it was that they were fighting about; they were incapable of exchanging any thought much more complicated than the equivalent of 'Yaah,' 'Drop dead,' and 'You're another.'

While they were still snarling at each other, Lavon pierced the nearest one all the way through with an arblast bolt. The surviving two were at once involved in a lethal battle over the remains.

'Than, take a party out and spear me those two Eaters while they're still fighting,' Lavon ordered. 'Don't forget to destroy their eggs, too. I can see that this world needs a little taming.'

The girl shot through the port and brought up against the far wall of the cabin, flailing in terror. Lavon tried to approach her, but from somewhere she produced a flake of stonewort chipped to a nasty point. Since she was naked, it was hard to tell where she had been hiding it, but she obviously knew how to use it, and meant to. Lavon retreated and sat down on the stool before his control board, waiting while she took in the cabin, Lavon, Shar, the other pilots, the senescent Para.

At last she said: 'Are – you – the gods – from beyond the sky?'

'We're from beyond the sky, all right,' Lavon said. 'But we're not gods. We're human beings, just like you. Are there many humans here?'

The girl seemed to assess the situation very rapidly, savage though she was. Lavon had the odd and impossible impression that he should recognize her: a tall, deceptively relaxed, tawny woman, not after all quite like this one … a woman from another world, to be sure, but still …

She tucked the knife back into her bright, matted hair – aha, Lavon thought confusedly, there's a trick I may need to remember – and shook her head.

'We are few. The Eaters are everywhere. Soon they will have the last of us.'

Her fatalism was so complete that she actually did not seem to care.

'And you've never cooperated against them? Or asked the Protos to help?'

'The Protos?' She shrugged. 'They are as helpless as we are against the Eaters, most of them. We have no weapons that kill at a distance, like yours. And it's too late now for such weapons to do any good. We are too few, the Eaters too many.'

Lavon shook his head emphatically. 'You've had one weapon that counts, all along. Against it, numbers mean nothing. We'll show you how we've used it. You may be able to use it even better than we did, once you've given it a try.'

The girl shrugged again. 'We dreamed of such a weapon, but never found it. Are you telling the truth? What is the weapon?'

'Brains, of course,' Lavon said. 'Not just one brain, but a lot of them. Working together. Cooperation.'

'Lavon speaks the truth,' a weak voice said from the deck.

The Para stirred feebly. The girl watched it with wide eyes. The sound of the Para using human speech seemed to impress her more than the ship itself, or anything else that it contained.

'The Eaters can be conquered,' the thin, burring voice said. 'The Protos will help, as they helped in the world from which we came. The Protos fought this flight through space, and deprived Man of his records; but Man made the trip without the records. The Protos will never oppose Man again. We have already spoken to the Protos of this world, and have told them that what Man can dream, Man can do. Whether the Protos will it or not.

'Shar – your metal record is with you. It was hidden in the ship. My brothers will lead you to it.

'This organism dies now. It dies in confidence of knowledge, as an intelligent creature dies. Man has taught us this. There is nothing. That knowledge. Cannot do. With it … men … have crossed … have crossed space …'

The voice whispered away. The shining slipper did not change, but something about it was gone. Lavon looked at the girl; their eyes met. He felt an unaccountable warmth.

'We have crossed space,' Lavon repeated softly.

Shar's voice came to him across a great distance. The young-old man was whispering: 'But – have we?'

Lavon was looking at the girl. He had no answer for Shar's question. It did not seem to be important.

BOOK FOUR

Watershed

The murmurs of discontent – Capt. Gorbel, being a military man, thought of it as 'disaffection' – among the crew of the R.S.S. *Indefeasible* had reached the point where they could no longer be ignored, well before the ship had come within fifty light years of its objective.

Sooner or later, Gorbel thought, sooner or later this idiotic seal-creature is going to notice them.

Capt. Gorbel wasn't sure whether he would be sorry or glad when the Adapted Man caught on. In a way, it would make things easier. But it would be an uncomfortable moment, not only for Hoqqueah and the rest of the pantrope team, but for Gorbel himself. Maybe it would be better to keep sitting on the safety valve until Hoqqueah and the other Altarians were put off on – what was its name again? Oh yes, Earth.

But the crew plainly wasn't going to let Gorbel put it off that long.

As for Hoqqueah, he didn't appear to have a noticing center anywhere in his brain. He was as little discommoded by the emotional undertow as he was by the thin and frigid air the Rigellian crew maintained inside the battlecraft. Secure in his coat of warm blubber, his eyes brown, liquid and merry, he sat in the forward greenhouse for most of each ship's day, watching the growth of the star Sol in the black skies ahead.

And he talked. Gods of all stars, how he talked! Capt. Gorbel already knew more about the ancient – the *very* ancient – history of the seeding program than he had had any desire to know, but there was still more coming. Nor was the seeding program Hoqqueah's sole subject. The Colonization Council delegate had had a vertical education, one which cut in a narrow shaft through many different fields of specialization – in contrast to Gorbel's own training, which had been spread horizontally over the whole subject of spaceflight without more than touching anything else.

Hoqqueah seemed to be making a project of enlarging the Captain's horizons, whether he wanted them enlarged or not.

'Take agriculture,' he was saying at the moment. 'This planet we're to seed provides an excellent argument for taking the long view of farm policy. There used to be jungles there; it was very fertile. But the people began their lives as farmers with the use of fire, and they killed themselves off in the same way.'

'How?' Gorbel said automatically. Had he remained silent, Hoqqueah would have gone on anyhow; and it didn't pay to be impolite to the Colonization Council, even by proxy.

'In their own prehistory, fifteen thousand years before their official zero date, they cleared farmland by burning it off. Then they would plant a crop, harvest it, and let the jungle return. Then they burned the jungle off and went through the cycle again. At the beginning, they wiped out the greatest abundance of game animals Earth was ever to see, just by farming that way. Furthermore the method was totally destructive to the topsoil.

'But did they learn? No. Even after they achieved space-flight, that method of farming was standard in most of the remaining jungle areas – even though the bare rock was showing through everywhere by that time.'

Hoqqueah sighed. 'Now, of course, there are no jungles. There are no seas, either. There's nothing but desert, naked rock, bitter cold, and thin, oxygen-poor air – or so the people would view it, if there were any of them left. *Tapa* farming wasn't solely responsible, but it helped.'

Gorbel shot a quick glance at the hunched back of Lt. Averdor, his adjutant and navigator. Averdor had managed to avoid saying so much as one word to Hoqqueah or any of the other pantropists from the beginning of the trip. Of course he wasn't required to assume the diplomatic burdens involved – those were Gorbel's crosses – but the strain of dodging even normal intercourse with the seal-men was beginning to tell on him.

Sooner or later, Averdor was going to explode. He would have nobody to blame for it but himself, but that wouldn't prevent everybody on board from suffering from it.

Including Gorbel, who would lose a first-class navigator and adjutant.

Yet it was certainly beyond Gorbel's authority to order Averdor to speak to an Adapted Man. He could only suggest that Averdor run through a few mechanical courtesies, for the good of the ship. The only response had been one of the stoniest stares Gorbel had ever seen, even from Averdor, with whom the Captain had been shipping for over thirty Galactic years.

And the worst of it was that Gorbel was, as a human being, wholly on Averdor's side.

'After a certain number of years, conditions change on *any* planet,' Hoqqueah babbled solemnly, waving a flipper-like arm to include all the points of light outside the greenhouse. He was working back to his primary obsession: the seeding program. 'It's only logical to insist that Man be able to change with them – or, if he can't do that, he must establish himself somewhere else. Suppose he had colonized only the Earthlike planets? Not even those planets *remain* Earthlike forever, not in the biological sense.'

'Why would we have limited ourselves to Earthlike planets in the first place?' Gorbel said. 'Not that I know much about the place, but the specs don't make it sound like an optimum world.'

'To be sure,' Hoqqueah said, though as usual Gorbel didn't know which part of his own comment Hoqqueah was agreeing to. 'There's no survival value in pinning one's race forever to one set of specs. It's only sensible to go on evolving with the universe, so as to stay independent of such things as the aging of worlds, or the explosions of their stars. And look at the results! Man exists now in so many forms that there's always a refuge *somewhere* for any threatened people. That's a great achievement – compared to it, what price the old arguments about sovereignty of form?'

'What, indeed?' Gorbel said, but inside his skull his other self was saying: Ah-ha, he smells the hostility after all. Once an Adapted Man, always an Adapted Man – and always fighting for equality with the basic human form. But it's no good, you seal-snouted bureaucrat. You can argue for the rest of your life, but your whiskers will always wiggle when you talk.

And obviously you'll never stop talking.

'And as a military man yourself, you'd be the first to appreciate the military advantages, Captain,' Hoqqueah added earnestly. 'Using pantropy, man has seized thousands of worlds that would have been inaccessible to him otherwise. It's enormously increased our chances to become masters of the galaxy, to take most of it under occupation *without* stealing anyone else's planet in the process. An occupation without dispossession – let alone without bloodshed. Yet if some race other than man should develop imperial ambitions, and try to annex *our* planets, it will find itself enormously outnumbered.'

'That's true,' Capt. Gorbel said, interested in spite of himself. 'It's probably just as well that we worked fast, way back there in the beginning. Before somebody else thought up the method, I mean. But, how come it *was* us? Seems to me that the first race to invent it should've been a race that already had it – if you follow me.'

'Not quite, Captain. If you will give me an example—?'

'Well, we scouted a system once where there was a race that occupied two different planets, not both at the same time, but back and forth,' Gorbel said. 'They had a life-cycle that had three different forms. In the first form they'd winter over on the outermost of the two worlds. Then they'd change to another form that could cross space, mother-naked, without ships, and spend the rest of the year on the inner planet in the third form. Then they'd change back into the second form and cross back to the colder planet.

'It's a hard thing to describe. But the point is, this wasn't anything they'd worked out; it was natural to them. They'd evolved that way.' He looked at Averdor again. 'The navigation was tricky around there during the swarming season.'

Averdor failed to rise to the bait.

'I see; the point is well taken,' Hoqqueah said, nodding with grotesque thoughtfulness. 'But let me point out to you, Captain, that being already able to do a thing doesn't aid you in thinking of it as something that needs to be perfected. Oh, I've seen races like the one you describe, too – races with polymorphism, sexual alteration of generation, metamorphosis of the insect life-history type, and so on. There's a planet named Lithia, about forty light years from here, where the dominant race undergoes complete evolutionary recapitulation *after* birth – not before it, as men do. But why should any of them think of form-changing as something extraordinary, and to be striven for? It's one of the commonplaces of their lives, after all.'

A small bell chimed in the greenhouse. Hoqqueah got up at once, his movements precise and almost graceful despite his tubbiness. 'Thus endeth the day,' he said cheerfully. 'Thank you for your courtesy, Captain.'

He waddled out. He would, of course, be back tomorrow.

And the day after that.

And the next day – unless the crewmen hadn't tarred and feathered the whole bunch by then.

If only, Gorbel thought distractedly, if only the damned Adapts weren't so quick to abuse their privileges! As a delegate of the Colonization Council, Hoqqueah was a person of some importance, and could not be barred from entering the greenhouse except in an emergency. But didn't the man know that he shouldn't use the privilege each and every day, on a ship manned by basic-form human beings most of whom could not enter the greenhouse at all without a direct order?

And the rest of the pantropists were just as bad. As passengers with the technical status of human beings, they could go almost anywhere in the ship that the crew could go – and they did, persistently and unapologetically, as though moving among equals. Legally, that was what they were – but didn't they know by this time that there was such a thing as prejudice? And that among common spacemen the prejudice against their kind – and against any Adapted Man – always hovered near the borderline of bigotry?

There was a slight hum as Averdor's power chair swung around to face the Captain. Like most Rigellian men, the lieutenant's face was lean and harsh, almost like that of an ancient religious fanatic, and the starlight in the greenhouse hid nothing to soften it; but to Capt. Gorbel, to whom it was familiar down to its last line, it looked especially forbidding now.

'Well?' he said.

'I'd think you'd be fed to the teeth with that freak by this time,' Averdor said without preamble. 'Something's got to be done, Captain, before the crew gets so surly that we have to start handing out brig sentences.'

'I don't like know-it-alls any better than you do,' Gorbel said grimly. 'Especially when they talk nonsense – and half of what this one says about space flight is nonsense, that much I'm sure of. But the man's a delegate of the Council. He's got a right to be up here if he wants to.'

'You can bar anybody from the greenhouse in an emergency – even the ship's officers.'

'I fail to see any emergency,' Gorbel said stiffly.

'This is a hazardous part of the galaxy – potentially, anyhow. It hasn't been visited for millennia. That star up ahead has nine planets besides the one we're supposed to land on, and I don't know how many satellites of planetary size. Suppose somebody on one of them lost his head and took a crack at us as we went by?'

Gorbel frowned. 'That's reaching for trouble. Besides, the area's been sur- veyed recently at least once – otherwise we wouldn't be here.'

'A sketch job. It's still sensible to take precautions. If there should be any trouble, there's many a Board of Review that would call it risky to have un- reliable, second-class human types in the greenhouse when it breaks out.'

'You're talking nonsense.'

'Dammit, Captain, read between the lines a minute,' Averdor said harshly. 'I know as well as you do that there's going to be no trouble that we can't handle. And that no reviewing board would pull a complaint like that on *you* if there were. I'm just trying to give you an excuse to use on the seals.'

'I'm listening.'

'Good. The *Indefeasible* is the tightest ship in the Rigellian navy, her rec- ord's clean, and the crew's morale is almost a legend. We can't afford to start gigging the men for their personal prejudices – which is what it will amount to, if those seals drive them to breaking discipline. Besides, they've got a right to do their work without a lot of seal snouts poking continually over their shoulders.'

'I can hear myself explaining that to Hoqqueah.'

'You don't need to,' Averdor said doggedly. 'You can tell him, instead, that you're going to have to declare the ship on emergency status until we land. That means that the pantrope team, as passengers, will have to stick to their quarters. It's simple enough.'

It was simple enough, all right. And decidedly tempting.

'I don't like it,' Gorbel said. 'Besides, Hoqqueah may be a know-it-all, but he's not entirely a fool. He'll see through it easily enough.'

Averdor shrugged. 'It's your command,' he said. 'But I don't see what he could do about it even if he did see through it. It'd be all on the log and according to regs. All he could report to the Council would be a suspicion – and they'd probably discount it. Everybody knows that these second-class types are quick to think they're being persecuted. It's my theory that that's why they *are* persecuted, a lot of the time at least.'

'I don't follow you.'

'The man I shipped under before I came on board the *Indefeasible*,'

Averdor said, 'was one of those people who don't even trust themselves. They expect everybody they meet to slip a knife into them when their backs are turned. And there are always other people who make it almost a point of honor to knife a man like that, just because he seems to be asking for it. He didn't hold that command long.'

'I see what you mean,' Gorbel said. 'Well, I'll think about it.'

But by the next ship's day, when Hoqqueah returned to the greenhouse, Gorbel still had not made up his mind. The very fact that his own feelings were on the side of Averdor and the crew made him suspicious of Averdor's 'easy' solution. The plan was tempting enough to blind a tempted man to flaws that might otherwise be obvious.

The Adapted Man settled himself comfortably and looked out through the transparent metal. 'Ah,' he said. 'Our target is sensibly bigger now, eh, Captain? Think of it: in just a few days now, we will be – in the historical sense – home again.'

And now it was riddles! 'What do you mean?' Gorbel said.

'I'm sorry; I thought you knew. Earth is the home planet of the human race, Captain. There is where the basic form evolved.'

Gorbel considered this unexpected bit of information cautiously. Even assuming that it was true – and it probably was, that would be the kind of thing Hoqqueah would know about a planet to which he was assigned – it didn't seem to make any special difference in the situation. But Hoqqueah had obviously brought it out for a reason. Well, he'd be trotting out the reason, too, soon enough; nobody would ever accuse the Altarian of being taciturn.

Nevertheless, he considered turning on the screen for a close look at the planet. Up to now he had felt not the slightest interest in it.

'Yes, there's where it all began,' Hoqqueah said. 'Of course at first it never occurred to those people that they might produce pre-Adapted children. They went to all kinds of extremes to adapt their environment instead, or to carry it along with them. But they finally realized that with the planets, that won't work. You can't spend your life in a spacesuit, or under a dome, either.

'Besides, they had had form trouble in their society from their earliest days. For centuries they were absurdly touchy over minute differences in coloring and shape, and even in thinking. They had regime after regime that tried to impose its own concept of the standard citizen on everybody, and enslaved those who didn't fit the specs.'

Abruptly, Hoqqueah's chatter began to make Gorbel uncomfortable. It was becoming easier and easier to sympathize with Averdor's determination to ignore the Adapted Man's existence entirely.

'It was only after they'd painfully taught themselves that such differences really don't matter that they could go on to pantropy,' Hoqqueah said. 'It was the logical conclusion. Of course, a certain continuity of form had to be maintained, and has been maintained to this day. You cannot totally change the form without totally changing the thought processes. If you give a man the form of a cockroach, as one ancient writer foresaw, he will wind up thinking like a cockroach, not like a human being. We recognized that. On worlds where only extreme modifications of the human form would make it suitable – for instance, a planet of the gas giant type – no seeding is attempted. The Council maintains that such worlds are the potential property of other races than the human, races whose psychotypes would not have to undergo radical change in order to survive there.'

Dimly, Capt. Gorbel saw where Hoqqueah was leading him, and he did not like what he saw. The seal-man, in his own maddeningly indirect way, was arguing his right to be considered an equal in fact as well as in law. He was arguing it, however, in a universe of discourse totally unfamiliar to Capt. Gorbel, with facts whose validity he alone knew and whose relevance he alone could judge. He was, in short, loading the dice, and the last residues of Gorbel's tolerance were evaporating rapidly.

'Of course there was resistance back there at the beginning,' Hoqqueah said. 'The kind of mind that had only recently been persuaded that colored men are human beings was quick to take the attitude that an Adapted Man – any Adapted Man – was the social inferior of the "primary" or basic human type, the type that lived on Earth. But it was also a very old idea on the Earth that basic humanity inheres in the mind, not in the form.

'You see, Captain, all this might still have been prevented, had it been possible to maintain the attitude that changing the form even in part makes a man less of a man than he was in the "primary" state. But the day has come when that attitude is no longer tenable – a day that is the greatest of all moral watersheds for our race, the day that is to unite all our divergent currents of attitudes toward each other into one common reservoir of brotherhood and purpose. You and I are very fortunate to be on the scene to see it.'

'Very interesting,' Gorbel said coldly. 'But all those things happened a long time ago, and we know very little about this part of the galaxy these days. Under the circumstances – which you'll find clearly written out in the log, together with the appropriate regulations – I'm forced to place the ship on emergency alert beginning tomorrow, and continuing until your team disembarks. I'm afraid that means that henceforth all passengers will be required to stay in quarters.'

Hoqqueah turned and arose. His eyes were still warm and liquid, but there was no longer any trace of merriment in them.

'I know very well what it means,' he said. 'And to some extent I understand the need – though I had been hoping to see the planet of our birth first from space. But I don't think *you* quite understood *me,* Captain. The moral watershed of which I spoke is not in the past. It is now. It began the day that the Earth itself became no longer habitable for the so-called basic human type. The flowing of the streams toward the common reservoir will become bigger and bigger as word spreads through the galaxy that Earth itself has been seeded with Adapted Men. With that news will go a shock of recognition – the shock of realizing that the "basic" types are now, and have been for a long time, a very small minority, despite their pretensions.'

Was Hoqqueah being absurd enough to threaten – an unarmed, comical seal-man shaking a fist at the captain of the *Indefeasible*? Or—

'Before I go, let me ask you this one question, Captain. Down there is your home planet, and my team and I will be going out on its surface before long. Do you dare to follow us out of the ship?'

'And why should I?' Gorbel said.

'Why, to show the superiority of the basic type, Captain,' Hoqqueah said softly. 'Surely you cannot admit that a pack of seal-men are your betters, on your own ancestral ground!'

He bowed and went to the door. Just before he reached it, he turned and looked speculatively at Gorbel and at Lt. Averdor, who was staring at him with an expression of rigid fury.

'Or can you?' he said. 'It will be interesting to see how you manage to comport yourselves as a minority. I think you lack practice.'

He went out. Both Gorbel and Averdor turned jerkily to the screen, and Gorbel turned it on. The image grew, steadied, settled down.

When the next trick came on duty, both men were still staring at the vast and tumbled desert of the Earth.

If you've enjoyed these books and would like to read more, you'll find literally thousands of classic Science Fiction & Fantasy titles through the **SF Gateway**

✶

For the new home of
Science Fiction & Fantasy . . .

✶

For the most comprehensive collection
of classic SF on the internet . . .

✶

Visit the SF Gateway

www.sfgateway.com

James Blish (1921–1975)

James Blish studied microbiology at Rutgers and then served as a medical laboratory technician in the US army during the Second World War. Among his best known books are *A Case of Conscience*, for which he won the Hugo Award for Best Novel in 1959, and the Cities in Flight sequence: *They Shall Have Stars*, *A Life for the Stars*, *Earthman Come Home* and *A Clash of Cymbals* (published in the US as *The Triumph of Time*). He also wrote almost a dozen books adapting episodes of the *Star Trek* television series, and the first original spin-off novel, *Spock Must Die!*